GROWL

GROWL

Eve Langlais   Kate Douglas   A. C. Arthur

 St. Martin's Griffin ⋘ New York

GROWL. Copyright © 2015 by St. Martin's Press.
Legal Wolf's Mate. Copyright © 2015 by Eve Langlais.
Feral Passions. Copyright © 2015 by Kate Douglas.
The Alpha's Woman. Copyright © 2015 by A. C. Arthur.
All rights reserved. Printed in the United States of America.
For information, address St. Martin's Press,
175 Fifth Avenue, New York, N.Y. 10010.

www.stmartins.com

Designed by Molly Rose Murphy

Library of Congress Cataloging-in-Publication Data

Names: Langlais, Eve. Legal wolf's mate. | Douglas, Kate. Feral passions. |
    Arthur, A. C. Alpha's woman.
Title: Growl / Eve Langlais, Kate Douglas, A. C. Arthur.
Description: First edition. | New York : St. Martin's Griffin, 2016.
Identifiers: LCCN 2015040039| ISBN 9781250078582 (trade paperback) |
    ISBN 9781466891050 (e-book)
Subjects: LCSH: Werewolves—Fiction. | Shapeshifting—Fiction. |
    Paranormal fiction, American. | Erotic stories, American. | BISAC:
    FICTION / Romance / Short Stories. | FICTION / Romance / General. |
    FICTION / Romance / Paranormal.
Classification: LCC PS648.W37 G76 2016 | DDC 813/.0873808375—dc23
LC record available at http://lccn.loc.gov/2015040039

Our books may be purchased in bulk for promotional, educational, or
business use. Please contact your local bookseller or the Macmillan
Corporate and Premium Sales Department at (800) 221-7945, extension
5442, or by e-mail at MacmillanSpecialMarkets@macmillan.com.

First Edition: January 2016

10 9 8 7 6 5 4 3 2 1

CONTENTS

GROWL

LEGAL WOLF'S MATE

Eve Langlais

CHAPTER 1

"Absolutely not." Funny how Gavin kept repeating it and yet Broderick continued to pester.

"Come on, dude. Do this one favor for me."

"One? Don't you owe me like a dozen at this point?" And yeah, he kept track. A practical man, Gavin fully planned to call them in one day.

"All I'm asking is that you talk with the girl. Once you meet her, you'll agree with me. She's innocent, and if someone doesn't step in and do something to help her, they're going to throw her ass in jail and toss away the key."

"As I recall, you said the same thing about Simon, your lawn guy."

"So I misjudged in his case. How was I to know he was an ex-biker with a brother in jail for murder? He seemed like such a nice guy." Gavin could practically see his friend squirm at the reminder. "This time, though. I'm telling you, the girl is innocent and could use someone on her side."

"My answer is still no."

"But I haven't mentioned the best part. I'm pretty sure she's being framed by Fabian Garoux."

The juicy tidbit dangled before him, surefire bait to pique

his interest. At the mention of Fabian, Gavin stopped drumming his fingers and swung his chair away from his lofty view of the city—the advantage of a penthouse office suite. Expensive but worth every damn penny. "What the hell does Fabian have to do with this?"

"Did I forget to mention that the man this woman supposedly murdered was his enemy?"

As were lots of other people. Fabian didn't have many close friends, probably because he was a prime example of an asshat.

"Have you stopped to consider that maybe she was hired to do the hit?" While it was not exactly common, women were just as capable of assassination as a man. Gavin remembered a pair of twins in bikinis he once crossed paths with whose victims often died with a smile. A smart man, who intended to live ripe into his old age, he steered clear of the invitation to celebrate their acquittal. Winning didn't make his clients innocent. He was just that good.

"No way was she hired. My gut says she's telling the truth about being framed."

"Your gut also keeps dragging you back to that Mexican place, even though you have to chew antacids like a candy-stricken addict for days afterward."

Broderick groaned. "Such pleasurable pain. And stop changing the subject. Talk to her. Hear what she has to say. If you don't believe her, then no harm. She keeps her public defender and goes to jail. But if you believe her . . ."

Then Gavin would take on the case pro bono just for a chance to screw with the dirtiest dog around. Fabian Garoux, biggest crime lord in the city. Slippery bastard with too many bodyguards, always a ready alibi, and the wolfsbane of Gavin's existence. Also known as his creator—and the alpha Gavin refused to roll over for.

"Fine. I give up against your expert nagging. I'll see her. What jail are they holding her in?"

"Funny thing you should ask. Someone posted her bail. Anonymously. A hefty half-million dollars. Know anyone with cash like that?"

That piece of dangling steak just got bigger. Fabian had that kind of money. The thought of tying him to a serious crime practically made Gavin wag his ass in delight. Good thing it remained planted in his chair. Wolves could get away with shaking their tail. Grown men in suits? Not so much.

"That is some serious dough." But chump change for Fabian. "Get her to set an appointment with my secretary."

"No need to delay. She's already there."

"What do you mean, she's there?"

"I mean there, as in sitting in your reception area. I dropped her off at your office just before I called."

And Gavin never knew of his visitor because his secretary had left to fetch them both lunch.

As Broderick hung up, midchuckle, Gavin grumbled under his breath. "No-good, meddling feline, always trying to help every bloody stray that comes his way."

A less nice guy would have eaten the furball. However, Gavin counted Broderick as one of his closest friends and had since his *change*. It was Broderick who calmed Gavin down the first time he morphed into a wolf at the insistent brilliance of a full moon.

As Gavin was suffering from a full-blown panic attack,

first from the pain of shapeshifting, then from dealing with the horror of the knowledge he'd chased down a rabbit and eaten it raw—which still made him want to heave—Broderick was the one who'd found him and offered him a towel to gird his naked loins when he awoke the next morning, naked on the forest floor. Pine needles, for the curious, did not make the best of cushions, unless attempting a homeopathic version of acupuncture.

Back to Broderick, though. If his bud wanted something, then Gavin would provide it. He always did. Why did it prove so hard to hate the good guy? *Dammit, I keep trying.* And failing. Stupid best bud. *I gotta remember to chase his mangy butt up a tree the next full moon.* Watching him climb down bare assed the next day always gave Gavin a good chuckle.

Fabian Garoux, on the other hand, wouldn't get the same courtesy. This was one instance where Gavin was kind of glad Broderick had involved him. Anything to do with Fabian was of interest to Gavin. Especially anything that might allow him to punish the arrogant jerk through legal means.

Standing, Gavin stretched to his full height of six feet three before heading to his door, a thick, double-hung, steel-framed, and insulted vault of a portal, which he'd had installed when remodeling the office. A safe place to change if caught unexpectedly downtown during a forced moon shift. While werewolves in London might run rampant, werewolves in New York City got shot at. For those who wondered, silver or metal bullets hurt and could kill, while buckshot was a literal pain in the ass to remove.

Opening the door a crack, Gavin glanced out and, at

first, didn't see anyone. His visitor blended that well. Head ducked, shoulders curved, the woman blended into the background.

When he cleared his throat, she immediately startled and raised her head. The biggest brown eyes framed in long, dark lashes met his. Met and snagged his gaze.

Punched him as well in an emotional sense.

She's the one.

Like hell.

He stepped back and, as if afraid the devastating—unwanted—conviction would follow, slammed the door shut.

Then stared at the thick portal.

What the heck just happened?

Nothing . . . and yet everything. The world had obviously tilted on its axis because nothing felt the same. He teetered as if off balance and he couldn't deny a change within him. He couldn't have said what it was or what it meant—*liar*—but he sure as hell felt it. And it had something to do with the woman.

A woman he'd just rudely ignored and slammed the door on.

Oops.

Not being a pussy—unlike Broderick, that big feline hairy bastard—Gavin took a deep breath and told himself to man the hell up. There was nothing scary about a frightened human woman.

A woman who was gone.

Ah hell.

As he stared at the empty reception area, he realized he'd have to do something he'd sworn never to do. Chase after a woman. And he'd thank his inner wolf to simmer the hell down. He wouldn't lope or run or loll his tongue while doing it. Even a wolf in legal clothing had an appearance to maintain.

CHAPTER 2

Perhaps a little more aggressively than needed, Megan jabbed at the elevator button. Then stabbed it again for good measure, even though the light illuminating the down arrow showed her request already in progress.

But she needed the cab to arrive faster.

I need out of here.

Now.

I should have never come. How had she let herself get talked into it?

Oh yeah, she remembered, Broderick with his husky purr and genial smile. She'd happened upon him by accident exiting from her attorney's office, her vision flooded with tears because she'd stubbed her toe on the way out, anger making her clumsy. Why the ire? Because the courts saddled her with an idiot for a lawyer, one who wanted her to plead guilty. *Even though I'm damn well innocent.*

Peeved, her toe throbbing, her eyes watering in the most annoying fashion, and then her colliding clumsily with a broad-shouldered man, when he'd asked, "What's wrong, sweetie?" she'd replied.

"Wrong? What isn't wrong? That idiot is talking twenty-five to life. But I didn't do it." Although she was tempted to murder her public defender for his treatment. Then at least she'd deserve incarceration.

Who knew blurting her woes to a stranger would result in a chance to make things right? Next thing she knew, Broderick had dragged her—almost literally, since he wouldn't take no for an answer—to a café and plied her with a whipped-cream-topped café mocha. Sugar and sympathy soon had her spilling her story, which was totally unlike her. She didn't usually unburden to strangers. She blamed it on stress.

It felt good to have someone to talk to. Someone who didn't assume the charges against her had any merit. Good to vent and have someone pretend to believe in her innocence.

She wouldn't have thought any more of her chance encounter with the man or his promise he'd look into her case. What did Broderick think he could do? He wasn't a lawyer or a cop, just some kind of numbers guy who worked for an agency that investigated fraud.

But apparently he knew a lawyer, some hotshot, who could maybe help her. While charity didn't sit well with her, with almost nothing in her bank account Megan knew without help she was going to jail or going to have to flee to a country that didn't allow extradition—all to avoid a conviction for something she didn't do.

Hope for a different outcome meant she let Broderick lead her to the impressive chrome-and-glass building downtown. Hope also let her perch in the outer reception area of the lavish penthouse office.

Talk about swanky. Furnished old style in polished wood,

thick carpeting, and leather club chairs, Megan had never felt more out of place. A swanky, high-priced lawyer who could afford this kind of work space wouldn't want to take on her case pro bono. But she couldn't extinguish the tiny flame of hope that hoped he would. She'd run out of other viable options—other than flight, which meant ducking the law the rest of her life.

Her current lawyer's optimistic prognosis? "If you plead guilty, then maybe we can whittle down the verdict from life to something like twenty-five years and eligible for parole."

As for her retort of, "But I'm innocent," "Not according to the evidence you're not."

Framed. Just like a certain rabbit.

It was while thinking of rabbits that she heard the office door open and a guy stuck his head out.

He stared at her. She stared right back because, really, who in their right mind wouldn't? The man was freaking gorgeous. Tall, way taller than her five-foot-eight frame, and while she couldn't see his body, he bore the face of a god, chiseled from stone—square-cut jaw, aquiline nose, and a regal air. Add to that bright blue eyes, short, layered dark hair, and a frown, which creased his slightly tanned brow, and she locked her jaw, lest she gape.

Before she could take a breath and say hello, he ducked back into his office and the door slammed shut.

It stayed shut, and her nerve fled.

I knew this was a bad idea. Her gut yelled at her to leave.

Up she popped from her seat, and she quick-stepped to the elevator. For some reason, it suddenly became imperative she escape. That instant.

While she didn't hear sound of pursuit, the hairs on her nape tingled. Again she jabbed the button.

"Why is this taking so long?" she muttered. A more athletic girl might have tackled the stairs, but Megan's rounded thighs, formed from a love of donuts and French fries dipped in ketchup, protested loudly against this plan. Much easier to poke a button and bitch. "Come on, damn you. Hurry."

"Leaving so soon?"

The low, husky tone, coming from right behind, startled a small cry from her. With her pulse racing, she whirled and confronted a chest. A nice chest, mind you, wide and covered in a suit that she could swear cost more than she made in a month as a secretary, but also a daunting wall that blocked her view.

How could a man so large, with an unmistakable presence, sneak up on her, especially given how she'd been raised by a father and large extended family who preached constant vigilance?

Forcing her gaze upward, she fought not to gape. Even in close proximity, the guy appeared gorgeous. Too bad he was such an ass.

Slam a door practically in her face indeed.

Tilting her chin at a stubborn angle—her fighting angle, as her dad would say with a chuckle—she netted the butterflies in her stomach and managed to say, "Sorry if I disturbed you. It seems I visited the wrong office."

"You're the woman Broderick wanted me to see." He didn't ask. He stated.

Should she lie? What was the point? "Yes, but I see now this was a mistake. Sorry to have wasted your time."

A *ding* from behind and a swish of a door sliding open indicated her ride down had arrived. It left empty, as she found herself propelled down the short hall back to the opulent office, not of her own volition. As if she were a piece of flotsam, he left her no choice but to go where he shoved her.

"What are you doing?" she managed to say instead of reacting in a more childish manner, wanting to duck out of his grasp and race for the stairs. Chubby thighs be damned.

"What does it look like I'm doing?"

Other than firing up her libido?

The big guy, with his rather large hand firmly placed against the small of her back, firmly guided her in the direction of his office. It wasn't too late to protest or to give in to her instinct for flight. However, given the insistence of his push and the uncompromising set of his jaw, she doubted she'd make it far.

The guy had a lot in common with a giant boulder. She got the impression that once he set his mind, not much budged it. Perverse as it sounded, it made him more attractive. She rather liked decisive people.

Two other reasons compelled her to follow him. One, that darned flicker of hope that refused to die. And second, at the touch of his hand, everything in her both tensed and relaxed at the same time.

That a thrill of excitement could ease her anxiety didn't make much sense, but it did confuse her enough that she found herself quick-marched through his reception area and into the most ridiculously awesome office she'd ever seen outside of a television drama.

Jaw surely hanging yokel-wide, she stared in fascination at the wall of glass that conveyed a panoramic view of the city.

"How the hell do you manage to work here? Isn't that distracting?" Good to know she wasn't tongue-tied around him, but it made her cringe to note her awed compliment.

"When you work long hours, having a view and a flood of daylight is a must. Especially for a guy like me. But we're not here to discuss my amazing view but rather your current situation. Broderick says you've been charged with the murder of your former employer." He pushed her in the direction of a fabric-covered armchair before his desk. He circled the massive wooden expanse and seated himself in a smooth-appearing leather chair.

Ah yes, the reason for her being here. How should she handle it? "I didn't do it," she blurted out. Way to shout her innocence. Heat infused her cheeks as she found herself the focus of his piercing blue eyes. He drew the oddest responses from her. She really needed to find her balance and start acting instead of reacting.

"Why not?"

The odd question saw her blink. "Excuse me?"

"I said why didn't you kill him? Was he a good boss?"

"Not really. But he wasn't the worse one I've had either," she hastened to add.

"Were you fired?"

"No."

"Fucking?"

She couldn't help a wrinkle of her nose at his profane question. "Most definitely not."

"Are you seeing anyone?"

A frown creased her forehead. "What does that have to do with anything?"

"I'm going to take that as a no then. Did you owe him money?"

"No."

"Was he cooking the books?"

"Not that I know of."

"So, in other words, you have no motive?"

"No, I don't have a motive. And even if I did, I still wouldn't have killed my boss."

"Too squeamish?"

"What? No. Yes. What the hell is wrong with you? I wouldn't kill him or anyone because it's just not something normal people do. Something you're apparently unaware of. What is it with you lawyers? Whatever happened to innocent until proven guilty?" She had managed to only stand before she found herself pushed back down. Her ass hit the chair and she stared in consternation at the man. He'd leaped over his desk to stop her from departing and now towered over her.

How did he manage to move so fast? Only her daddy ever moved as quick.

"I think you need to tell me everything, from the beginning. Starting with how you came to work for the guy."

"I saw an ad online looking for a secretary."

"And that was how long ago?"

"Not long. I just celebrated my one-month mark."

"So you weren't referred to this job? Subcontracted in any way?"

"No. Does it matter?"

"Maybe. Maybe not. When it comes to establishing motive,

these are questions that will arise during the course of your trial. The prosecution might attempt to show premeditation, which is why these little details are important. Speaking of details. What do we know of the evidence gathered that implicates you?"

Instead of replying, she dug into her voluminous purse—a secondhand Prada that she loved dearly, even if she paid way more for it than she should have. But nice secretaries didn't buy hot Pradas from the back of a truck. Being nice sucked.

"I brought a copy of my file." A folder filled with papers the lawyer gave her detailing the circumstantial evidence pointing her way. Even she had to admit it appeared damning.

Her fingerprint on the weapon, mysteriously located in her closet when the police executed their search warrant. Traces of her deceased employer's blood on her clothes in the hamper. The facts shone a bull's-eye on her, and yet . . .

I didn't do it.

Forget the truth. Her assertion fell on deaf ears. No one had listened to her when she told her story. She'd gotten home from work with her take-out Thai food, and from that point on she didn't remember a thing until she awoke the next day, face-first on her bed in bra and panties, when the cops came pounding on her door to arrest her and toss her apartment.

Gavin took the thick bundle of papers from her and tossed them onto his desk. "I'll read those later. I'm less interested in what the reports say and more in what you have to say."

"So you believe me when I say I'm innocent?"

"I'd like to"—she perked up in her seat—"but I barely

know you." She slumped back down. "Which is why you and I are going to dinner."

"We are?"

"Now."

"But—"

He fixed her with those amazing eyes, and her mouth snapped shut. "If you're going to be my client, then you need to start doing what I say without argument."

Not argue? Ha. Like that would happen. "Who says I'm your client?"

"I do."

"Even though you don't know if I'm innocent?"

"I enjoy a challenge. Besides, defending only the innocent is for the altruistic."

The word "altruistic" reminded her that her bank account was hovering awful close to zero and she refused to call her daddy. "I have no money to pay you."

"Don't worry about it. We'll figure something out."

The way he stared at her, his gaze smoldering and his body intruding on her personal space? A lightbulb suddenly illuminated.

Megan's lips pursed. "If you think I'm going to sleep with you to pay for your services, then you're sadly mistaken. I'm not a whore." She'd do a lot of things for money, if the price was right, but sell her body? Not one of them.

White teeth flashed when he laughed. The sound sent a shiver, a pleasant one, racing down her spine. "I never said you were, and I guess I should have made myself clearer. I won't be requiring payment for your case, at all. I have money. Lots of it. Which means if I'm intrigued I can indulge in the occasional pro bono case."

"So you'll take me on?" The flutter of her heart now had more than one reason to stutter fast.

"Oh, never fear, little rabbit. I fully intend to *take* you."

How did he make that sound both ominous and promising at the same time?

CHAPTER 3

Initial panic conquered, Gavin, while not resigned to his fate—yet—could now take a mental step back and analyze his situation.

Less situation, more like dilemma, as he contemplated what role the woman who sat across from him would play in his life. Not just a woman, his mate.

My mate.

Even just thinking it made him want to run for the woods. Or get really, really drunk.

Before anyone came to the conclusion he was blowing things out of proportion, perhaps a few facts would help. When it came to his kind, in other words, Lycanthropes—men who became werewolves if the wolf virus took a fancy to them after a bite—it was said that there was only one woman destined to share their secret and heart.

One woman. One lover.

Forever.

One.

Ha.

Until now, Gavin had scoffed at the very idea. He'd spent the last ten-plus years as a werewolf, tasting the delights of the nubile fairer sex. Indulging in erotic pastimes—bad, bad wolf.

Sex with whomever he fancied was part of his lifestyle. In his world, he couldn't imagine why anyone would give up variety for monogamy.

It was Broderick who first tried to dispel that notion over way too many tequila shots.

"Once you meet the one"—and yes, Broderick used some ominous finger quotes—"you're fucked."

Leaning back in his chair, Gavin grinned as he eyed the scantily clad gyrating bodies on the dance floor. "Fucked? I like the sound of that."

His feline buddy made a rude noise. "Not that kind of fucked, you idiot. I mean screwed, as in hand in your man card, harness your balls, and prepare to dedicate over half your closet and bathroom counter space. Once you meet the woman destined to be your mate, you're a goner."

"You're drunk and full of shit," was Gavin's reply.

"Drunk, yes. But as to the shit part? Sorry, dude, I wish. The mating thing? It's totally real. Think of it as just another weird quirk of our kind."

"Weirder than swapping human skin for fur?"

"Okay, maybe not weirder, but definitely part of our package deal."

"Just fucking great. Yet another aspect to our curse."

At times, when he let alcohol render him nostalgic, Gavin missed his previous ignorance about the shapeshifting world. A world fraught with pain—because no matter what the movies showed, morphing into a different shape and growing fangs and fur freaking hurt. A world where secrecy was paramount, lest you wanted to push up daisies in an un-

marked grave. A secretive life where even his own family could never know of the society that lived among them, viewing humans as little more than ignorant sheep.

Okay, that was more the vampire view, but there was no denying Lycanthropes and other specially enhanced beings saw regular humans as beneath them.

"Can you really still say you think it's a curse? I've seen the exhilaration in your eyes after a successful hunt. I know you use your keen senses to help you find clues other lawyers could never hope to find. Or are you going to still deny that what you've become has made you better? Stronger?"

"Fine. It does have some benefits." A grudging admission. "But I refuse to believe that this virus, which changed us, also predisposes us to settle down with one woman. I mean, there are billions of people inhabiting this planet. No way can we expect some intangible force to decide there's only one." Although, when he viewed it like that, it seemed he didn't have much to worry about. The chances of him running into this so-called one and only were slim to none.

"On the surface, I agree with you. It seems beyond far-fetched, but I've seen it too many times to ignore. Guys, like you and me, happily playing the field until one day we turn a corner, and boom, we run into her. I don't know how it works. Call it magic or dumb fucking luck. When it's time, you'll meet her and once you do . . ."

Gavin couldn't help but draw an imaginary knife across his throat and choke.

His buddy rolled his eyes. "It's not a fate worse than death. More like a relief because even if your urge to play the field disappears, at least the one you're fated to be with is not only

*allowed to know your secret, but somehow, the same magic
that draws you together enables her to handle it."*

Capable of handling the fact that their boyfriends turned
furry at least once a month and liked to chase things and
bay at the moon? Or, in Broderick's case, yowl.

Impossible to believe such a crazy thing as a fated girlfriend or, as the old-timers called it, fated mate.

Gavin had pretty much forgotten about that drunken
conversation, until he saw the woman.

The world had stopped. Something in him shifted.

Initially he tried to deny it, even as he chased her down
and prevented her from escaping him. But one smell . . .
One touch . . .

That was all it took for the jaws of monogamy to slam
shut around him. Hear that? It was the pitiful whine of a
man who knew his life was about to change.

Exaggeration? He wished. Case in point, he already
noted a huge change in his behavior. He deliberately took
Megan to a restaurant where he knew the waitresses wore
low-cut blouses and slim, hip-hugging skirts that showed
an indecent amount of leg. Usually Gavin would have admired the wares. Not tonight.

Tonight he could focus on only one person. A cute person. But still. Was he not even allowed to ogle and leer
anymore?

And another thing, no one had warned him she might
argue with him every chance she got.

Shouldn't she be simpering at me or batting her eyelashes?
Nope. Not his woman. Megan, who claimed innocence in the
face of damning evidence, scowled at him.

"I thought the purpose of this dinner was to talk about my case."

"I lied. We don't need to talk. I know all I need to know."

"What's that supposed to mean?"

"I needed food, and you definitely needed food."

"I wasn't hungry."

"Says the liar whose stomach was growling louder than my neighbor's long-haired rat and who has since consumed not only a large salad, but a steak, a baked potato, and a gigantic slice of cheesecake."

"It's rude to pick at your meal. I don't get what my eating has to do with anything. I thought we came here to talk about my case and to see if you'd take me on."

Oh, he'd take her all right, he hoped sooner rather than later. This proximity to her was a special form of torture. "I already told you I'll handle your case. As to asking you more questions, what's the point until I have any pertinent ones? You've already admitted you didn't do it, so there's not much you can currently add to the situation. I will need to comb through the evidence and dismantle it to discover the true culprit."

"So you believe me?"

"Would I be here risking my life against your deadly killer skills if I didn't?"

Her lips twitched as she fought not to smile. "You are deranged."

"Thinking outside the box is not a bad thing in my line of work. Sometimes looking at things from a different per-spective is what it takes to spot the thread that unravels a web of lies."

She rolled her eyes. "Do you always speak so melodramatically? I mean really. We're not in a courtroom, and you don't have anyone to impress."

On the contrary, there was a lady he intended to impress, but unlike with the previous women of his acquaintance, his cultured veneer didn't seem to appeal.

Determined to regain control of the situation and throw her off balance for once, he tossed out, "Why are you single?"

"Who says I am?"

"Says the good-looking lawyer you're having an intimate dinner with."

"First off, conceited much? Second, how do you know I don't have a boyfriend waiting for me at home?"

"Me, conceited? No. Merely confident enough to accept myself as I am. Also confident enough to state there is no significant other, else you would have called him at one point since our departure from the office. But not only have you not called or texted anyone; you haven't received any either."

"I can see someone is a control freak when it comes to dating. Not all women are required to report their every move to a guy."

"Is there a reason you feel a need to argue with everything I say?"

"You're a lawyer. Isn't arguing, like, your thing?"

"In the courtroom. Outside of it, I prefer more relaxed conversation."

"So sorry. Perhaps I should start nodding my head and just agreeing with everything you say. Ooh, and asking you to tell me about yourself."

He couldn't help a wide grin at her sarcasm. "That would

be a good start. How else will we connect unless we get to know the intimate details?"

"Connect? You talk as if we're dating. We're not. I just met you a few hours ago. You're my lawyer, or maybe not. I'm really beginning to rethink this whole idea."

"Ah yes, because you'd rather take your chances with your public defender, who has advised you to what? Oh, that's right, plead guilty."

She glared at him. "He might have advised it, but it doesn't mean I would have."

"Whereupon, I, on the other hand, will have you proclaim loudly your innocence."

Innocent when it came to the crime, but by the time the case was over he'd work on licking the innocence from every inch of her skin. If he could last that long.

Ethics said he should wait until he'd absolved her before making his move.

Hormones and the ridiculous pull he felt toward her mocked his oath to the legal bar.

I will have you, and before the next full moon.

CHAPTER 4

"Surreal" didn't come close to describing her evening repast with Gavin. Megan had heard of slick lawyers with their legal talk meant to make your eyes roll back in your head. Met with a disinterested one who made her actually want to murder someone. Given her current experience, she didn't hold lawyers in very high regard, so she certainly never expected to lust after one.

I'm a grown woman. And yet, much like a moon-struck teenager, she clung to Gavin's every word, trembled inwardly every time they innocently touched. Even worse, she couldn't help hoping he'd touch her more.

It completely and utterly annoyed her, yet she couldn't stem the reaction, but she could make sure things didn't go any further.

Once dinner was over, again he led her with a firm hand in the middle of her back. He held open the door for her and tucked her hand in his arm as he walked them to the parking lot. His courtly gestures didn't do anything to help her attraction.

Why can't he act the uncouth jerk? It made it so much easier to dislike him.

Refusing a ride home wasn't an option, not when she lacked cab fare. However, she'd not counted on the intimacy of his two-seater sports car. Did he purposely brush her knee and thigh with his fingers every time he shifted?

Did it matter? The result remained the same; she shivered each and every time. *God, I hope he can't guess how he affects me.*

Could she blame her extreme attraction on some kind of psychological syndrome? Wasn't there one that made women fall for men who swooped in like a hero promising rescue from a dire fate? In her case, was she mistaking her gratitude that he wanted to defend her as attraction?

Nah. Face it. The guy was hot. Handsome. Sexy. With a voice made for late-night radio and dirty words.

Or, even better, dirty acts. *It's been much too long since I've indulged in some naughty fun.*

The purring engine shut off a moment after he pulled to the curb in front of her building. Miracle of all miracles, he'd managed to scoop a spot. Displaying, once again, an uncanny agility and speed that nagged at her, he somehow managed to make it to her side of the car within seconds of parking.

After opening the passenger door, he held out a hand to her, and as she clasped it she couldn't help a quiver in her lower belly as their flesh touched. Was it her or had he sucked in a breath? With a firm clasp of her hand, he aided her from the low-slung vehicle.

Once on the pavement, he didn't immediately release his grip, and she bit her lip, uncertain of what he expected from her. She'd meant what she said earlier. She wouldn't put out. *I'm not that kind of girl.*

Her body, on the other hand, disagreed. *We could totally be that kind of girl, and enjoy it.*

"Thanks for the ride," she said, even if it was the banal kind.

"You're welcome."

"I guess I'll be hearing from you." And probably dreaming, her imaginative sex life so much more active than her reality-based one.

"I'll be in touch tomorrow," he said as he laced his fingers through hers and walked her to the glass door of her building.

"You don't need to escort me to my apartment. I am more than capable of seeing myself the rest of the way."

"A gentleman always sees a lady home."

"Are you always a gentleman?" she blurted out. She bit her lower lip a moment later at the implication he wasn't. He wasn't her family or a close friend to whom she could just speak her mind or, as her cousins complained, insult at every turn.

Instead of taking offense, he laughed, a low baritone that again set her nerves atingling. "Most definitely not. Most would actually compare me to the wolf."

"Because you're wild?"

"Partially, but more because I'm a hunter. When I see what I want, I go after it."

"And what do you want?"

As the elevator door closed, encasing them in a small space where she remained much too aware of him, he didn't immediately reply, but he did stare down at her, an intense gaze that had her dropping her eyes to study the scuffed floor.

A finger tipped her chin, forcing her to meet his gaze. "Would you run like a scared rabbit if I said I wanted you?"

"No, but I might hurt you in your man parts if you try to take liberties."

A wicked smile curved his lips. "Is that a challenge?"

No. Yes. Conflicted, she managed to stammer, "N-n-no, it's not a challenge. We need to keep things professional. Don't you lawyers have to swear some kind of oath about not sleeping with clients?"

"Who said anything about sleeping? But, in answer to your query, yes, we are ethically obliged to try and keep a distance and not engage in personal relationships. However, once I've acquitted you, all holds are off."

"You're that confident you're going to win."

"Yes. I rarely lose, especially when it's something I really want. So prepare yourself. Once I've cleared your name, I will pursue you. And we will become involved."

Cocky. Self-assured. So utterly male . . . and sexy. But she was a modern woman. Surely she wasn't falling for his caveman tactics? How dare he dictate. "You make it sound so ominous. As if I don't have a choice."

"You don't. Don't you remember what I said? I'm a wolf, and I always get what I want."

The sound of a *ding* prevented her from replying, as did the swish of the elevator doors opening. Hiding her racing pulse and flustered thoughts proved easy as Megan stepped from the elevator cab and, with quick steps, marched to her door.

When she fumbled the keys to unlock it, his hand covered hers, which didn't help, not when such awareness flared between them.

The tumblers clicked, but she didn't open the door, instead turning to face him.

He stood close, much too close. It made her much too aware once again of the size of him, of the overwhelming maleness of his bearing. *What is the matter with me?* She'd dealt her whole life with imposing men. She'd never had a problem before putting them in their place.

Peeking upward into his chiseled countenance, she uttered a polite and dismissive. "Thank you for everything."

"No thanks needed. I'm doing what I must."

Despite her insistence on nothing personal between them, she couldn't help a miffed squirt of irritation that he'd relegated her to the status of a chore. "Must? I didn't realize you felt forced."

"You misunderstand. I am representing you because I can't stand by and watch a gross miscarriage of justice. Nor can I allow the woman I intend to pursue, ardently I might add, to suffer against obviously false charges."

When put like that . . .

Before she could reply, firm lips pressed against hers, stealing words and breath. No time to react. No time to reciprocate. The electric touch was there one moment, gone the next.

"What was that?"

"Since I didn't have a contract, I sealed our deal with a kiss." With a naughty wink, he strode away from her and back to the elevator.

She stared at his receding back. Even in a suit, the rear of him shouted, *I'm hot!*

With her lips tingling and body screaming for more, Megan could only numbly blink as he tossed her a sensual grin over his shoulder and said, "See you tomorrow, little rabbit."

Then he was gone, in body perhaps, but not in mind.

Enclosing herself in the comfort of her apartment, Megan leaned for a moment against the door, struck dumb by the kiss and the promise she read in his parting words.

As her new lawyer, yes, he'd have to see her, but why did she suspect he meant more than that?

Probably because he's stated quite emphatically that he's interested in me as more than a client.

Forget indignation at his caveman intent to claim. The woman in her couldn't help but flush in pleasure.

He wants me.

And God help her, but despite the complication, she wanted him, too.

CHAPTER 5

Making an appointment and giving warning was never any fun, which was why Gavin showed up on Fabian's doorstep right after leaving Megan.

Give the cameras that recorded everything that dared encroach on his territory, Gavin wasn't surprised when the master of the house himself opened the door, a dark brow raised. Fabian presented him with a cool, "To what displeasure do I owe this visit?"

At least the older wolf—who in his early forties counted as older than Gavin's early thirties—no longer pretended a fondness for his creation. In the beginning, Fabian had tried to take Gavin under his wing, more like have him bend on a knee to his overlord paw, but Gavin would have none of it. The ruthless manner in which the crime lord had turned Gavin in the hopes of having a lawyer join his legal team had stroked Gavin the wrong way.

Changing Gavin into a Lycanthrope hadn't cured him of his stubborn nature, or his desire to be his own man—and now wolf.

How dare Fabian upset the carefully ordered life Gavin would have enjoyed, and for what? So that Fabian's own selfish needs were served. How dare the man try to assume a dictatorship over Gavin? Alpha and Lycan pack politics be damned, Gavin wasn't about to start taking orders. He enjoyed his status as lone wolf, and he made sure Fabian knew it at every turn.

"I see no one has managed to shoot your criminal ass yet. A shame."

"Not for lack of trying," was Fabian's dry reply. "I assume you want to come in."

"But of course. Unless you have something to hide." Gavin's feral smile dared Fabian to deny him. They both knew how much Gavin wanted to pin him to a crime. Any crime. Something for payback. Alas, it hadn't happened yet. But the night was young.

"Despite your conviction that I am related to the devil and constantly up to nefarious deeds, I am simply a businessman."

"Who dabbles in things skirting the edges of the law."

"Skirt, perhaps, but still within the letter."

"One day you'll slip up and I'll catch you."

"We'll see, pup. But I'm sure idle threats aren't the real reason for your visit, so why not cut the bullshit and get to the point. Perhaps over a glass of whiskey?" Fabian strode away and through an archway into an opulently appointed living room. Gavin followed.

Only an idiot would refuse the aged amber liquid offered in the tumbler. Fabian's image might show up under the definition for "asshat," but he stocked a fine liquor cabinet.

Gavin took the proffered glass and enjoyed a sip of the velvety smooth, yet kick-packed, alcohol. "Damn, that shit is good," he admitted.

"Only a dozen bottles of it left in the world."

Which meant a price tag Gavin didn't even want to fathom. Before things got too relaxed, Gavin went for the jugular. "So I hear you hired some little secretary to knock off your rival Pierre Jonquin?"

His creator didn't quite spew his mouthful of whiskey, but it definitely didn't go down the right tube. Fabian coughed, then gasped before laughing. "Well, that was certainly unexpected. You think I'm now resorting to hiring, what is it you said, little secretaries to rid myself of people? Where on earth did you get that ridiculous idea?"

"Well, this Pierre fellow is dead. His employee, one Megan Alexander, stands accused. According to sources, with him out of the way the one who stands to benefit most is you."

"Your sources are misinformed. The man was hardly a rival. As a matter of fact, he wasn't even a blip on my radar. Pierre, at one time, might have been a man of power, but these last few years he's allowed certain vices to deplete his finances and common sense. It was only a matter of time before his business interests flopped. Why would I kill him when, in but a few short months, I could have swooped up his assets for a song?"

"What do you mean, 'could have'?"

"His death was most inconvenient. Because of the legal matters surrounding his demise, his assets will now be tied up in endless rounds of litigation and legal tape. I'm rather annoyed that his paramour took matters into her own hands and killed him. He was more useful to me alive."

Jealousy tightened Gavin's grip around the glass. "Why do you say she was his paramour?"

"Isn't that the most likely scenario? Married man has affair with his secretary, and when he refuses to leave his wife, in a crime of passion, she murders him."

"Except they weren't lovers." Gavin couldn't help his stark response.

His vehemence was noted by a certain observant wolf. Fabian's eyes narrowed. "What exactly is your interest in all this? It's not like you to brashly appear on my doorstep spouting feeble accusations without merit."

No point in hiding the truth. Gavin just didn't divulge the entire truth. "I've taken on Ms. Alexander's case. It is my belief she is innocent and being framed."

"And you automatically assumed I was the one doing the framing? How unsurprising and shortsighted. Pierre had many enemies, and while I guess one could count me among those who didn't care for him, I assure you, if I wanted him dead, I'd handle it much more *personally*." The toothy grin easily conveyed Fabian's method. In the Lycan world, justice was mostly dealt hands-, or should he say paws-, on.

As much as Gavin wanted to continue to believe Fabian had orchestrated the murder and frame job, he couldn't ignore his gut, which said the powerful wolf spoke the truth. But if Gavin's damned creator hadn't killed Pierre, then who had?

As if reading Gavin's mind, Fabian answered him. "Might I suggest that if you're looking for culprits, you take a closer look at those he owed money to? I wasn't kidding when I said Pierre teetered on the brink of ruin. Those wanting their payout may have very well acted."

"But why frame the secretary? And then bail her out?" Because a half-million dollars wasn't exactly chump change.

Whoever put up the cash surety for her release did so for a reason.

Fabian shrugged. "I think the better question is why they felt a need to so publicly kill him instead of having him discreetly disappear."

Tossing back the rest of the whiskey, because he couldn't bring himself to waste the delicious liquid, Gavin didn't bother thanking the other wolf for his forced hospitality. He just marched out of the house to the mocking shout of, "Nice to see you. We should do this again sometime!"

Jerk. Even more irritating was the fact that if Fabian hadn't forcibly changed Gavin he might have liked the man—even if he was a criminal lord.

The drive home was done at high speed, mostly because Gavin found himself perturbed. However, outracing his thoughts, and most especially his tumultuous emotions, didn't work.

With his visit to Fabian out of the way, and without a lead to pursue on his new case, he couldn't help but think of the client herself.

His woman.

My mate.

Not quite mate. Yet.

Despite his having met Megan only hours ago, every nuance of her features was etched into his brain. Mahogany-colored hair, upswept in a messy chignon with curling wisps escaping to frame her face. Bright, and at times bold, brown eyes framed in silky dark lashes. A curvy figure, perhaps a touch on the plump side, but pleasantly so. A perfectly padded frame for strenuous bedroom activities. Inches of creamy flesh for him to explore. Or so he imagined as she sat all

prim and proper across from him at dinner in her buttoned-
up blouse and knee-length skirt.

How easily he could picture the perfect Cupid's bow of her
mouth, a mouth he briefly tasted. Torture, because now he
couldn't help but crave more.

More of her. Now. Tonight.

Not happening.

Fuck.

Need thrummed through him. A primal urge to hunt his
female down and claim her. Gavin understood some of the
intensity of his emotions had to do with his base side, his
wolf side. It wasn't as if he were two beings in one body—
man and wolf—and yet, at times, certain aspects of his wild
side pushed for dominance. Such as now, when a part of him
thought he should return to Megan, knock on her door—*kick
it down if she doesn't answer*—sweep her into his arms, and
seduce her until she clawed his back and cried his name.

The more civilized part of him still wanted to seduce her
but had a hard time assimilating the whole claim-her thing.

He barely knew the woman.

But I want her.

She was a client who should have been hands-off.

Yet I want to put my hands all over her.

She was nothing like the usual high-maintenance model
types he went after with their superslim bodies, peroxide
hair, and teensy bites of salad.

She's a curvy handful with an appetite to rival my own.
And he didn't just mean when it came to food.

He predicted when it came to bedroom play she'd show
an enthusiasm and passion to bring any man to his knees.
And that thought did not help his situation. Partially erect,

and with him alone with only his hands for company. His five-finger massage did little to ease his tension.

Which was why he was terse and irritable when he showed up at her door the following day, only to find her gone.

An old codger stuck his head out his door as Gavin insistently pounded, wondering at her lack of answer. Where could she be at eight thirty in the morning? *Where is she?* Had she fled town, trying to escape the charges? Had she slept over somewhere—with a man? Claws popped from the tips of Gavin's fingers and scored her door as he pounded again.

"She's not there."

Whirling, hands tucking into his pockets until certain things retracted, Gavin eyed the neighbor. In his house robe loosely sashed over plaid pajamas, the old guy didn't offer any danger, which eased the coiled tension in Gavin's body.

"Any idea where she is?" Getting a coffee? The newspaper? Perhaps gone for a jog or a walk? Waking up beside a dead man? *Because anyone touching my woman is asking for it.* Lawyers called it justifiable cause.

"Cops came and got her late last night. Apparently, the prosecution got her bail revoked. Managed to convince some judge she was a flight risk."

"You seem rather well-informed."

The old guy shrugged. "I was listening at the door. It's not often I get to witness something this exciting. Felt sorry for the poor girl, though. I mean, I know she's supposed to have killed a guy and all, but she was always real sweet. She used to drop me off cookies and stuff when she baked some. Damn shame what happened."

A shame indeed given she should have never been picked

up in the first place. Someone had posted her bail, anonymous or not. She'd not breached her conditions that Gavin knew of, so for the prosecution, in a vindictive move, to have it yanked spoke of something deeper than just a public district attorney keeping the public safe.

Someone didn't want Megan out and about and someone obviously was denying her the right to contact her counsel, because his cell phone didn't show any missed calls.

Simmering within, but not outwardly showing it, Gavin sped his way to the courts to kick some legal ass. It didn't take him long to get a wrong righted. It seemed someone had called in claiming Megan was seen at a train station buying a ticket. They should have done their homework, seeing as how she was at dinner with him, with more than enough witnesses to prove it.

Paperwork accomplished, his displeasure duly noted, and her release secured, Gavin made his way over to the jail.

The cops on duty there knew him and didn't waste time. In short order, he was seated across from Megan.

Dark circles ringed her haunted eyes, and her shoulders hunched. She presented the picture of someone who'd given up. It totally pissed him off, so he barked a little more tersely than she deserved given the upheaval she'd gone through.

"Why the hell didn't you call me?"

She shrugged. "I asked to call my lawyer. They didn't know you'd taken over, so I got my public defender's voice mail."

"Did you tell them they fucked up?"

"I tried, but . . ." Again with the helpless shrug.

The urge to leap over the table, gather her in his arms

and hug her took him by surprise. Gavin wasn't a cuddle type of guy. Nor was he usually overcome by an urge to protect, but seeing Megan brought so low created all kinds of new emotions within him. He also wanted to growl. Loudly. He told his inner wolf to chew on a bone in the corner of his mind. He'd take care of this.

"Lucky for you, I was at your apartment bright and early and heard about this mockery. I've already had the bail reinstated. Now it's just a matter of waiting for the paperwork to go through. We should have you out of here mid- to late afternoon."

"Really?" For the first time since he entered the room, she perked up.

"Of course really. You didn't honestly think I'd let you rot in here, did you? Like hell. Have some faith, little rabbit. I am good at what I do, and when it comes to my clients"—and especially this woman—"no one fucks with them." *Or me.*

"Thank you."

"While we're waiting for them to get their heads out of their asses and release you, I'd like to talk a bit more about your boss. It was brought to my attention that he was dealing with some financial difficulties. Can you elaborate?"

Her nose wrinkled. "Money problems? Not that I knew of, but then again, I wasn't in charge of his books. I can say he always paid me on time and he didn't skimp when it came to spending, especially when he wanted to impress someone."

"Notice anyone coming to his office recently that left your boss agitated, maybe worried?"

"Lots of people. Mr. Jonquin ranted often. Heck, he even went on a tirade when his wife came around."

"Not a happy couple?"

"Oh, he worshiped the ground she walked on. I don't know how many times I ordered flowers for her or had to score some tickets to some event he thought she might enjoy."

"So why would he get upset when she visited?"

"Because she accused him of cheating."

"Was he?"

"Honestly, I don't know, but if you want my opinion, I'd say no. Like I said, he worshiped her. It drove him nuts that she thought he didn't love her. Hence the gifts."

"Did she ever come out and accuse you of sleeping with him?"

"Only once, when I first came to work for him. He was late coming back from a lunch meeting, and she told me if I ever set my sights on him, I'd pay."

"Sounds rather confrontational. I'm surprised you didn't quit."

"It was rude, but I needed the job, so I told her quite frankly that I wasn't into old, balding, short guys and that I'd probably buy a vibrator before I'd let him touch me."

He couldn't help but chuckle. "How did she react?"

A smirk curled Megan's lips. "After she got over the initial mouth-gaping shock that I'd compared her husband to a troll, she told me that I'd better not ever change my mind and stalked off. After that, she never really paid me any mind."

"Who posted your bail?"

"I don't know."

"Come on, little rabbit. Half a million dollars. Someone who obviously likes you must have posted it. Who do you know with that kind of dough?"

A shrug lifted her shoulders. "I don't know. I barely have enough to buy groceries for the week. My family lives out on the West Coast and doesn't know about my situation yet. I was never more surprised than when they told me that I was going free."

A freedom that nagged him. Initially he'd wondered if whoever she claimed framed her for the murder was the person who posted the bail. By having her on the loose it wouldn't prove hard to have their scapegoat suffer a fatal accident, resulting in an open-and-shut case.

Then someone had falsely accused her of fleeing and made sure she got her delectable ass thrown back into jail. Someone who obviously didn't know about him yet. But would now.

Him versus an as-yet-faceless threat to his woman. Too bad for them, they'd picked the wrong rabbit. The chase was on.

CHAPTER 6

Tired and feeling kind of grubby, Megan couldn't wait to get home, strip, and take a long, hot shower. When the police showed up in the middle of the night—which truly was a cruelty given even the birds weren't awake yet—and dragged her away, they'd not given her time to bathe or dress properly. Why bother when they had her exchange her pajamas at the station for a lovely orange jumpsuit? Apparently, they'd expected her to stay awhile.

She'd thought herself a tad bit screwed, too, until Gavin arrived with some good news. It appeared as if her new lawyer might prove himself useful after all. He'd manage to spring her with the most simple of logic, the truth.

It seemed someone wanted Megan's butt in jail. Question was, why? Wasn't it enough she stood accused of murder? Did they have to compound the insult by taking away her freedom to find justice?

As she bounced from one foot to another—clad in some truly comfortable purple fleece-lined Crocs—she almost wished she'd ask to keep the orange suit rather than trade back into her oh-so-sexy puppy dog pajamas. Her jammies, made of cotton, had shrunk in the dryer so the top didn't quite end at her waistband and the pants hugged her a touch more than she considered proper. Best part of all, though? No bra.

When she emerged from the station, she crossed her arms over her chest, very conscious of the fact that her tight, almost crop top clung to her breasts and outlined a certain part of her anatomy currently reacting to the chillier temperature.

A familiar sleek car purred at the curb. The passenger door popped open, and she saw Gavin leaning across the vehicle, arm still outstretched.

His keen gaze took her in, and a corner of his lip curled. "Cute outfit."

Her cheeks burned. *Not again.* What was it about this guy that made her so self-conscious? "They didn't give me a chance to change when they came for me. And I see someone didn't think to bring me spare clothes."

"You won't have to wear them for long."

At his words, her jaw might have dropped open. "Excuse me?"

He laughed. "I like the way your mind works, but in this case, it's wrong. I meant, you won't have them on for long because I'm taking you home."

Surely she wasn't disappointed? Nothing like feeding another hunger to distract herself. "Can we do a pit stop on the way? I'd rather we got some food first. I am freaking starving, and I know what's in my fridge." Nothing humanly edible.

Rich laughter filled the car, the intimate space wrapping the baritone sound around her warmer than any blanket. "You're not exactly dressed for a fine dining establishment."

"Who said anything about 'fine'? Can't we just hit a drive-thru and grab something ridiculously greasy and bad for me?"

"Bad." He practically growled the word. "I like it when you say that."

"You are such a dog."

"Wolf."

Yes, a wolf, a predator, one seeking to destroy her promise of remaining aloof. Getting involved with Gavin spelled danger. She needed him to defend her, which meant she had to keep a professional distance. A pity he seemed hell bent on doing the opposite.

"Why is it men only have one thing on their minds?"

"One? You wound me. I am a man capable of many thoughts at once. I have several right now as a matter of fact."

"Are any of them not about sex?"

To her amusement, which she tried her best to hide, he pretended to think about it before lavishing her with a sensual grin that should come with a warning. "No, they're all about you and something utterly decadent. When you're around, my mind seems to have only one track."

"Well, you need to get off that track to nowhere and get your mind back in the game. Because one, I really, really need some food, or we're going to have an issue." Make that a major meltdown that just might result in her nibbling on flesh because, dammit, now he had her thinking of sex, too. "And two, am I the only one noticing the fact that there's a blue Toyota Corolla that's been following us since we left the station?"

Gavin spared only a cursory glance to his rearview mirror. "Possibly a coincidence."

"Really? Then humor me. Turn left. Now!" she shouted at him, and to her surprise, he complied, spinning the wheel and angling his car in a sharper-than-ninety-degree turn. His sports car handled it with ease, not so the Corolla. Having half-turned in her seat, Megan peeked out the back window and frowned as she saw the other car's driver had slammed on its brakes. Too late. The vehicle shot past the intersection and almost got rear ended.

"Well, that was interesting," she murmured, turning back around.

"Very. I wondered if someone would try something once they heard you got sprung," he mused aloud. "I just didn't expect it so soon. My bad. Good eyes by the way."

"You mean you expected someone to follow us? And you didn't say anything?"

"It was just a theory, one I didn't want to worry you with."

"Well now I'm worried."

"Don't be. I'll make sure you're kept safe."

Exactly how her lawyer thought he could protect her from someone who might wish her ill intent she couldn't figure out. But the way he promised it . . . Sigh. While unnecessary, it was totally sexy.

"Keep me safe from who? And why? You still haven't answered me."

"Given the blatant attempt to get you off the street by having your bail revoked, I hypothesized that if you were indeed framed—"

"I told you I was," she grumbled.

"—then whoever is screwing with you might escalate things. The best way for them to have an open-and-shut case on your old boss's murder is to have you unable to talk.

Getting you tossed in jail proved troubling. I'll admit I was glad to see you unharmed. I kind of worried something unfortunate would happen to you in jail."

Hmm, like the drunken broad thrown in with her who turned out to not be so drunk once the cops left the holding block? A good thing Megan knew a thing or two about defending herself. When the cop returned, he looked from her sitting primly on the bench to the drunk snoring on the floor and simply raised a brow. Megan didn't feel a need to let him know that, when the hussy came at her, she knocked her out cold. *Thank you, Cousin Harry, for teaching me that left hook.*

"Well, I'm fine. Even better, we seem to have lost our friend in the blue car, and look, there's a Burger King up ahead."

As she practically inhaled a Whopper made of decadent goodness and hummed a happy sound while munching fries, she noted Gavin executing a lot more turns and taking a lot more time than needed to get to her condo complex. His eyes constantly flitted between his mirrors, and he didn't talk as much, intent on the happenings around them.

They made it to her apartment without mishap, where he parked a block down, his previous luck having not held. At least she wasn't completely uncovered, though, as he donated his coat a moment after handing her from the car. She wrapped herself in it, glad of the cover, not just from the cooler twilight air but also from the stares of the curious.

How she must look with her hair sticking out from a messy ponytail, wearing her bright slippers, escorted by a clean-shaven, towering hunk in a suit. With a freaking tie.

The ridiculous thing made her want to grab it and yank him down so she could plant a kiss on those tempting lips.

Bad. Very bad. And to think she'd accused him of having the dirty mind. It seemed she wasn't innocent when it came to letting her mind play in the gutter.

As before, he insisted on accompanying her right to her door. Once again, the elevator felt much too small for the two of them, especially when he planted himself before her and tilted her chin.

"Feeling okay? You seem rather subdued."

"While I appreciate what you've done so far, I have to admit that a part of me is a little tired at whatever game is being played at my expense." Tired and annoyed.

"We'll find whoever is doing this. Because once we find them, we'll find the true murderer."

"And you'll get the charges dismissed."

"Yes, which will then mean you're no longer my client."

"And back his mind goes into the gutter," she said with a laugh as she exited through the elevator doors when they slid open to her floor.

Striding up the hall, she smiled, a part of her flattered at his insistence on courting her. How long since a man had shown such ardent interest? Actually, she didn't think any man had seemed so intent to convince her to bed him as Gavin. Most suitors tended to last only a short time, especially once they met her family. And Daddy wondered why she'd fled to the East Coast.

At her apartment door, she stopped, chagrined to realize her keys were inside, sitting in the purse the police wouldn't let her bring.

"Shoot. I don't have a way of getting in," she grumbled. "I'll have to find the superintendent."

"Allow me. Wait here."

Given her fatigue and outfit, she didn't argue and enjoyed the rear view of Gavin as he strode back to the elevators.

Since she didn't know how long he'd be, she let herself slump until she sat on the floor. Instead of focusing on her sexy lawyer—who came to her rescue—she tried to use her brain to figure out who the hell had it out for her.

She'd not lived in this town long enough to make any enemies. As a matter of fact, no one knew she'd moved here. Not even the friends she'd left behind as she made her fresh start. As for her family, they just called her cell phone when they wanted to talk. This place wasn't a permanent thing for Megan. Just a temporary job she'd taken on her path to better things.

A job she now regretted.

Someone framed me for Pierre's murder. Someone who wanted him dead. Who stood to benefit the most? According to most crime shows, the spouse was the first suspect. With the evidence against Megan, no one bothered to look at the widow. But Megan had to wonder. Much younger than her husband and volatile, Vivienne certainly had a temper that could lead to murder. But a crime of passion wouldn't have involved the meticulous planning that led to Megan getting accused.

Which begged the question that nagged most. How did they plant the evidence? *I was drugged. Had to be.* How else to explain her lack of memories from the moment she entered her apartment to the next morning when the cops beat down her door? Drugged so they could plant a bloody knife and a blouse she'd left two days before at the dry cleaners stained with Pierre's blood. Those elements combined spoke of forethought.

"Got it," Gavin announced, breaking her train of thought as he exited the elevator, key in hand.

In short order, she entered her place, Gavin on her heels. It seemed he'd elected to stick around for a while. She ignored him, hoping he'd take a hint and leave. But when she emerged from the shower, she heard him talking on his phone in the living room.

Dressing first, and blow-drying her hair before wrapping it in a scrunchie atop her head, she exited her bedroom to find him completely at home, sprawled on her couch.

"Don't you have to work?" she asked as she busied herself in the kitchen making a much-needed coffee.

"I am. Working your case as a matter of fact. So, no surprise, the wife has an alibi."

"You checked?"

"Of course I did. Spouses are the usual suspects in these kinds of cases."

Funny how he mirrored her earlier thoughts.

"Now mind you, she could have hired someone to do it, but given the red tape now involved with his estate, I doubt it. Most hired killings for inheritance try to make it look like a benign accident. So I've veered my inquiries into his business dealings and discovered something interesting." Gavin stopped talking.

Megan took a sip of coffee and waited for him to continue. When he didn't, she prodded. "And?"

"And if you want to know what I found, then you need to sit over here."

"I'm fine where I am." Where she was being across the room from him, seated on a stool by the kitchen counter.

A getting-familiar deadly and sexy smile curved his lips. "But I'm not fine. If we're going to be together—"

"To work."

"—then you're going to have to learn to trust me."

"I do trust you. You're my lawyer."

He patted the cushion beside me. "Don't be a scared rabbit. Come here."

The taunt was an obvious ploy. That didn't stop her from falling for it. "I'm not scared," she stated as she plopped herself down on the couch beside him. Accepting dumb challenges ever was a vice of hers. Her mother said Megan got that trait from her father's side.

"Of course, you're not scared," he murmured, draping his arm along the back of the couch and tickling fingers across her exposed neck.

Shifting would have given him too much ammo. She pretended to not notice his feathery touch. "I'm sitting. Now do you mind telling me what you found?"

"It seems Pierre had a certain fondness for a strip joint, one known to also partake in certain illegal gambling activities."

"You think they might be the ones behind my framing?"

"It can't hurt to find out. I'm vaguely acquainted with the manager. She works for a mutual acquaintance."

"You're friends with a criminal?"

"Hardly friends, but in my line of work, I tend to meet

interesting people. I'll go and talk to Lulu. See if she knows anything about Pierre. She might be able to shed some light on who he was dealing with and if he owed any large sums of money."

"I'm going with you."

"To a strip joint?" He couldn't hide his incredulous tone.

"Sure. Why not? It's not like I haven't seen a woman's naked body before. How bad could it be?"

CHAPTER 7

This was bad. Oh so bad.

In his defense, when Megan had told Gavin she wanted to go he'd tried to say no. Several times as a matter of fact. Then she leaned in close, placed a hand high up on his thigh, and whispered, practically against his lips, "I'm going, and you can't stop me. So either we go together, or I go alone."

Bested. By a woman. Which was how he found himself in a den of iniquity, with his future mate, regretting his decision. Especially when he noted the interested leers of the men patronizing the place.

His lip curled in menace, and he couldn't help a low growl, which Megan, thankfully, didn't hear. But it did force him to put a lock on his more primitive side.

This wasn't the time or place to get jealous. He knew on a rational level that he needn't fear competition from the men in this place, but his possessive side, which until now he never suspected existed, really didn't like the male attention directed her way.

With a boldness he would not have suspected her capable of, Megan strode to the bar, head held high, as if she were in charge.

Behind the granite-topped surface, a woman with a wild mane of red curls, a freckled nose, and a top a few sizes too small dried a glass with a towel.

"What can I get you?"

"We are looking to speak to the owner or manager please."

"About?"

"It's a private matter."

Primly said. Gavin almost laughed. He positioned himself behind Megan, close enough to feel her shiver at his proximity. Nice to know his presence affected her. "Hey, Lulu. Short staffed today?"

"Bloody idiot who bartends this shift got himself thrown into jail for a DUI, which means I'm stuck until a replacement comes in. Who's the broad?" asked Lulu with a head dip in Megan's direction.

"My client. We're here looking for information on a certain Pierre Jonquin. Does the name ring a bell?"

"Wait a second. Isn't she the one accused of killing him? I heard it was an open-shut case. Overwhelming evidence and all."

Megan stiffened. "I'm being framed."

"Sure you are, doll." Lulu didn't roll her eyes, but her tone said it all.

"Certain inconsistencies have led me to believe there is more to this case than meets the eye, like the certain matter of money owing."

"Not to me, he didn't."

"So you're familiar with him?"

"Sure. Pierre was a regular. Every day at lunch, right when Mitzy's set started."

"He was cheating on his wife?"

Lulu fixed Megan with a hard stare. "Eyeballing some scantily clad dancers isn't cheating."

"But his wife—"

"Is a psycho who used to work here once upon a time. Betcha didn't know that. Vivi, or Vivienne as she now likes to call herself, was a popular act until she got hitched to Pierre last year."

"So they met here then? Perhaps I was hasty in dismissing her as a possible suspect. Given how they met, I can see how she might have let jealousy consume her if she discovered his noontime activities," Gavin mused aloud.

"Discovered?" Lulu snorted. "She usually joined him. And it wasn't for the floor show. The pair of them like playing the odds."

"And losing?"

"Actually no. They did surprisingly well. Too well. Bruno was thinking about cutting them off. Their wins were cutting into his profit margins."

Gavin couldn't help but frown. "If that's the case, then what about the rumors saying he owed large sums?"

Lulu shrugged. "Hell if I know how those started. But if he did, it wasn't here. You know the big man doesn't allow bets that aren't covered."

Indeed, Fabian might enable illegal gambling, but he also had a policy that demanded money up front.

"I don't suppose you know anything else?"

"Nope. But hey, we just lost a girl last week. Darned chit ran off with her boyfriend. Given your client is now unemployed, she should think about a change in career. We've got guys who'd pay her big bucks to take those clothes off."

Gavin's fist struck the counter before he could stop it, and he growled, "Megan won't be working here. I forbid it."

Leaving Lulu staring at him in openmouthed shock, probably because he had referred some ladies looking for cash her way before, he grabbed Megan by the elbow and steered her out of there before his simmering anger got the better of him.

He didn't make it completely out.

"Hey, buddy, how much for your—"

The man never finished his sentence, probably because Gavin punched him.

As Gavin and Megan exited the bar to see twilight had descended, she pulled from his grasp and whirled on him.

"What the heck was that?"

"What? Me hitting the guy? He implied you were for sale. A man never lets scum insult a lady."

"I wasn't talking about that. The hitting was totally deserved. I meant the whole I-forbid-it thing. I'm not saying I'd take up stripping for money, but what gives you the right to decide what I am allowed to do? I don't belong to you."

That was where she was wrong.

She. Was. His.

And it was time she started to realize that fact.

He dragged her toward him, arms wrapped around her so she couldn't escape, not that she fought him. But in case she tried to flee, he trapped her against his chest. He caught her protest before it could leave her lips, his mouth slanting across hers, claiming them in a torrid kiss.

A very hot kiss.

A kiss she returned.

In that moment, Gavin didn't care they were on the sidewalk in plain view. He didn't care about ethics or rules. He also didn't give a damn that he was announcing his affection for the world to see.

I want her.

Simple. Undeniable. So right.

Which was why he could have ripped the tongue out of the guy who let out a wolf whistle from a passing car along with a shouted, "Twenty bucks if you get her to blow you in public!"

Megan froze, her pliant lips stiffening along with the rest of her as she resisted his embrace. He didn't force the issue, letting her escape the confines of his arms.

She glared at him. "I thought I said no touching."

"And here I thought you'd changed your mind, given your tongue in my mouth."

To his delight, pink suffused her cheeks. Embarrassment, though, didn't prevent her from retorting, "Only because I was attempting to push it out."

"Such a liar," he chided her, his tone low and teasing. "A good thing for you I'm a man who can hear the truth beneath the lie. Are you ready to go back to your place now, or shall we indulge in more *oral* argument?" He couldn't resist the inflection, not when he knew it would drive her nuts.

Eyes flashing, she shot him an eloquently raised finger and stalked to his car. Enclosed within its confines, he wouldn't allow her to simmer in anger.

"Come now, it wasn't that bad."

"No. It wasn't. It was a great kiss. The best I've ever had," she admitted, completely taking him by surprise.

"Why do I sense a but?"

"Because there is one. Let's say we get involved. You're my lawyer. Now tell me what happens if, before the trial or during, you suddenly decide we're no good together. Or I find out you suck in bed."

"I don't."

"Even if you don't, let's say you're a god in bed. An utter erotic genius. What if you hate kittens?"

"Love the little furballs." Especially when he got a feisty one he could chase up a tree.

"Don't like garlic."

"Is there such a thing?"

"Discover I snore and you can't sleep with me. Or maybe I'll suck in bed."

"I highly doubt that."

Again she blushed.

"You're deliberately missing the point. What if we do take things to the next level, and it doesn't work out? Where does that leave me?"

Did there exist a delicate way of telling a woman she need not fear he'd ever leave her because his werewolf heritage had deemed she would mate with him for life and that they'd live happily ever after? Or so he assumed. He'd never exactly ascertained that point.

He stuck to a partial truth. "No matter what happens between us, I would never allow it to affect my duty to you and this case."

"I wish I could believe that. Really I do, because I am insanely attracted to you."

Yes!

"However," she continued, "I'm afraid attraction can't

come before my future and well-being. So please respect my wishes and keep your distance."

"For now."

While he could understand her concern, he couldn't stop himself, though. The more time he spent with her, the more he unraveled about her personality and discovered the spit-fire she hid within, the more he craved her. Wanted her. Would have her.

And he wasn't going to let weeks or months of tedious investigation while he cleared her name stop him.

So I'd better solve this case quick.

CHAPTER 8

Once again, Gavin insisted on accompanying Megan to her apartment door. Talk about dancing with temptation.

Bad enough dealing with him in the closeness of his car, especially after that devastating kiss, then having the scent of his cologne enveloping her as other building tenants forced him to invade her space. But she doubted her willpower if he entered her apartment, a place that would offer privacy and a bed. A bed that hadn't seen any exercise since her move here.

I need him to go. Quickly. Exiting the elevator, she took brisk steps to her apartment, only to slow as she approached the door to her place, a door not quite closed.

Key in hand, she hesitated.

"Move away from the door," he ordered, but she didn't jump to obey.

"Maybe I didn't close it properly when we left earlier," she muttered, reaching out with trembling fingers to push at the portal. It swung open.

Before she could truly comprehend what she glimpsed, Gavin had inserted himself between her and the open doorway, blocking her view.

But a second was all it took. One second to see that a tornado had apparently visited her home and left only wreckage in its wake.

Her trembling coalesced into a cold anger at the senseless destruction of her apartment.

Sure, she'd not lived here long or truly given it her stamp, but darn it, this was her space. *My home.* And someone had dared enter and destroy what little she had.

Someone would pay.

CHAPTER 9

It didn't take a keen sense of smell for Gavin to realize something was amiss as they approached Megan's apartment door. The fact that it sat ajar screamed intruder, especially since Gavin knew for a fact that they'd closed it when they left earlier. Hell, he'd watched her lock and test the knob before they set off.

When Megan didn't heed his warning to move aside, he simply inserted himself between her and the doorway, ensuring that should any intruders wait within, they'd have to deal with him first.

Or should he say, he'd deal with them?

Mess with my woman, mess with me. Apparently, wolves and cavemen had a lot in common.

Stepping into her apartment, Gavin focused on the possibility of the attackers—attackers in the plural because he smelled more than one. His focus didn't mean he missed Megan's gasp of dismay, but he'd focus on that in a moment. The broken detritus of her belongings could be replaced.

She couldn't.

Someone had gone through and left a very potent message, even spray-painted it on the wall.

Plead guilty or else.

"Not very subtle, are they?" he said aloud as he came to the conclusion he and Megan were alone.

"They trashed my place to try and convince me to go to jail for a murder I didn't commit? Are they out of their freaking minds?" Far from being terrified, Megan sounded disbelieving. "What idiot would ever agree to something like that? So what if they destroyed my place? I'm not going to spend my life behind bars."

"Fear can be a powerful motivator."

"Fear?" She snorted in clear disdain. "This makes me mad, and even more determined to fight this."

"That's my girl." He couldn't help pride in her stance, even as her fighting spirit took him by surprise. Most women he was acquainted with would have taken this opportunity to sob and fling themselves at him, begging he protect them. They would have hinted at sleeping over. He would have refused of course. An active social life didn't mean he invited his bed partners to get too close. He did have secrets, after all, and a need for personal space. But Megan was different.

"I'd better get the bucket and rag out."

"You don't want to call the police?"

She snorted. "What for? We both know break and enters don't rate high on their list of priorities. Especially for a suspected murderess. If you'll excuse me, I have a mess to clean up."

As Gavin glanced around the place, he noted it was more than just a mess. She needed a Dumpster, and pretty much everything replaced. She obviously couldn't stay here and surely acted so brave out of pride.

"You can stay with me until we catch the culprit," he told her. He waited for the smile of gratitude. Maybe a hug. Or a kiss?

"No."

The unexpected reply threw him for a loop. "Er—what?"

"No. Totally inappropriate and unnecessary."

"You can't stay here. Not only is this place unfit, but how do you know the culprits won't come back?"

She pursed her lips. "Good point. I'll find a motel."

"I thought you were broke."

Her nose wrinkled, and she made a noise. "Ugh. Dammit. I keep forgetting about that. I guess staying here is the only option. I doubt they'll come back tonight, and if they do, good luck getting in. I'll wedge a chair under the door." She walked away from him, stripping off her coat and draping it on the leg of an overturned armchair. She headed to the bedroom, still speaking. "It won't be that bad. I'll just vacuum up the glass and stuff so I don't cut myself and—"

The stream of curses she let out would have made even the most obscene comedian blush. How could such a pretty, demure woman know the most painful way of brutalizing a body part? Even more shocking, how could she utter it with complete conviction that she could accomplish the physically impossible feat? The flip from sweet victim to violent vixen rendered Gavin speechless.

Needing to know what had set her off, he entered her bedroom, only to stop as the scent of urine hit him.

"They peed on my bed!" She stood at the foot of it, hands on her hips, and glared.

Despite the nasty environ, her evident anger, and her dirty, dirty mouth, he'd never seen anything sexier. Grabbing her by the hand, he yanked her back out into the main area.

"What do you think you're doing?"

"Getting you out of here."

Digging in her heels, she halted her movement. "I am not going with you to your apartment."

"Fine. But you're going somewhere. I know of a hotel downtown we can go to with decent security and tight lips. Before you argue about the price, let me state that I consider this part of the cost of taking you on as a client. If you get killed because I was lax in your protection, then it looks bad on me."

"Do I have a choice?"

"No. And let it be known, right now, that I will carry you out of here kicking and screaming, caveman-style if needed. So swallow your pride and stubbornness. We're going."

"Fine," she grumbled. "I'll go to a hotel."

Hallelujah, he'd gotten her to agree. It probably wasn't a good time to mention he'd be staying with her and that he planned to get a room with only one bed.

For her protection and to save on costs of course. Already he prepared his argument, because no way would she allow it without a fight.

He rather looked forward to it.

CHAPTER 10

Megan fumed all the way to the hotel.

I can't believe they invaded my space like that.

Did they really think the loss of some stuff would make her plead guilty?

Like hell.

But she did find it worrisome that someone would go to such destructive lengths to try to pin a murder on her. Who hated her enough to want her in jail? Or was it she was just that the most convenient scapegoat?

Of other concern was the ardent interest of her lawyer. When he'd issued his invitation to have her stay with him, her first impulse was to say yes, especially since she got the feeling he didn't mean in the guest room. Then sanity kicked in, and she found herself refusing.

Getting involved with the man who was supposed to convince a jury and judge of her innocence wasn't in her best interest. Neither was accepting any favors from him. But what choice did she have?

She couldn't very well pull money out of a secret offshore bank account so she could hire some other swanky lawyer. Poor little secretaries didn't have that kind of luxury.

I am well and truly stuck. Stuck with a man who engaged her senses. A man who had her erotic imagination working overtime as she kept wondering when he'd kiss her again— because he would. She couldn't keep holding her breath and trying to suppress a shiver whenever he inadvertently—or purposely—touched her. She didn't even fool herself into wondering if it would happen. It was just a matter of when he'd make his next seductive move.

Lucky for her, she didn't have to wait long.

After handing the keys to the valet at the front entrance to the elegant downtown hotel, Gavin proceeded to book her into a lavish room that probably cost more for one night than the rent for her current apartment. Key card in hand, he insisted on accompanying her up to the ninth floor, going so far as to entering the space first on the guise of checking it out.

Once in there, he wouldn't leave.

Kicking off his black leather loafers, loosening his tie, he flopped onto the left side of the king-sized bed and laced his hands behind his head.

"Comfy," he observed.

"I'm sure it is. Shouldn't you be getting home?" she asked as she removed her own shoes by the door. She hung her coat neatly in the closet. Considering the clothes on her back were the only things she currently owned, she'd better take care of them.

"Yeah, about me leaving, it occurred to me that I should stay."

"Stay? For what reason? No one knows I'm here."

"I do. My credit card does. The clerk saw you. Hell, for all we know, someone followed us."

Doubtful. Megan had kept watch in the side mirror. "I'll lock the door."

"What if they kick it in?"

"And how will you being here stop anyone that determined?"

How a man, dressed in a suit, and a yuppie lawyer to boot, could smile and manage to look so predatory, so dangerous, Megan couldn't have said. But he managed it. And damn, but he wore it well. The shiver that went through her had nothing to do with fear. Desire on the other hand?

He made it hard to resist his charm. Especially when he patted the mattress beside him and said, "Care to join me?"

"Do you treat all your female clients like this? Giving them the personal *touch*?"

"Never. In that you are special, little rabbit. With you, I am finding myself in uncharted woods, a hunter snared by the sensual allure of a nymph."

"Nymph?" She couldn't help but giggle at the comparison. "Hardly that. A nymph implies some supersexy buxom woman with hip-length locks and a phone-sex giggle. While I might have the cleavage, the rest of me hardly fits the bill."

"I disagree." One moment he lounged on the bed, and the next he loomed before her, once again displaying an uncanny speed for a man his size. A finger tilted her chin and forced her to meet his mesmerizing gaze. "I am extremely attracted to you. As you are attracted to me. I want to explore every inch of your curves. Taste the softness of your skin."

She couldn't help but swallow at the husky purr of his words. "What happened to keeping things professional?"

"You're the one who keeps insisting. I, on the other hand,

have made my intentions clear. I want you, Megan, and I don't think . . . actually, I know I can't wait a moment longer."

She might have protested, but his lips claimed hers in a sizzling kiss that wiped away all the reasons why they shouldn't touch.

On the contrary, his lips just reinforced her own belief that they needed to embrace. She needed the molten feel of his lips on hers. Wanted the moist tongue that danced and twined around hers with a sensual decadence that drew a groan.

Somehow they went from standing to lying upon the bed, hands roaming and tugging at impeding garments. How dare the fabric get in the way of their skin touching?

Ripping. Tearing. Buttons pinging.

They weren't gentle in their haste. The need within her pulsed. It hungered. She'd never before been so caught up in her desire for a man.

As clothes went flying, their flesh met in a sizzling clash of skin. Yet, despite their frenzy, their lips remained locked and their hands never paused in their stroking.

On her back, on the plush sateen comforter, she watched him through partially lidded eyes as he reared back, revealing a perfect chest with rippling, mouthwatering muscles. He visually devoured her.

"As perfect as I expected," he said in a husky tone as he reached out to flick an erect nub.

She sucked in a breath, then gave in to temptation and touched his inviting skin, dragging her nails, applying a little bit of pressure, as she scratched him from his pecs to the waistband of his unbuttoned slacks.

He sucked in a breath, and she smiled. So much for him being in control. She'd finally found a way to throw him off balance.

Only problem? She teetered as well.

Under his scorching gaze, her nipples puckered and her breathing stuttered, especially as he slowly lowered his face until his lips hovered over her erect nipple.

Megan couldn't help but arch in invitation, willing him to suck the tip. He couldn't resist. The hot flick of his tongue forced a moan from her, then another as he circled the tip wetly. She grasped his hair and tugged, attempting to force him to take the engorged nipple deeper. In this he didn't let her dictate.

"Such impatience."

"I know what I want," she replied.

"So do I, and I'll give it to you, when I'm good and ready." A sensual threat that sent shivers rocketing through her.

In a show of strength—which melted instead of angered—he clasped her hands and held them above her head. This served to expose her to his touch. Exposed her to the hot mouth that couldn't stop torturing.

How her body hummed. How she strained, her quivering sex begging for release. While he'd removed her bottoms during their stripping tussle, he still wore his pants, unbuttoned but still a barrier. It didn't prevent him from grinding his evident erection against her. Determined to not let him take that source of enjoyment away, she locked her legs around his waist, cinching him tight.

"You're going to have to let go if you want more," he murmured against the soft roundness of her belly as his lips finally moved to new territory.

Only that erotic promise could get her to loosen her grip. Standing, he didn't take long, stripping his pants and tossing them to the side to land—who cared?

She stared at him, at the thick shaft that jutted proudly from his body. As she stared, she couldn't help but lick her lips as a drop pearled on the tip.

She reached for him, but he growled, "Don't move."

More orders? Ha. She tucked her hands behind her head, spread her legs, and drew her knees up. She exposed her moist core to him and saw the shudder that trembled through him.

"You're making this hard."

"Then come here so I can make it soft." A bad joke, but he didn't seem to care. He dropped to his knees on the bed, right between her spread thighs. One hand guiding him, he rubbed the tip of his cock against her wetness.

She sucked in a breath and grabbed at the headboard. He did it again, and her hips arched off the bed.

Then his cock was gone, and she mewled in protest as she opened her eyes.

A cry was torn from her as he blew hotly on her plump lower lips. Big hands cupped her ass and raised her, positioning her at just the right height for—

Her body arced in a giant letter C at the flick of his tongue on her clit. Unexpected, the sudden touch proved too much. She might have caught him off guard with the first lick, but by the second and third he'd anchored her to the bed. A good thing, too, because once he latched his mouth to her she went mindless with pleasure.

She couldn't have said what she enjoyed more, the light flicks of his tongue against her clit or the probing between her lips, teasing her channel. But he wouldn't let her come.

She tensed. She trembled. She shuddered on the brink. He pulled back until she could have screamed.

A whimpered, "Please."

All that got her was a different kind of penetration. His tongue was replaced by one finger. Two. In and out, he pumped his digits. It wasn't enough. He knew it and added a stretching third. He also changed his angle, and the pitch of her moans changed to a high note as he repeatedly stroked her G-spot.

"Come for me," he murmured. "I want to feel it on my fingers." And his tongue apparently, as he began his oral tease again.

This was one order she gladly obeyed. Her channel tightened almost painfully around his pumping fingers before the climax ripped through her. Spasm after spasm, quivering and panting. And still he fingered and licked her.

He gave her intense pleasure and kept going, building her tension again until she keened and cried for relief.

He withdrew. Fingers. Tongue. All gone.

She could have cried. Instead, she sighed as the swollen head of his cock pressed against her moistness.

Inch by torturous inch, he fed his wonderfully large cock into her sex. It took forever, and it was wondrous. She couldn't help but have the muscles of her channel cling to him tight.

His turn to groan and throw his head back, the cords in his neck deliciously taut.

Braced on his forearms, Gavin hung just out of reach. She couldn't kiss him or lick his skin the way she wanted, but she could touch him. Rake her nails down his chest so that he hissed and his hips jerked, seating him deeper.

She could pinch the tips of his nipples and see the goose bumps rise on his skin as he reacted.

She could also say, "Get down here so I can kiss you."

And taste herself on his lips.

Their mouths clashed and clung in a fiery embrace while his hips pistoned his hard length. Her legs locked around his waist, urging his furious pounding. How she loved the fleshy smack of his body against hers, the delightful friction as he thrust in and out.

She clawed at the skin on his back, her breathing and cries incoherent grunts and pants, which matched his lower tenor ones.

Together they rocked and undulated, two bodies joined, lips meshed, hearts racing as one.

Their rhythm took on a primal life as rapture built. Built and built, much like a teetering tower of blocks until, with one teeny push, it fell over. Or, in their case, exploded.

Hers wasn't the only voice yelling as her orgasm hit and shook her.

Above her, Gavin gave one final thrust and went still, but she felt the hot spurt of his climax and heard his utterly possessive, "Mine."

But she allowed it because, in that moment, she couldn't help but think it, too.

CHAPTER 11

How the fuck did a cat get in the room? was Gavin's first thought when the caterwauling started. It took only another second to realize he was getting a call. His phone sang the old Purina cat commercial song, which involved a lot of meows, which drove his inner wolf mental.

Bloody Broderick. The irritating feline had gotten his hands on Gavin's cell somehow and put it as his ringtone. Gavin had yet to figure out how to change it.

I've really got to try that brownie recipe I found on the Internet but replace the marijuana with catnip. The resulting blackmail video might atone for some of his pal's pranks.

Sliding out of bed, leaving the warm and cuddly body of his mate—*after last night she's mine, even if she doesn't know it yet*—he padded naked, but for the phone in his hand, to the bathroom and shut the door.

"What do you want?" he answered, forgoing a hello.

A tad grumpy? *Damned right.* He'd harbored other plans for waking up that didn't involve speaking to his friend while a naked delight waited in bed.

"Good morning to you, too."

"It's not morning yet." Not even close.

"Doesn't matter. You need to get up. Where are you?"

"Does it matter?"

"It could. I don't suppose you've got a certain lady with you?"

In the past, Gavin might have bragged, but this was his woman. Things were different now. "I don't see that it's any of your business."

"I'll take that as 'yes' and hope there are witnesses, since her apartment was set on fire last night in what the cops are calling 'an attempt to conceal a crime scene.'"

"What the hell are you talking about? Her place was trashed, yes, but to accuse her of torching it is nuts."

"I don't know anything about her place getting ransacked. I'm talking about the body."

Turning on the water tap to muffle his conversation in case Megan awoke, he asked, "Rewind. What fucking body?"

"The one you apparently don't know about yet. About eleven p.m. last night, an off-duty fireman, coming off shift, smelled smoke coming from Megan's place and grabbed an extinguisher from the hall to put it out. Given he had to kick the door in to spray the place, he was the one to spot the body inside. The very dead and obviously murdered body of a male."

Good thing Gavin knew where Megan was or the news might have sent him off. As it was, the revelation of more shit aimed his mate's way didn't sit well.

"Any idea who the body belongs to?"

"You're going to love this. It's Jacques Lamontaine."

The name seemed familiar. "Isn't he a bookie?"

"Yes, and he works for—"

"Fabian." Funny how the case had veered back in Gavin's

creator's direction. "What the hell was Jacques doing at her place?"

"The cops have a theory, but you're not going to like it, as it just reinforces the case against Megan."

"Tell me."

"They think that Jacques hired Megan to kill Pierre as a public example of what happens to people who shirk on their debt. They think Megan called him over to her place to extort money from Jacques, except he refused to give her more money, so she shot him."

"Well, their theory is wrong. Not only did Megan not kill the guy, but she didn't set fire to her place either."

"So you can alibi her?"

"Yeah, me and a bunch of others. Not to mention the hotel we're holed up in has cameras on all the floors and in the elevators for security. I can easily prove she didn't leave this room after we entered it last night just after seven."

"Good thing, because someone's got it out for the lady."

"No shit. Question is, who? Fabian swears he's not involved."

"And you believe him?"

Much as it pained Gavin to admit? "Yeah. It's not his style. He'd either do it himself and not leave any evidence or make it so subtle no one would suspect murder in the first place."

"Good point. Whoever is behind this isn't afraid to get their hands dirty and has it bad for your little secretary. What are you going to do?"

Apparently, go furry, because, even over the sound of the water running there was no missing the distinctive thump as the hotel room door got kicked open, and he somehow doubted it was room service.

Of more concern, though, was who slept defenseless in the room.

Megan!

"I gotta go. We're being attacked," he said as he tossed the phone down without bothering to hang up.

As he was already naked, it took Gavin but a moment to let the adrenaline surge until claws popped from the ends of his fingers, fur sprouted from his skin, and teeth elongated.

With a howl, he rammed into the bathroom door, cracking the frame and slamming it into the wall. Teeth bared, he lunged to meet the threat and surprise his mate.

More like she surprised him.

What the fuck is she doing?

CHAPTER 12

The meowing ringtone woke Megan, but comfortable in the bed, she didn't bother to stir—although she did crack an eyelid to admire the flexing, tight buttocks of her lawyer/lover.

My lover.

Not quite the stupidest thing she'd done lately but, given her situation, not the brightest either.

At least her lapse in judgment resulted in a phenomenal night of sex. Apparently, Gavin's skills weren't just in the courtroom. The man knew how to play her body, leaving it pleasantly sore and, more surprising, hungry for more.

Indeed, just thinking about the pleasures of the previous eve had arousal stirring and her skin tingling. How rare to find a man who attracted her and on more than one level. Not only did his body attract; his mind wasn't too bad either.

Another unexpected aspect about Gavin was her ability to sleep with him. Sleepovers weren't her forte. Something about the vulnerability of sleep made her restless and unable to enjoy but the lightest of slumber, a habit she'd not managed to drop since she went out on her own. A lone woman never liked to be caught unaware.

For some reason, Megan relaxed her guard when around Gavin. For a three-piece-suit kind of guy, he managed to exude an aura that screamed, *I can take care of myself and you!*

He'd certainly taken care of her last night. She only had to stretch a little to feel the pleasant soreness of certain muscles.

The low murmur of his voice rose as he practically yelled, "What the hell are you talking about? Her place was trashed, yes, but to accuse her of torching it is nuts."

He's talking about me?

Straining to hear, she silently cursed as the sudden whoosh of water coming from a tap drowned his words.

That wouldn't do. Slipping from the bed, she tiptoed to the bathroom door, not bothering to put on any clothes. She wanted to hear. Who was calling him at this ungodly early hour? And what were they talking about?

Pressing her ear against the door, she couldn't quite make out his words but caught enough. "Fabian." "Kill." "Fire."

The plot thickened, and she needed answers. But first she needed pants. Confrontation was always less effective when naked. Especially when someone kicked in a door and rushed in aiming a gun.

Good thing she'd honed her reflexes over the years. "Chubby" didn't mean she couldn't move.

Instinctively, she ducked, so the first shot fired went right overhead. Before the gunman could trigger a second, she lunged and hit him in the knees, tackling him. Down he went, landing with a hard thump on his back. A moment later, her bare thighs pinned his arms, her forearm was pressed against his throat, and he stared at her with wide eyes.

Occupied with the intruder under her, Megan only vaguely noted the bathroom door smashing open as Gavin rushed out. Poor guy. He probably didn't expect to find his supposedly sweet and innocent client—and bedmate—restraining a hired killer.

A low growl rumbled from behind her. A very ungentlemanly growl. One would say even inhuman.

What the hell.

Despite the threat beneath her, Megan couldn't help but crane to peer behind her.

Her eyes widened. Her breath was caught. Her rigid pose relaxed, and the gunman took advantage of her lapse to fling her away from him.

She hit the wall with an oomph, but the shock of impact was nothing compared to the mental one as she beheld a veritable wolfman looming over the blubbering gunman, who aimed his gun with shaking hands and pulled the trigger.

Red blossomed as the bullet hit the massive beast, but the wound, which went right through his shoulder and leaked blood, didn't stop him. The wolfman emitted a snarl of rage while a paw tipped in claws swiped at the hired killer.

But the wolfman didn't strike to kill. Rather, he grabbed the man by his jacket and lifted him, shaking the large fellow much like a dog with a stuffed toy. Then the wolfman tossed him, clear across the room.

The hired killer hit the wall, hard, then the floor. With a single bound, the beast reached him and picked him up again.

It was at this point that Megan came to a few realizations. One, that wolfman was Gavin. No mistaking those gorgeous blue eyes of his, and besides, given there was no human lawyer in the bathroom, or anywhere else for that matter, simple logic prevailed. Two, this was not a place for her to stay.

While Gavin played with his new squeaky toy, Megan snagged some clothes off the floor, his keys off the desk, and dashed for the door.

Stark naked, she streaked up the hall, which, to her surprise, remained quiet. Even better luck, the elevator was still at their level. As the doors slid shut, she saw through the shrinking crack wolf-Gavin emerge in the hall in all his furry splendor and glance in both directions.

His gaze caught hers at the last moment.

Through a jaw not meant for human words, the wolfman managed a gruff, "Come back."

As if. "Like hell," she muttered, not without a smirk.

And then the doors slid shut but not before she heard him howl.

A shiver went through her.

No wonder he called her little rabbit. The man truly was a wolf. And she'd just done the one thing prey should never do.

Run.

CHAPTER 13

Emerging from the bathroom, Gavin expected to encounter a few things. An intruder with nefarious intentions. Maybe some screaming from Megan, because a normal woman would be frightened by not only someone kicking their door down and shooting but also the appearance of a living and, yes, viciously snarling Lycan.

What he didn't expect was to find his mate expertly taking down a hired thug.

Naked.

Straddling a stranger's chest, her forearm across the man's throat, her boobs hanging practically in the guy's face, Megan had things under control—but the guy under her had a much too intimate view.

That more than anything set Gavin off.

His woman was touching another man while not wearing a stitch of clothing. The fact that she did so to protect herself—with a skill Gavin would question later—didn't matter.

Red, roaring jealousy infused him, followed by icy rage as the gunman, during her shocked moment of inattention, flung her away, causing her harm.

He hurt my woman!

Unacceptable. A civilized man wouldn't stand for it, and for a wolf it was grounds for a serious assault. Gavin went after the bastard, ignoring, for the moment, the rules governing his kind—specifically, "thou shalt not let humans know about us." He quite enjoyed smacking the thug around while carefully ensuring he didn't accidentally kill him. After all, dead bodies required explanation, whereas thugs claiming a wolfman beat them up got tossed in the loony bin or put in rehab.

The satisfaction of hitting something somewhat mollified his jealousy and rage. He might even say he was having a grand ol' time, too, hitting the bastard. That was until Gavin caught the sound of steps running away. While he showed Megan she could count on him to protect her, she escaped.

Dropping his blubbering victim, Gavin loped after her. He hit the hall and stopped. Which way did she go, down the stairs or toward the elevator? He sniffed and turned just in time to spot her in the elevator as the door shut. As for his demand she return? Yeah. She didn't quite give him the middle finger salute. However, the are-you-kidding expression on her face said it all.

For a moment, he debated taking to the stairs and beating her to the ground floor. Then he looked down, noted his hairy, naked, wolfy frame, which, for the curious, was very anatomically correct—and large. Oh, and let's not forget noticeable.

Only seconds before a curious hotel patron peeked in to the hall, Gavin ducked into his room and closed the door—but couldn't quite latch it, given the splintered doorjamb.

The thug still inside lunged at Gavin. Stupid human. Gavin knocked him out and then leaned against the portal so he could furiously think. He needed to get to Megan, not only so he could explain but also to keep her safe. However, at the same time . . .

I can't go out like this. He'd draw a little too much attention. Not to mention he couldn't leave the unconscious man here because eventually the intruder would awake. Gavin didn't fear the idiot blabbing to the police. A thug like this wouldn't go to the cops, and if he talked he'd soon see Gavin wasn't the only Lycan he needed to fear. No, Gavin's reasons for keeping the intruder weren't to protect him but because he had questions.

Big questions. Such as, why was the guy sent to kill Megan? Did Fabian orchestrate the attempts? And more important . . .

Who. Was. Megan?!

It didn't take a genius like Gavin—he had the Mensa score to prove it—to realize she wasn't the delicate secretary and little rabbit he'd taken her for. More like a vixen, wily and beautiful.

A vixen who ran, which called for a chase.

What fun.

Before he could sniff out her trail, he first needed to flip back into his human skin and locate some pants—and a tie, because anything less just wasn't civilized.

Closing his eyes, he concentrated, willing his humanity to take charge again. For some reason, shedding his wolf exterior hurt a lot less than putting it on. He could almost hear the teasing thoughts of his wolf say, *Because I'm tougher.*

"Let's see how tough you are if we get something waxed while we're furry."

On second thought, he'd probably never resort to that because even just the threat made him wince. Yet he faced down a thug wielding a gun without flinching. So sue him for being inconsistent. He'd defend himself and win.

Apparently, though, he'd lost the first round to his mate. "What happened to her accepting my wolf side?" he muttered as he washed the wound in his shoulder, which, luckily for him, had already stopped bleeding. While he didn't heal instantly, he did enjoy quicker-than-human regeneration power. In a few days, the bullet hole would be nothing but a scar.

As he dressed, he pondered the recent events. More specifically what happened with Megan.

He'd claimed her last night. Marked her as his, even if he'd yet to tell her. Yet she still panicked when she encountered his beast. What happened to her accepting his wolf side? Were the rumors about mating wrong?

Only one way to find out, but that involved confronting her. A task that would prove easier if she'd not taken his keys

"Bloody fucking hell!" Before he could call for a ride, the busted hotel room door opened. Gavin didn't bother to turn around.

A Lycan should never deign to acknowledge a feline as a threat. The one lesson of Fabian's that Gavin remembered and adhered to—mostly to drive the arrogant cats he knew yeowly.

"Damn, Gavin. Another body?" Broderick sauntered in,

only slightly flushed. He must have jumped in his car and raced all eight blocks from his place when Gavin abruptly ended their call, then, knowing his penchant for small places, jogged up the stairs. "One body you might explain to the cops, but two?"

"This one isn't dead."

"I thought the rule was don't play with your food."

"Ha. Ha. Aren't you just a comedian?" was Gavin's mocking reply. "The guy attacked us."

"Because he obviously didn't know what a stupid idea that was. Boy, did he choose the wrong room."

"You don't say, especially given it wasn't my wolf who actually took him down but a certain little secretary."

"Megan?" Broderick snorted. "She couldn't hurt a fly."

"And yet she pinned an almost-three-hundred-pound thug to the floor. Is there something about her that you're not telling me?"

"No. Not quite. That is . . ."

The more Gavin fixed Broderick with a hard stare, the more the feline pretended disinterest in him. Instead, his friend crouched by the snoring thug and hoisted him onto a shoulder.

"Let's get this fellow somewhere a little less likely to get a visit from the cops. I don't think your antics went entirely unnoticed."

Not so fast. "Spill what you know, or I am going to turn you into a bobtailed cat."

"Not the tail! Don't ever threaten the tail!" Broderick exclaimed. "Talk about sacrilege."

"Talk and you won't have to worry about it."

"Swear you won't freak."

Not exactly promising words. Gavin arched a brow. "How about I promise not to kill you?"

Broderick pretended to think on it. "Fair enough. If you insist. Fabian asked me to ask you to defend Megan."

"He what?"

"He's also the one who put up the bail money, or so I hear."

"How the hell is she connected to him?"

"I don't know."

Gavin growled, and Broderick, in the process of peeking in the hall for observers, took a second to peer back and say, "Seriously, dude. I don't know. I'd never met her before I not-so-accidentally bumped into her."

"And yet Fabian knew about her." *He lied to my face. Sly fucking wolf.*

As Broderick jogged for the stairs, Gavin close behind, he said, "I really do think she's innocent, though. I mean, look at everything that's happened and the shit that is still happening. Somebody wants her out of the picture."

Indeed. Someone did. And there was only one name Gavin could think of. Someone who probably wanted to cover his tracks.

Fabian.

CHAPTER 14

Such a nice bedroom, decorated in light blues and grays. Very tastefully appointed. What a shame it was about to get messy.

From the comfortable club chair she sat in, Megan aimed the gun she'd taken off the guard she'd assaulted in the garden at Fabian's forehead.

It was highly doubtful she'd taken him by surprise. The man was a renowned mob lord for a reason, but his cocky self-assuredness meant he took his time acknowledging her presence.

She couldn't help a grudging admiration. It took a set of megaballs to act as if he didn't fear her and to ignore the gun she held pointed at him with unwavering hands. He knew for a fact that she never missed.

"Megan. Darling. To what do I owe this lovely crack-of-dawn visit?"

"I was in the area and thought I'd pop in."

"Did you make my guards look incompetent again?"

"Just the one guy. He's out cold in the garden. The others don't even know I'm here."

Fabian blew out a breath of disgust. "Bloody hell. I'd really like to know your tricks."

"And give away my mystique?"

"Don't you mean give away your advantage?"

She smiled in reply.

"I'm sure you're not just here for a friendly chat and reminder that my staff need more training. I thought we'd agreed to keep our relationship on the down low until certain matters were settled."

"Certain information came to light, so the plan has changed."

"You mean the murder charges?"

A scoffing noise came out of her. "Annoying but not the end of the world. While I'd prefer to not have murder charges hanging over me, in the event of a conviction I would have escaped and ditched this identity."

"Only you would blow off murder charges as nothing. So if that's not what has you in a tizzy, then what is so momentous you just had to pay me a visit?"

She blurted it out. "Gavin is a wolf."

Not by one iota did Fabian's eyes widen. He already knew. Then again, considering Fabian bore the title of alpha wolf leader for the Lycans in this city, it didn't surprise her.

"Yes, he's a wolf."

"And my lawyer."

"You forgot to also add your 'lover.'"

The fact that Fabian could scent her lingering passion with Gavin didn't surprise her, but his next words did.

"When I told Broderick to convince him to take your case, I didn't expect that to happen."

"You maneuvered this?" she queried, waving her gun around, not averting her gaze when Fabian slid from bed—a bull of a man with a wide chest, defined pecs, and more muscle and size than any red-blooded woman would look away from.

Just because Megan didn't like the older man—who, in his forties, was just a touch too old for her—didn't mean she didn't admire him.

With a lack of modesty, Fabian strode past her and snagged a robe from a chair. He slung it around his body only moments before the door to his room flung open.

A scowling Gavin entered, dragging an unconscious man behind him. The same thug she'd taken down in their hotel room.

"And here I thought it was only cats who dragged in prizes to show off," was Fabian's response to his bedroom invasion.

"Why waste my energy dragging when I can get him to be the muscle?" Broderick quipped as he entered on Gavin's heels. He smiled in her direction. "Hey, Megan. Fancy finding you here."

The situation still didn't make much sense, but one thing was becoming clear. Her meeting with Broderick and Gavin wasn't by happenstance. Heads would roll. She shot Broderick a teasing smile and mouthed, *You're dead.*

"Now, now, Megan. No killing the help. The cat is rather useful to me. I'd prefer we not use up any of his lives."

"Fine, he lives." Because he probably only followed orders, but as for Gavin . . . She turned her sights on him next. "But that one." She waved her gun Gavin's way. "Him I want to maim." Now if only when she imagined him trussed to her bed she wasn't also inching her way up his body torturing him with her tongue. *I'm going soft.* Probably because she was already addicted to a certain *hard* part of his anatomy.

Dumping the body on the floor first, Gavin stared at her as he straightened his tie—what psycho lawyer wolf stopped to put on a tie when involved in a kidnapping of a thug? He ran a hand through his already perfectly coiffed hair and brushed imaginary lint from his suit. *Holy hell, he's a neat freak.*

"I think maiming is a little harsh, don't you, little rabbit? On what grounds do you think you're owed such violent restitution?" Trust a lawyer to couch a rebuttal in fancy words.

"Grounds? You want grounds? I'll give you grounds. You work for Fabian and didn't tell me." In other words, Gavin hadn't taken her on because he'd truly wanted to help her or liked her. He did what he was told.

"I do not work for the man. I abhor him as a matter of fact. So much that I plan to celebrate the day they finally toss his mangy ass behind bars."

"He would, you know," Fabian said, turning from the coffeemaker he kept stashed behind a panel in his bedroom wall. "He's the most ungrateful pup I've created."

Created? And the plot thickened. Gavin might claim to not like Fabian, but that didn't sever his ties to him. "Thanks for pointing out yet another strike against you. You're a wolf." Yet she'd never spotted it, even if she suspected something was off about him.

How could I have missed it? It seemed so obvious now.

From his arrogant self-assuredness to the lanky and smooth way he moved. Not to mention all the other subtle verbal hints. Hell, he'd even told her he was a wolf when she'd accused him of being a dog.

But what sane person would have taken his words literally?

I should have.

"Yeah, I'm a wolf. So?"

How like Gavin to act so blasé about the admission. "You didn't tell me." She managed to stifle the petulant note.

"Nope. I didn't tell you."

Said with absolutely no sign of repentance. "Didn't you feel like this was information I should have?"

"I would have eventually gotten around to it."

Eventually? She blinked in disbelief. Never mind she knew the first rule Lycans learned was "tell no one," for some reason she felt he should have divulged the truth. "And exactly when was that going to be?" Because it sure as hell wasn't before they'd jumped into bed.

"Probably about the same time you told me that you were working for Fabian. Because you are, aren't you, as a spy on Pierre? Only Fabian double-crossed you, had Pierre killed, and then framed you to take the fall."

Not quite. "The whole Pierre assassination was my job." She flung that at Gavin with a cocky smirk and waited for his reaction.

While Gavin's face went through a myriad of emotions, Fabian exuded only one, mirth. "Oh, this was so worth waking up early for. Broderick, why aren't you taping this? I swear, I've not been so amused in ages."

Broderick held up empty hands. "Sorry, boss. I left

my phone in the car in case I had to suddenly shift. Things were a little tense between me and my best bud on the way over."

"Thing still are tense," Gavin growled. "But I'll deal with you later. I'm kind of busy right now trying to wrap my head around the fact my client did indeed kill the victim. You lied to me."

Draping a leg casually over the armrest of the chair, she waved her gun, which she'd yet to tuck away. "Not quite. I said his death was my job. I was hired by him"— she jerked a thumb at Fabian, who raised his coffee cup in acknowledgment—"to keep an eye on Pierre and feed him certain information. As his secretary, I had access to files and codes, which allowed me to discreetly shuffle a few business interests. Once the moves were done, Pierre was to have an unfortunate accident."

"But he caught you fucking with his shit, and you killed him."

"Bzzt. Wrong. I said I was supposed to, but someone got to him first and framed me." She couldn't help the incredulity in her tone. It still galled her that someone had dared screw with her like that—and scoop her job from under her.

"Framed?" Gavin snorted. "That's priceless coming from an assassin."

"Says the guy who turns into a freaking wolf."

He glared at her, and she arched a brow and smiled.

Strange and tense as the moment was, oddly enough she enjoyed herself. Something about Gavin truly brought her alive. She found his alpha tendencies and uptight attitude highly entertaining. What a shame about his howl-at-the-moon condition.

The silence stretched, Fabian and Broderick steering clear of the conversation but avidly watching.

Widening her grin, which only deepened his scowl, Gavin broke the standoff. "Why?"

"Why what?"

"Did you agree to kill Pierre, of course?"

Fabian replied. "You mean other than the fact it's her job and she's good at it?"

Oh, way to make her sound mercenary. The fact that it was true didn't mean she liked it bandied about. Megan tossed Fabian a glare that screamed, *Zip it!*

As if he'd listen to her. He grinned, completely unrepentant. The jerk knew she wouldn't kill him.

Stupid family. He might only be a distant cousin on her dad's side, but it still made him someone she couldn't kill—and hope to make it out alive at Grandpa's Thanksgiving dinner. Unusual were the extremely rare times when their clan gathered and things didn't get a little hairy. Grandma said it wasn't a true family reunion unless some blood was shed.

One hundred percent human or not, no one messed with Grandma. The most excellent cook went everywhere with a knife. And food. Megan was pretty sure Grandma could probably pull the ingredients to make a gourmet seven-course meal—for fifty—from her large canvas purse covered in tropical flowers.

It was a talent Megan, sadly, didn't inherit. But Grandma forgave her since her only granddaughter, who was also human, could at least wield a knife and a gun, plus a myriad of other weapons.

However, Gavin knew nothing of her history, and the arrogant wolf snapped at her cousin, "Do you mind? I was talking to Megan." He practically snarled the words.

Despite Megan having grown up around a father and other male relatives who could do the same thing, having Gavin do it took it to a whole new level. A sexy one.

But his primal wolf attitude was also silly, and she rolled her eyes. "Why else would anyone do it? For the money, of course. It's not the first time either."

"Megan here has been working for the family for quite some years now. Mostly on the West Coast, but she recently moved to the big city to take a more active part in my empire."

"Actually, I did it to drive my dad nuts. He's a touch overprotective," she warned Gavin. As a matter of fact, if dear old dad knew that Gavin had seduced her things could get hairy. Especially if her other cousins got involved. And her uncles. And Grandpa. As for Grandma, she'd probably cackle, pull a cow from the walk-in freezer, and start cooking a feast for when they were done playing with Gavin.

And he wondered why she'd become an assassin—other than because of the money. She came from a family of somewhat psychotic wolves. And before anyone began assuming they'd been born that way, it should be made clear that Lycanthropy was given, usually intentionally. It was triggered by a bite, several of them, while a male was in wolfman form, not human or full wolf—which usually happened only during full moons. Only when a Lycan stood with one foot in both camps was his bite contagious. Yet the chomping didn't always turn a man.

Some died; the weaklings, her dad said, not without a little scorn. Some recovered, victims of an attack. But some . . . some turned Lycan, the first moon triggering the full change. After that, with practice a male could control his inner beast and allow only parts of it to emerge. Except when the full moon shone in the sky. Then they all went 100 percent hairy, no matter what.

Not that she'd ever experienced it. Megan, to this day, remained human.

So how, some might wonder, if it took a bite to infect, was she descended from a line of male wolves that went back generations? Simple. Her family was freaking nuts.

Each generation birthed a son or two, sometimes more. And each generation got bitten by their dads on their sixteenth birthday. It was barbaric. It was also tradition.

It was also for guys only.

Girls couldn't turn wolf. Women were immune to the bite.

No one was sure why. Daddy said many had tried. Hell, apparently Grandma made Grandpa bite her because she wanted to be furry like her boys. It failed.

Luckily, the men could still marry human women and father children. Mostly boys in her family, with the occasional girl like Megan, who was raised among wolves.

Had she mentioned the psychotic part?

"Ahem." Fabian cleared his throat. "You know, while all these lovely introductions are fascinating, I'm finding myself less intrigued with your banter than I am with the body on my floor. Doesn't he work for me?" Fabian asked as he nudged the thug with a bare toe.

At that announcement, Megan snapped her attention to

her cousin. "He's one of yours? I can't believe you sent a gunman after me. Wait until my daddy finds out."

Alpha of a contending clan or not, Fabian vehemently denied it and perhaps even blanched a little. "I most definitely did not send him after you. I'm not insane enough to challenge your father."

Dear Daddy. His reputation since his return from the war preceded him.

"Then if you didn't send him, who did?"

They all stared at the thug, who groaned as consciousness returned to him.

With so many violent personalities in the room, it didn't take much threatening to have him spill his guts. The verbal kind, not the messy intestinal ones.

His voice earnest, the hired gunman told them what he knew, which wasn't much. "I was hired for the job. Well, less hired, more like I accepted an open call."

Broderick, who tapped away on a laptop Fabian had fetched by his guards, confirmed it. "What do you know? I'm on the forum he was talking about, and here's the posted bounty."

The forum he referred to was an online Web group under several layers of security and encrypted so that only those in the business could decipher the contents.

Megan, gun tucked in the waistband of her pants—no panties because she couldn't find them when she'd fled earlier—peered over his shoulder.

Sure enough, as she scanned the board she saw the announcement.

A whistle blew past Fabian's lips. "Five million to end your life. That's not what I would have paid."

Affronted, Megan shot him a dark look.

He grinned. "I would have paid more of course, dear cousin."

His face set in a perpetual scowl, it seemed, Gavin paced before Broderick. "How do we get this message taken down?"

"We don't. Only the poster can erase it."

"But we can nullify it to a certain extent," Fabian added. "We will post a message saying that if anyone succeeds in killing dear Megan they will incur my wrath and I will hunt them down myself and ensure they die screaming."

"I was planning on doing that anyway," added Gavin, his tone quite ominous.

And sexy. *Damned wolves and their protective ways.* To think Daddy wondered why she had fled to the East Coast. Grandma and Megan's mother understood and had abetted her departure. Now Daddy sulked because his little girl left him.

"Gavin, I am most delighted to see this violent side. And to think I'd wondered if you were soft when it came to justice."

"Sometimes the law just isn't enough," Gavin replied.

Megan shook her head. "Men. Always promising more violence. I'll take care of this. After all, this person dared to screw with me."

"What do you plan to do?"

What a dumb question. "I'll kill whoever is behind this of course. No money getting paid means no attempts on my life. Simple."

"Easier said than done. We don't know who is bankrolling this."

"Yet. Given their erratic behavior, I'd say it's not long now before they reveal themselves."

"But do we have that long to wait? They've set a pretty trap around you, Megan," Broderick reminded. "The cops are currently looking for you on account of the body in your apartment."

"What body?" she asked. They brought her up to speed, and she lost her smile. "This is getting ridiculous. What the hell did I do to incur this kind of vendetta?"

"I'll admit I'm a tad jealous. No one puts this kind of effort in their attempts on me," Fabian huffed.

"It's because you're soft." She coughed it in her hand, and her cousin glared.

She beamed.

"What if we could get the charges dropped?" Gavin said.

"Exactly how are you going to do that? You have seen the pile of evidence they've gathered, right? The best we can hope for is having the most current arson and murder charges dropped."

"That's what you think. I have a plan."

And it was a good one, too.

In return for their letting Larry—the hotel intruder—live, he would not only confess to his part in the murder and arson at Megan's place, which resulted not long after her threat to remove his ability to procreate, but also admit he'd killed Pierre and framed the innocent secretary for it. It should be noted that, despite the measures they used to make him speak, Larry swore, and quite unimaginatively, that he didn't have a part in that plot. Not that it mattered. Given the choice between life in prison and facing their wrath—which again, Megan punctuated with more bodily threats, good ones that made all the men wince—Larry wisely chose the least harmful route.

With their plan in place, it was decided that Gavin would bring Larry in on a citizen's arrest. Gavin would concoct some story about having taken down Larry when the thug visited Megan at her hotel room. Brave lawyer traps criminal intent on killing his scapegoat. Why Larry wanted to kill her they left vague. With a confession in hand, it was doubtful the cops would dig too deeply, especially once one of Fabian's men on the inside pushed the paperwork through.

"I'm going to time it so that I arrive about a half hour before the end of shift. The cops will just want to process the paperwork as fast as they can to get out of there." Gavin eyed the watch on his wrist and tapped it to set an alarm.

Wearing no underpants and no bra, Megan felt quite unprepared beside his impeccably turned-out attire. She didn't let his suave exterior beside her grubby one, though, daunt her.

After all, I've seen him naked. And dirty. Oh, so dirty. She crossed her legs in the chair she'd once again commandeered.

"With Larry's confession, it will be a cinch to get the arrest warrant for Megan canceled. Then I'll work on the rest of the charges. You'll be a free woman. That is, if you can stay out of trouble. Anything else I should know about? Some other crime that will pop up to mess with my plan? Did you perhaps sneak out and kill someone while I was sleeping?" He fixed her with a dark stare.

She snorted. "As if you gave me enough time. I barely got any sleep." Too late she realized what she'd admitted, aloud, to an audience. Killer since her college days or not, she blushed.

Wisely, no one remarked on it.

Gavin shot a look at Larry, who sat quietly on the floor, no longer so intimidating when surrounded by real predators. "Broderick, zip tie his hands, would you, and put him in the car."

"Why me?"

"Because you owe me. That and I need to speak to my client some more before I handle the cops. Also"—he poked Broderick in the back—"after you're done with that, I want you to work on unscrambling the identification of whoever posted the bounty. While you"—he jabbed a finger in Fabian's direction—"need to do something criminal that I can tie back to you so I can at least throw you in jail for a few nights for irritating the fuck out of me."

"Only a few nights? I take it I am forgiven for introducing you to Megan."

"I forgive you nothing, but I am willing to forgo the exhilaration of seeing your ass in an electric chair out of deference to the fact you're related to Megan."

"You would show me mercy because of Megan? How interesting," Fabian mused aloud.

Megan frowned. What did her cousin mean? Before she could speculate, Gavin dragged her from the room. Only because she allowed it, though.

Now that she didn't need to hide who she was, she could have broken his hold—or his wrist. Daddy made sure his little girl wasn't defenseless. Besides, Gavin was right. They did have some things to discuss in light of recent events and revelations.

They didn't go far, only to a small parlor with a pair of hidden sliding doors, which Gavin whisked shut as soon as he had her in the room.

He whirled on her. His presence—large, confident, and oozing primitive maleness—filled the room while his gaze drilled her. He advanced on her with the slow steps of a predator.

Despite her upbringing, she couldn't help mincing steps back. The cautious retreat of prey. A prey with a racing heart, heated blood, and tingling parts.

"So, little rabbit. It seems I've misjudged you. It's not often someone can say that."

"My ability to blend is why I'm paid the big bucks." Her wan joke didn't crack a smile.

"Speaking of big bucks. You could have afforded a lawyer but didn't hire one. Why?"

"And ruin my cover? Part of my defense was the whole benign-secretary thing. If I could keep it and have the charges dropped, then I wouldn't need to reinvent myself. I've heard new fingerprints are painful."

"You didn't need me to take on your case for free."

"Are you about to complain about me wasting your time? Would you feel better if I offered to pay you the going fee, discreetly, of course?"

He'd kept advancing as they spoke, and she couldn't help but retreat from him until her back hit the wall. Did she retreat from fear? Not quite, more like an excitement that had her heart racing and her body tingling.

He framed her body with an arm braced on either side of her head. "I don't need your money."

"Because Fabian is paying for my defense of course."

"No, he's not, and I would never take a penny from him." Gavin invaded her space, not quite touching her but close enough for her to feel the heat of his body.

"If he's not paying you, and you don't need my money, then what do you want?"

"Other than the truth?" He rubbed his face against hers, a jaw shadowed in stubble against her smooth skin. Having been raised among wolves, literally, she knew what he did. He marked her with his scent.

That didn't bode well. "What if I promise you the truth from here on out? No more surprises."

"I don't think we need to go that far. While I will expect forthrightness from you, as for surprises . . ." He blew warmly against the lobe of her ear. "Some surprises are delicious." He nipped the tip, and she shuddered, arousal tensing the muscles of her sex.

"I'd have said 'dangerous.'" Her voice emerged a touch more high-pitched than she wanted as she tried to distract herself from his mouth. "You do know I'm a trained killer." An assassin who was thinking if she hooked her foot around his ankle and caught him off guard she could tip him onto the floor, straddle him, and do things on the plush carpet that would totally be more fun than this conversation.

"I like danger." Wolf or not, he practically purred the words.

Jump him. How she wanted to, but she knew what a bad idea that was now. Distraction was what she needed. "So what happens next, with my case, that is?"

Talking didn't stop his lips. On the contrary, the hot puff of air as he spoke so close to her skin was almost worse. "Larry will be charged. You go free, and we find the real culprit behind all these acts." He dragged his lips down the column of her throat.

"Whoever it was initially didn't want me dead, or they would have killed me when they planted the stuff."

"True, but they definitely wanted you punished. Which reminds me. I've been wanting to ask, how did such a savvy assassin get caught and framed in the first place?"

She babbled in an effort to fight his tantalizing mouth, which sucked the sensitive skin at the base of her throat. "I should probably begin by telling you my plan in regards to Pierre. Given I was almost done with the deed and asset transfers Fabian wanted, I concocted an office-robbery scenario. Business guy stays late because I create a bit of a panic with one of his distributors. He's alone. Unarmed. A junkie breaks in and shoots him, the junkie being me. First, though, I had to establish an alibi. On the day of the murder, I went home and got some Thai takeout on the way, making sure I kept a time-stamped receipt and that my credit card was used. I made sure the lobby camera for my building saw me coming in. Once I was at my place, my plan was to change into some concealing clothes and whip back out using the fire escape. A tenant, two floors down, who's in Florida for the week, leaves her bike chained by her window. I planned to borrow it and use it to get there and back, with no one the wiser."

His suckling of her skin paused. "Except you never left your apartment that night."

The lips resumed their roaming adventure. "I never even made it in the door. I'm assuming someone darted me with a heavy-duty sedative, because the last thing I remember is juggling my bag of food so I could unlock my door."

She barely held in a disappointed sigh as his lips stopped again.

"So you really didn't kill him?"

"No." The reminder helped put a damper on her burgeoning arousal. "Which is why I was so pissed the next day when the cops showed up and began pulling the supposed evidence from my apartment. I was framed."

His blue gaze met hers, and a lilt curved his lips.

"This isn't funny," she pouted.

"Yeah, it is, because I can't believe an assassin is complaining about getting framed for murder."

"Hey, you would, too, if it happened to you. I mean, not only did I not get properly paid for that wasted month of working for my target, but I now have to clear my name and find the real culprit."

"Your name will be clear by the end of the day."

"But whoever started this war against me is still out there." Only for as long as it took her to find them. Once she did—

Gavin's lips moved upward, hovering over her mouth, taunting her with their closeness. "I take it asking if you have enemies is a moot point."

"Are you implying I'm not well liked?" She batted not-so-innocent lashes at him.

"I'd say that anyone who likes you too much is asking for trouble."

"A good thing you discovered this sooner than later then," she replied, somewhat miffed.

Sure, she'd not exactly expected their one night of passion to change things between them. Hell, she'd been the most vocal about not indulging, but it rankled knowing that her profession and true self were too much for Gavin to handle. It seemed she'd grown to like Gavin, despite their short acquaintance—and the fact that he turned furry.

Well, at least I know where we stand now. Not that things would have gotten much further. Once her family found out about him, it wasn't just her daddy who might have an issue with her taking up with an unknown wolf—and a lawyer at that.

"Yes, it is a good thing I know what a troublemaker you are. I'll have to call my security company and have them increase their service if I'm going to keep you safe."

"Excuse me?"

He leaned in close, forehead leaning against hers, his lips but a hairsbreadth from hers. Intimate, close, heart-stopping. "Oh, you didn't think something like you being an assassin would chase me away, did you? I am a wolf, little rabbit. I thrive on danger. And now that we're both unmasked, we don't have to hide who and what we are anymore."

"I'm not looking for a relationship."

"I wasn't asking. I'm stating that, like it or not, we're a couple."

The feminist in her bristled at his domineering statement. The woman in her melted and then puddled as his lips tugged at hers, a slow, languorous embrace that had her breath stuttering.

If only they had the time. *No, what am I thinking? Bad idea.* She'd grown up with wolves, and she knew better than to get involved with one. "Aren't you supposed to go to see the cops?"

"I will, in a minute. First, I think we need to take care of more pressing business." His business pressed against her lower belly.

Again, so tempting, but Megan wasn't some doe-eyed idiot who thought having sex in her cousin's house, with him just up the hall, probably on the phone to her dad, and with a contract on her head sending every Tom, Dick, and Hairy— as in furry shifter—coming after her was a good idea.

She ducked down and slid sideways out of Gavin's intimate grasp. Only the sparring she'd done growing up gave her the dexterity needed to evade his lunging hand. *Oops. Nope.* He caught her, moving fast, like only a Lycan could.

Or did she allow him to catch her?

"I wasn't done with you." Such heated promise in those words, and damn if she didn't melt as he, once again, dragged her into his embrace and plastered his lips over hers.

Megan wanted to blame her racing pulse on her indignation at how he manhandled her without permission. Perhaps a fever was to blame for the heat coursing through her frame. But what excuse did she have for the arousal moistening her sex? The tingling anticipation prickling her skin?

She said screw it to the little voice that told her she should run from the wolf. She pressed herself against him, clutched at his muscled biceps, and let herself enjoy the kiss.

What a kiss. His hard mouth claimed hers with a fervor she'd never experienced before. This. This hard, hot, breathless embrace was passion, not the tepid acts of her past with boys.

Gavin was a man. All musk, power, and intent.

He didn't waste time coaxing her lips apart. He demanded they open. He took over and went on a quest for her tongue that he might twine with it and draw soft cries of pleasure from her.

While her knees might buckle, he didn't let her fall. He braced her with his body and the wall, pinned her with his solid frame, and rubbed.

Oh God. He rubbed, the hardness of him pressing against her core. She throbbed between her legs. She needed more than just rubbing.

She made a noise, an incoherent one, but he deciphered it, and next thing she knew, her pants were around her ankles and he nudged her legs apart. He inserted his thigh, and she ground against his muscled leg. Her breath caught at the sweet friction this created on her delicate sex. Her clitoris pulsed with each pass.

Her fingers dug into his biceps, the cruel fabric of his jacket keeping her from his skin. So she went after the flesh she did have access to, nipping his jawline and hearing him finally groan.

"Megan." Her name emerged on a husky note. The sound of a zipper lowering had her shivering as anticipation hummed through her.

The head of his shaft rubbed across her lower lips, and she gasped at the heated steel length of his cock. So erect, and ready for her.

So big. For her.

She couldn't help a long, slow moan as he penetrated her, the length of him sliding into her moist heat, inch by slow inch. Tighter, she clawed at him, arching her pelvis forward.

"Impatient, little rabbit," he chided. He stopped all movement, and she could have screamed. Especially when he used the gap still between their bodies to place his hand. More like his fingers, which delicately rubbed her clit.

Oh my. With him partially inserted, along with the decadent pleasure of his stroke, she quivered and cried out, hips rocking in an attempt to drive him deeper.

She only partially succeeded, as he refused to let her take what she wanted. He was very much in control, only allowing himself partial entry into her sex.

His finger worked her fast and she made a frustrated cry as her body tensed. Everything within her coiled as the pleasure built. And built.

When he did finally slam the rest of the way in, she yelled and pretty much came. Minor quivers rocked her channel as he stroked, in and out. Each thick thrust hit deep within, deep enough that a second round of bliss built and throbbed.

Both his hands now gripped her, cupping her ass cheeks so he could hoist her to the proper height. Deeply seated within her, he thrust, each smooth strike hitting her sweet spot making a mockery of her first miniorgasm as he rolled her into a proper second one.

A mind-blowing, mind-blanking, body-shuddering climax.

Still coming down from her high, she felt him come, the heat of him bathing her womb. He went still, buried to the hilt, hands cupping her, body pressed tight, his head lowered so, once again, their foreheads touched and their ragged breaths merged.

It was an oddly emotional moment, and yet nothing was said. She wasn't sure either of them had the mental capacity or words in that moment.

Why ruin utter perfection?

Why unless you were a man, and he did it with just two words.

Softly said.

Intimate.

Possessive.

"My mate."

"Excuse me?"

Wisely, he slipped away from her, a wolf in a lawyer's suit, calmly buttoning his pants and straightening his tie.

As for her? There she stood, more like slumped against the wall, with her pants in a puddle at her feet, hair sticking out all over, and eyeing him with dawning suspicion—and a touch of horror.

"I don't know how much you know about our kind," he said as he wisely stayed out of reach.

"Enough." She didn't elaborate on the how. She wasn't in the mood to share secrets, not when he'd just dropped an epic bombshell.

"Wolves have this thing. Some call it fate. Some call it—"

"The mating fever. You'd better not be saying what I think you are." But didn't she already know? Hadn't she suspected once she knew what he was? But then again, what were the chances in a city this size she'd run into a wolf? It wasn't like they were that common.

She closed her eyes as he confirmed it. "You're my mate."

"No. You're mistaken." This wasn't happening.

"I'm quite sure."

"I refuse." Because she could just imagine the havoc this would wreak.

"Too late."

It had been too late the moment they'd met. And especially so once they slept together.

"You trapped me." How that galled, and after all the lessons from her father.

"Claimed you."

"Same thing. You made me yours without permission."

"It's not like I had much of a choice. Once I saw you . . ." He shrugged. "I'll admit at first I was kind of freaked out by it, but I've come around to the idea."

"I'm going to kill you."

"Now, little rabbit. There's no need to—" He ducked as she threw the glass bowl of candy on the table.

"I see you need time to process this, and I really should go get that paperwork done." He just couldn't help himself. He flashed her a cocky grin and said, "See you later . . . *mate*."

The lamp hit the door a second after he shut it. However, the crashing noise couldn't erase the echo of his words.

Mated. To a wolf.

Oh no. This couldn't be happening. Why, oh why hadn't she spotted his beast side before it was too late? A side she failed to recognize, distracted by her situation and his good looks.

I'm a wolf's mate.

Life as she knew it would never be the same.

The knowledge made her rash.

CHAPTER 15

While Gavin hated leaving Megan after having declared her his mate, given her somewhat temperamental reaction he thought a cooling-off period might work in his favor. And possibly keep him alive longer.

Sure, he'd not exactly sprung the news of their wolfish nuptials on her in a romantic way.

However, the whole situation since he'd met her had proven less than normal or ideal.

He still couldn't wrap his mind around the fact that the woman he'd tied himself to for life was a proclaimed assassin and spy for his nemesis.

What would this mean for their future? Would she insist on pursing her career? *If she does, at least she'll have a damned good lawyer to keep her sweet ass out of jail.*

Speaking of law, how did he feel about the fact that his mate was a woman on the wrong side of it?

The answer took less than a second to arrive. It didn't really bother him. Gavin was used to defending criminals. Innocent or not, he'd not previously cared. It was up to him to give them their chance in court. To battle against the myriad levels of legal mumbo jumbo, discredit evidence, and tear apart witnesses—verbally, not physically—to win.

Did that make him a bad person? Depended on who you asked. The clients he acquitted loved him.

But treading a gray line with the law didn't mean, though, that he'd cave to Fabian's repeated request to come work for him because, as his creator claimed as Gavin left the mansion, "Now that you've claimed my cousin, that makes us family."

Ugh. The reminder put him in a foul mood, which Larry wisely didn't test as he sat in the backseat of Gavin's car, hands tethered and mouth clamped shut. Wise man.

The police station antics went as expected. Gavin showed up to proclaim Megan's innocence. The officer in charge laughed and said they had all the evidence needed. They changed their tune once Gavin presented them with the hotel evidence that she hadn't been home the previous night, and then, when Larry began to talk, it wasn't long after that the warrant for her arrest got canceled and the murder charges were dropped.

Simple really, except all that took a few hours. A few hours away from Megan. A few hours for her to come to grips with the situation or stew over it. A few hours for her to get in trouble.

When Gavin's phone meowed, he welcomed the distraction, especially when Broderick announced, "I think I have a lead on the culprit."

As Broderick relayed his findings, Gavin exited the police station and jogged to his car, phone pressed to his ear with one hand while the other dug out his keys from his suit—which he'd stopped and changed quickly at his office, lest people note the distinctive scent of passion it bore. A pity he'd not gotten to enjoy the perfume of his mate longer. Megan's erotic response to him was something to revel in. However, that scent belonged to him alone.

He growled as he realized his keys were in the other pocket and he had to switch hands. As he juggled the phone to the other ear, he asked, "Are you sure of the identity?"

"Are you seriously questioning my ability to follow money trails?" an aggrieved Broderick replied.

"Have you told Megan?"

"Not yet. I actually haven't seen her since you left this morning. But then again Fabian's place is huge. She could be hiding anywhere."

Such as in his backseat with a garrote. Gavin flicked a glance in his rearview mirror but didn't spot his sexy mate. *A shame.* Even if she planned to murder him, he wouldn't have minded seeing her.

I have it so bad.

"Do me a favor and don't say anything to her. I want to take care of this myself." Because he had a score to settle with the person who'd orchestrated the attacks on his little rabbit. The knowledge she could handle herself didn't mean Gavin could so easily force his protective instincts into a box and tell them to stay there.

In this instance, he reverted to a primal driving force. *My woman. Must protect.*

"I'll keep my lips sealed, buddy. By the way, I never had a chance before to say congrats on the whole found-your-soul-mate thing."

"Congratulate me in a few months if I'm still alive. She was less than pleased at the announcement."

"She'll come around."

He sure hoped so.

Perhaps gifting her the mastermind behind her arrests and attacks would pave a truce and a starting point for his forgiveness.

Not that he planned to allow Megan to sulk or punish him for doing what came naturally. If she protested too much, he'd just seduce her. It seemed to work well on the other occasions he'd resorted to it. *It works well for both of us.*

Arriving at the address Broderick gave him, Gavin noted the lack of guards for the estate. Unusual, but not unheard of. It could be they were subtle and hidden. Perhaps the owner didn't believe in twenty-four-hour on-premise security. *Or maybe I'm walking into a trap.*

The possibility didn't affect his step or purpose. He knocked firmly on the solid wooden door. When no reply was forthcoming, he pushed on the levered handle. The portal swung open without a creak, and he stepped in.

No butler greeted him, or an army of guns. Not even the owner of the house. In a glance Gavin took in the empty, soaring hall with its polished marble floors, wide archways leading off into the house, and the waft of perfume from the left.

Smelled like someone dunked herself in the cloying fragrance. At least the stench provided him a direction. He entered a dining room, where a lone figure sat at the head of the table, a bottle of wine and a glass partially filled with amber liquid set on the gleaming wooden surface.

One person. A woman who looked like anything but a criminal. On the contrary, she could have graced any high-row social event with ease. Hair layered in perfect golden waves that spilled over the shoulders of her red tailored suit. It matched the crimson of her lips and went well with the darkness of her kohled eyes and the big shiny gun she held aimed at him.

What was it with him running into deadly women lately?

"Do you always greet your guests with a revolver?"

"I was expecting someone else, not a legal wolf in lawyer's clothing," the blonde said with a hint of a Russian accent.

The expression went "a wolf in sheep's clothing," as if he'd get caught—or really drunk—in anything so ridiculous.

Gavin only ever wore Armani. Anything less was simply uncivilized—kind of like him during a full moon.

Vivienne, who also went by the name Scarlet Widow—a fact Broderick had only discovered with some deep digging—didn't bother rising from her chair as he strode farther into the room. Nor did she drop the gun.

"So you know who I am?" he said.

"As if I wouldn't recognize the lawyer who's taken on the case of that awful woman who murdered my dearly departed husband."

"Gee, I hadn't realized I'd accepted a retainer from you." His subtle jab didn't go unnoticed.

"Are you implying I killed Pierre? Have you not read the police file yet? The evidence is irrefutable."

"And missing. A funny thing happened last night. The original knife and bloody clothes have disappeared from the precinct. No one knows where they went. Not that it matters, given the search where they obtained them was illegal. It seems the warrant to toss her place was issued after the cops showed up at Megan's apartment. Since they didn't have it, everything they found is—" He made a noise as he splayed his hands, miming an explosion. "Gone. And even if recovered, inadmissible. Lucky for the police, I came across some evidence that led them in a new direction. They're investigating it right now and have someone in custody."

A slight moue of displeasure momentarily creased Vivienne's features. "So you've freed the secretary. How nice for you. That doesn't explain your presence here. Or did you feel a moral obligation to offer me closure by telling me who truly killed my husband?"

"We both know who killed him, and he isn't sitting in a jail cell."

"Are you telling me you've implicated an innocent man in a crime?"

"Oh, we both know Larry's not innocent. His hands are covered in blood, just like yours. You've got quite the reputation, *Vivienne.* Or do you prefer your nickname, Scarlet Widow?"

The rouged lips parted in a wide smile that flashed white teeth. "I see someone did some intensive homework. But I don't see what good it does you. My electronics detector at the door shows you aren't wearing a wire. Your phone signal is jammed, and you are unarmed."

"Am I?"

"Ah yes, the wolf thing. I've run across your kind before. Tough to kill in a hand-to-hand battle but still susceptible to a well-aimed bullet."

He didn't flinch as she raised the gun, aiming it at his head. As a matter of fact, he still smiled. Against a human man she might have held the upper hand, but Gavin didn't play by human rules, nor was he bound by human speed. She might know his secret, but he doubted she'd ever come across a truly strong Lycan. Or one as determined as Gavin to protect his mate.

"Aren't you going to beg for your life?"

"I don't beg."

"Perhaps some final words? I'm sure you'd like to know why I did this."

He shrugged. "Actually, I don't really care. I'm sure you think your reasons are valid. Even if they were, they don't matter. You tried to hurt something of mine, and I won't allow that." Murder might be against the law; however, something had to be done, especially against a woman who wouldn't hesitate to use deadly force again. The list of killings attached to her reputation staggered. *I wonder how Megan's own accomplishments would rank.*

"Won't allow?" Vivienne let out a husky laugh. "Such cockiness. Such a shame I have to kill you. With your looks and that attitude, I'll wager you would make a wonderful lover."

"He does. But that's not something you'll ever know."

With those words, Megan, who'd arrived without a sound or warning scent—damned heavy perfume—shot Vivienne dead.

Gavin, no stranger to violence, blinked as he processed the quick and quiet efficiency of it. "Did you seriously just do that?"

"I did."

"Even though I had the situation under control and didn't need your help."

"You call that under control?"

"Yes."

She snorted. "From my perspective, I'd say you were taking too long. My daddy taught me that letting your enemy talk is a sign of stupidity or suicidal tendencies. Efficiency always comes first."

"What about answers?" Gavin asked. "Don't you want to know why she was after you?"

"I already figured it out. Work-based rivalry. I stole a few hits from under her. Even though we never officially met, I guess she recognized me when she saw me at Pierre's office. She might have also held a grudge that I killed her stupidly rich fiancé a few years back before she could get her claws on his fortune."

"You killed her boyfriend?" That explained the vindictiveness.

"The guy was a drug lord and trafficker of women. He deserved it."

"Do they all deserve it?"

"Are you asking if I have a moral code that only allows me to kill the guilty?"

"Do you?"

She smiled. "Everyone has sinned at one point in their life. But if it's any consolation, I do have lines I won't cross." Piece spoken, Megan, wearing gloves, pressed Vivienne's fingers around the stock of the gun before letting the limp arm flop, dropping the weapon. The other gun, which Vivienne never fired, was tucked into the waistband of Megan's tight jeans.

Moving his focus away from the way the denim showcased the curve of her hips and clung to her thighs proved a chore. Especially since he couldn't stem a visual of himself peeling the fabric from her skin. He shook his mind free from the distracting image. "Forensics will dispute the suicide because the angle is wrong."

Again she made a disparaging noise. "Forensic folk are overworked and underpaid. Cops will find the despondent note she left behind, see the mountain of debt, and think exactly what they need to think. Forensics will make the facts fit and move on to their next case."

"You have this all figured out, don't you?"

She tapped her chin before grinning. "Yup."

"I'll allow it, this time. However, in the future, as my mate, I'm going to have to ask that you not go around just killing things. At least not without talking to me first."

That wiped her smirk off. "Like hell."

"If we're going to make this relationship work, we need some ground rules." He knew he was sticking his foot in his mouth, could see it by the way she stiffened, but he couldn't seem to help himself.

Nothing about Megan was going the way he'd expected. She didn't just fall in his arms. She made him work for it. She did what she wanted and to hell with consequences. And she didn't seem to care that seeing her pop up out of nowhere, putting herself in danger, just about made his heart stop.

Unacceptable.

But, of course, she just had to argue. "There will be no rules because this isn't happening. I don't care what you think you feel for me. I'm not your mate. I can't be."

"Why not?"

"Because, for one, my family would never stand for it."

Was that her biggest argument? "Does your family have a thing against lawyers who do well for themselves?"

"No, they have a thing against unapproved wolves messing with me. You know how Fabian leads the wolves out here and is considered a big shot?"

"Yeah."

"Well, on the West Coast, my granddaddy is the other big shot. Really big shot."

"He's not—" *Shit.* Fate really had it in for him. Even Gavin, who preferred to stay out of Lycan politics, knew the West Coast was ruled by the Bianchi family. And only idiots messed with them. Or a beloved granddaughter.

Apparently, he wasn't so smart, after all, because Gavin didn't care. *Megan is mine.*

"By the look on your face, I see you grasp why this won't work."

"On the contrary." He edged around the table, approaching her where she stood framed in the second entrance to the dining room. She stood her ground. "I think you're perfect for me. I worried when Broderick explained the whole mating thing to me. I wondered how a woman could learn to accept a wolf as her husband. Who better than a woman raised among them?"

"I don't love you."

Yet. He didn't let her words deter him. Love and trust took time, but they did have one thing she couldn't dispute. "But you desire me."

At the intent he made sure shone in his eyes she retreated as he stalked her.

"Desire is a physical thing. It goes away."

"Not in this case and you know it."

"My family will kill you."

"Will they? Or will they welcome a strong wolf into the fold, one perfectly ready and able to handle a headstrong woman?"

"Welcome? Like fuck. There isn't a man good enough for my baby girl," was the only gruffly snarled warning Gavin received before the lights went out.

CHAPTER 16

A week later and Megan still pouted. She just couldn't have articulated exactly why, though.

Yes, her daddy had shown up and decided things for her, his well-aimed throw of a statuette knocking Gavin out. Her hollered, "What did you do that for?" was met with an implacable, "I didn't like him."

Funny enough, Megan couldn't say the same. Despite Gavin's pompous assertions, she rather liked him. Not that it mattered. Her daddy literally abducted her and took her home.

Megan didn't fight much.

Really, leaving was for the best. She couldn't just allow Gavin—no matter how sexy or yummy or anything—dictate the course of her life.

So what if he thought fate had designated her as the one woman he'd spend his life with?

No one asked her.

No one asked her if she wanted to more or less marry an almost stranger—who made her body sing and brought her to life.

No one asked her if she could handle living with a lawyer

whose ethics depended on whom he defended—and who accepted the fact that she sometimes killed people for money.

No one asked her if she wanted her heart broken, because, despite his claim that she belonged to him, a week had passed and he'd made no attempt to contact her.

Such a jerk.

Yet she missed him.

Sigh.

The slap to the back of her head, though it rocked her, didn't even make her scowl. Love taps were common in her family. "Hey, Grandma."

"Hay is for horses." A familiar retort. Grandma settled herself on the rocker and snagged a ball of wool and a pair of needles out of a basket. "Stop sulking," she admonished.

"I'm not sulking."

"Says the girl with the lip hanging so low it's dragging on the floor. I thought you were tougher than this."

"I am. Or haven't you seen Kit's black eye?" Stupid cousin had dared mock her getting framed. She mocked him for getting hit by a girl.

"I'm not talking about that kind of strength, but the one to go after what you want. Or, more specifically, who you want."

"I don't want anyone."

"Oh please. I've heard enough of what happened out east to know you wanted that lone wolf, or else he'd have been singing soprano before he ever laid a hand on you."

"So he was hot."

"More than hot or you wouldn't be pining for him."

It occurred to her to lie again, but given Grandma held

two sharp objects—and wouldn't need much incentive to use them—Megan wisely stuck to the truth. "Yes I miss him, even if I shouldn't. We knew each other only a few days, and in that short time I discovered he's arrogant, with no scruples. He seduced me. Lied to me about what he was. Ordered me around. Drove me crazy." In bed, out of bed, in her head . . . She just couldn't shake him, much like a tick that burrowed under the skin.

"You love him."

Megan snorted. "I don't love him."

"Why not?"

"What do you mean, why not? Did you hear what I said?"

"I heard that he engaged you on so many levels you didn't hesitate when it came to mentioning a few. I heard he doesn't stand for your stubbornness and that he liked you in spite of it. His lack of scruples makes him a perfect fit for our family, or have you forgotten who you are?"

Why did her grandmother have to turn Megan's arguments against into reasons for? "But he doesn't love me." Because if he did, once he'd regained consciousness he would have come after her.

"Doesn't love you?" Grandma made a noise. "Look out the window and tell me that's not a man in love."

Say what? Megan flew to the window and peeked out. Bright sunlight shone down on the short, trimmed grass of the front yard to her grandparents' place—where Daddy had dumped her after Megan decorated his beloved gun collection with stickers, cute, really gluey ones with dancing unicorns and rainbows.

The image of her father staring in incredulous shock at

his decorated arsenal paled before the image of Gavin striding up the front walkway, in his suit, tie and all, determination in his stride.

"He came." She could barely believe it.

He came for me. And was stopped.

From behind bushes, from around the corners, from anywhere a Lycan could hide, slunk forth family members, male ones, Daddy, Uncle Bernard, Cousin Robert, another cousin.

Oh dear.

They'd kill Gavin.

"What are you waiting for, girl? Get out there before they get blood all over my begonias. I already watered them once today."

Megan didn't need the order to already be flying out the door. She paused on the front step, caught by Gavin's stare as he immediately noted her appearance.

"There's my little rabbit." He smiled. Slow. Sexy. And hungrily.

A little too hungrily. Daddy punched him.

Gavin barely budged, and his only concession to the blow was to rub a hand on his jaw. "I'm sorry, sir. I don't believe we were properly introduced last time we met."

"You should have stayed back east, boy."

Growls from her other male family members agreed in chorus.

Faced with a threat that would have made more than one wolf piss himself, Gavin remained tall and undaunted. Such a sexy idiot.

"Staying east wasn't an option. Megan is here. Which means I'm here. She's my mate."

Even louder grumbling from the assembled males.

"It took you long enough to remember that," she muttered.

A sardonic grin tilted his lips. "Miss me, little rabbit? I would have been here sooner. However, the police finding me at the apparent scene of a suicide created a bit of havoc. It didn't help that once Larry saw me in the cell alongside his he recanted and tried to pin the blame on me and you."

"I'll kill the thug," she snarled.

"No need. Larry was taken care of. Between the evidence uncovered at his apartment, courtesy of my maker"—Gavin made a moue of distaste—"and the unfortunate slip he suffered in the shower, Larry is no longer an issue. Leaving me free to pursue more important matters." His stare left no doubt as to what matters he meant.

"Megan is not available for the likes of you," her daddy said.

Gavin flicked his gaze to the man standing in his path. "You, sir, are placing me in a difficult situation. All of you are. On the one hand, as my mate's family, I am to treat you with respect. Which, for normal people, means no violence. But on the other hand . . ." Gavin loosened his tie, and his eyes took on a dark glint. "She's mine, and I will allow no one to stand between us."

Daddy cracked his knuckles. "A pity she doesn't want you, boy. I could almost admire your balls."

Didn't want him? "Hold on a second. Who said I didn't want him?" Megan demanded as she skipped down the porch steps.

"If you did, you would have never let me put you on a plane and take you back home," her daddy argued.

"You zip-tied my hands and gagged me for the trip," she reminded.

"Well, you didn't try and go back once we got here," her father announced. "If you truly cared for him, none of us could have stopped you."

"Well, maybe I was still making up my mind," she sassed.

"And what does your mind say?" Gavin asked.

Seeing him again, she finally had to admit the one thing she'd tried to ignore. *I love the idiot.* Even if he drove her nuts and she couldn't see how it would work. Damned if she didn't want to run to him right now and plaster herself against him, and not just because it would possibly give the entire male side of her family an apoplexy.

"I missed you," was what she said. Only that.

Yet the admission was enough for his entire face to brighten, and he stupidly took a step forward, only to have her cousin step in his path.

"Where do you think you're—"

Poor Robert, he never did finish his sentence, as Gavin just grabbed and tossed him out of his path, her cousin landing and squashing Grandma's roses. Grandma would have words with him for that. Not Gavin, of course. Wasn't his fault Megan's idiot cousin didn't know how to get out of the way of a man on a mission.

Her other cousin and uncle went to stand in his way, but Gavin wouldn't allow himself to be deterred, and when Megan said, "Let him through, or else," she shot them a look that promised painful retribution. They knew she didn't issue empty threats and wisely scattered.

Except for Daddy.

He crossed his arms and glowered. "I don't think he's good enough for you."

"I'm probably not, sir. But I can promise to do my best to do right by your daughter."

"You know she's a killer."

"Yeah."

"And a pain in the ass."

"So I've noticed."

"She's evil, too. You don't want to know what she does when she's pissed." Her father stroked the butt of his pistol, which still held a faint sparkle from the glitter glue she used for the less cooperative stickers.

"I kind of like that about her, sir."

Awwww. Megan had never heard anything so sweet.

"It's your funeral, then. Which mated or not, I'm not paying for," Daddy grumbled as he stalked away.

"But you will pay for the wedding," she hollered at his back just so she could see his step stumble, his shoulders tighten, and a shudder rock his body.

Then she saw nothing but a broad chest as arms swept her up and hugged her close. "Married?"

"I might kill people for a living, but I refuse to live in sin."

Gavin snorted. "Your warped set of values is really going to take getting used to."

"It's not too late to walk away," she offered.

He declined. "Like fuck. It's been hell these last few days. It's been much too long since I saw you."

"Not my fault you aren't as good as you think. A hotshot lawyer like you should have had the charges dropped before they got filed," she teased.

"I see life with you will never be boring," he declared before dipping his head to kiss her.

She allowed the embrace, savored the taste of him, the excitement of his touch, before whispering, "Run!"

"What?"

She grabbed his hand and tugged. "I said run, unless you want to eat some buckshot. I think someone forgot to tell Grandpa we got Daddy's approval and he's coming with the shotgun."

Lucky for them, Grandma tackled him before he caused any damage.

And by the time the wedding came around, a few days later, because the testosterone half of her family said it wasn't proper her sharing a room with a man, Grandpa had even managed an almost friendly scowl and a wedding gift that consisted of a promise not to kill the damned lawyer.

The warm welcome to the family almost brought a tear to the eye—probably because Grandma stamped a few toes with her pointy-heeled shoes.

Later on that night, alone in the honeymoon suite, her skin dewy from passion, Megan traced the line of his jaw. "Say it again."

"I love you, little rabbit."

Just like she loved him. And to think it was murder that had brought them together.

Beat that, Cousin Kit.

EPILOGUE

Back east, in an office tucked at the back of a strip club . . .

Having nine lives was well and good in theory, but when a woman straddled a man, held a gun to his head, and said, "What are you doing in my drawers?" it probably wasn't a smart thing to say, "Hoping to lick some delicious cream."

Broderick could blame his stupid statement only on the fact that his mother claimed he'd landed on his head instead of four paws more than was healthy for a kitten.

He could also blame hormones, as it took only one look and scent to realize the goddess threatening his life was his mate.

Meow. And he meant *ow!* as she dug the barrel into his skin, not at all impressed by his compliment. "Give me one reason why I shouldn't shoot."

Apparently, "Because I'm pretty sure we're soulmates," wasn't the right answer.

FERAL
PASSIONS

Kate Douglas

This tale is dedicated with much love to Margaret Riley,
owner and publisher of Changeling Press,
who convinced me many, many years ago that yes,
I really could write stories about shapeshifters
and werewolves. Thank you, M! I guess you were right. ☺

ACKNOWLEDGMENTS

My thanks as always to my beta readers, Ann Jacobs, Rose Toubbeh, Jan Takane, Lynne Thomas, Karen Woods, and Kerry Parker—six women with busy lives who always manage to find time to read for me. Thanks also to my editor, Eileen Rothschild, who has given me a chance to play once again in the world of make-believe.

CHAPTER 1

Thursday

"Aw, c'mon, Cherry. It'll be so much fun. Please?"

"Cissy, I . . ." Cherry turned away. She hated to disappoint Christa, but there was just no way. No way at all.

Her sister's BFF, Stephanie, chimed in. "If you don't come with us, that fully paid reservation is just going to go to waste. We bought the package for three because Gina said she wanted to go, and then she bailed on us."

Cherry ran her fingertip through the salt on the rim of her margarita glass and stuck her salty finger in her mouth. Damn. Did she or didn't she? She stared at Stephanie. "There has to be someone else who can fill a third spot. Especially since it's paid for."

Christa chimed in. "Gina bailed an hour ago. We leave Sunday morning, so we don't have time to hunt for anyone. I know you have time off coming. Talk to your boss tomorrow and let her know you'll be gone all next week. Please?"

"C'mon, Cherry."

Cherry glanced from her sister to Steph and pulled back feelings that were more about envy than irritation. She'd never had a close friend other than Christa, aka Cissy, not the way Steph and Christa had each other. They'd been inseparable since they'd been, quite literally, in diapers. Two adorable little girls in day care together when they were toddlers, two stunning and perfectly slim, trim twenty-five-year-olds.

On top of that, each of them was smart and successful, and they were almost too nice to be true.

When she was with them, Cherry felt like a toad. A very fat toad. The idea of spending a week at a luxury resort with her gorgeous dark-haired baby sister and Christa's equally beautiful blond best friend—each girl perfectly sleek and toned while Cherry had to lie on her back on the bed to get her fat pants zipped—was beyond depressing.

Except she really loved her little sister, and Steph had never been anything but nice, and Cherry did have vacation time she had to use or lose . . .

"Think about it, Cherry." Christa touched Cherry's chin with her fingertips and gently forced her to make eye contact. Damn. She was definitely bringing out the big guns.

"I already . . ."

"No. You haven't even listened to us. It's not your typical Club Med kind of place. This is a rural setting up in the north part of the state, almost to Oregon. Men run the place and do all the cooking and everything, but there're only women as guests. And not even a lot of women. Only six guests—all women, I remind you—at the club at one time. We will be three of them."

"That's half. The only men are the guys who work there," Steph said, "but the resort is set up to allow women to get in touch with nature without the hassle of guys and all that testosterone-driven need to hike farther, climb higher. You know, a relaxing and *fun* vacation?"

Christa interrupted with, "They don't plan every single minute of your day. You're encouraged to bring books, knitting, paints, whatever it is that makes you happy. In fact, I'm hoping you'll throw in some of those really sexy romances you like to read."

"Me, too," Steph said. "I never have time to read for fun and Christa says your books are . . . stimulating." She poked Christa in the ribs. "We might actually learn something about men."

"You're not kidding." Christa poked Steph back. Then she once again focused that laser-eyed stare on Cherry. "What's really unique about it is that it's at a wolf preserve."

Wolves? Their enthusiasm must be contagious, since Cherry was actually thinking of doing this. *But wolves?*

"You can interact with the wolves in their natural setting." Laughing, Christa let go of Cherry and hugged herself. "Can you imagine? Being close enough to touch a wild wolf? Going swimming where there are only other women— no guys ogling your butt?"

"Or your boobs," Steph added drily. She was much more generously endowed than Christa. "I'm off men for now, anyway. A week at a resort just for women sounds like the ideal vacation."

Cherry spun her head to stare at Steph. "What about Mike? I thought you guys were . . ."

"That is a name not to be mentioned in my presence."

Cherry glanced at Christa, who merely shrugged and said, "He was boinking the receptionist."

Steph practically growled. "Not just boinking, but do-ing such a great job at it that she was absolutely starry-eyed." She took a big swallow of her margarita. "I was most definitely not starry-eyed, but that's not what we're dis-cussing, Cherry. You're going with us. No argument."

"Wolves?" Cherry glanced at the painting over her faux-fireplace mantle. A pack of wolves racing across a meadow in the moonlight, teeth gleaming, eyes alight with the joy of the hunt. She'd always loved wolves, but she'd never seen a real-live wolf before. Only pictures. "They're actually tame enough to interact with people?"

"That's what it says." Steph laughed. "I would think it's poor business practice to allow them to eat the guests."

"Because it's a preserve," Christa added, "the Web site says, a lot of them were rescued as pups, hand raised, and then returned to the wild, but that's why they're here—they aren't entirely wild, but they're not really tame, either. It's thousands of acres where they can roam like wild wolves and they still have to hunt to eat. And no, they don't hunt the guests."

Christa was still smiling as she tapped away on her cell phone for a few seconds. Then she raised her head and grinned triumphantly at Cherry. Or was that a smug grin? Cherry grimaced. She'd lost this argument—losing was a given when Christa had her mind made up.

"There," she said. "I just sent you the link to the resort. It's called Feral Passions, and it's up in the Trinity Alps. No arguments. You're coming with us. The wolf preserve is only open to guests of the resort, and if the pictures on the Web site are anywhere close to the real thing, the place looks rustic, but the lodge is all new and everything is set up for comfort and convenience. No!" Christa held up her hand when Cherry opened her mouth to argue, at this point, merely for the sake of not giving in too easily. "No argument. You're going. We're picking you up Sunday morning at seven. It's over five hours of driving, and we'll need to stop for lunch and potty breaks along the way. Pack comfortable clothes, good hiking boots, and a warm coat. There's a list of things on the Web site. It says the nights can be chilly. They provide all camping gear if we do any overnight trips. We'll come home the following Saturday. And bring your swimsuit. The pool's heated."

Cherry shook her head. "No. No swimsuit." She didn't even own one. Not since she was little, too young to realize how awful she looked when she wasn't covered up. She was fully aware of Steph and Christa exchanging glances. They just didn't get it, but neither of them carried fifty extra pounds around, either.

"Ladies, I've gotta go." Steph grabbed her bag, leaned close and hugged Cherry, and then patted Christa on the head.

"Me, too." Christa hugged Cherry. "Hon, we're gonna have such a great time. I want you to relax and enjoy yourself. No Wi-Fi or cell phone reception, so it really is a vacation. No one from your office can even text you. You'll love it."

Cherry sighed. She hoped she'd love it, but she didn't expect to. Still, Christa never asked for favors. A week at an exclusive resort with real-live wolves shouldn't be too bad.

"Okay, gentlemen. What's your take on our first month of business? Is Feral Passions going to work, or did I just sink a shitload of money into a stupid idea?" Traker Jakes stared into his mug of draft beer as if it offered up the secrets of the universe.

"It's a great design." Brad Martin wiped down the polished redwood bar with a damp rag and then threw it into a bin under the sink, but he turned and winked at his buddy.

Cain snorted. "Of course you think it's a great design—you designed it." Laughing, he swiveled on his barstool and faced Trak. The guy might be a century and a half old, but like the rest of them, he didn't look a day over thirty.

None of them did. One of the upsides of werewolf genetics, though their long lives could be a downside, too. A lonely downside. "We've had four groups of women come through and they've all had a great time," Cain said. "We've ended the month with a better financial picture than any of us expected, and you're not the only one with a shitload of money tied up in this, Trak. We've all invested. Give it time. I think it's going to pay off."

"Financially, sure." Trak shook his head, frustration evident. "Except making a profit isn't the point of this project. The point is not just to give a bunch of women a good time. The point is to find mates for the guys, you two and me included. So far, not a single pairing has come of this."

"We've only been open a month, Trak. Cain's right. Give it time." Brad glanced at Cain.

"Have you enjoyed meeting the women?" Cain forced eye contact with Trak, which was not an easy thing for a subordinate to do with his alpha, but the bastard could be so hardheaded sometimes, not to mention a die-hard pessimist. "Don't tell me you didn't have a good time with that absolutely sensational redhead last week."

Trak grunted.

Brad poured himself a glass of iced tea, carefully squeezing lemon over the top. "C'mon, Cain. She was hot, but a little too aware of her own hotness. And she most certainly didn't like having wolves around."

"What? She was afraid of the wolves?" Cain must have missed that part of the visit. He'd given her a massage and thought she was okay—a little too skinny for his taste, but . . .

Brad shook his head. "Afraid of the hair. It's spring. Wolves shed. She thought it was disgusting."

Trak's sigh was a bit too dramatic. "She ran Brad and me out of the pool area. Threatened to complain to management. Said it was unsanitary having wolves shedding near the hot tub, not to mention the fact that we were all males and probably peed on everything. What a bitch."

"Too bad you couldn't just shift right then, tell her you were management and, hey, what's the problem, sweetheart?" Cain took a swallow of his beer. "Well, we haven't had any trouble filling up the slots. We've got a new group coming in tomorrow. Three smart, young professional women from San Francisco. They're driving, should be here by three or four. Another group of three out of LA. They're coming in by private plane and plan to land in Weaverville. They have a rental car waiting, so they might show up earlier. They all work in the movie industry, but not as actors. Their reservation info said they're into the production end of things. We'll need to be careful around them. They might be more in tune with the weird and wonderful, and we can't risk them finding out what we are."

"Which is why Feral Passions is the perfect venue for a lonely werewolf to find a mate." Brad glanced at Trak but focused on Cain. "In a beautifully designed setting, of course. We get to see the women in our habitat, see if anyone is drawn to any of us in both our human and wolf forms. And if they are, if they really seem to go for anyone . . ."

"And don't mind a little shedding in the hot tub." At least Trak was sort of smiling. A good sign.

"Then we bite, and voilà! Instant mate." Brad's cocky grin was actually . . . wolfish.

"Or a really pissed-off female werewolf." Cain didn't like that part at all. Yeah, it was important to keep their existence secret, but it wasn't like the old days when a guy could go out and kidnap a nice, uneducated woman out of a small, rural village, bring her back to the pack, let her choose which guy she liked best, and then the guy could bite her. Women didn't expect as much back in the old days. Now they had equal rights and cell phones, and Facebook, where they could blab about everything.

And post pictures. The last thing the pack needed was a video on social media of one of them shifting from human to wolf. Cain shuddered at the mere thought. "I like the accepted 'werewolf lore,' that we each have a true mate waiting for us. It would make this all a lot easier, but we're on our own. My biggest fear is that women are so different now. They're independent and well educated, and they expect to have an equal say in their lives. They're more fun than they used to be, but they're not chattel, guys. We have to remember that."

"Well, we're going to have to figure out something, and do it soon," Trak said. "None of us is getting any younger, and it's been too long since any of the pack has had young. Brad, you're the youngest and you were born . . . when was that? Nineteen-thirty?"

"Nineteen-thirty-one." Brad shook his head. "I'm only eighty-five. Still a pup, Trak. Not nearly as old as you." He tilted his head, stared at Trak's head. "Hmm . . . is that a bit of gray I see?"

Brad might be laughing, but Cain felt the desperation behind the humor. Even though they all looked and felt like they were in their thirties and they each had many hundred more years left in them, the pack was dying. Some of them had been around since long before the Declaration of Independence—they'd come over on the first sailing ships to colonize North America not long after the Pilgrims; a few even fought in the Revolutionary War. Most of those old ones were showing their age now, not participating as much in pack life.

Some stayed in wolf form all the time, spending their days basking in the sun, waiting for the time when that afternoon nap never ended. Trak had been born during the Civil War, which made him over a hundred and fifty years old, and he wasn't even considered middle-aged, but if they didn't do something about it now while they still had time to find mates and have young, time to teach their pups about their amazing heritage, the Trinity Alps pack was going to go the way of the passenger pigeon. Cain had never seen one of those—he'd been whelped around 1910—but Trak remembered them. He'd seen them by the millions when he was a kid, flocks so big they filled the sky.

Then they were gone.

Exactly what was going to happen to the Trinity Alps pack, if this experiment with Feral Passions failed.

CHAPTER 2

Sunday

It was almost five when Cherry parked the car in front of a sprawling log building nestled in a large clearing with forest all around. Towering pines and dark green fir trees shadowed part of the area, and the tangy scent of cedar filled the air. The lodge was surrounded by a beautiful deck, and it was all absolutely breathtaking—even better than the pictures online.

"Okay, ladies. Rise and shine." She turned and poked Stephanie, who slept soundly in the backseat.

Grunting, Steph slowly pivoted and sat upright. Sort of.

Christa stretched her arms overhead and arched her back. She'd ridden shotgun the last seventy miles or so. The sound of popping vertebrae made Cherry wince. She hated to think what her own back was going to sound like. "I'm surprised neither of you ladies thought to mention that the last eleven miles were nothing but a dirt road." It was well marked, so she hadn't been afraid of getting lost, but the forest was so thick and impenetrable looking, it was scary when you didn't know your way.

Then, at a wide spot in the road not a quarter mile from

here, there'd been a professional-looking sign pointing toward Feral Passions Resort. Of course, on the opposite side of the road was a cute little bar that really fit the surroundings, though she wondered who the customers were, since they were on the preserve and there hadn't been any houses along the way. There'd been a couple of beat-up trucks parked in front and a hand-painted sign that said "Growl" nailed over the door.

Seemed apropos. She'd looked for wolves. She might have caught a glimpse of one shortly after they'd come through the electric gate marking the entrance to the fenced wolf preserve. That was back where the paved road ended. A long way back.

She still felt as if Christa and Steph had pushed her into this trip, and Cherry wasn't quite able to give up the feeling of resentment, the sense the elusive Gina didn't exist and she'd been manipulated. At the same time, it was hard to stay grumpy in a setting this peaceful. Craggy mountains cut into a brilliant blue sky and a thick forest grew below with trees in all shades of green.

There was even wild dogwood blooming among the tall evergreens. She'd seen a few deer and wondered if she'd really spotted that wolf a couple of miles back, but the best part was the smell. Air so fresh it made her want to breathe deeply and just hold that clean air deep inside her lungs.

Unfastening her seat belt, she glanced at the front of the lodge. Three young women sat at a table on the deck with glasses in front of them.

Any kind of drink sounded really, really good about now.

"Holy shit."

"Christa!" Cherry snapped around and gaped at her sister, who was staring out the passenger window.

At what could only be a male model. Maybe a god. Whatever. Cherry almost swallowed her tongue. The man walking toward their car was tall, dark, and sexy, and he walked with that loose-hipped swagger that hinted at all kinds of things he could do with those hips.

Hands shaking, she opened the door and got out. No way was she sitting in the front seat and staring up at a man that hot. She needed to plant her feet firmly on the ground.

"Welcome to Feral Passions." He walked directly toward Cherry with his hand out. She shook hands with him, but hers totally disappeared in his. She bit back a nervous giggle as that old cliché popped into her head, about the size of a man's hands and feet correlating to his . . . No. She was not going there.

"You ladies must be Cheraza, Christa, and Stephanie. I'm Traker Jakes. We were getting worried about you. I hope the trip wasn't too difficult."

He still held Cherry's hand. His palm was rough, his skin dry and warm. She knew hers was starting to sweat. "No. Just long," she said, slipping her fingers free of his light grasp. "I'm Cheraza, but everyone calls me Cherry; that's my sister, Christa, and our friend Stephanie."

Steph crawled out of the backseat, looking deliciously rumpled. Cherry just looked rumpled, but she'd learned not to let it bother her. Too much.

Steph grinned. "Hi, Traker. Nice to meet you." Then she covered her mouth and yawned. "Oops. Just woke up." Laughing, she turned away to grab her handbag from the backseat.

Christa got out of the car and slung her huge leather

purse over her shoulder. She looked adorably messy with her ponytail hanging sideways and a sleep crease on one cheek. "Nice to meet you. Cherry, hon, thanks for driving the rest of the way. I thought we were going to switch off."

Cherry merely shrugged. "Not a problem." She flipped the lever inside to pop the trunk. Traker beat her to the back and laughed at the huge number of bags shoved into the tight space. Glancing toward the lodge, he called out, "Hey, Brad. Grab Cain and get your asses out here." Turning to Cherry, he said, "We'll get you ladies settled in your cabins. As soon as you're unpacked, come on up to the lodge and Brad'll fix you a drink and let you take a look at the menu for tonight. That work for you?"

Cherry could only nod. The term "speechless" had never had more profound meaning than it did right now. That had to be Brad and Cain walking across the deck, now coming down the steps. She'd thought Traker was handsome. These two took her breath.

"Hey, ladies. Glad you're here. We were getting worried." The dark-haired one stopped beside Christa and tugged his baseball cap off. Then he turned his full focus on Cherry. "I'm Brad. Why don't you show me which bags are yours." It was the oddest thing—he looked as if he was sizing her up, but instead of giving her a dismissive glance, he continued looking right at her. His brown eyes actually twinkled, and then he winked.

Her knees turned to jelly. She pressed her hand to the side of the car, unobtrusively, she hoped, but it was that or fall on her butt. Men never looked at her for long. A quick glance to check out her oversized assets, and then they moved on.

Brad didn't. He grabbed her bags out of the trunk and

lifted them with ease. She'd needed help from Christa to load the large one. Brad held it lightly in one hand.

"C'mon," he said. "Your cabin's all ready, and I'll help you get settled."

She had to swallow to speak and then decided merely nodding was easier. He smiled and nodded to Traker. "Trak, I'll be back behind the bar in a few minutes."

For some reason, Trak looked like he was trying not to laugh. "No rush. Take your time. I'll cover for you."

A cloud coasted right over the top of Cherry's sense of well-being. Of course, Trak was probably thinking of how he was going to tease Brad later, about getting stuck with the fat one.

She let out a breath she didn't realize she'd been holding. "Meet you two in the bar in about half an hour, okay?"

"Sounds good."

Christa grabbed her overnight bag and followed Cain, while Trak led Steph in the same direction.

As Brad led Cherry toward a trail that angled away from the big lodge and away from Christa and Steph, Cherry felt a moment of panic. She hadn't thought about the fact that they'd be in individual cabins—she'd pictured the lodge as a large hotel with separate rooms. Not only were they rooming by themselves, she didn't even know which cabins Steph and Christa would be staying in. She glanced over her shoulder as her sister and Steph disappeared into the woods, and then she turned and almost ran into Brad.

"Oh. I'm sorry." Flustered, she realized she'd slapped her hand to her chest like an old lady with the vapors, which had her feeling like a fool. Heat raced over her chest and face and she knew he was thinking she was an idiot, a complete loser. Her eyes filled with tears.

"You okay?" He set the bags down on the hard-packed trail.

She dug through her handbag for a tissue, but she didn't look at him. "Fine," she mumbled. This was all a mistake. She never should have come; it was—

"Hey, Cherry. Whatever it is, it's not worth tears."

Arms wrapped around her. Strong, warm arms pulling her close against a broad chest, so close she heard his heart beating, felt the steady *thud, thud, thud* against her cheek. He smelled so good. She couldn't remember the last time a man had hugged her, and there'd never been one that smelled of pine forest and wood smoke. She should pull away, she really should, but he was holding her close and stroking her hair, and whispering stuff she couldn't really hear, and she was just so damned tired from the long drive, and so . . . she wasn't sure what to call it. Vulnerable? But somehow, even though he was a stranger, even though he was probably the most beautiful man she'd ever seen and that alone should scare her to death, it settled her.

He settled her.

She sniffed, drew in a shuddering breath, and sniffed again. He shoved a clean white handkerchief into her hand. "I'm a firm believer in the healing value of a good hug. You okay?"

When she nodded, he leaned over and grabbed her heavy suitcase in one hand and threw the strap to her second bag over his shoulder. She wiped her eyes and blew her nose and then didn't know what to do with the handkerchief.

He took it from her with his free hand, wiped a tear she'd missed, and then stuck the soggy thing into his pocket.

"I'll wash it—"

"Forget about it. I'll take care of it. You must be exhausted after that long drive. Let's get you to your cabin."

They were only a short distance away, but with the trees all around and ferns lining the trail, it was as if they'd stepped into the deepest, darkest woods. Still rattled, Cherry followed him up the steps, across a small front porch and into the cutest little log cabin she'd ever seen. Surrounded by trees but with the front of the cabin in sunlight, it fit like a natural addition to the forest. Inside were a large bed at the back, a sitting area near the front window with four chairs, a bathroom with a huge shower, a tiny kitchenette with a coffeemaker and a microwave, small refrigerator, and a cupboard stuffed with chips and all kinds of other munchies.

Brad set her suitcase on a stand beside an old-fashioned Shaker-style armoire that was well over six feet tall. Her smaller bag went on the floor beside it. Inside, there was more than enough space to hang the clothes she needed to hang, and plenty of drawers along one side for all the little things.

"That's beautiful." She ran her hands over the smooth wood, glanced around the small room, and realized all the furniture matched. Simple, solid, and very utilitarian, but also an incredible fit to the style of the rough-hewn log cabin. "Is it antique? It looks really old."

"Some pieces might be, though I don't know which ones. Depends on whether Trak made it, or his father, or his grandfather. Their woodworking skills are a family trait."

He turned to Cherry and lightly rubbed her shoulder.

She automatically tensed, but his warm hand quickly had her feeling about as tense as sun-warmed honey.

"Relax, Cherry. You're wound too tight for this place. You need to let it all go, relax, and just put yourself in my hands. Or Cain's." He slowly turned her to face him and rested his hands on her hips. She felt their heat through her yoga pants and almost sighed—but she didn't even think of pulling away.

"Cain's the resort's masseur, and I swear the man has magic fingers. I have to go back to the bar, now. The ladies on the deck are probably ready for a refill. Don't be too long."

She loved the way his voice rumbled up out of his chest. Deep and sexy, to go with those soulful brown eyes and thick, dark hair. "Tonight's all about relaxing," he said. "A drink, a good dinner, maybe a massage later, a walk in the moonlight, or time to sit by the fire in the main lodge with a glass of good port or a decadent dessert. We're all about helping you relax so you can enjoy the peace and quiet."

With his hands still resting loosely on her hips, his lips curved up in a smile she felt all the way to her toes. The man was dangerous. Her heart had to be hammering a million beats a minute, but he was just so . . . so . . .

Cocking his head to one side, he gazed intently into her eyes. "Now are you going to be able to find your way to the lodge? It's only about fifty yards. Just follow the path out the front door and go back the way we came. If you're not at the bar in twenty minutes, I'm going to send someone after you."

"I think I can find the way." She couldn't shake her gaze from his. He blinked once and she wondered what it would be like to kiss him. Almost as if he read her mind, his head lowered and his lips met hers. Shocked, Cherry gasped, her lips parted, and Brad deepened the kiss. She lost herself in the warm pressure of his lips, the minty taste of his mouth, the unexpected but welcome thrust of his tongue.

Surprise quickly faded into desire, and when he pulled her close Cherry didn't even think of fighting his embrace. No, because all she could think of was the heat and the size of the larger-than-life erection pressing against her stomach. Much too soon, he slowly, sweetly ended the kiss. Then he leaned his forehead against hers and whispered, "Eighteen minutes."

She felt his heart pounding in his chest, almost as loud as hers. He rubbed his bristly chin across the side of her throat, sending chills along her spine. "I'm sorry you're only here for a week. That's not going to be nearly long enough."

She didn't know what to say, could barely make her lungs work to draw each breath, but it didn't seem to matter. Brad smiled at her, and he was even better looking, if that was at all possible, when he smiled. Then he leaned close and kissed the tip of her nose and without another word was out the door and gone.

Stunned, Cherry stared at the door he'd closed on his way out. Her heart pounded in her chest and all her girl parts clenched as if she'd just spent an hour with her favorite vibrator. She might have thought he was leading her on—just playing with her—but when he kissed her she'd felt him. Brad was erect, the hard length of him pressed close against her belly, so long and solid she was actually wet from wanting him.

Guys could fake a lot of things, but she'd never known one who could fake an erection.

CHAPTER 3

Cherry clipped her hair into a knot on top of her head and took a quick shower. Long trips always made her feel grimy, but that wasn't the only reason. The old cliché about horny guys taking a cold shower to cool down actually made sense. Her body was on fire after Brad's kiss. The man kissed like he'd meant it. She'd only known him for what? Fifteen minutes?

How would he kiss her after a few days? After they got to know each other.

Why wasn't she freaking out? She never kissed men she didn't know. Actually, they never kissed her. But Brad did. And damn it all, he kissed her like he meant it.

The shower helped, though the minute she got out and thought of him she flushed hot all over again. "Oh. My." Fanning herself, Cherry stared at the woman in the mirror. Her cheeks were pink, her eyes sparkled, and she could swear her lips were swollen from kissing. She'd never, ever reacted to a guy the way she did to Brad, but then she'd never had a totally hot guy kiss her just minutes after meeting her.

Who was she kidding? She'd never had a totally hot guy kiss her. Ever.

She really needed to get her act together. She added some lip gloss, unclipped her hair, and brushed it out so that it fell in thick waves past her shoulders. Wrapping the towel around herself, she opened the suitcase she hadn't had time to unpack and dug through it, looking for clean underwear and her favorite knit maxi dress.

She wanted to look as good as possible, but she was too tired to stress over it.

A strange noise had her spinning around. Something had clunked against the cabin door—not quite a knock, but someone was obviously out there. Cherry glanced at the little clock beside the bed. Brad had left a little over twenty minutes ago.

He wouldn't really send someone after her, would he?

Heart thudding, she wrapped the towel tighter around herself and opened the door just a crack.

An absolutely spectacular silver and gray wolf sat on the front step. He raised his head and whined, stood, and pushed at the crack in the door with his nose as if he had every right to come inside.

Cherry didn't think. She merely stepped aside and let the wolf into her cabin. He walked past her and straight to the bed, where he stopped, turned, and, if she didn't know better, posed for her. He really was beautiful, and obviously friendly. She felt absolutely no fear of the animal—in fact, she wanted to pet him but wasn't sure if she should.

Holding her towel tightly between her breasts, she studied the beast. He appeared to be studying her right back.

"Did Brad send you?"

The wolf looked at her, tongue lolling, and yipped. Then

he planted his butt on the little rug beside the bed and stared at her suitcase.

Talk about Mr. Obvious, but if that wasn't an answer—she couldn't wait until she told Christa and Steph about her visitor. "Okay, already," she said. "I'll get dressed." She almost dropped the towel, but then she took another look at the wolf, at the way he watched her out of those perceptive evergreen eyes, and she blushed. Again. He seemed much too intelligent for an animal, that direct stare, his obvious responses to her questions.

She'd read that wolves were really smart.

But not this smart.

Still, did she want to strip down in front of him?

Absolutely not. Instead, she tightened her towel around herself, tucked the end in between her breasts, and unpacked her cotton knit dress with a pattern and fit that disguised her extra weight. She laid it out on the bed and quickly pulled her underpants on under the towel.

She took a quick glance at the wolf.

He was staring toward the window, totally ignoring her, which made her feel really stupid. He was an animal. There was absolutely no reason at all for her to feel embarrassed being naked in front of an animal.

With that thought in mind, she dropped the towel on the floor and reached for her bra.

The wolf whined. She turned. He'd moved. He stood beside her, his green eyes focused on her breasts. Cherry yanked the dress up and covered herself. The wolf dropped to his belly and covered his eyes with both front paws.

Stunned, Cherry watched him. Then she turned away

and set the dress aside, quickly slipped into her bra, waited a couple of seconds, and spun back around. His head was up, eyes wide open.

The moment she turned, his head went back to the floor and his paws covered his eyes.

"No one will ever believe this. A peeping wolf?" Definitely too bizarre for words. She pulled the dress over her head. "Go ahead," she said. "You can look now."

The wolf sat up, mouth open in a big doggy grin while she slipped her feet into comfortable sandals and grabbed a soft shawl in case the weather turned cool. She wasn't sure what got into her, but Cherry went to her knees in front of the wolf so that she could look at him eye to eye. "I'm not sure what your game is, big guy, but I like you. I didn't want to come on this trip with my sister and her friend. I think they tricked me into coming because I'm not really comfortable in new places, but so far this has been the best time I've ever had. Though you, my friend, are a bit of an enigma." She stood, and then shook her head. "Great. I can't believe I'm having a conversation with a wolf. Maybe *I have* been working too hard."

She stood, glanced around the cute little cabin, and realized it already felt familiar and comfortable. The wolf watched her, and if she didn't know better, she'd think he looked concerned. Maybe she did need a drink. "C'mon," she said, snapping her fingers as she opened the door. "Why don't you show me where the bar is."

Then she opened the door and followed the wolf outside.

The sound of laughter drew Cherry to the broad deck in front of the lodge. Christa and Steph were seated at a long picnic table with the three women they'd seen earlier. She glanced back to see if the wolf was still with her, but he'd faded into the forest.

Disappointed she couldn't show off her new friend, Cherry climbed the stairs to the deck.

"We were just wondering where you were." Steph scooted over and made room for Cherry on the long bench.

"I needed a shower. Driving that far makes me feel grungy." She sat in the vacant spot and faced the three strangers. They were each beautiful, and, as usually happened in situations like this, it would take two of them to make up one of her.

It used to bother her. She'd learned to accept she was who she was and there was no point in wishing she could be different. Not that her personal philosophy totally stopped her agonizing, but still . . .

Smiling, she reached across the table to shake hands with the closest woman. "I'm Cherry."

"I'm Fred." The tiny blonde laughed at Cherry's raised eyebrows. "Fredericka, but if you call me that I'll have to kill you. This is Suni on my right, Darnell on her right."

"They're up from L.A.," Christa said. "Suni's a costume designer, Darnell does makeup, and Fred's a hairstylist. They just finished work on a movie they can't talk about yet."

"Wow. A secret movie?" Cherry glanced at the three.

Fred rolled her eyes. "We had to sign an agreement not to talk about it. The director's superstitious."

"But he's really good," Darnell added.

"And we all got paid on time." Suni poked Darnell in the shoulder. "That's never a given in this business."

"Hey, Cherry." Brad stepped out of the lodge with an empty wineglass and a newly opened bottle of Chardonnay. "I was beginning to wonder if you were coming."

She took the glass and held it while Brad poured. "Are you saying you didn't send that big, beautiful guy to my cabin?"

His smile was so damned sexy she broke out in goose bumps from head to toe. "I take it you had a visitor?"

"You might say so." She took a sip of her wine. Brad winked and then turned away to refill the glasses for the other women.

Christa reached around Steph and poked Cherry's arm. "I wanna know more about your visitor."

Cherry had no idea why she blushed, but it never took much to set her off. Sometimes she wondered if she were the only woman in the world who spent as much time showing everyone just how embarrassed she was.

"Cherry?" Laughing, Christa cocked an eyebrow. "Who was it?"

"More like 'what was it,'" she said. "Did you send him, Brad?"

"I'll never tell." He tipped the brim of his ball cap and headed back into the lodge.

Cherry called after him, "You're no help."

He turned at the open door and made a deep bow before going inside.

"Men." She almost snorted but bit it back in time. "I was just getting out of the shower when I thought I heard someone at the door. When I opened it, an absolutely magnificent wolf was sitting there. He just shoved the door open with his nose and walked into my cabin like he owned the place."

"Oh! I am so jealous. I've been hoping to see a wolf." Suni was practically vibrating with excitement. "That's the whole reason I talked these two bums into coming with me."

"I was thinking someplace a little more, um . . . upscale?" Fred rolled her eyes. "I'm not much of an outdoors girl. I grew up in Brooklyn."

"Where the wildlife consists of pigeons and stray cats?" Darnell checked a nonexistent hangnail.

"Pretty much."

"Was he friendly?" Christa was leaning forward on the table. "What was he like?"

"Weirdly smart. I mean almost human intelligence. I asked him if Brad sent him to get me, because Brad had threatened to do just that if I wasn't down here in twenty minutes. The wolf showed up almost exactly twenty minutes after Brad left. Anyway, when I asked him, he yipped like he was answering me. And then when I went to change clothes, I just felt really weird with him sitting there staring at me, so I actually told him not to look."

"Well?" Steph laughed. "Did he cover his eyes?"

"Yes." Cherry stared at her.

"No, he didn't." Steph stared at her, and her eyes went wide. "He did? You're not kidding, are you?"

Cherry shook her head.

"He really covered his eyes?"

"With both paws. But then he peeked."

"What?" Christa's shriek had all of them laughing.

"You heard me. He peeked. I turned around to see if he still had his eyes covered, but he was watching me. The moment I turned, he covered them again. It was just weird. I was laughing but I felt really exposed, ya know? I mean, he's a wolf, but he was obviously watching me, and he understood when I told him not to. He actually looked embarrassed that I'd caught him."

Christa suddenly grabbed Cherry's hand. "Is that the same wolf? Look. Over by that big pine. Isn't he beautiful?"

"Yes! I think it's him." Cherry walked down the steps and across the green area in front of the lodge. The wolf spotted her, trotted across the parking area, and sat at her feet.

He just stared at her, but she could swear he was grinning. "Okay, big guy. Now don't make me look stupid. I told them you were really smart. Will you come up on the deck and meet the girls?"

The wolf tilted his head and then nudged her hand. Taking the hint, Cherry placed her fingers in the thick fur around his neck, and the two of them walked back up to the deck. "Yep," she said. "Same wolf. I think he's a voyeur."

The wolf hung around while the women had their dinner inside the lodge. Two men they hadn't met had set out a beautiful buffet and the six women loaded their plates and sat at a large table inside. The service was quiet and unobtrusive, and Cherry couldn't remember an evening she'd enjoyed more. The three women from L.A. were funny and smart, though Fred could be a bit abrasive. Brad kept the wine and drinks flowing.

Time seemed to fly, but before long the L.A. contingent, as Darnell, Suni, and Fred were calling themselves, headed off to their cabins, following the trails lit by twinkling lights. Brad called them fairy lights, but they were really just white Christmas lights hidden in shrubs along the pathways, bright enough to make it safe for the women to find their cabins.

It wasn't much longer before Christa yawned and Steph joined in. Wide awake after her shower and a sense of excitement she hadn't expected, Cherry hated to see the evening end, but she wrapped her shawl around her shoulders and followed her sister and Steph out to the deck.

The lights twinkled and shimmered along the paths to the cabins. Christa hugged her sister and yawned again. "I hope you're having a good time. You okay going back to your cabin alone?"

Cherry hugged Christa and then Steph, too. "Are you kidding? Look." She pointed toward the path that led to her cabin. The big silver and gray wolf sat there, waiting patiently. "With a bodyguard like that, what's there to be afraid of?"

Laughing, Steph and Christa left. The night seemed to close in around Cherry, but in a comfortable, soothing way. She leaned against the railing, feeling more at peace than she could remember. She'd only been here a few hours, and already she was having a better time than she'd thought she would. Maybe this week wouldn't be terrible after all.

CHAPTER 4

Brad heard the women telling one another good night. He'd really enjoyed all of them, but Cherry called to him. He wasn't quite sure what it was about her, but both he and Cain had felt drawn to her from the moment she crawled out of the car looking tired but delicious. Thinking about her swollen lips and the soft sounds she made when he kissed her, he finished wiping down the bar and checking the kitchen to make sure the stove was off and everything was ready for morning.

He'd just hung up the damp towel to dry when he sensed someone near, looked out the front window, and saw Cherry standing on the deck, staring at the twinkling fairy lights in the forest. She looked lost in thought, leaning against the railing, her hands clasping the top rail.

He realized he wasn't nearly as tired as he'd thought and spending some quiet time with Cherry was just what he needed. She had absolutely no idea how she affected him. Why was that so refreshing? It was definitely attractive. She wasn't a doormat as far as he could tell, but she wasn't hitting on him like he was some sort of male stud. She was more reserved than her friends, but he already knew she had a wicked sense of humor—he'd eavesdropped, and her story about the wolf in her cabin had cracked him up. He hoped Cain had heard her telling it.

Tucking some chocolate in his pocket, he poured a couple of glasses of dark port and carried them outside. Cherry glanced up and smiled at him, and he knew he'd never seen a lovelier woman. Her thick dark brown hair hung in glossy waves past her shoulders, and while she looked tired, he could tell she was still wound up, still excited about her first night here at Feral Passions.

He hoped she was having a good time. Hoped she didn't feel bad about him kissing her earlier tonight. He honestly hadn't been able to help himself. Kissing Cherry felt right, as if the wolf side of him wanted to claim her in some small way.

He'd heard a few of her comments, subtly self-deprecating, enough to know she thought she was overweight. She'd eaten very little tonight, and that bothered him. He hated to think that, even on vacation, she would be depriving herself. How did a guy tell a woman he barely knew that he thought she was absolutely perfect?

He walked out and leaned against the railing beside her. "Here. I brought you something." It was a dark, rich wine, sweeter than the Chardonnay the women had been drinking earlier.

"Thank you." She held up the goblet, admiring the dark, dark color, more purple than red. "What is this?"

"It's late harvest port—a friend of Trak's makes it. He's got a vineyard near the coast."

She took a small sip and sighed. "Delicious."

He pulled the chocolate out of his pocket—two small bars wrapped in a napkin from the bar. "Try this with it."

She reached for the chocolate, paused, and curled her fingers into her palm. "I can't. But thank you."

"You don't like chocolate?" He took a small bite of his bar and then sipped the wine. The melded flavors exploded on his tongue, and he wanted to share the taste with Cherry.

"I love it, but it likes me too well." She patted her hip. "It likes to stick around."

"I don't see that as a problem for you. I think you look pretty amazing." He gave her a long look when what he really wanted to do was pull her into his arms, hold her against his chest so he could feel those full, tantalizing breasts, bury his hands in her beautiful dark hair. And kiss her. Kiss those luscious lips, nibble on her throat—tell her what he was, that he already knew she was perfect for them.

That he and Cain wanted her as their mate.

Except that wasn't going to happen—couldn't happen, at least not yet—though he loved the way she blushed over his simple observation.

They stood there, leaning against the deck, just talking. She told him a little about her life in San Francisco, he told her about going to college in Southern California and getting his degree in architecture, how he'd been asked to design the resort when Trak decided he wanted to build one on the preserve. Cherry seemed interested in everything. She was easy to talk to, with a sense of humor that synced way too closely with his.

He'd never met a woman before that he'd felt this comfortable with so quickly. He wondered what Cain thought of her, if he'd had time even to form an opinion.

He sensed movement, and turned just as Cain stepped out of the forest. He wore his faded blue jeans, beat-up moccasins, and no shirt. Brad knew the exact moment when Cherry noticed him walking toward the lodge.

Her heart rate picked up and the sweet scent of her arousal filled the air. He'd sensed it a while ago when he'd walked out onto the deck, and now for Cain? This was looking better by the moment.

"Hey, Cain. I wondered when you'd show up. Where've you been?"

"Checking on the den by the creek. Mama wolf has three beautiful new pups. Two females and a male."

"Really?" Cherry's eyes actually sparkled. "Did you see them?"

"I did, sweet Cherry." He took the steps up to the deck two at a time and stopped in front of Cherry. He looked to Brad and they shared a look; sometimes it was like Cain could read his mind. "I might even tell you about their birth and my heroic, lifesaving rescue . . . for a kiss."

"A kiss?"

Her eyes went wide. Brad inhaled the addictive scent of her arousal. From the look of surprise on Cain's face, he'd caught it, too.

"Just a simple kiss," he said. Then he leaned close and kissed her before she had time to duck, even if she'd wanted to. Brad didn't think she wanted to miss Cain's kiss, but he couldn't help throwing a rather possessive arm around her waist.

She gave him a sidelong glance that told him she knew exactly what he was doing, but she smiled.

Cherry was smiling, and Brad was falling hard and fast. But what if she wasn't right for them? What if he was reading all the signs wrong? It wasn't as if they'd had much contact with human women or even mated couples. Even in the old days, mated members of the pack lived in their own communities, raising their sons and doing their best to fit into the human population. That left the single males on their own. Now, except for a few much older mated couples, the guys here—both young and old—were all that were left of the Trinity Alps pack. Single males, surrounded by a whole pack of other single males.

"Thank you, Cheraza." Cain stepped back after their kiss and leaned on the railing beside Brad. "I helped her deliver the first pup. It wasn't ready to leave such a nice, warm place."

Cherry sighed, but Brad caught Cain's fear, the sense that if he'd not been there, they might have lost the pup, possibly the mother, and the entire litter. "She okay?"

Cain nodded. "She'll be fine. The pups look good." Frowning, he said, "I did a little chest compression and mouth-to-snout resuscitation, and by the time the first one was breathing and squirming to find Mama she'd delivered the other two."

"I'm glad you were there." Brad clapped Cain's shoulder.

"Me, too." Cherry watched him with her heart in her eyes. It appeared she was as big a softy as Cain. At least when he wasn't acting all badass. "How did you know she needed help?"

Cain merely shrugged. "We keep an eye on them, make

sure everyone's healthy. This is her first litter, so I've been checking on her. Plus, they're used to us. We can get close enough to help when there's a problem." He described the den under a fallen tree near the creek, the way the mother had licked her pups and nuzzled them close against her to nurse. Cherry hung on every word.

Brad leaned close and kissed her cheek. "Be right back," he said, and stepped inside the lodge to grab a goblet for Cain. When he got back, Cain and Cherry had moved to the big picnic table, Cherry at the end, Cain on her left. Brad sat on the other side, across from Cain and next to Cherry, and poured a glass of port for Cain.

"Here's to new life," he said, raising his glass. Cherry and Cain raised theirs. The crystal chimed softly when they touched glasses.

"Where's the chocolate?" Cain stared at Brad and shook his head. "Don't tell me you shared some of Trak's port with Cherry and didn't offer chocolate!"

Brad shrugged. "I did, but she didn't want any." He dug it out of his pocket—only he'd added a couple of extra pieces and put one in front of Cain, another in front of Cherry, and kept one for himself.

"You're trying to sabotage my diet." Cherry sipped her port, but she stared at the small piece of dark chocolate in front of her.

Cain picked up the chocolate and held it in front of her lips. "You don't need to diet. I love the way you look. Your breasts are begging for my attention and my hands really want to clasp those incredible hips. You are a voluptuous woman, Cheraza DuBois. You would not be the same without your curves. They make you absolutely perfect."

No man had ever said she was perfect. Not ever. Now, tonight, two hot-as-hell men had told her just that. "Just a taste," she said, and she wasn't sure what gave her the courage, but she nibbled at the piece Cain held for her.

"Now the port," Brad said, smiling at her over the rim of his glass.

She took a sip, closed her eyes, and moaned. And to think she'd almost missed this. "Amazing," she said. Brad held a piece to her lips, and she nibbled that one as well, sipped her port, and then yawned. And blushed. Damn. She so wished she didn't blush over everything.

"I think someone's sleepy." Cain stood. "I'm going to find one of the wolves, have him walk you to your cabin. Is that okay? I need Brad to help me with some stuff before he gets too cozy with the rest of Trak's port." He leaned over and kissed her and, just as quickly, disappeared around the back of the deck.

Brad wrapped a curl of her long hair around his little finger.

Cherry'd never been with men who kissed and touched so easily, so naturally. She took a sip of port and merely enjoyed the slight tugging as Brad played with her hair.

"I hope you don't think we're running you out," he said. "Cain asked me earlier to help him with a couple of projects tonight, and I totally forgot."

"No. I think I just hit the wall, anyway." She yawned again, covering her mouth with her hand, her skin flushing hot and probably beet red. Again. "Trak's port is better than sleeping pills."

The silver and gray wolf trotted up the steps and sat beside Cherry and she quit worrying about blushing.

"It appears Cain found my escort. He's so beautiful." She stroked her hand over his head and down his shoulders. The wolf rested his chin on her knee, but Brad leaned close and kissed her, pulling her to her feet with his strong arms wrapped around her, his lips moving over hers.

He tasted of chocolate and wine.

After a moment, he broke off the kiss and rested his chin on top of her head. Her heart was pounding in her chest, her breasts felt as if they might burst from the bra she wore, and she knew the taut points of her nipples were obvious even through the fabric.

"I think you're right," he said. "I'm tired, too. I just hate to think of you leaving."

She laughed. "I'm only going about fifty yards, and I'll see you in the morning. Does my escort have a name?"

"This guy?" Brad scratched behind his ears; the wolf leaned against his thigh and moaned. "He may not act like it, but he's a wild wolf. We don't name them. We've all learned to recognize the ones who like to hang around the lodge, but it doesn't seem right to give them names. I'm sure they have their own."

"I like that." She stared at Brad for a moment, losing herself in his dark brown eyes, thinking of what he'd just said. He was telling her they had enough respect for the wolves not to treat them like pets.

She had a horrible feeling she was falling for a guy she'd only known for a few hours.

But then she thought of Cain and realized she felt almost as drawn to him after merely a few minutes in his company. She wanted to laugh at the surfeit of male riches suddenly thrust into her life. She couldn't wait to tell Christa and Steph what they'd missed by leaving early. "Go help Cain, Brad. This guy will get me back to my cabin. Thank you for the port." She glanced away. "And the chocolate. That was amazing."

"I'm glad." He rested his hands on her shoulders. She had no idea what he was thinking, but she was almost certain it had something to do with kissing. The fact that he seemed to enjoy kissing her so much sent a small jolt right through her midsection.

When he kissed her again, when those talented lips molded hers and his tongue made a swift foray across her lower lip, she didn't even try to suppress her needy moan. He nipped gently at her lower lip and ended the kiss.

Tonight had been like a fairy tale, but she had absolutely no idea what to say. Brad and Cain were unbelievable, and—The wolf caught the hem of her dress in his teeth and tugged. "It looks like my chaperone wants me to go to bed." She smiled at Brad and wished she could just invite him to join her in that big bed.

"Good night, Cherry. Sleep well."

The wolf tugged. "I'm coming." Laughing, she glanced once more at Brad and then followed the wolf down the steps. When they reached the edge of the forest, she looked back, hoping to see Brad once more.

The deck was empty.

Sighing, she followed the wolf along the path lit by sparkling fairy lights.

They were almost to the cabin when a second wolf joined them. He was big and dark, his coat streaked with russet and gold, and he planted himself in the middle of the trail, blocking their way. Cherry let out a startled squeak and buried her fingers in her companion's thick ruff of fur. "I really hope you're friendly."

Her wolf wagged his tail and yipped, and the new wolf went down on his front paws as if he wanted to play. "That looks promising. C'mon, boys. Take me to my cabin, and then the night is yours."

The porch light was on, but the cabin was dark. She opened the door and the russet-colored wolf walked in first, almost as if he was checking to make sure she'd be safe. Cherry followed him, flipped on the light by the door, and stepped inside.

She left the door open in case the wolves wanted out, grabbed her nightgown, and took it into the bathroom. After she'd changed and brushed her teeth, she stepped back into the main part of the cabin.

Both wolves were curled up on the braided rug beside the bed, almost as if they planned to spend the night. She sat on the rug between them and looped her arms over their backs. "Boys, I would love to have you stay with me, but I know you'd probably want out in the middle of the night, and I'm tired."

The russet wolf whimpered and rested his chin on her knee so he could stare at her. It was unnerving, to say the least. His eyes were dark brown, darker than the chocolate she and Brad had tonight, just as dark as Brad's beautiful eyes.

She glanced at the silver and gray wolf. His eyes were green. The same color as Cain's.

No. She was just tired, and these were merely wolves. Beautiful wolves. Wolves who, somehow, reminded her of two very sexy men.

It had definitely been a long day. Cherry stood and walked to the open door. The wolves watched every step she took. When she stood by the door, she could have sworn they glanced at each other, but then both of them slowly stood.

Cherry held the door open. "Time for bed, fellas. You two need to go out."

Tails and heads down, the two of them slowly walked out the door.

The russet one glanced her way as he stepped onto the front porch. She heard him sigh. The other wolf was right behind him. Cherry waited, watching as they faded into the forest.

She closed and locked the door but left the porch light burning and crawled into the big comfortable bed. The big *lonely* bed. But she couldn't get her mind off the wolves. That was just too weird for words. The feeling they were more than they appeared would not leave her.

She picked up the romance she'd been reading. *Dying Room Only*—not a sexy title, but the werewolf and vampire heroes in the story were two of her favorites. Actually, the werewolf was her favorite, but she loved the ménage fantasy. Funny, how she loved stories where two sexy men fell in love with the woman. She didn't even have one.

She stared at the cover for a moment, at the wolf standing beside a woman with his amber eyes glowing, and thought of her two wolves. Yawning, she set the book aside. It had been a very long day. Dreams were about all the excitement she could handle tonight.

They did not disappoint. Dreams so graphic, so real, that when she awoke she was actually surprised she didn't have four legs and a tail. She'd spent the night racing through dark forests and moonlit meadows with the two wolves—wolves her dream self knew as Brad and Cain in their human form.

It might have been a bizarre night of crazy dreams, but the sense of running beneath a full moon with the granite mountaintops gleaming silvery beneath its light, the steady thunder of wolven feet racing beside her along the hard-packed, shadowed trails, had felt so real.

They'd even howled, all of them standing on a hilltop, howling at the moon. She'd awakened with tears on her cheeks, overcome by a sense of belonging.

She'd come awake a number of times throughout the night, sometimes breathing hard, as if she'd truly been part of a small pack of three, the two familiar wolves on either side. The last time before dreamless sleep finally claimed her, Cherry awoke sprawled crosswise on the big bed with pale moonlight slanting across her body.

It was only a quarter moon. In her dreams, the moon had been full, hanging directly overhead. That slice of moon left her sighing in relief. She hadn't run as a wolf. No, that had all been the result of an overactive imagination, thank goodness.

Relieved, yet oddly disappointed, Cherry straightened out on her bed, punched the pillow a couple of times for effect, and finally rolled over and went back to sleep.

CHAPTER 5

Monday

Cherry was actually disappointed when she finally crawled out of bed, dressed, and realized she'd be walking to the lodge without her wolf escort. They'd certainly been busy last night, escorting her through her dreams. There weren't any wolves at the lodge to greet her, either, but Christa and Steph were on the deck having coffee, the sun was barely peeking over the tops of the pine trees, and it was an absolutely breathtaking morning.

"Good morning. When did you guys get here?"

"About five minutes ago." Christa held up her coffee cup. "Coffee's inside, and it looks like Trak's cooking breakfast."

"As long as it's not me. Morning, Steph." Cherry and Christa both laughed when Steph merely grunted. She was most definitely not a morning person. Cherry opened the door and walked into the lodge. Trak was visible through the pass-through window, standing at the stove in the kitchen with an apron tied around his trim waist, and the dining area was filled with delicious smells. Inside, the lodge was like an old-time café, with a bar for a quick meal or drinks, and the big pass-through window into the kitchen. A couple of small tables were placed by windows at one end, and there was one long table in the middle, where they'd eaten last night.

There was no sign of the other three women, but Brad smiled from behind the bar. "Good morning, Cherry. Coffee?"

Cherry nodded and took a seat on one of the barstools. "Yes, please. Good morning."

"You're up early."

"Blame the day job. I'm usually in the office by seven."

Brad handed Cherry a big mug of coffee, black, just the way she liked it. Then he propped his elbows on the bar with his own steaming cup between his hands. "What do you do in the day job?"

"Statistics and market analysis, which sounds really high-tech and boring, but it's not."

He laughed. "Yeah, but what do you *do*?"

She was used to this part of the question. "Figure out what ads work best for companies and why. I research algorithms and how to optimize ads, create methods for measuring the effectiveness of ads, that sort of thing. Essentially I try to help people use the most effective advertising for a particular product. It's fun. I love my work."

Brad just laughed. "If you say so. How did you end up doing something like that?"

"I love numbers and majored in statistics, with a minor in computer science."

She heard the door open and Christa added, "And she's actually *Dr.* Cheraza DuBois." Christa plopped her butt down on the stool next to Cherry and draped an arm around her shoulders, laughing. "It is so easy to make you blush."

"You're a pain in the ass, Cissy." And Cherry might be

embarrassed by Christa's praise, but she was damned proud of that PhD, even if it ran men off, if they'd even gotten past her plus-size body. But Brad actually seemed impressed, not put off by it. Now that was interesting.

"Hey Trak," he said, calling out to the cook. "You've got to come out here."

Trak poked his head through the window. "Morning, ladies. What do you want, Brad? The chef's at work."

"Yeah, I know, but do know what this lovely lady does?" And without waiting for an answer, Brad said, "She's a statistics and computers expert, and there's a 'PhD' after her name. Her focus is marketing."

"Really?"

Trak's eyebrows went up and he and Brad exchanged a very quick but obviously meaningful glance. Cherry had no idea what the meaning was.

"I need to get back to work," Trak said. "But Cherry? I'm impressed. I'm going to want to hear more about your work."

"Anytime." That was interesting, but obviously all he was going to say, at least for now.

The door opened once again. "Where'd you guys go?" Steph wandered in and took the barstool on the other side of Cherry. "It was lonely out there."

Christa glanced at Cherry. "What that means is, she just woke up enough to realize we weren't sitting with her."

"I know."

"Poor baby . . . are they picking on you?"

Steph's eyes lit up as Brad took her cup for a refill. "Yes. Do you have any idea what I put up with?"

He set the freshly filled cup in front of her and sighed. "I can only imagine."

"Milk it, Steph. Go for the sympathy." Cherry nudged Steph's shoulder, but she really loved the fact that Brad looked directly at her and winked. He'd singled her out while teasing Steph. Silly, that such a small thing made her feel warm inside.

They were all laughing and picking on Stephanie, who'd had enough caffeine to tease them right back, when the L.A. contingent wandered in looking for coffee, but the three of them took one of the smaller tables, all of them half-asleep and not saying much. Brad carried a tray over with filled cups, cream, and sugar. The women thanked him but kept their conversation low.

Two men Cherry hadn't seen before walked in a few minutes later. Christa poked her in the shoulder and whispered, "Are all of the guys who work here drop-dead gorgeous?"

"It appears so." These two were big and brawny and absolutely beautiful, but Cherry was surprised when she didn't feel that same little flip in her midsection that she'd gotten from both Brad and Cain. Obviously it wasn't her reaction to sexy men in general—just those two sexy men.

Steph, however, had finally come awake, tracking the two with her gaze as they stepped up to the bar beside her. "Good morning." She smiled, and the one closer to her nodded.

The other man shot her a bright grin. "Don't mind Ronan. He's just grumpy because we were out of coffee."

Brad set two cups in front of them. "Ladies, the sparkly one is Wils and the grump is Ronan. Behave, gentlemen."

Ronan planted his butt on the stool beside Steph, gave her a long look, and dipped his head. "My apologies. I had a late night and then the shmuck with the pretty blue eyes forgot to stock up on coffee."

Steph took a swallow of hers. "That's absolutely unforgivable. The fact that his pretty blue eyes aren't black is an obvious tribute to your good nature."

Ronan nodded seriously. "That's what I was trying to explain to him."

"You weren't very nice about it." Wils glanced at Cherry. Easy to see where Ronan's reference came from. Wils had the most brilliant blue eyes she'd ever seen. "He turned the hot water off when I was in the shower."

Cherry almost snorted her coffee. "You didn't?"

"I did." Ronan actually smiled at this point. "He screamed like a little girl."

"I'd be careful about insulting the women if I were you, Ronan." Brad walked around the bar with a couple of large serving trays that he set under the heat lamps in the buffet counter. Trak was right behind him with more trays of food. Both Wils and Ronan went back to the kitchen and carried out baskets of rolls and bowls of fresh fruit.

Within a couple of minutes, the buffet was loaded and even the three from L.A. managed to find a spot in line. Once the women had served themselves, the four men loaded their plates.

Brad sat next to Cherry.

"Where's Cain this morning?"

"Checking on mama wolf. He'll be here any minute."

"Mama wolf?" Steph leaned around Christa. "There's a new litter?"

"Yep." Brad slathered butter on a piece of toast. "Cain helped the female last night. She was having a tough delivery and he pulled the first pup."

"And then he did chest compressions on the pup and said he gave it 'mouth-to-snout' resuscitation." Cherry couldn't stop smiling. "Now that's something I'd like to have seen."

Conversation flowed as the food disappeared. Cherry enjoyed her meal and realized she'd actually eaten breakfast without feeling self-conscious about putting food in her mouth. Of course, the amount she ate didn't come close to what the men put away, but they were so busy talking and planning the day that she hadn't had a chance to feel as if anyone noticed or cared what was on her plate.

She'd have to think about that. She was so used to looking for problems, for perceived insults. Was she creating an issue where none existed?

"So it's agreed?" Brad glanced about the group.

Agreed? "On what?" She hadn't been paying attention.

"Ronan and Wils are going to lead a hike up to Blackbird Lake," he said. "It's only a couple of miles from here, but there's a bit of a climb, so you'll need hiking boots, and long pants would be best. We'll have daypacks ready for you with water and a bag lunch. If you've got cameras, take them. You're sure to see wildlife along the way, possibly a wolf or two."

"I'm going." Cherry didn't even have to think about it. "What about you guys?"

Steph shrugged. "That's why we're here. To get some exercise and see new country. Christa?"

"I'm in. What time are you leaving?"

Wils glanced at Ronan. "Can you ladies be ready in half an hour?"

"I think I'm going to stay here." Fred yawned. "I had a really rough week, and that swimming pool looks awfully appealing. Darnell? Suni? What are you guys up to?"

"I'm with you." Suni gathered up her plate and utensils.

"Leave it, Suni. We'll take care of that." Brad glanced at Darnell. "What about you, Darnell? Are you up for some hiking?"

"I am." She glanced uncertainly at her friends. "Fred? You're really not going?"

"I'm sorry, hon. I'm beat. Too much time on my feet last week."

Suni shook her head. "Same here. I just want peace and quiet and a long nap."

"Darnell, come with us. It'll be fun." Cherry stood and stretched. "Trak, that was absolutely delicious. Thank you." She checked her watch. "Half an hour? I'll be here."

It was almost four when they finally returned to the lodge. Darnell broke off from the group first when they paused near her cabin. She claimed she was exhausted, but she couldn't stop laughing.

"I have never worked so frickin' hard in my life, or had that much fun. If that's what you call a moderate hike, Ronan, I don't even want to imagine your idea of a tough one. And believe me, if anyone had told me a few days ago that today I'd be skinny-dipping in an ice-cold mountain lake with three white girls and two dudes I'd known all of a couple hours, I would have said, you are shittin' me! No way!"

She and Steph did a fancy knuckle-bump that included bumping hips at the same time.

"She's right, you know." Christa waved to Darnell as she turned off toward her cabin. "Today wasn't like anything I've ever done in my life."

"Me, either." Cherry'd gotten naked in front of everyone; she'd stripped out of her dusty clothes on the edge of the crystal-clear lake and gone into that icy water, gasping and screaming with the rest of them. Not only hadn't she even thought about her weight; she'd also been well aware that both Ronan and Wils were giving her what could only be described as admiring looks.

Definitely an amazing day, though she'd laughed hysterically when Christa complained about "freezing my ass off." If only!

"Certainly not me," Steph said. "I've never been skinny-dipping with anyone. Ever." Then she poked Wils with her elbow. "I think it was all your fault."

Wils laughed and wrapped an arm around her waist. Cherry'd noticed that the two of them had definitely hit it off. "C'mon, darlin'. Your cabin's just through here."

"It is? Mine's next to Darnell's?"

"Yep. And Christa's on the other side. I'll see you to your door, poor thing. I mean, since you're obviously so exhausted and all. Besides, then you can complain about me all you want since I'll be your only audience."

The two of them peeled off to the left and disappeared in the thick forest, though Cherry could hear them talking.

Then she heard the sound of them walking up the steps to Steph's cabin. The door opened and closed. There wasn't any sound of Wils's returning footsteps.

Ronan was watching the trail. A moment later he grinned. "It appears Wils decided to escort Steph inside." He started walking again.

"I thought we were more isolated, a lot farther from each other." Cherry turned to Ronan.

"You're really quite close to one another," he said. "You can thank Brad for the sense of privacy. The design is all his baby. He's an architect who plans his structures to blend with the landscaping. He's pretty well-known, actually, but he has a personal interest in this place. Brad wanted guests to be more aware of the forest around them than of the other cabins, so the six cabins form a half circle behind the lodge, but each is hidden from the others, and the lodge."

They'd only walked a few more steps before Ronan stopped and pointed to a small trail leading into the woods. "Cherry, I'm going to walk your sister to her cabin. I'll be right back."

Except Cherry had a feeling Ronan would much prefer to linger, and just as strong a sense that Christa hoped he would. "Take your time," she said. "The trail's easy to follow and I think I know where I am. Thank you, Ronan. Today couldn't have been more fun."

He really did have a beautiful smile. "You're welcome," he said. "You're sure you'll be okay on you own?"

"Not a problem. Now if it was Christa . . ." She grinned at her sister.

Christa groaned. "She's referring to my nonexistent sense of direction. I can get lost in the parking lot at Walmart."

Ronan merely shook his head. "Then I'm definitely walking you to your door. Thanks, Cherry."

Cherry gave Christa a hug and whispered, "Enjoy yourself."

Ronan grabbed Christa's hand; she waved and followed him down the trail. Cherry took the wider trail that would take her directly to the lodge. Giving Christa time with Ronan was the least she could do for a sister who cared enough to trick her into coming along on this most amazing adventure.

CHAPTER 6

Cherry'd only taken a few steps before she saw the back side of the lodge through the trees. She decided to go that way first—just in case Brad or Cain was there. Brad was behind the bar making margaritas for Fred and Suni, but there was no sign of Cain.

"Hey, Cherry. You're back!"

"Hi, Brad. Those margaritas look so good." She slowly parked her butt on one of the stools at the bar. Her legs were really sore from all the hiking.

"Trust me, they are," Suni said. "Did you have fun on the hike?"

"It was terrific, though my muscles might disagree. You'll have to ask Darnell about the day's activities. Ronan and Wils are better than any cruise directors for making things fun."

Brad set the drinks on the counter for Suni and Fred. After they each took theirs and left, Brad smiled at Cherry. "Would you like one?"

Regretfully, Cherry shook her head. "I'd love one, but I need to go and get a shower. I stopped by on the way to my cabin because I wondered if Cain had checked on the pups today, if they were doing okay."

"He's there now. I'm sure we'll get an update later this evening."

"Thanks. I'll see you at dinner, then."

Before she could step down from the stool, Brad said, "Hang on a minute," and turned back to the blender. In mere seconds he was pouring a fresh margarita into a broad glass with salt coating the rim. "It's plastic," he said, tapping the side of the glass. "Shower proof. Can you think of anything more decadent than a cold margarita and a hot shower?"

She laughed as she took the drink, then took a sip and stared at him over the salted rim of the glass. "Delicious. And yes, Brad, I can. It would be a lot more decadent if you were sharing the shower and the margarita with me." The second the words left her mouth, she knew she had to be fire-engine red. She never talked like that, flirted that openly.

But Brad didn't seem to mind at all. His eyes lit up and the look he gave Cherry curled her toes. "I have to agree with you on that one," he said. Then he leaned close, tipped her chin up with his fingertips, and gave her a kiss that included the sweep of his tongue against hers.

"Go, Cherry. Leave the door unlocked. If I can get away, I'll come join you."

She left the door unlocked, but she didn't really expect him. It didn't matter. Not really. She had her fantasies and her margarita, but she'd set the drink aside and was rinsing conditioner out of her hair when she heard the shower door click.

"Don't be frightened. It's just me." Warm hands caressed her shoulders, warmer lips found the side of her neck, and she shivered, though she couldn't blame it on the air temperature—that had to be rising from the heat coming off Brad's body.

She kept her eyes closed as Brad caressed her and the water beat against her neck and back. He cupped her full breasts and she moaned when he teased the tips of each one with his tongue and teeth. Then he pulled her close and hugged her, resting his cheek against her wet hair.

She sucked in a quick breath at the heat of his erection pressing against her belly. He was huge and so hot it felt as if he branded her.

"I'll wait for you in the other room."

She hadn't opened her eyes, hadn't said a word, but he was gone.

She finished rinsing herself and then turned off the water with shaking hands. She hadn't brought her night-gown into the bathroom, so she wrapped a big towel around herself and walked out into the main room.

Brad lay on her bed, all sprawled out and relaxed, with a big smile on his face and very little else. The workout shorts he wore didn't hide much at all. His chest was all hard planes and ridges, and she wanted nothing more than to run her hands across his flat stomach. But it was the blatant arousal tenting his shorts that took Cherry's breath. She sucked in a sharp gasp.

"Sorry," he said. "I hope I didn't frighten you."

When Cherry didn't say anything—catching her breath took all her concentration—he curled easily into a sitting position and patted the bed beside him. "Sit down, Cherry. Talk to me. I'm not going to do anything you don't want or aren't comfortable with. I will never do anything without your full consent. Are we clear on that?"

She nodded and took a big swallow of her margarita. The ice was mostly melted, the salt all gone, but thank goodness there was still enough tequila in the glass to burn all the way down.

It reminded her she was way too sober for this. Whatever this was.

But she liked Brad. A lot. He wasn't just a really nice guy—he was totally hot, his muscles rippling under satiny skin, the shadow of his beard this late in the day so sexy she wanted to stroke his cheek and nibble along his jawline. Instead, she sat.

On the edge of the mattress, as far from him as she could get.

He reached over and took her empty glass out of her hand and set it on the table beside the bed. Then he patted the covers beside him. "Move closer?"

She really couldn't find her voice, but she nodded. Closer was okay. She could do closer.

She scooted over, careful to keep the towel wrapped tightly around her breasts, covering her belly and her hips and thighs. Thank goodness it was a big towel.

"You did invite me here, remember?"

She nodded. Felt her skin flush, knew she was beet red. She didn't trust herself to talk.

"Do you have any idea how much I've been thinking of you since you crawled out of that car yesterday, all sweet and sexy and rumpled from your long trip?"

This time she shook her head. How could anyone think she looked sexy when they'd gotten here? She'd been dirty and sweaty, her hair in tangles from driving with the window open, her clothes all wrinkled.

He laughed. "I know what you're thinking, that you were travel worn and I must have a screw loose, but you were—you are—the sexiest woman I've seen in so long. That's mainly why I'm here, so I could tell you that. Well, plus I wanted to see that luscious body of yours. I can't stay long—I have to go get some things ready for dinner to feed all of you starving women and your voracious appetites."

She smiled at that, at the thought that there were only men seeing to their every need. Brad merely traced the line of her jaw with one finger.

"I hope you realize I'm living proof that, yes, men can cook."

She bit her lips to keep from laughing. He made her feel so good, all warm and tingly, and it wasn't all about sex. It was about being happy as much as anything.

She hadn't really thought of that. Brad made her happy, mainly because *he* was. She turned to him and ran her fingers through his thick hair. "I think you're living proof that men can do a lot of things."

He shot her a sexy grin. "That's good to know. Does that mean you'll let me kiss you?"

Shrugging, she smiled and said, "I haven't stopped you before, have I?"

"No," he said. "You certainly haven't."

She bit her lips to keep from laughing, but Brad grabbed her around the waist and lifted her onto his lap, moving so quickly she didn't have time to come up with a reason for him not to pick her up as if she weighed nothing at all.

And wasn't that a nice surprise . . . he was definitely strong, and he made her feel so—well, not small. She would never think of herself as small, but he made her feel feminine. Desirable.

His big arms came around her, large, warm hands stroking her bare back above the damp towel. Her breasts, while covered in the towel, were pressed against his broad chest, while his lips covered hers in the sweetest of kisses. He nibbled at her mouth and ran his tongue along the seam of her lips until she parted for him.

He deepened the kiss until "sweet" wasn't the word that came to mind at all. His tongue tangled with hers, his lips moved over her lips, but his hands . . . his hands had somehow slipped beneath the towel to stroke her naked back, and it was all so amazing, the pressure of his mouth, the sensual delight of his big hands roaming the length of her spine, stroking the flare of her hips.

Her breathing grew labored and so did Brad's. She felt the thick length of his erection against her hip and didn't complain at all when he lifted her once again, turning her so that she straddled his lap and that thick length rode between her legs, the soft fabric of his shorts hiding nothing as they connected beneath the rumpled towel.

He growled—that was the only sound she could compare it to—and tugged the thick towel from between them, freeing her breasts, her whole body, to his gaze. When she was entirely bare, he groaned, lifting her breasts, one in each hand, palming the fullness of them, pinching her tender nipples until Cherry was the one moaning.

Not from the pain—this was the sweetest pain she'd ever known. She felt each pinch like a bolt of lightning streaking from her nipples to her clit. Brad dipped his head and took one nipple in his mouth, sucking hard, using his tongue and teeth, while he continued pinching and kneading her other breast, driving her higher, further, than any man had taken her before.

She wasn't a virgin, but she wasn't experienced, either. Even so, what Brad was doing, what he made her feel, was so incredible she didn't want him to stop.

He lifted her again and she thought he might push his shorts down and enter her, but they weren't using any protection and she had a moment of regret that they'd have to stop.

Except he laid her on the bed with her legs over the edge, and then he knelt on that small braided rug, gently pried her legs apart, and merely gazed at her for what felt like a very long time.

She pushed herself to a sitting position and he glanced up and grinned at her.

"Dinner might be a few minutes late tonight," he said. "I'm starting with my appetizer."

She was trembling when he leaned close and kissed her with lips already damp from their kisses. Trembling so hard her arms wouldn't hold her like this, she lay down on the bed with a soft whimper of absolute pleasure and complete surrender.

He slipped his hands beneath her and lifted her closer to his mouth.

Used his tongue and teeth the way he had when he'd kissed her mouth, except now he was licking between those nether lips, using his tongue to circle her clit in a steady swirl that took her so close to the edge that she bucked her hips. His fingers tightened on her butt and she wanted him inside her, wanted to feel the full, hard thrust of him, his solid weight over her.

Instead, he used his tongue and then his fingers, slipping his hands from her bottom, pinching her nipple with one set of fingers, while thrusting two fingers deep inside her.

The sensations rocked her from her breasts to her crotch, spread to her fingers and toes. She cried out and arched against his mouth, flying apart in a most spectacular explosion of sensations. Totally caught in her climax yet so aware of Brad, of his strength, of his flawless touch as he laved between her legs with the flat of his tongue, licking the fluids of her release.

She heard his deep groan, felt the tight clasp of his fingers on her as her body finally began to relax from the taut spasm of her climax. She should have been embarrassed— she'd never before put on a show like that for any man, but then, no other man had ever done this to her before. She lay there gasping for breath while Brad eased her down. Then he crawled up over her naked body until she felt the damp press of his erection between her legs.

She opened her eyes and he was right there, smiling at her, those dark brown eyes twinkling.

"I have to go," he said. Then he blushed.

"I wish you could stay. I mean, that was just . . . but you didn't—"

His blush went even deeper. "Actually," he said. "I did."

Cherry frowned. He still had his shorts on. She was the only one who had climaxed.

Wasn't she?

"I need to go back to my cabin and get a quick shower so I can go to the lodge and take care of the last-minute details for dinner." He kissed her and then pushed himself away from the bed. Away from Cherry. And when he stood, there was a decidedly dark stain on the front of his shorts.

He was still red in the face when he turned and walked into the bathroom. Cherry sat up and wrapped the towel around herself and then finger-combed her damp hair. She heard the water running, and a few minutes later Brad walked back into the room. He'd rinsed his shorts off and now, at least, the wet cotton was all the same color.

He walked up to Cherry, put his arms around her, and kissed her. "For what it's worth," he said, "that was a first for me. I have never, not once, come all over myself while making a woman orgasm." He kissed her again. "Now, when I tell you that you're hot and you turn me on, will you stop arguing with me?"

She had no words, not one, so she dumbly nodded as Brad kissed her once again and opened the door.

He paused there for a moment. "I almost forgot. I have a surprise for you tonight. Don't make plans, okay?"

She stared at him, still shaken from her climax. From the knowledge of his. "Okay."

He shut the door and just like that he was gone. Cherry stood there for a full minute, staring at the closed door, thinking of how he'd made her feel. Smiling over what she'd made him feel. It might have been a first for him, but it was definitely a first for her.

A truly handsome guy, the sexiest guy she'd ever met, lost control because of her. *Oh. My.* She sat down on the edge of the bed and laughed.

It was a long time before she stopped laughing.

And then she wondered what kind of surprise he had for her tonight.

CHAPTER 7

Cherry watched the small group sitting together at one end of the long table and wondered if she'd ever wipe the smile off her face. Steph was next to Wils, Christa had latched on to Ronan, and Brad hadn't left Cherry's side all evening. Just when she thought it couldn't get any better, Cain walked in, grabbed a couple of plates at the buffet, loaded them with enough food for at least four people, and sat on Cherry's opposite side.

The moment he sat, she turned, practically bouncing in her seat, and asked, "How are the pups? Are they okay? Is the mother okay?"

Cain paused, his fork filled with grilled salmon almost to his mouth. "Great, yes, and yes, and I'm starving. Give me a minute!"

Cherry sat back, laughing, as he neatly shoveled in salmon and rice, roast beef and potatoes, a couple of pieces of French bread, and an entire plate of Caesar salad. Conversation went on around them as before, though Cherry was fascinated that a man as trim and slim as Cain could polish off so much food in such a hurry—and still manage to do it with impeccable manners.

Finally, he pushed his plates away and sat back. "Okay, Cherry. Barring any unseemly belching, I can now give you an update." He glanced toward Brad and both of them burst out laughing. "Hey," Cain said, giving Brad and Cherry a look that said he was being terribly misunderstood and mistreated. "While you, Cherry, were out hiking through the woods with Wils and Ronan, with bounteous lunches, I'm sure, and Brad was here cooking and nibbling as he worked, I was watching over mama wolf and her pups. I haven't eaten since around six this morning."

Brad held up both hands. "Did I say anything?"

Cherry shook her head and looked at Brad. "No, you didn't, but in defense of poor, mistreated Cain, here, I bet you were thinking of something horrible." Then she turned toward Cain. "Okay, Cain. I defended you. Now I want to hear everything."

"Well . . ." He grinned and then carefully wiped his mouth with his napkin, making Cherry wait even after she'd so graciously defended him. She was ready to throttle him.

"The pups are really healthy and strong in spite of the fact that they were born so late in the year. Generally, the mothers give birth in early spring, and it's almost June. The pack is healthy, so I imagine these little guys will do fine. The male brought Mama a couple of rabbits today, and she appears to have plenty of milk. The deer herd looks healthy, so there should be more than enough game for the pack next winter."

As they talked, the dining room emptied out, until it was just the three of them. Christa and Ronan had left early with Steph and Wils. Another big, sexy guy named Evan had arrived and proceeded to put all the food away and clean up the dishes. When he left, Darnell went with him. Suni and Fred had grabbed a bottle of wine and the two of them left with Trak, each woman holding one of his hands. He'd winked at Brad and said they'd be in Fred's cabin if anyone needed him.

"Be sure and knock first," he'd drawled as the girls dragged him out the door.

Which left Cherry here in the lodge, alone with two very hot men. Brad smiled at her. She read it as a smile that promised all sorts of things.

She just wished she had an idea what they were.

Brad stood and held out his hand for her. "Remember I told you I had something for you?"

Like she'd forget anything he said? Cherry nodded.

"Tonight, you get Cain."

"What?" Cherry glanced from Brad to Cain and back at Brad. "What do you mean?"

"He's teasing you, Cherry." Cain stood and held out his hand. "Though you're more than welcome to me, should you be interested." He wriggled his eyebrows and then laughed. "Actually, Brad asked me to give you a massage tonight. He thought you might be sore after hiking up to Blackbird Lake. I'm the official masseur for Feral Passions, and tonight, gorgeous girl, now that I'm no longer starving, I will be at your service."

"Oh. Wow . . ." She glanced at Brad and then at Cain and thought of what she and Brad had done earlier. She'd kind of hoped they'd continue on with that bit of entertainment, though a massage sounded really good. But Cain . . . he was just . . . wow. He was Brad's polar opposite in looks and demeanor but still way too sexy for her own good. Shaggy, sun-bleached hair curled over his collar that occasionally flopped into his eyes, a few days' growth of beard, a body just as toned and ripped as Brad's, though lean and rangy where Brad was solid muscle.

But what really made all of her inner muscles clench, what made him uniquely Cain, was an indefinable bad-boy vibe. It wasn't in anything he said or did—it just existed. Whether it was the loose-limbed swagger when he walked or the way his eyes were always moving, checking out his surroundings, he carried the vibe that he'd be a dangerous man to cross.

And an exceptionally bad boy in bed—in a very good way. She sucked in a breath and said, "Okay. Where?"

He had the sexiest smile. "Your cabin. I'll go and get my equipment out of the office. The table's on your front porch. I dropped it off before I came to dinner, so it's ready to go. Why don't you and Brad meet me there? I'll be about five minutes behind you, okay?"

"Go ahead and turn out the lights when you leave," Brad said. He glanced at Cherry and she could have sworn she felt him touching her just from the heat in his dark-eyed gaze. "I'm not planning to come back here tonight."

"Gotcha." Cain winked. "See ya in a bit."

Cherry barely remembered the walk to her cabin. Brad was beside her, holding her hand, Cain was on his way over. To give her a massage. With Brad there? She hadn't thought about that, about what it would be like to be on a massage table, barely covered in a towel, with two sexy men in the same room.

One of them would be touching her. The other already had, and she couldn't get that touching out of her mind. Her bra felt tighter; her nipples were taut little points growing more and more sensitive the closer they got to her cabin, until she felt as if they were two charged contacts channeling sexual energy directly to her clit.

She almost laughed when she realized how much she'd been thinking about sex all day.

Amazing what associating with sexy men could do to a girl's libido.

There was a big black case with a handle on top sitting on Cherry's front porch. She went to help Brad take it inside, but after trying to lift one end she quickly gave up. "This thing weighs a ton. How did Cain get it here by himself?" Cherry opened the door and reached for it again.

Brad waved her off. "It's all in how you lift it. Why don't you turn the light on and move your poor little feminine self out of the way."

"Oh, you are so asking for it." She laughed and then did exactly that. Brad grabbed the handle, picked the table up, and carried it inside. The only sign it was any kind of effort for him was the delicious bulge of his muscles.

He set the case in the open space between the bed and the kitchenette and opened it. More opportunity to watch his muscles flex. Cherry didn't think she could ever grow tired of watching him move. He was so comfortable with his body that he didn't seem the least bit awkward in the worn jeans that rode low on his hips and cupped his package in a perfectly praiseworthy manner. His faded T-shirt stretched so tightly, it molded his muscular chest as if he'd painted it on.

It was at that point, while admiring said package and chest, Cherry realized that after a little over twenty-four hours at Feral Passions she wasn't even thinking of her own clothing or even her weight. It was a shocking revelation, since they were both issues that generally occupied a large portion of her frontal lobe when she wasn't stressing out over other stuff that was just as inconsequential in the overall scheme of things.

Obviously, her newfound change in focus was going to require some thought. Later.

A couple of quick flips and Brad had the table set up in the only open space in the small cabin, which made the cabin seem infinitely smaller. What had reminded her of an old folding cot her dad took camping was now a comfortable-looking massage table with a beautiful leather cover and a form-fitting attachment at one end with a hole for her face.

Cain knocked on the door as Brad was locking the table legs in place.

"You timed that right," Cherry said. She held the door open for him and Cain walked in with two large tote bags. "Brad just got the table set up."

"That's good." He set the bags down. "Okay, Cherry, before you get to take off your clothes and turn yourself over to my magic touch, I want you to set some candles out around the room. There are half a dozen of them—find places that feel right to you."

"Feel right?" Cherry took the basket filled with candles he handed to her. "I didn't picture you as the New Age sort, Cain."

He laughed. "I'm not, really, but I do know that candle-light is relaxing, and these have a mild vanilla scent that can calm anyone."

"Thank goodness it's not lavender." Cherry took the

basket and walked into the kitchen area to place the first candle. Anything to keep her from thinking about Cain's words. The ones about taking off her clothes. "Everyone says lavender's supposed to remove stress," she said, "All it does is make me sneeze."

"I'm glad I left the lavender at home." Cain pulled out a soft white flannel sheet and covered the massage table with it while Cherry hunted for places for the candles. One in the kitchenette on the granite counter, another went on the table beside the bed. She put one on top of the armoire and another on the little table in the opposite corner. There was a good spot on the bookshelf in front of the window—she hadn't even had time to look at the books in it yet—and the last one went on the bathroom counter in front of the mirror.

Cain was setting up what looked like a fancy TV tray for his lotions and oils. Cherry shivered. He was so capable looking, and it was obvious from his practiced moves that he did this sort of thing a lot. She'd had exactly one massage in her life—from a very nice lady—when Christa gave her a certificate for a massage for her twenty-fifth birthday over three years ago.

That masseuse was nothing like Cain, who was as masculine and sexy as Brad, who had taken his shoes off and sprawled on the bed as if he was already planning to spend the night.

The moment that thought flashed into her mind, the muscles between her legs did an involuntary clench and ripple that took her breath. Thinking about how sexy these two looked had her body taking control.

She was still trying to process the sensation when Cain

walked across the room and handed a glass of red wine to her. He'd pulled out a cold beer for Brad and one for himself and raised the bottle in a toast. "Cherry, to you and your week here at Feral Passions." He raised an eyebrow and added, "And to new experiences."

She clinked her wineglass against Cain's bottle and Brad's, and sipped thoughtfully, tasting the wine, thinking of the day she'd had. Wondering what these two had planned and what those "new experiences" might entail.

"Tell me about your hike," Cain said. He led her to one of the chairs at the small table in the corner, seated her as if they were out on a date, and then took the chair across from her. Brad stayed on the bed, but the cabin was so small, he was almost close enough to touch.

"It was so much fun!" She'd had a fabulous time with her sister and Steph, and Darnell had kept them in hysterics. She was funny and so very "L.A. Hollywood" that they'd really enjoyed her stories and sense of humor. "We hiked for what felt like forever, but it wasn't, obviously. We're just out of shape."

"Which is why I'm here. But finish your wine first."

She made a face at Cain. "Yes, master." And took a swallow of her wine.

"I think I like that," he said. "'Master' works."

"In your dreams, sweetheart. Anyway we got up to Blackbird Lake and it's so pretty and peaceful. We saw a couple of wolves along the way. One even trotted alongside us for a bit. Darnell was so excited she could barely even talk, but we got to the lake and had our lunch under a huge tree. There were wood ducks in the water, and their colors are so amazing they don't even look real. I'd never seen one before. Ronan and Wils are really fun and they finally convinced us we should all go skinny-dipping."

"Oh, they did, did they?" Brad appeared to have suddenly grown interested in her story. He got off the bed and took the third chair at the table. "And of course they didn't look when you girls all stripped down, right?"

Cherry almost choked on her wine. "Are you kidding? We told them we'd only do it if they'd strip down first. So they did, and we had to." She laughed. "It wasn't all that hard to convince us by then. It was hot, we were all dusty, and that lake is unbelievably clear. It's also damned cold, if you want the truth."

Cain stared past Cherry at Brad. "And we all know what happens to a man's equipment in cold water, right, Brad?"

"C'mon. I got a good look before they got wet." Cherry took another sip of her wine. She'd had plenty to drink at dinner, and this glass was already relaxing her. "Ronan and Wils are extremely well-endowed. They did not suffer any embarrassment from the cold water. In fact, I would say it appeared to invigorate them."

Both Cain and Brad laughed hysterically, for whatever reason. Cherry looked at her wineglass. She was definitely relaxed, and whatever they found funny had obviously gone right over her head. She tipped the glass to her mouth and emptied it in one big swallow.

Cain added a bit more. "Are you ready for me to work my magic?"

She blinked. Already? "I guess. What do you want me to do?"

"Not a thing. I'm doing it all, with Brad's help. He's my minion for the night."

Cherry glanced at Brad. "You don't look like a minion. They're little and yellow and have one eyeball in the—"

"I'm a Feral Passions minion. Trust me." He laughed. Then he shoved his chair back and pulled a large white towel out of Cain's tote bag. "Come with me." He crooked his little finger, and like a puppet on strings, Cherry grabbed her glass and followed him into the bathroom.

She finished her wine while Brad first turned off the light and then slipped her sandals off her feet. The tiny candle reflecting in the mirror over the sink filled the room with a soft glow. She set the glass aside so he could help her out of her dress, touching and kissing, even licking her nipples once he'd unhooked her bra.

She thought of asking Cain to go home so she could just spend the evening with Brad, but she figured that would be rude. Brad sucked on her nipple. She whimpered.

Next he slipped her panties down over her hips, but it wasn't until he'd wrapped her in the soft towel that Cherry realized he'd just seen her completely naked and she hadn't even blushed.

She glanced at the empty wineglass. It was probably a good thing Cain had brought the bottle with him, because she definitely wanted—and needed—to be relaxed.

One more kiss from Brad, and he opened the bathroom door.

CHAPTER 8

Brad kissed her again as they stepped into the main room. Cain had turned out the lights, leaving only the flickering candlelight. Forest sounds played in the background—the soft swish of wind, an owl hooting, and for a moment the haunting cries of wolves howling.

It reminded Cherry so much of her dreams last night, she broke out in chills.

"Are you cold?" Brad wrapped his arm around her shoulders and hugged her close.

She shook her head, unwilling to speak. How could Cain possibly have known to duplicate her night of amazing dreams? It was almost as if he'd read her mind.

Or had been there with her.

Impossible. It was just an amazing coincidence. It had to be.

Cain waited patiently beside the table, bare chested now, still wearing the pair of black sweats he'd had on when he arrived. They hung low on his hips, soft and clinging, faded almost gray. His feet were bare.

Candlelight sent a soft glow across Cain's chest while shadows emphasized the beautiful musculature of his upper body. Where Brad's chest was mostly smooth, Cain had a dusting of dark blond hair that caught the flickering light. She stared at the line of hair trailing down from his navel, leading her imagination beneath the waistband of his sweats.

Then Brad took her hand and her concentration shifted as he walked her over to the table and helped her lie down on the soft flannel sheet covering the leather. She'd never felt so aware of textures before—his hands were rough and callused, the flannel so soft it felt almost silky. The air in the cabin was warm, drifting over her bare shoulders. Cherry lay on her stomach with her face cushioned in the ring at the end of the table.

She closed her eyes. One of the guys—Cain, she thought—twisted her long hair into a knot and pulled it forward so that it hung over the end of the table. She scooted around a bit to make herself more comfortable as Brad gently tugged the towel out from under her.

She was naked with two men looking at her. If this had happened with anyone else, she would have been freaking out, blushing multiple shades of red, and trying to cover herself.

But not with these two. For whatever reason, she trusted them. Completely.

Instead of feeling humiliated and embarrassed, she listened as Cain whispered to Brad. "She's even more beautiful than you said."

"She is, isn't she? I think she's absolutely perfect."

Had they really said that? Or was she just hoping they had? Probably wishful thinking. She'd had a lifetime of doing that, and tonight? Everything had taken on a dream-like quality. The illusion of fantasy was a powerful aphrodisiac, and with the cushion that supported her face deadening the sound just enough to give their voices a faraway, almost mystical quality, it was so easy to relax and just let whatever happened, happen.

"I'm warming the oil with my hands, Cheraza, but please let me know if it's too cool for you."

"Hmmm." She loved the way he said her name. She rarely heard it. She'd been Cherry since before she could remember.

Cain's hands were slick with the scented oil. More vanilla, but subtle. He was right—the vanilla was soothing even as her skin shivered beneath his sensual touch. She wondered where Brad was, if he was watching while Cain touched her.

Would that bother him? She and Brad had been as close to intimate last night as two people could be without actually having sex, and now Cain was touching her, his hands working the knots in her shoulders and the sore muscles in her calves and . . . no. Two sets of hands. Brad was obviously helping. She sighed and relaxed even more as both men made magic happen to her tired muscles. Drifting, she lost herself in the recorded forest sounds, the haunting cries of the wolves, the ultimate fantasy of two totally sexy men with their hands all over her.

She wasn't sure if she'd fallen asleep or merely drifted under the sensual massage, but Cain leaned over and whispered in her ear that they were going to turn her, and it made her smile, picturing a big spatula flipping her over like a pancake, but she was really too limp and relaxed to care how they did what they did.

One minute she was lying on her stomach and the next she was on her back. She flashed on how exposed she was, her breasts and belly, even her sex, openly displayed, but the magic of Cain's fingers massaging her scalp and Brad gently tugging and rubbing her toes and feet left her sighing and relaxed once again. This was even better. They'd found the rhythm of the forest sounds Cain was playing, moving in time with the wind in the trees and the soft hoot of an owl.

Cain's massage moved lower, his fingers working along her jawline and then to her neck, while Brad had moved up along her legs to the muscles in her thighs. Quadriceps. That's what those big muscles were called, and hers were really sore from today's hike.

Brad was gentle, so very gentle, though it was hard to imagine that strong man with the big hands treating her this tenderly. But Cain was every bit as gentle, rubbing her arms, massaging her biceps and then her forearms.

She already felt like warm pudding, her body so relaxed and fluid she could almost imagine dripping off the massage table into a puddle of goo on the floor.

Not a pretty image, but at this point did it matter?

Cain finished her arms and she heard him reaching for the bottle of oil while Brad used his thumbs to ease the tension in her groin muscles. She'd been sore there this morning, probably from all the climbing uphill to the lake, and the smooth press of his thumbs and the palms of his hands had her sighing with pleasure.

Then Cain began massaging her hands, and she forgot everything else. Stretching her fingers, putting the perfect amount of pressure on her palms, working each finger individually—it was heaven. Absolute heaven.

After he finished her hands, he arranged her arms alongside her body, palms up. She really didn't want this to end, but when Brad paused she knew the fantasy was over. She'd totally lost track of time and had no idea how long she'd been lying there.

Cain's voice interrupted her thoughts. "Cheraza, Brad and I would like to continue, but we want to ask your permission. Will you trust us enough to give you a more sensual massage? Our touch will be more intimate, and we don't want you to hesitate to ask us to stop should you feel at all uncomfortable. Brad's going to blindfold you if that's okay. It might not sound like it, but the blindfold will help you relax."

She didn't have to consider his words at all. Two men she liked, one who'd already brought her to an absolutely mind-blowing orgasm with his hands and mouth? She'd obviously gotten past the fact that she was lying here naked in front of them, so yeah, she could get on board with more. Even so, she kept her eyes closed, easily re-entered her fantasy world, and nodded.

Brad slipped the blindfold over her eyes, and Cain was right. She relaxed even more.

She wasn't ready to watch what they did. She only wanted to feel.

Cain kissed her forehead. She knew it was him because his short facial hair tickled. It was much softer than it looked and she really wanted to rub her face against his, but his kiss had been so quick, there hadn't been time. The recording he'd been playing changed. The wild sounds were there, but the long, sad howls of the wolves were different, more upbeat, if that was at all possible, and there was a subtle but sure tempo behind the natural sounds. It had to be a drum, but it was timed precisely to the beat of her heart.

Or was her heart syncing to the beat of the drum?

At first, nothing felt different. The massage continued, though Cain and Brad's pacing was smoother, as they worked in time to the steady tempo filling the background more with each passing moment. The sound had been muted earlier, but now it filled the room, a low thrumming that could have been blood flow or a beating heart. She felt the sound deep inside, a primal beat that turned her body liquid, warmed her inside and out.

Cain's big hands cupped her breasts, and she thought of Brad's touch last night, the way he'd pinched and tugged her nipples until she saw stars. Cain massaged her, though, almost as if he purposefully ignored her nipples. It took all her willpower not to arch into his warm hands.

Not to beg for more.

Cain moved to her right side and she sensed Brad at her left. The two of them stroked her from shoulders to toes, their hands slick with oil. Hands along the outside of each leg moved slowly inward, sliding gently over her calves, her sensitive inner thighs, following the crease between her thigh and groin.

She thought of them as if they were disembodied things— not Cain and Brad, but two powerful sets of masculine hands stroking her body in a graceful dance of sensation. They massaged her breasts, teased her nipples—stroking, brushing, and then gently pinching. She wanted more, wanted that pleasure-pain that transferred so easily to her clit, but they teased her until she was slowly writhing on the table.

Strong hands pinned her ankles, and she arched her back in frustrated response.

The tempo of the drums beat faster, the thrumming deeper, invading her bones. Her heartbeat leapt, racing to catch the drums, her body slowly twisting and arching in response to the seduction of touch. Strong fingers pinched her nipples harder; other disembodied fingers traced her labia, barely connecting with her greedy body as they circled her clit, driving her insane with featherlight touches that led her close to but not over that precipice of orgasm.

She sucked in a breath as a mouth covered hers. Brad's lips. She recognized their fullness, the smooth upper lip where Cain's was prickly from his moustache, the taste that was all Brad. His tongue thrust against hers as fingers drove deep between her legs and her inner muscles clamped down, clinging in spasmodic response to such an intimate invasion.

She was still on the edge, her body straining to reach the precipice, but they held her there—Brad with his deep kisses and his fingers working the nipple on her left breast while Cain's fingers filled her sheath, his thumb circled her clit, and his other hand tugged at her sensitive nipple.

She tried to picture them, two powerful, sensual men pleasuring her while her body bucked and writhed beneath their expert touch, but the drums in the background hammered harder, faster, and her body followed, so close, so damned close, wiping everything else from her mind.

She sensed a shift in the air and the hands disappeared. Sensation fell away and she wanted to scream at the lack. The drums beat just as hard, pounded every bit as fast, and she lay there, alone and panting.

Lips pulled at one nipple; fingers plucked the other. She groaned and clutched the sides of the table to keep from arching right off the thing. Strong hands parted her thighs, holding her down, opening her wide. A tongue stroked from her perineum to her clit, circled that sensitive bud, and then drove deep.

Was it Brad? She couldn't tell. Honestly? She didn't care. All that really mattered was that he didn't stop!

Mouth at her breast, mouth between her legs, and they worked together, sucking and licking, pinching and stroking as the tempo increased and the drums grew louder, as her heart raced and tiny lights flashed behind her blindfolded eyes.

Her body raced the drums and there was a thundering in her heart, in her blood, until the tongues stroking and hands touching coalesced into a single firestorm of need, of desire and sensation, and then it was too much, too perfect.

Too amazing to be possible, and yet she was flying, screaming out as wolves howled and drums thundered, her body tensed, her back arched, and she lost herself amid a climax unlike anything she'd ever known, a celebration of her body that shredded her soul and repaired it, better, stronger, more complete, than she'd ever been before.

Soft touches brought her down. Sweet kisses led her into a quiet pool of sensation where she needed only to relax, to let her mind and body melt away, suffused in pleasure, enervated, entirely complete.

Cain pulled the blankets back on Cherry's bed while Brad carefully wiped away the oil they'd rubbed over her body.

She slept soundly, the culmination of a long day hiking, a good meal, spectacular wine, and the best sensual massage Cain knew he and Brad had ever given anyone. She was exactly the woman they wanted, and if she didn't want them it was going to be tough to get over her.

He hardly knew her, and already she fit into his life—their lives—more comfortably than he could ever have imagined. Was one week going to be enough to convince her?

Brad carefully scooped her up in his arms and carried her to the bed. He laid her on the clean sheet and Cain pulled the covers down so they could tuck her feet inside. The nights here could be cold. He moved toward the head of the bed and lightly worked the knot out of her hair.

The long, dark tresses felt like silk between his fingers. His eyes burned with the thought of not keeping her forever and he wiped away a tear he refused to let fall. Raising his head, he caught Brad watching him.

"Well?"

Brad whispered, but Cain clearly heard him. He shook his head. "I never imagined . . . Damn, Brad. She's beautiful and smart and funny, and she loves wolves. It really couldn't get any better. She's almost too good. Scary good."

"Don't do that to yourself, Cain. You're starting to sound like Trak. He's all about doom and gloom, though it's nice not to have you teasing me about falling so hard and fast for her."

Cain laughed softly. "Yeah. I take it all back. C'mon. Help me clean this stuff up so we can get out of here and get some sleep."

They had the table folded up, the candles extinguished and stashed in their container, and all of Cain's equipment ready to go. Brad stood by the bed for a moment, watching Cherry sleep. "I don't want to leave her," he said.

"Help me carry this stuff back to the lodge." Cain walked over to stand beside Brad. "I don't think she'd mind a bit if the wolves spent the night."

"Do you think it's safe? What if she makes the connection? How will we explain how they got inside?"

Cain could tell Brad really wanted to believe it was okay. "We'll just tell her we weren't comfortable leaving her alone sleeping so soundly, the wolves were waiting for us outside, and we asked them to stay. I think it sounds believable."

Brad's soft laughter had Cain grinning in response. "Good," he said. "Then if Trak gets pissed, I can blame you." Brad picked up the massage table and waited by the open door.

"He blames me for anything bad that happens anyway." Cain grabbed the tote bags. He took a quick look around the dark cabin, but his gaze lingered on Cheraza, sleeping so soundly.

They had a lot of mountains to climb with this one. Then he followed Brad out the door.

CHAPTER 9

Tuesday

She came awake in the early dawn darkness, blinking slowly, remembering. Cain's powerful hands stroking so gently, Brad's sweet kisses, his touch gentle when needed yet more than capable of so much strength. Both men treating her like spun glass one moment, like a powerful woman the next.

She'd never, not even in her wildest dreams or the sexiest romance she'd ever read, experienced anything remotely like last night. A massage like that had to be illegal, but it had definitely done the trick. Her muscles had been screaming after the hike yesterday. She didn't feel sore anywhere this morning. Of course, she hadn't tried to move anything, either.

She hadn't slept as soundly in way too long. She felt totally rested, and since she didn't remember coming to bed, her men had to have tucked her in.

The giveaway was the fact that she was naked.

She never slept naked, but how could it matter when they'd both spent hours touching her, kissing her, doing things she'd never imagined? She'd been naked, and she'd been fine with it. She was actually sorry the guys had been dressed. Next time she'd ask for a naked massage.

If there ever was a next time.

Naked or not, she was so toasty warm that she just closed her eyes again, lay there a moment, and tried to recall the details of last night. There'd been dinner with everyone at the lodge, and then Brad had walked her back to the cabin, Cain had arrived, and—

Her stomach clenched with remembered desire and she shivered. Aroused, chilled, she tried to hug herself, but her arms were trapped. In fact, the blankets were pulled over her so tightly that she couldn't move at all. That's when she heard soft snoring to her left . . . and her right. Had Cain and Brad stayed in her . . .

Rolling her head to one side and then the other, she stared at the dark shadows on either side and bit back a laugh. That explained the snoring—and the warmth. It was hard to be cold with furry wolves pressed against each side of her, trapping her beneath the covers.

She recognized the two she thought of as "her" wolves. She tried to sit up, but they had her trapped so completely she couldn't even scoot out from under the blankets.

It appeared she'd awakened her bedmates.

"Good morning, gentlemen." The green-eyed beast raised his head and yawned, and his look was so disgruntled she almost apologized for waking him. The brown-eyed wolf merely raised his eyelids and stared at her, almost as if he was waiting to see what her reaction to waking up with two wolves in her bed would be.

She watched him, enjoying the moment. This was its own kind of magic, to wake up with two beautiful feral creatures lying on her bed, almost as if they protected her. She scratched behind the silver wolf's ears and he groaned. Then she did the same for the brown-eyed guy, who rolled over on his back, obviously hoping for a tummy rub.

She managed to scoot up and out from under the blankets, which left her breasts exposed, but she figured that if she could show them to Brad and Cain, wolves weren't a problem.

Rubbing one wolf's head and now the other one's belly, she watched the two of them for a moment, studying their reactions to her touch, the way they subtly interacted with each other. Finally, she asked, "How did you guys get in here last night? Did Brad and Cain let you in?"

The green-eyed wolf made a little huffing noise, rolled his head to one side, and stared at the door.

"That's either a 'yes' or an 'I want out.' Either way, I think you boys need to go outside." She tried to shove the blankets back, which wasn't easy with wolves pinning them down. The wolves showed no inclination of moving. "Off the bed. Both of you."

They both gazed at her as if they didn't believe she meant it. "Now, gentlemen."

This time they both jumped down, though the brown-eyed wolf looked so sad she almost gave in and let him stay. He certainly didn't act like he wanted to leave. She walked across the room to the door, and even though the sun wasn't up and there probably wasn't anyone out there, she stood out of sight behind the door when she opened it. She'd never been comfortable under any circumstances parading around naked.

Though being naked certainly hadn't been an issue last night. The two huge wolves slowly walked outside and then trotted down the steps. The brown-eyed wolf paused at the bottom and turned to look over his shoulder, and she felt as if her entire body flushed dark red from his intent look, which was just weird. She didn't remember blushing all that much last night, but maybe that was because what she remembered was so far beyond embarrassment it made her shiver just thinking about it.

She quickly closed the door. She hadn't expected that all those little muscles between her legs would clench in sympathy, and it was just so awkward with both wolves staring at her. She'd noticed the green-eyed wolf's nose was twitching.

She'd been so turned on, remembering Brad and Cain last night, and the wolf was staring at her making sniffing noises?

"Cherry, girl, you've read one too many paranormal romances." In those stories, the shapeshifter could scent his mate's arousal. Pure fantasy, and an active imagination could get a girl into trouble, except there was no denying the fact that the wolf had been watching her, his head raised with his nose in the air. Sniffing.

Could he smell her arousal? He was an animal, damn it, with a good nose, so even if he could smell her, it didn't matter. She looked out the window. Both wolves had disappeared into the forest. She turned around and leaned against the door and tried to make sense of last night and this morning. Except the more she thought about it, the less sense anything made.

Brad and Cain were both highly intelligent, strikingly

handsome men, and yet, for whatever reason, they'd focused on her. But why?

Please, she begged. Not like that other time, another guy who'd treated her like a goddess. And then he'd done something so cruel, so horrible to her, that she'd never been able to move past it. He'd seemed sincere, too, but it was ten years ago and guys grew up.

She couldn't picture Cain and Brad being cruel.

The problem, though, was that she couldn't understand why they were so damned nice, either. She wasn't anything special—there were five other women here, any one of them prettier than her. Maybe caffeine would help. A healthy dose of caffeine pumping through her system always cleared her head. It was almost six. With any luck, Brad should have coffee ready by now. She thought about taking a shower first, but she'd showered before dinner last night and that oil that Cain used for her massage had left her skin feeling so soft— she loved the subtle scent of vanilla.

She wasn't quite ready to wash that off.

Nor did she want to wash away the memory of Cain's mouth on her, or Brad's, either.

Or the best orgasm she'd ever experienced in all her twenty-eight years. Even better than the one Brad had given her before dinner.

Laughing, she went into the bathroom to wash up. Of course it was better—two incredible guys trumped one incredible guy every time.

Cain was still in his wolf form well after Brad had shifted, but he was planning to go check on the new pups. The wolf was a first-time mother and the male was young—Brad was glad Cain was keeping an eye on them. He took a quick shower and dressed, but the two of them hadn't really talked much about last night. He wondered if part of Cain's reason for not shifting was to avoid a conversation.

They really needed to talk about Cherry. Cain was convinced she was on to them or at least suspicious, but Brad wasn't all that sure. But if she was and she still liked them, wasn't that a good thing? He glanced out the window at the trail that led to Cherry's cabin and wondered if she'd gone back to sleep after booting them out. She hadn't seemed at all concerned about waking up with two wolves on her bed. That had to be a good thing, too. At least he hoped it was.

But what about two men in her bed? He glanced at Cain. The big silver wolf sprawled on the bed, watching Brad, and his heart actually hurt, thinking how much he loved the man. He knew Cain loved him every bit as much. They'd been together a long time, but they'd both agreed there was something missing in their relationship—a woman.

Was he just dreaming of moonbeams, imagining Cherry accepting both of them, loving them equally? She was so beautiful, not to mention the way she clicked so easily with the two of them, filling that empty spot that was so much more noticeable when she wasn't with them. Cain was the worrier—he wasn't sure she'd be happy, stuck up here in the woods with a couple of werewolves. She was used to the city, used to having her sister close by.

Not used to loving or trusting one man, much less two. Brad had argued that they had to show Cherry that their feelings for her were real, that they weren't leading her on or playing with her affections. He was certain they could make her love them, but it wasn't going to be easy.

They'd always known that any woman they found to love was going to have to love both of them. Now, though, they didn't want just any woman. He and Cain agreed on that point—they wanted to keep Cherry. Not as one of a couple, but as part of a triad.

They weren't talking two guys taking turns, either. Both of them wanted her in their lives, in their bed, the two of them and Cherry. Brad had no idea how to approach the subject.

He sat down on the bed and ran his fingers through Cain's thick fur. "I'm going downstairs to get the coffee going," he said. "Trak will be here before long, even if the women come in later."

Cain yipped and, while they couldn't actually communicate all that clearly telepathically, they'd been together long enough for Brad to know what his guy was thinking. "Good point," Brad said. "I forgot Trak left with Suni and Fred . . . we may not see him until noon."

Cain leapt off the bed and waited by the door. They shared a suite of rooms on the second floor of the lodge, just above the kitchen area. The other men had cabins, some of them shared, others lived alone, but Brad and Cain had been together for years, a young man's friendship that had grown into so much more. Brad liked to think they each made the other stronger, better men, but for whatever reason, when they'd gone into Feral Passions as investors it had been with the idea that if they found a mate it would have to be a woman willing to love both of them.

If they'd had a checklist of their ideal woman, Cherry would fill every slot. Brad already felt a powerful connection to her, and while he couldn't yet call it love, it was damned close. Everything about her was appealing—the sound of her laughter, the joy in her smile. Her vulnerability. He wanted to be the man to protect her from the bastards who hurt her, because he knew she'd somehow been badly hurt along the way. He wanted to make love to that sexy body, lose himself in her soft breasts, bury himself between her perfect thighs, and he wanted to share all that was Cherry with the man he loved.

He wondered if Cain's hesitancy was because he'd fallen for Cherry. Cain had always been the one who pondered every nuance of every event, every person. Brad was one of the few who realized how deep Cain's emotions went, how powerfully he loved.

Was he afraid of loving Cherry and having to watch her leave?

Brad knelt beside the big wolf. "It's going to be okay. We'll make this work, Cain. I promise." Cain whined, a low, sad sound. "I know. It's a risk, but we have to believe."

Brad opened the door and let Cain out, but he followed Cain down the stairs, his mind on Cherry, on what the three of them had done last night. Brad hadn't been certain how well she'd handle the two of them, but she'd seemed to love every minute. She'd been amazing so far. It was already Tuesday. They had less than five days to convince her she really wanted to spend her life mated to a couple of werewolves.

At the rate they were going, it shouldn't be all that hard, should it?

It was growing brighter, but the sun still wasn't showing above the mountains when Cherry reached the lodge. The wolves were gone, probably back to their dens or wherever wild wolves went during the day. Or, if her growing suspicions were true, back to their human selves.

She stopped in the middle of the trail. "I don't believe I just thought that." Her imagination was definitely running away with her logic. They were just hidden away for the day, that was all. Brad had told her they weren't as active during daylight, but she'd still managed to see quite a few of them.

Waking up with two in her bed wasn't anything she'd counted on, that's for sure. Thinking about that, about last night, about what an amazing time she was having in spite of all her misgivings about this trip, had her looking for Christa and Steph. She really wanted to find out how their night had gone.

She wasn't sure if she was ready to spill the beans about hers. Smiling, remembering, she walked up the steps and pushed open the door into the dining room. The place was empty except for Brad standing behind the bar with a cup of coffee and a newspaper spread out on the counter.

"Good morning." She sat on one of the tall stools while he gave her a very serious once-over. Make that twice-over. She'd had some amazing orgasms, and the only one he'd had was an accident. He probably wouldn't appreciate a reminder.

He leaned close and kissed her, and she tasted coffee. "Hmmm . . . is this the only way I'm going to get my caffeine this morning?"

"Works for me." He laughed and turned around to pour a cup for her. "How'd you sleep?"

"Like the dead. You and Cain are better than any drug I've ever heard of. I didn't wake up once during the night, though I certainly might have if I'd known I had visitors."

At least he had the grace to look a little sheepish. "I hope you don't mind. You were out like a light when we put you to bed, and Cain and I were both worried that you might be disoriented if you woke during the night. The guys were outside when we got ready to leave, so we decided to let them in." He shrugged. "It was sort of a spur-of-the-moment decision."

She laughed. "I didn't mind at all. They were excellent bedmates, and they're definitely toasty to sleep with. Ya know, I never imagined sleeping with a wolf on my bed, much less two. It was actually pretty cool." She glanced around the empty dining area. "Where is everyone?"

"Well, Cain's checking on mama wolf and the babies, and none of the others have shown up yet this morning. Considering how everyone paired up last night, I have a feeling they'll come straggling in a bit later than usual."

"Does this happen every week? New women show up and the guys all find someone to sleep with?" She hadn't thought about it that way, that she might be one of a revolving carousel of women here for the men's pleasure. If that was the case . . . Damn. She didn't want it to be.

"Not usually." Brad took a sip of his coffee. "Granted, it's hard to meet women living so far out in the woods, but we've only been open a month, so that's four sets of guests, six each week, and this is the most interesting group we've had. You're certainly the most interesting one I've met."

She shook her head. "Why, Brad? I don't get it. Are you and Cain for real? Because believe me, I am not usually the focus of any man's desire. I'm more apt to be the best friend that guys come to when they're having trouble with their girlfriends or, even worse, the butt of their stupid jokes."

Crap. She hadn't meant to sound like such a bitch, but . . . She needed to take her coffee and go back to her cabin. Brad didn't deserve her anger.

"Cherry."

She closed her eyes and looked away. She really couldn't look at him, but then he tipped her chin up with his fingers and gently turned her toward him. "I think you're beautiful. Plus, you're funny and smart, and I personally don't find anything attractive about a girl who's so thin she looks half-starved. Do you have any idea how much I want to take you to bed? Last night it about killed me when you fell asleep, because I wanted to be inside of you."

She smiled at him. What a line this guy had. "That would have been difficult. Cain was there."

"Cain wants you, too."

"What?" She slapped her hand over her mouth. She hadn't meant to squeak.

Brad peeled her hand away and kissed her. He took his time getting it right, and Cherry was breathing hard when he finally pulled away, but before she could catch her breath and respond she heard voices outside. Steph and Christa coming up the steps and she was sitting here, most likely beet red, totally incapable of a coherent thought.

"Relax. We can talk later when Cain gets back." He raised his head and smiled. "Good morning ladies. Coffee?"

Suni and Fred arrived just behind them, and then Darnell wandered in. Cherry really wanted to talk to her sister and absolutely had to talk to Brad and Cain, but that would have to wait. Everyone was standing around, chattering about what a good time they were having, and yet she noticed that there was no mention made of the men they'd all gone home with last night.

That was good. It let her off the hook, at least for now. How could she possibly describe the night she'd had with Cain and Brad? It was a lot safer to talk about the wolves. Wolves were fine. They were so much simpler to deal with than two men who, for whatever reason, appeared to think she was sexy.

Which gave her an utterly superb opening. "Ladies, I need to tell you who spent the night in my bed last night."

The room went stone quiet.

Brad laughed. "That's definitely the way to get a crowd's attention." He leaned over and kissed her soundly before heading into the kitchen. "I need to get breakfast started. Behave, ladies."

"Behave? Are you kidding?" Christa snagged the barstool next to Cherry. "Okay, girl. Dish."

CHAPTER 10

Cherry sipped her coffee and took her time, at least until Cissy growled at her. "Okay," she said. "Well, first of all, I got a massage last night. Cain's the masseur and he's wickedly awesome, but Brad was there, too. He helped Cain carry the table and his tote bags of massage stuff, and it was just what I needed after that hike." And that was all they were going to hear about the massage. "I was so sleepy and relaxed when Cain was done that the guys dumped me into bed and left. Brad said he was worried about leaving me so zonked out, but the two wolves I've gotten to know were outside as they were leaving, so he sent them in."

"Two wolves? You had two wolves in your room?" Suni's shoulders slumped. "Damn. I've hardly seen any wolves at all."

"You'll see them. I'm sure of it." Cherry hadn't realized how unique her situation was—she appeared to have two wolves really interested in her. "If you're lucky, you might wake up the way I did, trapped under your covers by wolves lying on top of the bedspread."

"You're kidding! They were on the bed?" Christa laughed out loud. "And to think you didn't want to come on this trip."

"I planned to tell you this morning that I'd changed my mind. I'm having a blast."

Christa winked. "So am I, darlin'. So am I."

Cain walked into the lodge before Cherry could ask Christa to expand on that comment. He had three big wolves with him, and they drew everyone's attention. All the chatter in the dining room fell silent as the beautiful beasts paused beside the equally striking man. Then he smiled, and the moment was broken.

"I was coming up the steps when I heard Suni saying she hadn't seen hardly any wolves, and these guys were just lying around being bums. Suni, they know you mean them no harm, so feel free to come over and tell them just how rude they've been, avoiding you."

"Really?" She crept around Cherry, paused, and then walked up to the closest wolf. He planted his butt on the floor and waited until she came close enough and then he sniffed her hand. She rubbed his head and he leaned against her leg, but there was something about him, about the way he moved, that caught Cherry's attention.

He reminded her of Trak. It was hard to say why, but there was something about him that made her think of the man. That made her look more closely at the other two. The biggest one, silver with some light brown coloring, had gray-blue eyes, and there was something about the way he watched all of them that reminded her of Ronan, the man who'd gone with Christa last night. A man who also had beautiful gray-blue eyes.

The third wolf, a big gray and black animal, had brilliant blue eyes. Eyes just like Wils's.

Cherry shivered and rubbed her arms to warm herself,

even though it was warm enough in here. When she raised her head, she caught Cain staring at her, and those forest green eyes matched the eyes of the wolf she'd slept with last night. Just the way the brown-eyed wolf had made her think of Brad.

Cain was watching her, almost as if he knew what she was thinking. She shivered again, turned her head away to break eye contact, and took a sip of her lukewarm coffee.

Cain walked across the room, directly toward Cherry. He had a horrible feeling she'd figured them out, no matter what Brad said. The way she was watching him right now, like she was putting two and two together and coming up with anything but four.

He had no idea what he was going to say if she asked him. No idea at all. So he'd just act like there wasn't anything to worry about and see what happened. He smiled as he approached her, threw his arm over her shoulders when he got close. "How are you feeling this morning? Did the massage help?"

She blushed. Damn, but he loved the way her skin flushed that deep red. She'd had the same reaction when she was aroused, even more when she climaxed, and he'd better stop thinking about that or he was going to have a hard time hiding what he was thinking.

"You know it did. I can't believe I fell asleep on you guys."

"You're kidding, right?" He tightened his arm around her shoulders and kissed her cheek. Any more and he wouldn't be able to stop. Choosing to stay over with her as wolves had been its own sweet torture—it had also meant he and Brad couldn't take care of the problem at hand, so to speak, and just being this close to her already had Cain on edge. "You have to realize that's about the best compliment a masseur can get. It means you were totally relaxed."

"Any more relaxed and I would have melted right off the table."

"You didn't mind that we let the guys in to sleep with you last night?"

"Are you kidding?" She shook her head, and there was nothing about her that felt at all suspicious. Damn, he hoped he was right. They'd taken such a huge risk, opening up Feral Passions the way they had. Opening up the chance of their secret getting out.

"I told Brad they were great bed partners. Warm and quiet. Where are they? I thought when you walked in that you might have them with you, but these are all different wolves. They're so beautiful, each so unique. I never realized before how different wolves looked from each other."

He shrugged. Tried to look as nonchalant as he could, considering one of her wolves was pouring coffee behind the bar and the other one was standing here with his arm around her. "We don't keep tabs on any of them. They come and go; sometimes they're gone for weeks at a time. Other times they hang out here at the lodge, now that it's done. When we were building, they stayed away, but once the equipment and construction crews were gone, they've started coming back. I've never seen wild wolves as sociable as these guys."

"They're all males, the ones that hang around the lodge, aren't they? Isn't that unusual?"

She really was too damned observant. He shrugged as

if it wasn't any big deal. "Not really. The females, at least the ones close by, all have pups now, and they're not going to bring them around so many people. If you come back later in the summer, you'd be able to see the females with their pups, but they're a lot shyer than the guys."

Brad stepped out of the kitchen. Cain had forgotten he was cooking this morning. "Hey, Cain, can you help me with the trays? I've got breakfast ready to put out."

"Duty calls," Cain said, and gave Cherry a quick kiss.

She followed him into the kitchen. "I can help. I don't see any of your regular crew out there."

Brad just shook his head. "Too much fun last night, I imagine. Thanks, Cherry. Be careful—the handles are cool, but the pan's hot." He gave her a stainless pan filled with bacon and sausage. Cain had two with fried potatoes and scrambled eggs, and Brad followed them out with a big bowl of fruit and another with a large quiche. They had everything set up on hot plates or under heat lamps within a couple of minutes, and the line quickly formed.

Cain put the wolves outside, and Cherry got in line with Steph and Christa. They filled their plates and then found places at the long table in the center of the room. By the time they were seated, Trak arrived. Wils, Ronan, and Evan showed up a few minutes later.

Cain took a seat with Brad and Trak at one of the smaller tables, ostensibly to go over plans for the day's activities. He kept his fears to himself, but he'd watch Cherry closely.

Of course, he had no idea what he'd do if she asked him point-blank if he was a wolf. Why did he feel as if they maybe hadn't thought this plan through as well as they should have?

"I thought we'd never get a chance to talk." Cherry led Christa and Steph along a shaded trail, following a map Cain had sketched on a napkin that was supposed to take them to a large meadow filled with wildflowers and a small pond. "I am dying to know what happened with you and Ronan, Cissy, and you and Wils, Steph. I mean, those guys are just so hot!"

Christa snorted. Steph blushed.

"Steph! You're blushing. You never blush!" Cherry planted her feet and laughed. "Must have been one wild night."

Steph giggled and turned even redder. "Wils is amazing, and 'wild' doesn't even come close." She glanced at Christa and they both burst out laughing. "C'mon. I want to get a little bit farther from the lodge. I really, really don't want them to hear us talking about them."

"Them?"

"Uh, yeah. Them." Christa was blushing now.

"Okay, but then you guys are going to tell me everything."

Cherry led off at a good clip with her sister and Steph trailing along behind. They only went about a quarter of a mile before the trail dumped them out into a beautiful meadow. Deer grazed belly deep in thick grass on the far side near a line of trees, and a shallow pond stretched across the northern end.

Masses of wildflowers in shades of blue and gold, with patches of white and red scattered about, went so far beyond the "pretty flowers" Cain had described that the three of them just stood there at the edge of the meadow, staring.

There might not be any cell phone service, but Cherry was glad she'd kept her phone in her pocket. She pulled it out and snapped some pictures. This was just too beautiful not to. She glanced up when Christa called her.

"Over here." Steph had found a weathered log in the shade and parked her butt on one end of it. Christa sat next to her. Cherry sat on a smooth boulder facing them. She felt like the grown-up in the room with a couple of misbehaving kids. Christa looked at Steph and they both looked at Cherry—and both of them blushed.

"I'm waiting."

Christa turned to Steph. "You tell her," she said. "I can't. She's my sister!" She practically wailed that last part.

Steph giggled again. "Okay. But it was all your idea."

"No, it wasn't!" Christa covered her face with her hands.

"Was, too." Steph was obviously loving this.

Cherry had to bite back a grin. She'd never seen Christa embarrassed before. Ever. "I don't care whose idea it was; what happened?"

"Okay," Steph said. "So I was with Wils and Ronan had Christa, and—"

"Did he ever," Christa muttered.

Steph ignored her. "We left together. The guys knew which cabins we were staying in and they took us on a trail that led from the back side of the deck. We all ended up at my cabin. Wils had snagged a bottle of some kind of really good liqueur—"

"Tasted like pomegranate juice," Christa said. "It does amazing things to gin."

"Oh, yeah. And that gin did amazing things to you,

sweetheart." Steph rolled her eyes. "Well, we all went into my cabin, and the guys mixed drinks for us—we'd been talking about cocktails at the lodge and so they'd brought everything they needed to make them."

"They made a lot of them. They were really, really good. The next thing we knew . . ." Christa glanced at Steph.

"We were getting naked."

"All four of you?" Cherry burst out laughing. And she'd been worried about what the girls would think of her! "Well? Then what happened?"

Steph and Christa looked at each other and blushed. Again. Steph took a deep breath, let it out. "I guess you could say that anything that two men and two women who find each other attractive can do with one another got done. More than once."

Christa nodded sagely. "Those guys have got amazing stamina."

"Amazing," Steph said. "Really amazing."

Cherry sat there with her hand covering her mouth. She did not want to interrupt this story. Not one bit.

"Ya know those romances you read?" Christa glanced at Steph and then focused on Cherry. "The ones with all the wild sex in them? Well, I can now tell you that yes, it is possible for two men and two women to get it on and all get off at the same time."

Steph shrugged. "Well, it did take us a couple of tries to get it right."

"I know." Christa gazed at Cherry. "I think we need more practice tonight."

"Good idea." Steph glanced at Christa again and they

both broke out in giggles. It took a minute before she stopped enough to actually talk. Then Steph very calmly said, "So, Cherry . . . how did your night go?"

"Well, not like yours, that's for sure, but it wasn't bad. It was just me and Cain and Brad. The guys gave me a massage, including an unbelievable orgasm, and then put me to bed. I slept with two wolves for company and woke up in time for breakfast. Not like your night, that's for sure."

"Both of them?" Steph glanced at Christa. "Massaging you?"

"Yeah, but they had their clothes on." Cherry sighed. "I didn't." She almost laughed when she realized how much fun she was having with this. "I'm hoping we can change that tonight."

Christa stared at her so long it made Cherry nervous. "What? Why are you looking at me like that?"

"Because this is so not you, hon. You haven't had a boyfriend in, like, forever."

Cherry shrugged. "I don't think of Brad and Cain as boyfriend material. I do, however, think of them as a really fun way to enjoy a spectacular vacation. They're both sweet and sexy and they like me." She leaned close and pressed her hand against Christa's knee. "I know what you're thinking, but they're not like that other guy. He was a cruel, self-serving jerk, but he's over and done with, and he's part of the past. Brad and Cain are . . ." She paused and thought about it. "I guess they're more right now."

She laughed, but then it was her turn to blush. "That is, if I don't fall asleep on them again. But what about you guys? You know that whatever you find here ends when we go home on Saturday, right?"

"God, I hope so." Steph glanced at Christa. "If I had sex like that every night, I think it would kill me."

"I know." Shaking her head, Christa laughed. "At least they've allowed me to take a few fantasies off my bucket list. And talk about beautiful bodies. Amazing." She poked Steph and they both cracked up. When she finally got it together, Christa merely shrugged. "However, we never got into likes and dislikes, or anything personal, not even their last names. So yes, I can honestly say I'm not thinking long term with either of those guys, but I wouldn't mind a few more nights."

Neither would Cherry. Brad and Cain filled something in her that she hadn't realized was empty until now. She flat out had fun with them. They made her laugh and they made her sigh, and damn, but they made her feel like that sensuous woman she'd always thought might be inside. She liked that woman and she didn't want to lose her, this woman who could take off her clothes in front of two handsome men and feel voluptuous and sexy, not fat. It wasn't going to be easy to walk away from that freedom at the end of the week. Not when she'd let herself go with Brad and Cain more than with anyone else in her life.

Including the jerk who'd been so horrible to her during her senior year in high school. She'd been so shy and awkward, but she'd thought she loved him and thought that love was returned. Obviously, it wasn't. He'd been a classmate in her advanced college prep calculus class. She'd helped him with his homework, and she'd crushed on him. Seriously. He'd finally asked her out, and they'd had such a good time. She thought.

It wasn't until later she'd learned the truth, that he needed her to help him pass the class and he'd taken a bet from his buddies that not only would she get him through calculus, he'd get into her before the semester ended.

Whoopee . . . he'd won. If he'd only just quit there. But no—he'd wanted her total humiliation, and he'd gotten it.

The walk back to the lodge was quieter. She wondered what Steph and Christa were thinking, if they planned to get together with Wils and Ronan tonight. Cherry had no idea what she was planning to do. It depended on Brad and Cain.

And maybe just a little bit on her.

CHAPTER 11

Cherry stepped into the lunchroom just as Steph and Christa were leaving with trays of food. "Where are you headed?"

"Brad and Trak made a run into town for supplies, but they left plenty of stuff for lunch and told us to take what we wanted." Christa glanced at Steph and laughed. "We've both got books we've been wanting to read, so we're going to veg out at my cabin with food, a bottle of wine"—she laughed when Steph held up the bottle—"and the books. They're your sexy romances by the way. I'm reading *Hot Alphas*. Steph's got one called *Alpha's Woman*. Notice a theme, here? It's all about the alpha male. We're thinking of them as educational reading at this point." She laughed and jabbed Steph with her elbow. "And wondering, of course, which guys here are the true alphas." She laughed. "I'm voting all of them. Thanks for bringing the books. You're welcome to join us."

"Thanks, but . . . where's everyone else? Did the L.A. contingent go somewhere?"

"Just to the pool, but they loaded up on the drinks," Steph said. "If I drank that much, I'd be asleep by dinnertime."

"I probably will be, just on principle alone. I can't remember the last time I was this relaxed."

Steph snorted. "Me, either, but that's because we can't remember the last time we were getting such creative . . . um, workouts. I had no idea this place offered such fantastic entertainment. Anyway, Cherry, if you don't find something else to do, come join us."

Steph grabbed Christa and the two of them left. Cherry almost went with them. She really didn't want to spend the afternoon alone in her cabin, but an afternoon reading and eating sounded pretty boring. She made a sandwich, poured some iced tea, and went out on the deck, but she took a seat at one of the small tables—it would feel too lonely, sitting at that long picnic table by herself. Cain showed up a few minutes later. He stepped out of the lodge with a couple of sandwiches for himself.

"Where'd you come from? I didn't see you in the kitchen."

He took the seat across from her and spread his meal out on two paper plates. "I just had to walk down the stairs. Brad and I share a suite of rooms here in the lodge. It's more convenient, since he does most of the breakfast cooking and I need to be available in case anyone wants a massage."

"You're roommates?" That explained why they seemed like such good friends, but then she wondered if they were gay. They'd brought her to orgasm but hadn't gotten anything for themselves, but if they had each other maybe she really was just a job for them.

Her lunch lost all its appeal. Had she totally misread their interest?

"I can almost hear the wheels spinning in that busy brain of yours. What are you thinking, Cheraza?"

"Are you and Brad gay?"

He shrugged and shook his head. "I love Brad and he loves me. We've been together a long time. We have great sex together—really great sex—but Cherry, do not doubt that we both really love women."

There really wasn't much to say to that. She and Cain finished up their lunch at the same time. She gathered up her napkin and the plastic cup she'd filled with iced tea when Cain grabbed her hand. "I'm going to check on the mama wolf and her pups. Come with me?"

She sat back down. "Really? I thought you didn't want to frighten her. Won't I—"

He shook his head. "Not at all. She's used to me, and if you're with me, she'll probably ignore you. She'll be fine."

"Are my shorts and sandals okay?"

"The trail's pretty level, just one tree that's down. I can help you over it."

She glanced at her flip-flops and shrugged. If Cain could go in sweats and moccasins, it couldn't be too daunting a hike. "Good. Then yes. I definitely want to go. Give me a minute to dump my plate, and I'll help you put the rest of the food away. I think everyone's eaten."

That was another thing he really admired about Cheraza, and damn, but he loved the way her real name rolled off his tongue, too, but she had absolutely no problem at all about helping him clean up the leftovers from the meal or even bussing plates a couple of the women had left at the table. They were on vacation and paying a lot of money to be here, but so was she. It didn't seem to matter—she just stepped up and did what needed to be done.

Not a single one of the women who'd been to Feral Passions had been anything like her. He hoped like hell he hadn't scared her off, telling her about his relationship with Brad. They'd begun as friends and the friendship had grown. It wasn't uncommon among the shifters—they lived for a long time, and if they weren't mated it was good to have someone to love.

But if Cain and Brad mated Cherry, she'd live just as long. That was another thing he hated springing on her—as if turning furry weren't enough.

"C'mon." He handed her a bottle of water and grabbed one for himself and then slipped a light daypack over his shoulder. He liked to carry treats out for the mama wolf, and he'd packed a few necessities for himself. Just in case. The den wasn't far, but the day had turned warm. The creek near the den had a pool that was deep enough to cool off in, but that would require getting Cherry naked.

Nothing like setting goals, right? He grabbed her hand and led her into the woods.

She wasn't used to holding hands with any man, especially one like Cain. He was so overwhelmingly masculine. She found herself thinking of the books her sister and Steph were reading. Cain had to be an alpha, more so than Brad. Both were powerful, sexual men, but there was something ruthless about Cain—ruthless and earthy. Brad was sexy, but Cain wore his sensuality like a cloak, an almost visible aura that made her fingers itch to touch him.

But something about being held by a man like Cain had changed her. Over the past couple of days she'd quit obsessing about her weight, about how she compared to the other women, how she looked to the men in her life. Was it because she needed the validation of a couple of good-looking guys paying attention to her? She hoped that wasn't the only reason.

She'd like to think it was something more, something inside her that was suddenly, for whatever reason, breaking free, but holding hands with Cain had her wondering what her life would be like when she got back to San Francisco. Would she be taking any of this newfound confidence with her?

He led her down a trail that followed the meandering creek north from the lodge. They hadn't gone very far—and she'd made it over the fallen tree without help—when Cain paused just ahead of her.

"Shhh . . . See that fallen tree?" He pointed to a large pine that had toppled from a rise where high water had undercut the bank. The roots were sticking out of the ground and the trunk went entirely across the creek. Up at the top of the bank, a large boulder rested against the upthrust roots and Cherry saw what appeared to be a well-traveled trail down the bank and between the boulder and the trunk. She nodded and clutched Cain's hand even tighter.

"I'm going to go first and see how she's doing. I'll whistle if it's safe for you to come. Just follow the trail the same way I do." He reached into his daypack and pulled out a plastic bag. "I brought some hamburger. Bring it with you and I imagine she'll be a lot less nervous."

Cain worked his way close to the den and then disappeared beneath the fallen tree. A couple of minutes later, he whistled. Cherry followed the same trail and paused at the opening to the den. It was larger than she'd expected, part of it probably dug out by the wolf using a natural little cave created by the boulder, the roots from the fallen tree, and the rocky bank behind them.

Cherry heard Cain talking softly to the wolf, and then he was talking to Cherry. She followed his instructions and crawled under the tree. It was deeply shadowed but light enough to see Cain sitting with his back against the boulder and his pack on the ground beside him. She smelled a musty odor the deeper she went inside. It wasn't unpleasant and made her think of puppies. The wolf was about six feet back, curled against the rocky bank.

She growled when she saw Cherry.

Cherry shot a quick glance at Cain. "She doesn't look happy to see me."

"Toss her a little ball of the hamburger. Try and get it close—she's nursing the pups right now, so she's feeling protective."

Cherry did as Cain instructed and managed to drop the meat within a couple inches of the wolf's snout. She sniffed it and snapped it up. Her ears came up and she studied Cherry with more interest. Before long Cherry had emptied the bag of meat and the wolf had finished every bite. Then she turned to lick her pups, totally ignoring the humans in her den.

They stayed for almost half an hour while the mother wolf slept with her pups curled up in the curve of her body before Cain pointed toward the opening and they finally crawled out with Cherry in the lead. Once they were outside, Cain led her over to the creek where a deep pool of water had formed behind a natural stone dam. They sat on a flat rock in the sunlight, but it wasn't long before Cain pulled his moccasins off, pushed the legs of his sweatpants up, and dangled his feet in the water.

Cherry slipped off her sandals and did the same thing. "That feels so good. It's warmer than I expected."

"It stays dammed up behind the rocks long enough for the sun to warm the water. This is one of my favorite swimming holes. It's off-limits to guests because of the den. We don't want to spook the mother, but she's fine with me and a few of the other guys. She thinks Evan is her pack mate, because he's the one who raised her when she was brought to us. They bonded."

"Lucky Evan." She turned and looked at Cain. "How come you're the one checking on her? Shouldn't he be doing that?"

Cain shook his head. "No, because she was growing too familiar with him. Even though this is a preserve, we want them to retain their wild nature."

She snorted. "Yeah, like feeding her hamburger is enforcing that, right?"

He bumped shoulders with her. "Well, yeah. That sort of breaks the rules, but I wanted her to accept you. Let's just keep that our secret, okay?"

"I can do that. I really appreciate your bringing me here to see them."

"I'm glad. I get in there and lose track of time. It's so cool to watch her with her babies."

"I still can't believe I got that close to her."

"She's lived most of her life here on the preserve. Her mother and one of her siblings were killed—hit by a car when the pups were about eight to ten weeks old. The guy who hit them felt terrible, but he was able to catch the surviving pup and she was brought to us. Evan hand raised her until she was ready to hunt on her own. Hence, the bonding."

Cherry studied his profile for a moment. Strong with a tough edge and yet so tender with creatures who needed him. She found the two sides of Cain fascinating. "Your lives are so different here from what I'm used to. Different, but beautiful, too." Cherry stared at the water flowing around her feet. Awareness of the man beside her pulsed like a living thing, along with the sense that she was being shown a life totally foreign to the only one she knew. It wasn't at all frightening—she saw this as an amazing adventure, an exciting addendum to her otherwise mundane existence.

It was also wildly arousing. Sitting here dangling her feet in the creek after such an amazing experience, close beside a man she fully intended to have sex with before the week ended had her nipples tightly pressed against her bra and the sensitive tissues between her legs suddenly feeling swollen and wet. She turned and caught Cain staring at her. His jaw clenched, his nostrils flared. She frowned. What was—

"I need to cool off. I'm going in." Cain stood, ripped his T-shirt over his head, and shoved his pants down. Why she'd imagined him wearing underwear, much less, a swimsuit, was beyond her, but he was gloriously naked under his sweats and absolutely beautiful.

He was also quite obviously aroused. Had he somehow picked up her scent? She'd been almost certain the wolves could scent her, but Cain?

Trying to be flip, knowing she was blushing ten shades

of red, Cherry gestured at his huge erection, almost at eye level. "Is that for me?"

"Could be, sweet Cherry. You only have to say the word."

Good lord, but the man's smile was deadly. Even so, her eyes had to be as big as saucers.

It took Cherry a minute to find her voice. "You look awfully hot." She winked. "I think you need to cool off a bit, Cain." She stuck her hand in the creek and splashed him.

His eyes narrowed, he retaliated, and the battle was on. At some point she lost her shirt and then her bra. Before long, her clothes were drying on the flat rock and she was naked in the pool, in water deep enough to cover her breasts but so crystal clear it hid absolutely nothing. Cain stared at her with enough heat in his eyes to warm the entire creek— either that or the heat coming off her body was having the same effect.

They both stopped at the same moment. Cherry had never, not once in her life, been so aware of a man—the awareness had been there since she'd first met him, but something about the current circumstances had ramped up the arousal quotient way beyond anything she'd ever experienced.

Probably the fact that he was beautifully built, stark naked, and had a raging hard-on aimed directly at her helped, but along with the heat was the power, the physically intimidating strength of the man—strength she didn't fear in the least. He wanted her. She knew without any doubt he would never, ever hurt her.

She'd heard the phrase "smoldering gaze." Cain's had her slowly but surely going up in flames. She'd fantasized in vivid dreams, wondered what it would be like, to be the focus of that kind of arousal, to be desired by a man with such intensity. This was her chance, wasn't it?

It would only take a single step and everything between them could change. Would change, because she knew she would be a different woman after sex with Cain. She wouldn't call it making love. She couldn't call it anything but sex, but she wanted it just the same. Wanted it so damned much.

"Cherry?" Cain's voice was so deep she knew what she heard was the result of desire thrumming in his veins—the same desire that sizzled in hers.

She smiled and, for the first time in her life, felt powerful. "Cain?" She took a step toward him, not the least bit intimidated.

He held up his hand, as if reaching for her. His fingers trembled. "I don't want you to think that I planned this, but I have protection in my pack. Of course"—he shrugged and gave her a disarming smile—"I want you, obviously." He glanced down at himself, his erection easily visible in the clear water, "But only if you feel the same way."

"Will you kiss me?" She couldn't believe that was her voice, that those were her words. Her desires—and she was actually putting voice to them.

Cain stepped closer, moved into her space, and she swore the heat off his body was even hotter.

"I was actually planning on that, regardless." He slipped one hand around her waist and pulled her tightly against him. He was tall—at least six two—and his cock rested against her stomach. The wet hair on his chest was a slick and springy abrasion against her breasts. The same coarse hair on his thighs tickled her legs, and the heat from his shaft branded her belly. He pulled her close, lifted her against him. She stared into his eyes as his lips came down on hers.

Green eyes, as green as the pines in the forest, flecks of blue and gold this close, and then his mouth was on hers, his lips pressing, his tongue testing the seam between her lips until she opened to him. It was a vacation fling, a chance meeting with a guy who made her so damned hot; it was nothing, and everything, and her body went liquid in his arms.

He gripped her buttocks with his big hands and lifted her higher. She tightened her grasp on his shoulders and wrapped her legs around him, holding him close, preternaturally aware of the hot length of his cock resting between her legs, so hot that the water in the pool was suddenly icy in contrast.

She clutched his shoulders; their mouths sealed, their tongues twisted and explored until she finally broke away only long enough to breathe, long enough for Cain to whisper, "Condom," in a ragged voice.

He carried her to the shore and, still holding her with one arm, reached for his pack, dug through the thing one-handed, and pulled out a foil packet.

CHAPTER 12

She'd never had sex with a guy wearing protection. She'd had sex once in her life and not again, not since she was an eighteen-year-old virgin and the guy she thought loved her took what he wanted and then publicly humiliated her. Memories flashed into her mind, memories she'd never been able to bury, but Cain's hold on her tightened and he paused, holding her close, gazing into her eyes with an expression of care and concern.

"Cherry? Are you afraid? We don't have to do this."

"No, I'm not," she said, holding him close. "Yes. We do."

He turned and set her on the rock at the edge of the pool. "We don't, sweetheart. Not if it makes you uncomfortable."

"Cain, I'm going to be totally honest with you." He had no idea how hard it was for her to tell him this, but she wanted him to know why she had so many hang-ups, why she was such a freak. "I'm twenty-eight years old and I've had sex once. Just once, with a guy I thought loved me. He didn't. To him I was a joke and he made a point of letting everyone know how horrible I was in bed—except it wasn't in bed. It was the backseat of his car." Her voice broke, and it took everything in her to finish what she needed to say.

"That's my only memory of sex with anyone." She couldn't stop the tears. She hadn't wanted to dump this on Cain, but he needed to know what kind of basket case he was dealing with. "I want a good memory. I think that can be you. I hope it's you. Please?"

"Ah, Cheraza, my sweet Cherry. Tomorrow you give me the bastard's name and address and I will personally take him out." He smiled at her. "I can ensure a long and painful death."

She wiped her eyes with the back of her hand and laughed. Actually laughed, and it felt so damned good. "Thank you. I may take you up on that. Now, I really want to get back to what we were doing."

"So do I." His laughter was ragged, that of a man on the edge. "You have no idea."

He sheathed himself and leaned over her. It was shallower here by the edge, and he stood between her legs in water that reached his hips. Her legs were in the water, and he laid her down so that her back pressed against the smooth surface of sun-warmed granite. There were a few fluffy clouds floating by overhead, and birds flitted about the trees along the creek. A hawk screeched in the distance, water rushed into the pond, splashing over rocks and fallen trees, and Cain was there, leaning over her, kissing her, and then sliding lower, using his hands to plump her breasts, sucking first one nipple and then the other, and it felt so good she moaned. Actually moaned, lying on a sun-warmed rock in the woods with cool water up to her thighs and a gorgeous man between her legs.

She couldn't believe this was happening to her, until Cain moved lower and put his mouth between her thighs.

She gasped, sucked in a breath, and tangled her fingers in his long hair. He licked and sucked, twirling his tongue between her labia and then circling her clit, teasing her until she was ready to scream.

She whimpered and Cain raised his head. "Ready, Cheraza? It's been a long time for you, sweetheart. I want to be sure you're ready. I don't want to hurt you."

She let out a huff of breath she hadn't realized she'd been holding, raised her head, and glared at him. "The only one who's going to be hurt is you if you don't get busy and finish what you started."

"Yes, ma'am!" He ran his tongue between her folds once again and then slid up over her. The thick crown of his penis pressed between her legs, but he rested there, not pushing forward, just holding himself at her entrance. "You're sure, Cheraza? I want you to be sure, because I have a feeling that once we do this, I won't let you go."

He sounded so serious, his voice, his words, pulled her out of the sexual haze holding her almost immobile.

She opened her eyes and he was right there, his mouth so close, his gaze intense. "I don't think I've ever wanted anything more, Cain. I don't want to beg, but I will. Now, please?"

"Yes." His voice was rough with passion. His eyes held hers with laser focus, and he cupped her face in his hands. "This isn't going to be just sex, Cheraza. You had sex with that other guy. Not with me. We are making love. A beginning, okay? Will you think of this as a beginning?"

He didn't force an answer. Instead, he clasped her shoulders and his gaze never left her face as he surged forward. She was so wet, so ready, yet he entered her just enough to ensure he was going to fit. She felt the stretch and burn and remembered what it had been like so many years ago. Pain when the guy forced himself inside without preparing her for his entry, and while he was much smaller than Cain, he'd hurt her, and she'd bled.

Cain was so careful, taking it slowly, in a bit and then out, then in a little deeper. By the time he'd buried himself completely inside, they were both panting with the effort, with the pure sensation of connection.

He'd been right. This was a beginning. Cherry wasn't sure where it would lead. In the back of her mind, somehow she knew that what they did now was more than Cain making love to her. She felt Brad here as well, not between them, but part of them. The next time they came together, would he be with them? She wrapped her arms around Cain and held him close to her while he rested, regaining control, giving her time to fully accommodate his size.

She gazed up at him, at the strain etched in his features, the feral intensity in his eyes, and accepted that while she hardly knew him, she felt so safe, so entirely in sync with him, there was no fear. No hesitation. "When we do this again," she said, "Brad will be with us?"

Cain's smile changed everything about him. He was handsome and intense, a little scruffy with his long hair and clipped beard, but when he smiled this openly she felt as if he'd given her a gift, a sense of the man behind the laughter. It hit her then, a feeling so powerful it left her light-headed—she could love this man.

She could love Brad, as well.

She tilted her hips and, with that simple lift, invited Cain deeper.

"Thank you," he said. Then he laughed, and he began to move. She caught his rhythm and their bodies seemed to flow, one into the other. Together they were flawless and she reveled in that amazing synchronization, the way they fit so well together, the way each seemed to know exactly what the other needed.

She could do this forever—at least that's what she thought—until he tilted his hips just a bit and managed to find some magic spot deep inside, a part of her that was obviously the seat of all pleasure, because what had been a lovely, almost leisurely sensual journey had suddenly become a race, one that Cain started and Cherry knew she had to finish. Sensations rippled from her clit to her breasts and back again. Her toes began to tingle, her breath caught in her lungs, and suddenly, without enough warning at all, she was flying, her body arching beneath Cain's as the two of them crested that hill and flew together.

She cried out and birds in the trees overhead took flight. Cain shouted. A curse? A cry? She couldn't tell, only that he pulsed hard and deep inside her, his hands clenched her hips with enough force to bruise, and when he collapsed on top of her it took him a moment to realize he'd fallen hard enough to knock the air out of her.

Laughing, she shoved him to one side as he lifted himself away from her. He rolled to his back, lying beside her on the rock, laughing and gasping for air. It took him a few minutes to catch his breath, and when he did he turned his head until his face was inches from hers.

"Wow."

She grinned at him. "That's all you're going to say? 'Wow'?"

He took a couple of breaths. "Hell and holy shit, woman. What do you expect? Wow."

She sighed dramatically, in spite of the fact that her inner muscles were still clenching in the aftermath of a most amazing climax. "I guess I expected more eloquence. I mean, that was pretty spectacular, you know? Or is it always that way?"

The smile on his face disappeared. "It's never been that way, Cheraza. Not ever for me. I hope you realize, I am not letting you go."

He rolled over and reached for another condom. He was still hard.

Over the course of the afternoon, she lost track of how many times they made love, though the unfiltered thought in her head was that they'd probably still be fucking like bunnies if Cain hadn't run out of condoms.

Later, lying on the sun-warmed granite, Cherry noticed shadows beginning to creep across their sunny spot. She had no idea how long they'd been out here, but the day was passing and they'd have to get up and get dressed at some point.

Cain rolled to one side and propped his chin on his elbow. "Cheraza? When you asked me if Brad and I were gay a little while ago . . ."

She couldn't have kept a serious expression on her face for anything. "I think you've convinced me you like women, Cain. I may never walk again."

He smiled at her, white teeth against tan skin, lips slightly swollen from kissing. She touched her mouth and wondered if—

"The thing is"—he interrupted her thought with a smile and the gentle stroke of his fingertip along the line of her jaw—"we don't want women, plural." He gazed at her so intently, so passionately, her heart bolted. It pounded in her chest, thundered in her ears.

"You see, Cheraza, our dream has always been to find one woman, a very unique woman we can both love. One who will love us." He took her hand and played with her fingers. She was almost preternaturally aware of the strength in his hands—hands now intimately familiar with her body.

She looked at their joined hands, thinking of what he'd just said.

When she raised her head, he was gazing fiercely into her eyes, the moment so powerful that she wrapped her fingers tightly around his and held on.

"That is," he said, speaking so softly she could barely hear him, "until we met you. It's too soon to know if what we feel is love, and we have no idea how you feel about us, but what I'm trying to say . . ." He dropped his gaze, slowly shaking his head. "And obviously, not doing it very well . . ." He looked at her once again. "Is that we'd like to explore a relationship with you. Not just a vacation fling while you're here, but beyond this week. We've talked about you. A lot." He grinned then, a huge smile that lit up his face. "We want to spend more time together, exploring . . ." He let out a deep breath. "Everything."

She opened her mouth, realized she had no idea what to say, and shut it just as Cain's finger touched her lips. Shaking his head, he said, "No. Don't say anything now. I'm unfair to throw this at you so quickly, and for that I apologize, but one week is such a short time. Think about it. About us. Will you do that?"

She'd certainly not expected anything like this. Even a few days ago, such a suggestion would have had her running far and fast the minute he'd said what he and Brad were contemplating. Except hadn't she already been thinking of just this? She was curious enough to agree with Cain, to actually consider pursuing whatever it was he suggested.

Could she really be the right woman for two strong men such as Cain and Brad? Could she handle the convoluted ties that had to be part of a long-term ménage? It would entail so much change beyond the relationship. If they were involved, she'd have to move up here and live in the middle of nowhere, and what of her job? She really loved what she did and she could do it from anywhere, but they didn't even have cell service here, not to mention high-speed Internet, and—

She smiled at Cain. She was getting way too far ahead of herself. She could worry about Internet service later. Maybe she should be worrying about tonight . . . or just looking forward to it. "You don't need to apologize. I think I'd like to know more, maybe when Brad gets back," she said. When Cain's eyes went wide, she knew he wasn't expecting her answer. Everyone had her pegged as such a prude, but she wasn't. Not at all. She was just cautious. She had every reason to be.

"Really? You don't think we're crazy?"

"Well, I didn't say that." She gave him a cheeky grin and he wrapped his palm around her neck and pulled her close for a long, deep kiss.

If her lips hadn't been swollen before, they certainly would be now.

The walk back to the lodge only took a few minutes—not nearly long enough for Cherry to process everything that had happened today. She probably should have been sore, but she felt fantastic. Cain had been an ideal lover—thoughtful and sincere, teasing and funny—and his conversational subject matter after their marathon sex had certainly been fascinating.

Her head was still spinning, but in surprisingly great directions.

They passed by the pool where the three women from L.A. were hanging out with four men and a couple of wolves she didn't recognize. There was no sign of Brad or Trak, though she saw a large wolf lying on the deck in the shade. As she got closer, she recognized it as the one she'd decided—if these men actually were werewolves—was Evan.

A quick glance around the premises confirmed that Evan the man was nowhere in sight. Significant or merely coincidence? She glanced down at their hands—hers tightly clasped in Cain's—and wondered if she was merely losing her mind or if, at some point, Cain and Brad would tell her that no, she was just fine.

They were the ones with the issues. Furry issues.

And these were the same men who wanted her as the feminine third of their ménage?

She had to fight to keep from laughing. She really was losing her mind, but going off the deep end shouldn't feel this glorious, should it?

If she hadn't been such a huge fan of paranormal romances, hadn't steeped herself in the lore surrounding werewolves and the rules that governed their nature—and for every book she read there was a different set of rules—she'd never be wondering such an outrageous thing.

And if she was a truly intelligent woman and her suspicions were confirmed, would she actually be considering what Cain had suggested? Would an intelligent woman, with little more than suspicions that men were capable of changing into wolves, accept a proposal to become the mate of not just one, but two of them? *Hell, yes.* That decision was easy enough to reach. She was still smiling when they reached her cabin. Cain paused at the top step and rested his hands on her shoulders. "I don't want to leave you, but I have to go work on dinner, and you probably want a nap."

She nodded. A shower wouldn't sound bad, either. They'd gone back into the pond for a final dip after using the last condom, but she wanted a chance to wash her hair, and time alone to think about what she and Cain had done. What he'd proposed. "I'll meet you at the lodge for dinner, okay?"

"I'll be there. I'm cooking tonight." He rested his chin on top of her head as he held her close. "I'll warn you ahead of time, I'm not nearly as good a cook as Trak or Brad, but we all like to take a turn. Tonight you suffer through my feeble attempts."

"Oh, really?" She leaned back in his embrace. "And what are you making?"

"It's actually already made, thank goodness, because we're a lot later getting back than I expected. I just need to put it in the oven. Veggie lasagna, green salad, and garlic

French bread. Trak's got more of that good red wine his buddy makes, and I'll figure out something for dessert."

"Sounds yummy. I'll see you around six." She didn't even think about her next move—just went up on her toes and kissed him. She'd never, not once in her entire life, initiated a kiss with a man. What if that was a mistake?

Obviously not. He pulled her into his arms and kissed her breathless. As he turned to go, he ran his fingers along her cheek. "Beautiful," he said. Then he winked and left.

Cherry stood there on the porch, watching until he disappeared into the forest.

CHAPTER 13

After she showered, Cherry stared at the bed for a few seconds too long, finally gave in, and lay down. The next thing she knew, she heard someone at her door. A four-legged someone, from the soft whine and scratch of claws against the wood.

Cherry stretched carefully, well aware of an aching tenderness between her legs, a scrape on her shoulder where she'd rubbed a bit too much against a rough spot on the granite, and the sense that she'd not been exaggerating when she'd told herself that making love with Cain would change her life.

In a very good way—at least so far—and didn't that suck, that the best sex in the world came with the caveat that it could all be so much fairy dust.

Would she ever be able to put her *first time* behind her?

Whoever was on her front porch whined and scratched at the door once again.

Cherry had fallen asleep wrapped in her damp towel, so she tightened it around herself and glanced at the clock to make sure she hadn't slept through dinner. She'd only been lying down for half an hour, which meant she still had time to sleep another hour, and damn, but she felt like she needed every minute. Yawning, she went to the door to see who was out there. She wasn't surprised at the beautiful dark wolf sitting on her porch, black fur tinged with russet, eyes the color of bittersweet chocolate.

Brad's eyes. She almost said she was glad he'd gotten back from town, but she wasn't ready to go there. Not yet. Obviously, unless her imagination truly had taken her well beyond rational thinking and into the world of the truly committable, the wolves were keeping their secret for a good reason, and she really didn't want to blow it for them.

Besides, the fantasy was too much fun.

Instead, she stepped back and invited him in. "You can stay," she said. "But I just laid down for a nap, so you have to be quiet and let me sleep. I've had a really busy afternoon."

She wasn't sure, but if this really was Brad she imagined Cain had told him what they'd done. Since he'd also suggested she'd be with both men tonight, she didn't feel too guilty about making love with Cain, though Brad was the one who'd kissed her first.

Never in her wildest dreams had she imagined issues with too many men. She almost laughed, but then she caught herself just in time.

She didn't want to give herself away. Not yet.

She wasn't sure what made her drop the towel, but she let it fall to the floor and lay down on the bed, pulling a soft afghan up over herself. The wolf stared at her and whined. She patted the spread beside her and he jumped lightly up on the bed and then stepped over her to the other side. The springs creaked from his weight, but he lay down close to her. Wrapped in the multi-colored throw, Cherry snuggled against his warm back and drifted away.

An hour later, rested and dressed in one of her comfortable long dresses, Cherry followed the dark wolf back to the lodge. It was almost six and the valley was already in shadow. The tips of the craggy peaks on the eastern side of the valley shimmered in sunlight as the sun dipped below the hills on the west. She paused in front of the lodge and just stared— it was all so beautiful, and the towering peaks gave the resort a true sense of isolation.

She'd Googled it when Christa first sent her the link, and it wasn't all that far from the nearest town, if you could drive in a straight line. Which, of course, you couldn't, but there was such a powerful sense they were totally cut off from civilization, that this little community was entirely separate from the rest of the world.

If her suspicions were correct, there was an excellent reason for the men she'd met so far settling here, for wanting that isolation, if they really were shapeshifters. And funny, wasn't it, that she could think of them as shapeshifters much more easily than actually calling them werewolves! Amazing, how the human mind justified things. She wondered how long they'd owned this land, how long they'd been living in the backwoods of away and beyond, because it really did feel as if she and the other women had stepped into a totally different dimension, apart from the real world.

It wasn't as if the guys were totally isolated, though. Brad had studied architecture and environmental design and said he'd gotten his architectural engineering degree from a university in Southern California. She didn't know about Cain's education, though he spoke like a well-educated man. He'd told her he moved here from Idaho a few years ago. Trak was one of the owners of Feral Passions and also owned Growl, the bar the women had passed on the way in.

She wasn't sure about the other guys, though some of them were obviously employed by the resort. She'd seen Evan doing maintenance and some of the housekeeping, Wils and Ronan had led their hike, and the preserve probably required a certain amount of labor to keep it running.

But that wasn't her business, and she was on vacation. She had to shut that analytical part of her mind off if she was going to continue to enjoy herself. She glanced around, surprised to see that the wolf had disappeared. Probably got bored while she stood here woolgathering.

"Hey, Cherry. I thought I saw you out here."

She glanced up and smiled at Brad. At least now she knew where the wolf had gone. "Hi. How was the trip to town?"

"Long. I could go the rest of my life without shopping." He laughed as he reached for her and pulled her into a quick hug.

She just wished he hadn't made it such a quick kiss.

"C'mon," he said, tugging her arm. "Cain's got dinner on and you're the only one we're missing."

"Veggie lasagna?" She let Brad drag her up the steps, enjoying the tight clasp of his hand holding hers, the way his dark eyes twinkled as if he laughed at some secret joke.

How would he react if she told him she knew his secret? That thought alone had her smiling along with him as if she were totally in on the joke.

But wouldn't she feel stupid if she was wrong?

Christa waved as Cherry and Brad stepped through the door. The other women sat at the big table—Fred, Suni, and Darnell on one side, Steph and Christa on the other. "We saved you a spot," she said, patting the bench seat next to her. "Where have you been all afternoon?"

Damn. She should have been expecting that question, shouldn't she? "Tell you in a minute. I want to grab a plate first."

She turned away and hoped they didn't see her blush, but Brad certainly noticed. He smiled and raised an eyebrow. Then he leaned close, gave her a quick kiss, and walked over to the bar as Cherry stifled a growl and went to the buffet table. She glanced toward the pass-through window. Cain waved to her from the kitchen. He wore a white chef's apron and had a hat on with his dark blond hair tied back into a stubby ponytail. She thought he looked way too cute for words and not nearly as intimidating as she knew he could be, naked and aroused in a clear mountain pool, but even the bad boy had to follow rules in the kitchen, it appeared. She smiled, waved, and then turned away, fully aware she'd probably just gone another shade darker.

But it wasn't embarrassment causing her skin to flush. Not this time. Thinking about Cain naked, about making love with him, had her aroused all over again.

She hoped his nose wasn't good enough to scent her in the crowd.

Back at the table with her lasagna, salad, and French bread, Cherry sat beside Christa. The three from L.A. were in the midst of a heated discussion over a movie that had just been released, one that Darnell had worked on and Suni hated. Fred appeared to be playing devil's advocate.

At least that was better than her usual litany of complaints. Fred was not a happy guest, though Cherry wondered if she might be the type who complained about everything.

Christa and Steph listened avidly, which gave Cherry time to eat. The lasagna was delicious, as was the salad, and she'd cleaned her plate and was mopping up sauce with the French bread when it hit her that she'd been eating like an absolute pig the past few days they'd been here and enjoying every bite.

This was the first time she'd thought about her weight or how many calories she was eating since Cain had tempted her with the chocolate and port. She'd fallen hard and fast, giving in to temptation, and she hadn't looked back.

She didn't realize she was grinning, thinking about the joys of falling, until Christa called her on it.

"What's so funny? You look like you're cracking up inside."

Cherry set her last bite of bread on the plate and smiled at her sister. "Well, I'm certainly not crying on the inside. Just thinking about this afternoon." Which was the truth, wasn't it? Though she wasn't ready to dish, at least not with the three from L.A. suddenly watching her with more than a bit of interest.

"What'd you do?"

"Cain took me to see the wolf pups. They're adorable."

Darnell focused on Cherry. "Wow! Where are they?"

Shaking her head, Cherry said, "Not far, though the area is off-limits. Cain was headed out to check on them and let me come, but the mother is really shy, not at all friendly like the males hanging around the lodge, and you have to crawl inside the den. Claustrophobia, anyone?"

She gave an exaggerated shudder. "Cain went first and I followed him in, but believe me, I was checking for creepy-crawlies the entire time." Which wasn't at all true, but she honestly didn't want to encourage any of them to try to find the den.

"Well," Steph said, "you can count me out. I don't like small places or spiders."

"Me, either," Darnell said. "Especially the spiders."

"For me, it's snakes." Suni hugged herself, and the conversation took off.

Cherry grabbed her plate and carried it over to the bar to save anyone having to clear her stuff from the table. Christa and Steph followed suit and then went out the front door. Cherry followed them. "What?" She poked her sister's arm. "Not waiting for dessert?"

"It's later. They're going to have a campfire and we're having s'mores."

Steph gave an exaggerated moan. "Marshmallows, graham crackers, and gourmet dark chocolate." Fluttering her eyelashes, she added, "Be still, my heart."

"That sounds like fun." Cherry walked over and flopped down on a chair at one of the small tables. Of course, she really didn't know. During the summers when Christa and Steph went off to summer camp, Cherry's parents had made sure she attended fat camp. S'mores were most definitely not on the menu, but a weeklong course of intimidation and shame had been enough to ruin her appetite.

"Good." Christa sat next to her. "Now that we have that

out of the way, where were you all afternoon? We walked over to your cabin to return some of your books, and you were gone."

"I didn't see them there. Did you leave them?"

"No, and you're avoiding the question." Steph took a seat across from Cherry.

Surprisingly, Cherry didn't blush, but that was probably because she wasn't the least bit embarrassed over how she'd spent the afternoon. "I told you, I went with Cain to see the pups."

"For three hours?"

Three hours? How did they know she'd been gone that long? "I don't know how long I was gone, actually. Why? Did I miss something?"

"We walked over at one, again at two, and then stopped by just before three." Christa had a look of grim determination that was a bit unsettling.

"I was with Cain." Frowning, Cherry glanced from Christa to Steph and then back at her sister. "Why are you so concerned with where I was all afternoon? We went to see the pups and spent about an hour watching them, and then we cooled off in the creek, and had wild and crazy sex the rest of the afternoon. I was home by a little after three and took a shower and a nap."

She glanced from Christa to Steph and then back at her sister. Both of them had their mouths hanging open. Christa said, "Okay, Cherry. Would you repeat that, please?"

She almost laughed. Suddenly she was enjoying this conversation a lot more. "Uhm, you mean the part about watching the pups, the shower, the nap—"

Steph whispered with her jaw clenched and lips not

moving. "The wild and crazy sex part." She rolled her eyes and glared at Christa. "What is with your sister?"

Cherry flopped her head down on her folded arms and giggled until her sides ached. When she finally raised her head, Christa was staring at her.

"I thought you liked Brad? Why were you having sex with Cain?"

Her poor sister looked honestly perplexed, but Cherry didn't feel comfortable discussing Cain's and Brad's interest in her, or their personal relationship, so she shrugged. "Brad wasn't there and Cain was. And he's really hot and I am on vacation."

Steph threw her hands in the air. "But you never do that sort of thing. Not ever!"

"Well, Steph, maybe it's time I did." Cherry said it gently, but this was getting a bit old. She was older than both of them and maybe she was less experienced, but she wasn't an idiot. "Look, I'm having a wonderful time that will end in a few more days when I have to go back to the real world. Right now I'm enjoying the fantasy, okay? I don't think I should have to explain myself to anyone, especially when I'm on vacation, so please, stop worrying about me and just enjoy yourselves."

Christa took her hand. "I'm sorry, Cherry, and you're right. It's just . . ." She took a deep breath. "I had just turned fifteen when that asshole uploaded those horrible pictures of you all over the Internet, and I've never forgotten the hell you went through. I almost lost you. I don't ever want anything like that to happen again."

Cherry squeezed her sister's hand. "At least that's not a problem here—no Internet. I trust Cain, and I trust Brad, too. We've talked, I've gotten to know them, probably better than either of you know Ronan or Wils, and I'm having more fun than I've ever had in my life. Stop worrying. When the week ends, I go back to the day job, but with more than my share of incredible memories. I have both of you to thank for this amazing experience, so please, don't waste your vacation time worrying about me."

She understood Cissy's concern—her little sister had been as traumatized as Cherry by that bastard's actions and she'd had to deal with the fallout all through high school, but it was time for both of them to heal and move past it. Cherry was tired of feeling like a victim and even more fed up with acting like one. She wasn't about to waste any of this unbelievable week worrying. Not about anything.

CHAPTER 14

They'd all gathered on the deck as the sun went down—
Ronan and Wils with Christa and Steph, Trak with Suni and
Fred. Darnell sat in Evan's lap sharing a Long Island Iced
Tea that Brad had mixed for her and Evan had convinced
her was such a strong drink it really should be shared.

Cain and Brad had become Cherry's personal bookends,
one on either side of her, never intrusive, yet a sexy and
highly entertaining presence. The guys were relaxing this
evening while a couple of men she'd not met built a fire in
the pit near the swimming pool and got a good bed of coals
going.

"I hope you like s'mores." Brad had his arm around her
shoulders and squeezed.

"Doesn't everyone?"

She knew from the look in his eyes he'd easily caught her
noncommittal answer.

"Most everyone, but what about you?"

What was the point of lying? Shrugging, she said, "I
don't know. I've never tasted one."

His eyes went wide. "Cherry, every little kid's had s'mores."

She was really getting tired of being questioned over

everything. First her sister and sex and now Brad and s'mores. Of course, until this week she would have backed down and done anything at all not to make a scene, but she was learning that it felt good to stand up for herself, even if she might offend the person currently questioning her life.

Of course, she didn't mean to sound quite so antagonistic, but she'd missed out on so damned much growing up as the fat kid in the family. "Not every little kid's parents sent them off to fat camp when the other kids were eating s'mores at summer camp, so, no, Brad. I have never had a s'more."

Then she felt bad because he looked so sad at her answer.

He cupped her cheek in his warm palm and gently kissed her lips. "I'm sorry, Cherry," he said. "I really am, and I may be out of line, but your parents did a job on you. Little kids should be allowed to be just that—little kids. Some are fat, some are skinny, and they should grow up the way they're meant to be."

"Yeah, well a lot of little kids don't grow up with status-conscious parents concerned how their child might look while swimming at the club. My appearance was important to them and they worked really hard to make it important to me, too."

Then Christa chimed in, totally shocking her. "Yeah, Cherry, except I agree with Brad. Mom and Dad were totally wrong the way they badgered you about your weight. You got Dad's bones—he has a heavier frame and so do you. I've told you for years, you're not fat. You're bigger than me because I'm built like Mom and you take after Dad, so quit picking on Brad."

"Christa!" Cherry laughed, but she glared at her sister

and then put the evil eye on Brad, and Cain, too, even though he hadn't said a word. "Look, everyone, get over it. Whatever my body is, it is most definitely not skinny like you and Steph, or the other women here. I've tried to lose weight and it always comes right back, stops where I am now, and I'm okay with it."

"Well, you're eating s'mores tonight." Brad kissed her quiet.

"I agree you're eating s'mores, but you're not fat. You're sexy as hell." Cain leered at her, and then he leaned close and whispered in her ear, "I know what's under that slinky dress and she's all woman. I plan to get my hands on her later tonight."

Cherry blushed.

Brad whispered in her other ear. "So do I. Enjoy the s'mores. Cain and I are going to help you work the calories off later."

She was sure even the soles of her feet were red.

The s'mores were absolutely delicious. She ate three of them—one from Brad, another from Cain, and one she cooked all by herself.

Cherry stuck around with Brad and Cain after everyone else had gone to their respective cabins. She almost laughed when Steph hooked up with Wils and Christa with Ronan and the four of them took the trail that led to Christa's cabin. Cherry had made a point of not asking the details of their evenings, which she hoped might insulate her from giving out details of her night, though she was definitely curious to know if anything went on between Christa and Steph.

That would be a not-so-unexpected development. Cherry had had her suspicions, but it was Steph's and Christa's business to share, not hers to speculate. She was still grinning when Trak, Suni, and Fred took off and laughing hysterically when Evan tossed a giggling Darnell over his shoulder with a disgruntled laugh and carried her off to bed. To sleep, he said.

Darnell's Long Island Iced Tea had just about knocked her out. "I had no idea she was such a lightweight," he said. "If she asks for one tomorrow night, Brad, cut back on the booze."

Cherry watched Evan hauling Darnell back to her cabin and wondered if she should be worried. "Is Evan okay? I mean, she's definitely not sober. He wouldn't . . ."

She left the thought hanging.

"Darnell's safe with Evan. He's a truly gentle and honorable guy." Brad hugged Cherry close. "There's no one here we wouldn't trust with any guest who stays with us. Darnell will be fine. Of course, I'm only referring to her physical safety," he added, laughing. "No guarantees on how her head feels when she wakes up. Those drinks are potent, but she said she had to have it."

Cain bounded up the steps. He'd gone back to the pit to put dirt over the coals and make sure the fire was entirely out. "Actually, Evan told me he's planning to stay the night to make sure she's okay, that she didn't have enough alcohol to be sick. He'll keep an eye on her."

"Part of the Feral Passions full-service package?" Cherry shot Cain a quick grin.

He laughed. "No one beats our customer service. We can

handle any emergency, and our guests always leave satisfied."

"They do, eh? You can promise that? Absolute satisfaction, never a disappointed client?"

"Oh, yeah. For you, sweetheart, only the best." Cain slipped his arms around her waist. Brad paused as he passed behind her and hugged her from the back. She felt his lips nuzzling that sensitive spot behind her ear, Cain's beard tickling her jaw. Their powerful bodies were pure heat, blanketing her in bone, muscle, and warm, wonderful male, and all her synapses fired at once.

She didn't even try to hide the low, slow moan that escaped her lips. She was so ready for tonight. After her shower and nap, and then as she'd moved around more, the soreness from this afternoon had faded and now, with the campfire extinguished and the last of the guests departed, with her men blanketing her front and rear, her own fires were burning, the heat growing, her awareness of Brad and Cain and what the night promised expanding exponentially.

Brad slipped a tote bag over his shoulder and held her left hand and Cain grabbed her right as they walked across the parking lot to the trail that led to her cabin. They turned her loose along the narrow trail but kept her between them as they walked single file along the pathway. There was a slight breeze this evening and the fairy lights danced among the branches.

Cherry felt like dancing right along with them. When they reached her cabin, Cain held the door and she stepped inside. Both men followed her, and Brad pulled a chilled bottle of champagne out of his tote bag.

"What's that for?" Cherry reached into the cupboard and pulled out three champagne flutes. "What are we celebrating?"

"We're celebrating you, Cheraza." Cain pulled her into his arms for a kiss that lasted until Brad pulled the cork out of the bottle. The loud *pop* made her jump.

"Nervous, much?" She waved her fingers in front of her face, but it wasn't so much nerves as it was outright arousal. She wasn't certain she was quite ready to admit the truth—not to herself or either of the guys.

She wanted these men. Both of them, though she wasn't all that sure about the logistics. Two men at once? One at a time? And if so, in what order? Even she didn't know which of the two she wanted the most.

She wanted them both!

Brad poured champagne into each of the glasses. Cain held his glass up and stared at the bubbles for a moment. "To you, Ms. Cheraza DuBois. To new experiences—hopefully to be shared with the two of us."

Cherry was trying to wrap her brain around Cain's toast when Brad tapped the rim of his glass to hers.

"Cain told you we've been together for a long time," he said. "I don't now how much he said about our search for the perfect woman to complete what we've always felt was an incomplete triad. We have never met a woman before who fit so precisely the image we've always held on to and had hope for. Not until you. I hope you'll give us a chance."

She looked from one man to the other—both so different and yet so attractive. Brad was solid and muscular without an ounce of fat, his hair neatly trimmed and his beard little more than a dark shadow that merely outlined his strong jaw and emphasized the sexy curve of his lips. He looked the part of the successful young architect, and she could see him working in an office in the city, neatly attired in a suit or equally well dressed in chinos and a casual shirt.

Cain, though . . . she didn't know how to classify Cain. Scruffy where Brad was crisp and perfectly put together, Cain's long hair, short, thick beard, and sexy grin screamed bad boy and trouble. A lot of it was for show—he was a tenderhearted, caring guy who was gentle inside and out—but there was an edge to him, something dark and sort of dangerous lurking just beneath the surface. She had a feeling he wasn't someone you wanted on the other side in a fight.

It was so easy to imagine the two men together—so different on the outside, but inside, where it counted, both good, strong, honorable men.

And possibly both were wolves, but since she didn't know for sure and they'd not said a word about it, she wasn't even going there tonight. Tonight was her turn to be selfish—she wanted to experience sex with two men, but it couldn't be just any men. It had to be Brad and Cain, and it was going to happen now.

This time it was Brad setting candles around the interior of the cabin before turning out the lights. Cain set up his music—two small speakers and his iPod—but instead of wolves and night creatures, the room was filled with classical violin and cello. The sound was low, sexy, and slow.

Cain stepped up behind her, rested his hands on her shoulders, and whispered in her ear. "The massage worked really well last night. It relaxed you completely."

She nodded, shivering at the same time. No way in hell would she ever forget that massage.

Brad turned away from lighting the last candle and stood in front of her. "Cain and I thought we might try something different tonight. Since we want you naked for your massage—I mean, if we're going to do it right—it seemed only fair if we were naked, too. You okay with that?"

"Interesting." She tapped her forefinger against her cheek and honestly had no idea where this newfound confidence was coming from, but she liked it. A lot. "I had that same discussion with Steph and Christa. That it didn't seem fair, you guys fully dressed and me completely naked. The balance of power was out of sync, ya know?"

Brad nodded, as if this were the most serious discussion they could possibly be having. "I understand. You're right." He walked over to one of the chairs in the corner and kicked off his shoes, tugged his shirt over his head, and then unzipped his jeans. She was so busy admiring his beautiful chest that she almost missed the fact that he'd gone commando, at least for tonight. When he shoved his jeans down, first baring his taut butt and sleek, muscular legs before turning around, she saw him fully exposed for the first time.

She'd read a line in one of her books, where the heroine's mouth went dry when she saw the hero's package. Cherry could really use a tall glass of water about now. She had the champagne flute, at least, and downed the rest of her champagne in a single swallow.

Cain refilled her glass, and she drank that, too.

He leaned close and whispered, "He really is beautiful, isn't he?"

She nodded. Wasn't sure she could actually form words,

but this was Cain, and she'd already seen him naked. "How come you're still dressed?"

"You are, too."

She turned in his arms and rested her forearms on his shoulders. Right now, with a couple of glasses worth of champagne bubbles fizzing through her veins, she felt a lot braver than usual, even though she knew she hadn't had enough to feel it. Maybe this new confidence was going to hang around. "I realize I'm still dressed, but you keep telling me this is a full-service resort. Are you saying I need to undress myself? I assumed you and Brad would take care of that."

"You're right, sweet Cherry. I am remiss. It would be our pleasure. But first, may I?"

When she nodded, Cain ripped his shirt off over his head, kicked off his moccasins, and shoved his jeans to the floor in about twenty seconds.

She was biting back the giggles when she was once again sandwiched between two men—sans clothing. Brad scrunched the skirt of her dress in both hands and slowly pulled it up her thighs and over her body. She flashed on a sense of pure wanton sensuality—she felt so sexy; her body felt sexy. She'd never experienced such a powerful sense of herself as a desirable woman.

Of course, considering the two naked men, each of them sporting what appeared to be an almost painfully aroused . . . Why did she have such a difficult time saying "cock"? She read the word without a problem—it was used all the time in her books—but here she was faced with the real thing, and she couldn't say it.

Though the visual was giving her a better idea of what

she wanted to do as Brad peeled her lacy panties off, and Cain easily unhooked her bra. However, it took a great deal of cupping, squeezing, fondling—and a couple of licks—before he managed to take it off of her.

"Why don't you lie down on the bed, and we'll help you relax." Cain's smile was just too innocent for words. He had a hard time getting the word "relax" out without breaking into a grin.

"I have a better idea," she said. And while she'd never done this before, she'd certainly read about it often enough. With a small prayer that she not get it wrong, Cherry went to her knees between both guys, which put her right at eye level with those delicious-looking cocks of theirs. There. She actually thought the word and didn't faint.

She wrapped her fingers around both Brad and Cain and slowly stroked.

"Holy shit," Brad groaned, but Cain sucked in a breath and tangled his fingers in her hair.

She noticed neither man was circumcised, but it wasn't like she'd seen all that many naked men before Cain today and the occasional online shot of a naked guy. She found the sensation of touching a fully erect penis—and there was no doubt in her mind that these were about as big and hard as either guy could get—was absolutely exhilarating.

At least she hoped this was as big and hard as these things got.

The descriptions she'd read got it right; that "silk over steel" analogy nailed it, and so did the "velvety tip." She'd been so busy slowly stroking, she'd hardly noticed that the guys had both gone totally still. Glancing up, she caught two sets of eyes glazed with lust. She leaned close to Brad and licked the tip, and she was really glad she had a good hold on him, because his hips jerked forward.

"Tell me if I hurt you," she whispered. "I've never done this before."

"Trust me, Cherry." Cain hardly sounded like himself, his voice had gone so deep and rough. He cleared his throat. "You're doing really well."

She grinned up at Cain. "Thank you. If you have any suggestions . . . ?"

"No." Brad's voice sounded a bit strangled, too, and she remembered his faux pas the other night when he'd come in his shorts—of course, it was entirely forgivable, since it happened when he'd brought her to climax. Thinking of that had her paying closer attention, and that's when she noticed tiny drops of white fluid at the tips of each cock.

She was getting better. Cock. No, the world hadn't come to an end.

She leaned close and licked Cain's first, and then Brad's. Cain was saltier, Brad sweeter, but both tasted really good. She wondered how many calories there were in semen. Decided it didn't really matter. Sort of like s'mores—the taste balanced any calories.

Taste-wise? Brad and Cain? Sweet and salt. A perfect match.

CHAPTER 15

Cherry sat back on her heels. She really wanted to do this right, but for a first time, one guy at a time. If this worked out the way she hoped, she'd have a lifetime to practice on two at a time. Just the thought had her vaginal muscles clenching into a yearning knot between her legs.

She pointed at Cain. "You. Sit. You're next."

He grinned and saluted. And sat on the edge of the bed.

She knelt with her hands planted on Brad's hips. The drop at the tip of his cock had become a steady stream. She licked him, just, well . . . just because. "You can stand up or sit. Whatever you want."

"This . . ." He cleared his throat. "This is fine. Thank you."

"I like that. Polite." For some reason she'd slipped into the role she'd taken in graduate school when she was a teaching assistant. Then she'd known she was in charge of the classes she taught and she knew her stuff better than anyone else in the room. At least she let them think she did.

This was just the opposite. She didn't know anything about what she was doing except what she'd read—and once again she thanked those sexy romances—and what common sense told her. She'd have to let Brad teach her by leading her. She could do this—touching him had her even more aroused. She couldn't wait to take him in her mouth.

He still looked a little unsure, but then he and Cain had been planning on a massage, which meant she'd totally screwed up their plan, but that was a good thing. There really should be a balance of power, especially when there were two of them and only one of her.

They could do their massage later. They had all night. "I've never done this before, so please tell me what to do, anything you can think of. I won't mind, but I want to get this right. Look at it this way." And she glanced at Cain. "If you two are thinking long-term arrangement, you're going to want me doing what you like, just as I'm going to want you guys doing what I like. Does that work for you?"

"Oh, yeah." Brad tangled his fingers in her hair. "I'm all yours. Cain?"

Cain laughed. "Works for me. Besides, I'm getting off on watching you two. Live-action porn, but I find the actors a lot more appealing."

Cherry glanced over her shoulder. "You'd better. This is sensual, not pornographic. Pay attention." Then she wrapped her left fist around Brad's shaft and cupped his balls in her right. His whimper was the proof she needed. Obviously this was good.

She played with his balls for a moment. The wrinkled sac made a pretty good-sized handful. She'd never thought about how big balls were and honestly hadn't paid close attention to the details with Cain, but she loved the reaction she got from Brad as she gently squeezed and separated the orbs within his sac while slowly sliding her left hand up and down his shaft. More white fluid bubbled at the tip. She watched it for a moment and then licked up every drop. Definitely sweet. Then she opened her mouth and wrapped her lips around the velvety tip.

This time, she was the one groaning, especially when Cain knelt behind her and cupped her breasts in his palms. He straddled her legs with his knees, moving close enough that his chest pressed against her back and his thick shaft was riding between her thighs. She wanted him inside, but not now. Not yet. She forced herself to concentrate on Brad, which really wasn't that difficult, all things considered.

She'd always had an innate ability to focus, plus she was good at details. Brad seemed to appreciate that. He tangled his fingers in her hair and she sucked him deep inside her mouth, using her fist wrapped around his shaft to keep him from going too far. She wasn't ready to try swallowing his rather sizable cock—one step at a time.

He was long and thick and she circled the crown with the tip of her tongue, delving into the tiny slit at the tip before sucking all she could fit between her lips, pressing him hard up against the roof of her mouth with the flat of her tongue.

Brad's entire body trembled as she worked her tongue against the underside of his shaft, tracing the thick vein until she lost it beneath the folds of his retracted foreskin. She knew he must be really sensitive—that much she'd read about men who'd never been cut—and she was as careful as he seemed to need her to be.

But when he thrust his hips forward she sucked him harder and clasped her hands tightly against his muscular butt, holding his cock between her lips when he would have pulled away. Cain cupped her full breasts in the palms of his hands while he pulled and twisted her nipples between his fingertips. If she shifted her hips just right, the tip of his penis teased her clit, which made her work harder to bring Brad to climax.

They were three together, already working as a team for one another's pleasure, and she'd never imagined anything that could feel this good and be so much fun.

The music soared in the background, the fury of Vivaldi's "Storm" crashing into her consciousness, pulling her into the taste and the textures of the man she serviced, and yet there was nothing subservient about the act. She was in control, her mouth, her tongue, her hands—she was the one who was quickly bringing Brad to the brink.

Cain's softly murmured encouragement, the growing pressure of his thrusts between her legs, the sleek tip of his cock connecting with her clit on every drive until she realized she'd sucked Brad deeper than she'd thought she could. Her throat convulsed as she swallowed his length down rather than choke as he hit the back of her throat. He carefully eased out and then just as carefully moved forward, and again she took him deeper than she'd ever imagined.

Cain pulled away for a moment and then he was back, his erect cock covered in a condom, his thrusts now directed against Cherry's clit, but with the added protection came the knowledge that all she needed to do was let him know what she wanted.

She tilted her hips back and he sheathed himself within her, driving high and deep and bringing a gasp of pleasure from her lips. He held her right breast, pinching and teasing her nipple, but his left hand went low, over her thigh and between her legs where he timed the stroke of his fingers over her clit to his powerful thrusts between her legs.

They somehow moved in sync, the three of them, as Cherry took Brad ever closer to the edge. Her own climax hovered just out of reach, and she knew she was on the brink. Brad was losing his struggle to hold on. She felt the tension in his hips as he tried to pull out, but she held him close, sucking and licking until he finally gave in, gave up, gave it all to her.

"Cherry!"

His shout set off her own climax, her body clenching as the first sweet spurts of Brad's release hit her tongue, and she almost laughed with the joy of this moment. She, Cherry DuBois, resident misfit and horribly shy around men, was in the midst of a simultaneous climax with two incredible guys, and it was amazing.

Her body rippled with the release of tension, with the sparks of sensation from the sweet taste of Brad on her tongue, to Cain's short, sharp strokes as he joined them, collapsing against her back with a long, heartfelt groan.

Brad toppled over and landed on the bed. Cherry crawled up and over to lie beside him. Cain took a moment to dispose of the condom and then crawled over Brad and Cherry to take the other side. Once again Cherry was sandwiched between her men.

And they *were* her men. Smiling, because yes, she'd just officially claimed them.

Brad lay on his belly, practically comatose. Cain was on his back, still sucking air with each deep breath. Cherry snuggled between the two of them, all ready to do it all over again.

Plus, she still hadn't gotten her massage.

She licked her lips, tasting Brad. She'd not only sucked her first cock; she'd also swallowed. And she'd done it while another guy was taking her from behind while squeezing her boobs and then playing with her clit. The thought had her biting back an inappropriate case of the giggles. She knew if she ever started there'd be no stopping.

Instead, she lay there in her bed between two hot guys with a huge smile on her face. Never, not even after reading a really sexy romance where she'd imagined herself in the hero's arms, had she ever come close to dreaming anything remotely as awesome as this.

Or as much fun.

She must have dozed off, though she had no idea how much time had passed. Candlelight still flickered against the walls, and the classical music had segued from the wild rhythm playing earlier into a haunting, thoughtful tune.

Should she follow the musical lead to be thoughtful? Thinking of what they'd just done, she realized that no, she didn't want to dissect the way the two of them had made her feel. She'd felt glorious and so feminine, and she'd loved the way Cain had tied them all together when he'd entered her, had taken an act between Cherry and Brad and turned it into something uniquely intimate for the three of them.

There had to be a lot of other combinations for three people, right?

Now, thinking about that seemed perfectly apropos.

Cain and Brad slept soundly beside her and she wanted to wake them up, but first she carefully crawled over Cain and went in to use the bathroom. While she was in there she brushed her teeth and put on some fresh lipstick. If she ended up with Cain's cock in her mouth at some point during the night, the least she could do was give him a good visual.

Bright red lips around a darkly engorged erection should be just about right.

Brad awakened to the shift of the bed as Cherry crawled over Cain and went into the bathroom. He lay there a moment, thinking of what she'd done tonight, how it felt to watch his entire erection disappear between her lips.

The moment he had the visual, his damned cock surged to life once again. Cherry going to her knees had totally floored him, but watching her suck on him was something he'd never forget. He'd been with prostitutes long before she was born who hadn't made him come as hard, and the fact that this was her first time was definitely mind-blowing.

He was watching the bathroom door when she stepped back into the main room. She'd combed the tangles out of her hair and put on fresh lipstick, and he wanted her so badly he ached. He knew the moment she realized he was awake—her eyes lit up and her beautiful lips tilted up in a smile.

She walked around the end of the bed and lay down beside him. Cain was still asleep, so she shoved Brad into the middle, in her old spot, and snuggled close beside him.

He nuzzled her hair and then whispered, "That was pretty amazing."

She smiled and kissed his chin. "Definitely. Just think how good I'll be with practice."

"You'll probably kill me."

"Oh, I hope not." She ran her hands over his chest and traced the muscles on his arms. "Cain and I made love this afternoon, but you and I haven't."

She managed to pout and whisper at the same time. He'd never seen her pout before and thought it was a pretty sexy look. Of course, he thought everything she did was sexy. "I know." He pressed his forehead to hers. "I think you should take care of that grievous inequity."

She nodded against him. "I agree. He's sleeping—can we do it without disturbing him?"

"I doubt it, but he needs to wake up anyway. Besides, he said he likes to watch." And there would be something wonderfully prurient about knowing Cain was watching him with Cherry.

"Good point." She ran her hands across his chest again but this time stroked along his sides, raised goose bumps across his belly, and then tangled her fingers in the thick patch of hair at his groin. And tugged.

"Shit." He hissed the curse and thrust his hips close to her. Then he reached over her and grabbed one of the condoms Cain had tossed on top of the bedside table. "I really hope you meant what you said."

She shrugged and rolled to her back. "I'm waiting. Impatiently."

He ripped open the packet and grabbed his dick, but

then he noticed how avidly Cherry watched him. "Do you want to put this on me?"

She nodded and licked her lips. His dick reacted appropriately and grew. A lot. Cherry took the condom, sat up again, and stared at his erection. Hard as a post, it stood perpendicular to his body, and his balls had drawn up so tight they ached. She wrapped her hand around the base to steady him and then glanced at Brad. He shrugged and waited to see what she would do, but it didn't take her long to position the ring of latex over the distended crown and carefully roll it down his shaft. She smoothed it neatly, left plenty of room in the tip for all the spunk, and actually did a pretty good job.

When she was all through smoothing the sides, which didn't take nearly long enough as far as he was concerned, she glanced shyly at his face. "Perfect," he said, and pulled her over on him. He raised his knees, expecting her to sit on his belly so they could play, but instead she knelt over him, grabbed his dick, and slowly lowered herself over him.

It was the most amazing thing he'd ever seen. Her face was a study in concentration; a small frown wrinkled her brow and she had her lower lip caught between her teeth. He had a perfect view of her dark pink labia and the distended nub of her clitoris as she stretched to take him. His dick was bigger around than Cain's, though not quite as long, and it was fascinating to watch the methodical way Cherry slowly managed to take all of him.

Thank goodness his night vision was excellent. The candles were beginning to burn low, and he wouldn't want to have missed seeing her like this for anything. She finally got all of him inside and sort of wriggled her butt to get everything situated. Then it was almost as if she realized he might be watching, because she raised her head, met his gaze, and her eyes went wide. Even in the darkness he could see her blush.

"What?" He planted his hands on her waist and glared at her, trying really hard not to laugh. "Did you forget I was here?"

She started to giggle, slapped her hand over her mouth, and snorted. He bounced her a couple of times, lifting and dropping his hips, and she folded forward with her arms around his neck and her face buried under his chin. Laughing. This wasn't the reaction he'd expected, but he liked it. A lot. Almost as much as he liked Cherry.

He rolled her over and was on top of her before she had time to catch her breath, but he'd been dreaming of this moment since the first time he saw her last Sunday, and he wasn't going to wait any longer. He pulled out and slowly thrust forward. Then he did it again, and again. She brought her legs up and around his waist and locked her ankles behind his butt, and after a few more thrusts her eyes looked sort of glazed and her lips parted.

He rested his weight on his forearms and shoved her long hair back from her face. She was so beautiful he wanted to see her as he made love to her. Wanted to watch the expressions coursing across her face, the waves of color that suffused her cheeks as her arousal grew.

He leaned in and kissed her, exploring her mouth with his tongue, nipping at her full lips, breathing her breath. Tasting her. He and Cain hadn't had a chance to talk, but Brad was so positive that she was right for them he was ready to claim her tonight, which of course they couldn't do.

He'd read all the werewolf lore, how they were telepathic, which they weren't, that there was one perfect mate for them, but that wasn't true, either, or that they were forced into the shift beneath a full moon. Not at all. They were just typical guys with an atypical life span and the ability to change from human to wolf, but that meant they didn't get blind-sided by a mythical "One." A perfect woman who would bond to them forever—they had to be careful about choosing a mate, because eternity with an unhappy woman was its own kind of hell.

Which was why they'd all agreed that if a man met a woman at Feral Passions who could become his mate, he had to let her go home after her week was up, give her time to think about the relationship that might or might not prove to be strong enough to make sharing their secret a safe proposition. It had to be the woman's choice to stay.

He'd heard the old ones talk about carrying innocent young women off from their small towns and villages and turning them without giving them a choice. Some of those relationships lasted to this day, but the days of kidnapping women were long past. It was going to be so hard to let Cherry go, but he'd have to trust that they'd built enough of a bond over the past couple of days. Tomorrow was Wednesday.

She'd be leaving Saturday morning for the long drive back to San Francisco.

Desperation drove him as he realized how quickly the week was flying by. He felt the clenching muscles deep in-side Cherry as he pounded into her. She arched her back, driving him even deeper, and he watched her face as her climax rolled over her. The visual was too much—Brad was right behind her. His steady, deep strokes went short and sharp. Cherry screamed and her hands clutched at his shoulders.

Like a piston plunging in and out of her, he struggled to hang on, wanted to give her even more than he already had, and when her body rippled around him once again he finally let himself go, let the pleasure take hold and the emotions he'd been holding in check flow free.

He felt as if he emptied his soul into this woman, gave her everything he was, in the hope she'd understand how very much he cared. How much they both cared, because it could never be just Brad or just Cain. They were a pair.

They didn't want a woman who would divide them, who might try to tear them apart. They wanted Cherry, the first woman in their very long lives who seemed to understand what they needed, a woman who could bring them even closer together should she choose to stay.

CHAPTER 16

Stunned, Cherry lay there in the darkness. The last of the candles had finally gone out, and Brad's welcome weight covered her. He was still hard enough that she felt the gentle pulses of his cock deep inside, and he was conscious enough to hold much of his weight off of her, resting on his forearms, head hanging low with his face between her breasts.

She had fairly large breasts, but she knew she hadn't smothered him, and wouldn't that be a hard one to explain. *Yes, Your Honor, we were having wild monkey sex and he collapsed on top of me and I smothered him with my boobs. No, it was not intentional.*

She didn't know whether to laugh or cry, but then she turned her head to her left and there was Cain, lying beside them, resting his weight on his elbow with his head propped on one hand, slowly stroking himself with the other.

He smiled the moment she turned his way, and shook his head. "Good lord, Cherry, that has to be the most erotic thing I've ever seen. You and Brad together? You're both so beautiful, your bodies moving together perfectly. I wanted to be part of it, but I realized it was more important to watch, to imagine what you and I might have looked like together."

Brad slowly raised his head. "We're keeping her," was all he said. Then he rolled to his back, taking Cherry with him. Looking up at her, he smiled, blinking slowly as if he were just coming out of a sound sleep.

Or maybe a truly mind-blowing orgasm? "I'm sorry if I squished you, sweetheart. I felt a real need to wallow in you after that."

"You didn't squish me. You were holding a lot of your weight off of me. Thank you for that. You're heavier than you look."

He nodded. "Which is why you're now on top. Because you're not heavy at all." He tilted his head forward and kissed her. Then he lifted her up and off of him and settled her beside Cain. "I need to go take care of this." Hanging on to his semi-erect penis and the condom, he rolled off the edge of the bed and went into the bathroom.

"You okay?" Cain swept his fingers through her tousled hair.

She didn't answer right away. Instead, she took a moment to think about that. Was she okay? Her entire world had been totally blown away in the last three days. That's all this had been. Three jam-packed days of men and sex and experiences she'd never dreamed of, and a new sense of herself, a new confidence she had always wished for but never thought she'd have.

"I am," she said, frowning. "So much has happened in such a short time. It's sort of hard for me to process all of it."

Cain smiled and tapped her forehead. "It's that analytical brain of yours. If you can't fit things into an algorithm, you don't know how to deal with it. Brad and I don't compute with your internal content analytics."

She laughed. "How do you know about content analytics? Because I think you nailed it. Numbers, systems, things—they're something I understand. This?" She waved her hand in a loose gesture that encompassed the cabin and all it contained. "I don't have a frame of reference for any of this. Not for you and Brad, not for the awesome sex, not—"

He interrupted her. "Not sex, Cheraza. We've had this discussion. What Brad and you and I are doing is making love. Don't forget that. Sex is something people can walk away from. Making love is building a foundation that's rock solid. It has staying power. It's built to build upon. That's what this is, what we're creating."

"You've said that." She shook her head. "It's just hard for me to believe it." She glanced up as Brad came out of the bathroom. "But it's getting easier all the time, I think."

"What's getting easier?" he asked. "Turning me into a slavering beast?" He pounced on the bed and licked Cherry's throat. Then he pretended to bite her shoulder until she was giggling and trying to curl into a tight ball to get away from the mock assault.

Or was it all in fun? She still had her suspicions about these two and their wolfish ways, outlandish as they might be, but she went limp and lay there staring at him. There was a definite gleam in Brad's eyes, and then Cain laughed and punched him in the shoulder. Brad sort of shook himself and sat back on his heels, trapping her thighs beneath his butt, and the moment ended.

There was no doubt in Cherry's mind there had been "a moment." One Cain had very neatly brought to an end. Instead of making her wary of the two of them, it made her heart go out to both guys. If her suspicions were correct, they had a terrible secret. What would it be like, to live a life in hiding? To be creatures people either didn't believe in at all or feared?

She didn't fear either Cain or Brad or any of the other men at Feral Passions. As unbelievable as it was, as impossible, she was coming to the very strong realization that every day she was here she believed in and accepted that other reality of theirs just a little bit more.

Wednesday

Cherry came awake when the mattress dipped. Blinking her eyes, she saw Brad in the morning's dim light, pulling on his pants.

"Brad?"

"Shhh, sweetheart. Go back to sleep. It's only a little after five, but I need to get coffee going and breakfast started."

"But you were up all night." She glanced at the other side of the bed. Cain was gone. "When did Cain leave?"

"Just now. You must have heard the door—probably what woke you. He's going to help me with breakfast." Brad leaned over and kissed her.

She clung to him and hated that she felt the need to hold him close, but last night had been—She broke the kiss. "I'm going to miss you. Last night was amazing. I think you and Cain have wiped away all the horrible memories I've had for the last ten years."

Brad brushed her hair back from her eyes. "I'd like to say that was our goal, but neither Cain nor I are all that altruistic. You're hot and we wanted your body."

Smiling, she covered his hand with hers. "That works. I

hope you'll want it again tonight, because I know I want yours. And Cain's."

"I wish I could crawl back in with you right now, but duty calls." He kissed her again and then finished dressing. "I'll see you later, after you get some more sleep. We kept you awake way too late last night."

"I know. And I never did get that massage." She pouted.

"You're right. We got sidetracked. Tonight?"

"If I have to wait that long." Sighing, she scooted back under the covers. He kissed her once more and then he was gone. Cherry lay there for a few minutes, going over everything they'd done the night before. She'd had sex—no, make that "made love"—with two incredible men. They were sweet and caring and they'd put her needs first, but did they really mean it when they talked about forever? It was Wednesday already. She was leaving Saturday morning.

How could she possibly know for sure in just three more days?

Late that afternoon, Cherry wondered if she'd actually make it up the last few steps to the deck at the lodge, but Brad was standing in the doorway with a tray loaded with margaritas, and that was incentive enough. He gave her a kiss and handed her the icy, salt-encrusted drink. She wasn't sure which sounded better—the ice or the salt. "Don't stand downwind." She took a big swallow and licked the salty rim. "I probably stink."

"I heard Ronan was taking you to the bat cave."

Christa was right behind her, and she giggled. "He did, though while I was thinking Batman, he was obviously thinking of little brown bats. Gazillions of them." She grabbed a margarita off Brad's tray and sat next to Cherry.

Steph was right behind her. "And you know what you get with a gazillion bats? A gazillion tons of bat poop." Brad laughed and handed her a drink.

"You gonna make it up the steps, Darnell?" He held the glass out, tempting her.

"Oh, yeah," she said, staggering up the last two steps. "That was absolutely frickin' unbelievable." She plopped down in the last of the chairs at the small table and sighed when Brad put one on the table in front of her. "Bless you. I think Ronan tried to kill us."

"Was the near-death experience worth it?"

"Actually, yes. It was." Darnell took a swallow of her margarita and sighed. Brad pulled up a chair from the next table over and sat beside Cherry. "What'd you think of the cave?"

"It was beautiful." Shaking her head, Cherry took another sip. "I've never been in a natural cave before, and while the bat guano is pretty stinky, the cave was amazing. We could hear the bats squeaking, and Ronan used a shielded light that wouldn't startle them so we could see how many there were."

"A lot." Darnell looked at Cherry. "I am so glad you guys wanted to go see that. I'm pretty fed up with Suni and Fred. They haven't done any exploring at all."

Brad shrugged. "They're having the kind of vacation that works for them—quiet time by the pool with drinks on demand and nothing they have to do—but I'm really glad you're enjoying the chance to see some of the country up here. It's a beautiful area."

"I forgot to ask you." Steph sipped her margarita and grinned at Darnell. "How was your head this morning? I saw Evan hauling your skinny butt back to your cabin."

They all laughed when Darnell hid her eyes behind her hand. "Don't ever, ever let me drink a Long Island Iced Tea again. Never. They're evil. My head's fine, but Evan spent the night, and I didn't even know it. I woke up with him on top of the blankets, sleeping beside me on the bed. Can you imagine that? I wasted a perfectly good night with an absolutely drop-dead gorgeous guy, and all he did was babysit me." She sighed.

"I was a perfect gentleman." Evan bounded up the steps, grabbed a chair, parked his butt next to Darnell, and wrapped his arm around her shoulders. "Tonight, however, I intend not to be quite so gentlemanly. I will, however, be sexy as hell."

Everyone groaned, but Cherry laughed. So often she'd seen groups of friends sitting together, laughing, teasing each other, and just kicking back in the cafeteria at work or in the park near her apartment, but she'd never really experienced the sense of camaraderie she was feeling now. She sipped her drink and slipped into observer mode for a few minutes, watching how everyone interacted, but it wasn't long before she was drawn right back into the teasing.

A few minutes later, Ronan and Wils showed up, and Cain wasn't all that far behind. As the group grew and the laughter escalated, she knew she'd be taking home memories that would stay with her forever.

Except it was only Wednesday and she still had a massage coming. And more, if things worked out the way she hoped.

Trak wandered in a bit later, about the time Brad and

Evan went into the kitchen to get dinner together. Cherry looked around for Suni and Fred, but they weren't with him. Trak leaned against the deck railing. "Where's Evan?"

"Inside helping Brad fix dinner." Christa leaned back in her chair and looked at Trak upside down.

"Thanks. He's going to have to take over the bar at Growl tonight." Trak went on into the lodge.

Darnell put her head down on her arms. "Damn. I was really hoping to get laid tonight." She raised her head and stated at the others out of one eye. "Don't all go all teary eyed with sympathy, guys."

They were all laughing when Trak came back outside. "Darnell, if you want to go hang out at Growl while Evan works his shift later tonight, I can give you a ride to the bar. It's only a quarter mile, but I understand Ronan took you ladies up to the bat cave. I bet your legs are all walked out."

Darnell's head popped up. "They are, but I'd like that. Anyone else want to go?"

Steph and Christa shared a look. "Sure," Christa said. "Cherry? What about you?"

"I don't know." She finished her margarita and stood. "First I'm going to get a shower. The idea of sitting down to dinner reeking of bat poop doesn't really appeal."

"Good point." Christa stood and hauled Steph to her feet. "Shower and then dinner. And then we discuss a trip to the bar." She glanced down at her dirty jeans. "Wonder if I should just burn my clothes?"

"You can use the laundry service here if you like. Leave them in the basket in your cabin and Housekeeping will take care of them." Trak shoved himself away from the railing and turned to go back inside the dining room.

Christa, Steph, and Cherry all looked at one another and back at Trak. As far as Cherry was concerned, expecting one of these terrific guys to have to deal with her stinky clothes sucked. She shrugged. "Burning sounds like the best option."

Laughing, he threw his hands in the air. "Whatever. How do girls do that? You just look at each other and know what the other one's thinking? No wonder guys never have a clue."

Steph was the closest to Trak. She leaned over, wrapped her hand around the back of his neck, and pulled him close for a kiss. He blinked, but he obviously didn't object. Steph pulled away after a very long kiss and licked her lips. "You realize we do it just to keep you guys confused. I love that it's working."

"Oh, yeah." Trak looked a bit stunned. "Definitely working."

CHAPTER 17

Darnell sat with the three of them for dinner, and Cherry was once again laughing more than not. It wasn't long before Suni joined them, but Fred stayed with Trak and another guy Cherry hadn't met. For some reason, though, he looked familiar.

Wils and Ronan ended up at their table before too long and she forgot about the man, and then Evan showed up with a plate loaded with steak and salmon and two baked potatoes along with servings of everything else that Brad had put out on the buffet.

Cherry had her salmon and a salad, which was more than enough, but watching the amount of food the guys put away was entertaining all on its own.

Brad joined them once everyone was served.

"Where's Cain?"

"He wanted to check on Mama and the pups." Brad cut into his steak and took a bite. "They're growing really fast."

Cherry glanced at the table across the room. "Who's the guy with Trak and Fred? He looks a lot like Trak."

"Lawson. We call him Lawz. You're good—he's Trak's older brother."

"I knew it."

They were just finishing up dinner when Trak, Lawz, and Fred left. Cherry glanced up and smiled, but Fred glared at her as she left the dining room with the men.

Why would the woman give her such a dirty look?

Had to be her imagination. Cherry placed her utensils on her plate and turned her attention to whatever Suni was saying.

". . . and I've really had it with her attitude. This is such a great place," she said, "but all Fred does is find fault. There was a wolf on my front porch this morning and I was sitting out there on the step, petting him. He was so beautiful, I could have sat there all day with him, but Fred showed up and insisted I go to the pool with her." She glanced at Darnell. "I really wanted to hike up to the cave with you guys, darn it."

"You should have." Darnell sighed. "She can be really bossy. You don't owe her anything. I mean, you're paying for the same vacation she is."

"I know. I'm just not tough enough. I hate confrontation of any kind."

"I'm the same way. I'll do anything to avoid it." Laughing at herself, Cherry stood to take her plates over to the counter. She'd noticed that when she picked hers up the others did, too. It helped the guys out, if only a little, but then she thought of something totally out of context.

"Suni, what did the wolf look like? The one at your cabin? I'm trying to figure out how many different ones are around here."

"He was beautiful, but really dark, like a charcoal gray with black tips and brown eyes. And he was really big, but when I stepped out of the cabin he rolled over on his back. Otherwise he might have scared me half to death."

"It's hard to imagine them vicious when they do that." Christa grabbed her plate and the others followed suit.

Brad stood with the others and carried his over, but he glanced up as the largest man Cherry had seen at Feral Passions entered the dining room. Like the others, he was absolutely stunning.

"Hey, Tuck. You're just in time. Kitchen's all yours."

"You're too kind to me, Bradley."

"Meet the ladies, smart-ass. And behave." Brad took Cherry's hand, almost as if he were claiming her. She liked that. "This is Cherry, her sister, Christa, cohort in crime Stephanie, Suni, and Darnell. Ladies, this is Dr. Kentucky Jones, otherwise known as Tuck. He's our resident veterinarian, but he also has a practice that covers the whole valley. And tonight he's doing dishes, which is as it should be."

"Pleasure to meet you, and you know how it is, Brad. I need to keep an eye on the kitchen, make sure you don't poison any of these beautiful women." He grinned and rubbed the back of his neck, and his focus was on Cherry. "I've got to start hanging around this place more often."

Brad wrapped his arm around her waist. "You go right ahead. This one is taken."

"Got the message loud and clear." He grinned broadly, as if this was the biggest joke going, but Cherry didn't feel any animosity from him. It was more a sense of approval, or was she merely seeing what she wanted to see?

She and Brad walked out of the dining hall to the front deck. Christa, Steph, Suni, and Darnell sat at the big table waiting for their ride to Growl. Evan stepped out of the dining room right behind them. "Ladies, I think you've lost your ride to the bar. Trak's, uhm . . . tied up for a bit."

Evan laughed when Suni rolled her eyes and said, "Knowing Fred, you might want to take that literally. Are you walking to Growl?"

"I am. It's not far. Why don't you come with me if you're not too tired, and I'll make sure either someone walks back with you or we'll arrange a ride."

"Works for me." Christa stood and Steph was right behind her.

Brad stood behind Cherry with his hands on her shoulders. "Do you want to go?"

She shrugged. "When do you expect Cain back?"

"Anytime. We can leave him a note, or we can just go to your cabin and kick back."

From the secretive smile that lifted his lips Cherry had a good idea what kicking back entailed, and it had a lot more appeal for her than hanging out in a bar. "You guys go on ahead. I'm going to hang around here tonight."

She hugged Christa, waved good-bye to everyone else, and then she and Brad went back inside, through the dining room, and into the kitchen. Tuck was at the sink, sleeves rolled up over powerful arms as he scraped dishes and loaded the commercial-sized dishwasher. Brad packed up a meal of leftovers for Cain but kept Cherry in hysterics as he and Tuck tossed insults back and forth to each other.

They'd obviously been friends a long time.

She was still laughing when she and Brad went out the back door and followed the trail to her cabin. Lights twinkled along the path and the night was absolutely still. An owl hooted nearby, and something small scurried through the grass. It hit Cherry then, how much she was going to miss this place.

She'd only been here for four days, and already the beauty of the woods had seeped into her bones. She'd never felt this connected to San Francisco, even though she'd grown up in the Bay Area and had lived in the city since college. Somehow, she'd have to come back here someday, though seeing Brad and Cain and not having this same relationship would probably make that impossible.

Why was it that it was easier for her to believe that men were werewolves than the fact that they seemed to want more than a vacation fling? They'd said over and over how much they wanted her to stay, that she was special, but her logical mind had to accept the truth that Brad was right, her parents really had done a job on her. When she thought of the lifelong emphasis on her weight, she realized that everything she did, every thought she had, was governed by the sense that she wasn't pretty enough for anyone to love her.

Including her mom and dad. If they'd loved her, wouldn't they have loved her the way she was, not the way they wished she'd been? Her mind was still spinning when they reached her cabin, and she and Brad had barely gotten inside when he turned, set the box of food on the table, and wrapped his arms around her.

"I've wanted to do this all afternoon. I missed you today."

His mouth covered hers, so perfectly, his kiss so sweet, the sense of being protected and loved by him so strong, that she felt herself go soft and pliable in his arms, as if everything about her wanted to merge with Brad.

The oddest thing, though, was the sense that she missed

Cain. She wanted him here to share this time every bit as much as she wanted Brad. She couldn't help it—she smiled into his kiss.

"What's so funny?" Brad nuzzled her throat, teased behind her ear with the tip of his tongue. She shivered.

"Don't take this wrong, please?" And then she blew it by giggling. "You'll think I'm such a slut!"

"You? A slut?" Brad leaned away from her, but his hands held her waist, kept their lower bodies perfectly aligned. "I don't think so."

She rotated her hips against him, and he laughed. "Well, okay. Maybe a little, but mostly in the best possible way. So, why are you laughing?"

"Because you're amazing and hot and I want to get naked and rip your clothes off of you, and . . ."

"And there better be more, because I love what you're saying so far. Nothing slutty about it, either. Sounds like something that both of us want." He leaned close, kissed her, and then leaned away again, watching her.

She blushed. Damn! She'd been doing so well, too. "Except I want both of you. You and Cain. Last night with the two of you . . ." She sighed. "I have never felt so incredibly shameless in my life, or so, so . . ." She let out a huff of air.

"Loved?" He went very quiet, watching her with a feral intensity so powerful it made her ache. "When the two of us were with you, loving you, did you feel loved?"

She couldn't speak. Her voice couldn't make it past the lump in her throat. No one fell in love in four days. It just didn't happen. It certainly couldn't happen to her, which meant it definitely wouldn't happen for Brad. What did he mean? Why did he ask her such a stupid thing?

"Cherry? Why aren't you answering me?"

His gaze never wavered, and she saw in his eyes that same wolf that slept on her bed, the same light of the hunter in that searing intensity.

"I can't." It was all she could do to get those words past her tight throat.

"You're not afraid of me, of us, are you?"

She shook her head. Fear Brad and Cain? Absolutely not. "No," she said. "Never."

"I hope not, Cherry. It would break me if you were afraid of us. You're the most important person in our lives."

He kissed her then, and there was no hesitancy in the way he took her with his mouth, with teeth and tongue and lips, his hands clasping the fullness of her buttocks, pulling her close, breathing her in, and owning her with his kisses. With his strength.

A knock on the door barely registered. Cain's voice pulled them apart, both of them breathing heavily. With shaking hands, Cherry turned away from Brad and opened the door. She stood back with her head bowed.

"What's wrong?" Cain quietly closed the door behind him and locked it. The sound of the latch slipping into place echoed in the quiet cabin. "Brad? What's going on?"

Brad shook his head. "I don't know. I'm not really sure. I was teasing Cherry and she said she'd never felt so shame-less in her life. That even though she was with me, she wanted you here, too. Personally, I think that's a really good thing. But she . . ."

Cherry sighed. "I freaked. Cain, here's your dinner. You must be starved. Sit and eat. Brad? There's wine and beer in the refrigerator. Would you pour me a glass of wine? Get whatever you want." She grabbed Cain's box of leftovers, checked to make sure they were still hot, and got some silverware out of a drawer in the tiny kitchen area. Brad brought a glass of white wine to the table for her, a beer for himself, and one for Cain.

She stared at her glass of wine for a moment and thought of how she would have dealt with a situation like this merely a week ago. She wouldn't have been able to. No, she'd have taken off like a scared rabbit, which was probably an excellent analogy, considering she was having this conversation with two men she was almost absolutely positive were wolves.

"Give me some credit here, guys. I'm trying." She raised her head and smiled at Cain and then at Brad, but her gaze locked on him. He looked utterly confused, which made perfect sense. "I hear the *l* word and react like I expect most men to react. I panic." Shaking her head, she laughed. It was so stupid. "Brad, you asked me why I didn't answer you? I couldn't. My throat locked up. Froze solid. I think it's the beginning of a panic attack, but I've got issues that go pretty deep."

"I'm sorry." Brad wrapped her fingers in his big hand. Strong hands. She loved how they felt on her. Loved what they made her feel. "I had no idea and I pushed you," he said.

Cain didn't say anything. He just ate his dinner, sipped his beer, and paid attention. Sometimes she felt as if he processed so much behind that disinterested look of his. Maybe someday she'd get the chance to figure him out.

She stared at the way Brad's fingers wrapped around hers.

"I've told you bits and pieces about that guy in high

school. He was my very first boyfriend, which is a huge thing for a girl, especially when she's fat and nerdy and socially inept. The first guy who pays attention, who's cute and nice and makes her feel good about herself. The first—and only—boy to ever say he loved me. The first person. Even my parents withheld their love as long as I wasn't perfect, and that just made me eat more, but I was a needy idiot and I believed him when he said he loved me. Only he didn't. He needed me to help him pass calculus. Turns out, he'd bragged to his friends that I'd get him through the course and he'd get into me before the semester ended."

"Bastard." Cain glanced at her and his jaw clenched. He shoved the chair back, abruptly stood, paced across the room, and then returned. Grabbing the back of the chair, he stood there, hanging on with his head bowed. "I am so damned sorry, Cherry. I had no idea."

Cain's words meant a lot to her. It was the only thing he'd said since they sat down, and he already knew most of the story. Though not the worst of it.

Brad's grasp on her hand tightened. Knowing these two men—men, not boys—sympathized gave her the courage to tell the rest. Raising her head, she focused on Cain. On his anger. Somehow, it strengthened her, the fact that he was so blindly furious for her. "The thing is, he didn't just tell his friends; he showed them. This was before Facebook was popular, but he'd hidden a camera in the car and posted nude pictures I didn't even know he'd taken. They were up on another social networking site that was popular at the time, and I only heard about them when one of my friends, a boy in that same class, saw them. Christa freaked when I told her what happened, but not as badly as me. I tried to kill myself. Christy stopped me and told my parents what had happened. They were able to get the pictures taken down, but the damage was done. My parents and I have hardly spoken since. There was no recourse against the boy, since the sex was consensual and I was eighteen."

"That is so fucking wrong." Cain glared at Brad, who nodded silently in agreement.

"It is what it is. I was supposed to be valedictorian, but once the pictures got out, my name was removed from the list. I quit school, but I already had enough credits to graduate. I'd been accepted to college with scholarships to pay most of my expenses. My parents gave me the money they'd put away for my education, but then they cut ties and so did I."

"That explains why Christa and you are so close, why she's so protective of you."

She wiped tears off her face with her free hand. She wasn't about to turn loose of Brad's "Exactly, Brad. Cissy is an absolute saint. She had to put up with so much crap in high school and it was all my fault."

"None of it was your fault." Cain grabbed her hand, rubbed his thumb through the tears on her fingers. She raised her head. He was absolutely furious.

"It was that bastard's fault, and the school's for not protecting you. Your parents failed you. They should have stood by you, supported you, not 'cut ties' with you. Damn it all, Cherry. Was that prick allowed to graduate?"

When she nodded, both he and Brad cursed.

"Cherry?" She turned to Brad. "Do you see how wrong that is? That you, the victim, suffered, and the asshole who

attacked you and your good name got off without any reper-
cussions at all?"

"He didn't force me."

"He lied to you," Cain said. "He set you up and victimized
you. You told me you were a virgin when that happened,
which means he stole something very precious from you.
Don't let him keep winning. When you make decisions based
on what he did to you, you're letting that son of a bitch win.
Never again, Cherry. No matter what happens, you're never
to feel like a victim. You're better than that, and you're a
damned sight better than him."

She almost laughed. It was either that or cry. "I've been
telling myself that for years, that I'm better, but unfortunately I'm not very convincing. In the internal debate, my
inner coward appears to hold the upper hand."

"This one week may not be enough time to reprogram
your inner coward." Cain smiled at her when he pushed his
chair back under the table. "You'll need to stay with us at
least another week to turn you into a powerful Amazonian
warrior."

He was teasing, but she really wished . . . "I doubt my
boss would agree. I didn't give her much warning when I
took off for this week."

Cain dumped his empty box and paper plates in the
trash and rinsed out the silverware in the sink. Then he
turned and leaned against the counter with his arms folded
across his chest. He really looked like he needed to be leaning against a big Harley, not the cute little kitchen counter
in her cabin. There was something so elemental about the
man. Brad had that same sense of wildness, but where his

was gentle and kind with merely a hint of the beast, Cain was the alpha in the room.

Which was another thing—one she was still too cowardly to ask. Was he an alpha wolf? If she had to choose between Brad and Cain, she'd pick Cain as the more dominant, but if she were to look at the group of men here as a whole—the pack, in wolf terms—she would name Trak as the alpha. He was a big man, though not the biggest. So far, that would be Tuck, the vet, but there was something about Trak, an indefinable sense of leadership, that set him apart, whether human or wolf. Except she had no proof. These two terrific guys probably already thought she was certifiably nuts. If she was wrong and asked them if they were werewolves they'd probably run for the hills.

Of course, they were already in the hills, but—

"Cheraza?"

Jerked out of her wandering thoughts, she looked at Cain. "What?"

He laughed. "What's going on in that head of yours?"

She shrugged and improvised. "That I'm tired of rehashing my old news and I'd really much rather see you naked." She turned and pointed at Brad. "And you, too."

"Works for me," he said. Shoving his chair back from the table, he stood—and very methodically began stripping out of his clothes.

CHAPTER 18

"Now look who's the only one dressed." Brad raised an eyebrow and glanced at Cain, who nodded. Then they both focused on Cherry, and she felt that damned blush crawl across her skin. The two of them watched her for a moment longer. Once again they looked at each other.

Then they stalked her.

Brad came in from her right, Cain from the left. Each of them took hold of an arm. Her gaze flashed right then left and right again. "What are you doing?"

"This." Cain nodded to Brad and they both leaned over and caught her beneath her back and thighs and then carried her to the bed.

Giggling, she pretended to struggle, but they dropped her on the bed and methodically stripped all the clothes off of her. Holding down her shoulders and thighs, they gently restrained her, but she was still totally immobile.

Of course, she wasn't trying to get away. Her heart was thundering, but it wasn't fear.

It was arousal, pure and simple.

Brad offered a suggestion. "Should we tie her up?"

"What?" They wouldn't. Would they? Maybe they would!

She shivered—anticipation, not fear, and that alone was a turn-on. She'd never thought she'd enjoy being restrained, but with these two . . .

"It would be more fun." Cain gave her an innocent look. "Well, it would."

"Fun for whom?" She was not going to give in easily. She stared at Cain, then at Brad.

"For us," he said. "That's two out of three who are guaranteed a great time." He gave her a wide-eyed look. "Not to say you wouldn't enjoy yourself. I'm almost certain you would."

"Almost." Cain shrugged. "It's hard to say. Depends on what we do to . . . uh, with you."

She knew they were teasing, and yet the most delicious shivers raced through her when she imagined what they might do.

Then a new idea filtered into her head. She'd loved sex with the two of them when she was their focus. What if the two of them had sex with her assistance?

The mere thought made her wet and tied her feminine muscles into a knot.

Cain's nostrils twitched. So did Brad's. She kept her mouth shut, but knowing they were aware of her arousal turned her on even more. Knowing they didn't realize she was on to them—or at least she thought she was on to them—was an even bigger turn-on. "Do I get a say in this?"

"I don't really know," Cain said. "I guess it depends on what you say. Right, Brad?"

"Of course. I mean, we're basically democratic, right?"

"Except when we're not." Cain's smirk sent more shivers

that—even though he wasn't touching them—originated in her nipples and shot straight to her clit.

"What if I want to watch something?" She first gazed at Brad and then settled on Cain.

He cleared his throat. "Watch what?" He shot a nervous glance at Brad.

"You. And Brad. You sat and watched me having sex with Brad. It seems only fair."

"Brad and I are holding you prisoner. Fairness doesn't enter into the discussion."

She looked at each of them again, only this time she lowered her gaze. Eyes could lie, but those erections looked like the real thing. "True, but honesty should. I mentioned me watching, and both of you, uhm . . . reacted. Most dramatically."

They were holding her shoulders, but her hands were free. She grasped both men's hard shafts in her hands and gently squeezed.

"Oh, shit." Cain's hips thrust forward. "You're cheating."

Brad didn't speak, but the hiss escaping his parted lips was fairly eloquent. And why was it, lying here naked with two naked men standing over her, she had all the confidence in the world? They'd given her this awareness of herself as a sensual woman, but how the hell did she get past the emotional issues? Freezing up at the *l* word she couldn't think, much less say, and yet she was lying here hanging on to the cocks of two aroused men, calmly trying to convince them they should let her watch them together.

She kept stroking, her hands moving slowly up and down their hard cocks. "You realize, I don't necessarily want you to do anything all alone." She tried a sultry glance, at first Cain, then Brad. Her growing proof she'd nailed the look was tightly grasped in both her hands.

Smiling, knowing they didn't have a clue what she was thinking, she added, "I want to play, too, but I guess what I want is to see what it's like when the emphasis is on you guys, not me. When it's on me, I'm too whacked-out to pay attention to what you're both up to."

"Whacked-out?" Cain's eyebrow went up and he smirked.

She shrugged, not easy to do with the two of them holding her down and her still holding on. "I've discovered I'm not quite in my right mind when one of you is in me. Which reminds me—I want to see what it's like to have both of you in me. There are all kinds of things I want to try, and we're running out of time."

"I like that idea. A lot. But what do you mean? We have a lot of time. It's early."

"Brad, I leave Saturday morning. Early. It's already Wednesday night. Tomorrow and Friday, and then I'm gone. There's still a lot I want to explore with you two."

She caught the look he shared with Cain. She had no idea how to read it, wasn't sure what it meant. They'd said a lot of nice things to her, about wanting to keep her, wanting her to stay, but nothing she could take seriously. She'd worked so hard to build a successful life on her own. It wasn't nearly as exciting as life these past few days with Brad and Cain, but it was real and it was all hers.

She'd learned a long time ago you couldn't count on dreams. Too often they dissolved with the morning light, nothing more than mist and fantasy. But this? Right now? This was real and her libido was telling her to go for it. They could talk about making love and building things to last all they wanted, but Cherry wanted what she could count on—the here and now with two sexy guys who honestly seemed to find her attractive.

At least for the immediate future.

Brad slipped out of her grasp—obviously she hadn't been paying attention—and lay down next to her on the bed. He rolled half over her and sucked one nipple between his lips. She let go of Cain to wrap her arms around Brad, while Cain walked around the room and dimmed the lights until there was only a small lamp in the kitchen area and a night-light glowing from the bathroom.

Then he lay down next to Cherry on the side opposite from Brad. "You are really hard to convince, aren't you?"

Cain palmed her breast and rolled her nipple between his thumb and forefinger. "Damn, these are just beautiful." He leaned over and sucked the turgid bud between his lips, drawing a moan from Cherry. "Tell me more about what you want, sweet Cheraza. What fantasies have you got that two country boys can help make real for you?"

"Country boys? That's a stretch." She gasped when Brad sucked harder and slipped his fingers between her legs at the same time. She had so many fantasies, but it was hard to think of any when they were stringing her tighter than fence wire—and that was definitely a country boy analogy. Where the hell did that come from?

"Do you kiss each other?" She barely gasped that one out before Brad's fingers plunged deep inside.

"Of course we do. I love Brad. He loves me. We kiss; we touch; we make love. When people love each other, they need to touch, want to share that physical connection."

"Brad, what do you like the best?"

He nipped at her breast. "What I'm doing right now. Usually it's just Cain and me, but adding you makes it all feel better. More meaningful, if that makes sense. As if what we do together is stronger when you're here with us."

"What do you like when I'm not here, silly?" She watched him as he smiled at her, but then he stopped what he'd been doing, raised his head, and gazed at Cain, who stared back, trapped in Brad's intense study.

Brad never took his eyes off Cain, and after a moment he smiled and slowly shook his head. "It's difficult to explain, but when Cain holds me, he makes me feel safe. My favorite? When he tops me. I'm on my hands and knees—it's a very submissive position for a man and that kind of sex can hurt—but he's always so careful not to hurt me. I know he likes it rough, but he's always gentle unless I let him know I'm okay with it. It's a very sensual experience, very emotional. The way he is tells me how much he loves me. That he cares for my comfort."

Cain coughed and cleared his throat, and it took him a moment to speak. His eyes glistened, closed for a moment, and he clenched his jaw. Struggling with emotions. Cherry struggled with her own—she wanted to grab on and hold him.

"I didn't know," he said. "I wasn't sure you realized that, how I feel when I enter you. I love when you show your trust in me. You let me in; you tell me what you want. What you need. I'm always so afraid of hurting you. It's good to know I don't."

Brad shook his head, his attention riveted on Cain, and Cherry realized she could have been gone altogether, for

all they noticed her, but at the same time there was no denying the love between these two strong men. The powerful emotional connection they shared. What would it be
like, to be included in that love? Was this what their offer to
her was all about?

Brad's hand still cupped her breast, but Cain's fingers
rested on her hip. She'd not even noticed when they moved,
so caught in the intense communion between the men. A
conversation she'd started, and yet it was one they appeared
never to have had. Would they resent her for forcing them to
examine their relationship so closely?

Cain reached across her and wrapped his fingers around
the back of Brad's neck, pulled him close for a deep kiss.
Cherry's breath caught in her throat. They were so beautiful together, two totally different men, both in appearance
and manner, and yet the love between them was real, so
powerful, there was no denying how they felt.

She wondered what it would feel like, to be a part of that
kind of love, a once-in-a-lifetime love that was absolutely
real.

She flashed on the logistics—how she could involve herself with the two of them—because it was obvious that's
where this kiss was leading when Cain planted his knee
beside her on the bed, giving him better access to Brad.

Cherry slipped to one side as Cain tugged and Brad came,
the two of them still kissing, kneeling together beside her,
their bodies pressed from thigh to chest. Brad clutched
Cain's lean hips, but both of Cain's big hands wrapped
around the curve of Brad's skull, holding him in place as he
took over the kiss, easily dominating Brad with his mouth.
They kissed deeply, fervently, until Brad pulled away to suck

a deep draught of air before pressing his forehead against Cain's.

Cherry was drawing deep breaths as well, so aroused by the two of them she hovered on the edge of her own climax. Then Cain lightly kissed Brad once more before directing him into position on his hands and knees where Cherry had been stretched out only moments before. Brad raised his head and caught her watching. An expression passed over his features that she couldn't read at first but then realized was one of apology.

He was afraid of leaving her out of what he and Cain shared.

Well, tonight she was sharing. She turned and moved beneath Brad on her back, wrapped her fingers around the length of his erection, and pulled the dark, plum-shaped head down to her mouth.

"Ah, Cherry."

His soft words escaped on a sigh, and then his mouth was between her legs and Cain was kneeling behind Brad. She smiled around her mouthful—the view from this angle was amazing, but when Brad's tongue connected with her clit she forgot all about the view.

She knew the moment Brad felt Cain's entrance—his back arched and his cock filled her mouth. She kept one hand wrapped around the base to keep him from going too deep, but Cain was right there, up close and personal, and he was too much temptation to resist.

He paused for a moment. She figured he must be all the way inside Brad, because their thighs were touching and if their testicles hadn't been drawn up so tight they would touch, too.

She reached between Brad's legs and stroked both men's balls, cupping Brad's and then Cain's. He cursed, and she might have giggled if Brad hadn't chosen that moment to circle his tongue around her clit and then suck on that sensitive little bud. She moaned, careful not to bite down, but the laughter hovered in the back of her mind, as she thought that no matter what came of this one week of vacation, she was getting one hell of an education in the male anatomy.

Then Cain began to move and Brad concentrated on Cherry and she focused on Brad with the occasional foray into Cain's territory, but it made a lot of sense to pay attention to the pleasure she could give her men because it helped take her focus off herself.

She didn't want to come. Not yet. She wanted this to last forever. Brad's tongue was doing amazing things and she hovered on the edge, but her concentration on his pleasure kept her from going over. She had a feeling Brad was using the same process, and she wondered how Cain held on. His legs trembled and his heavy breaths were proof of his efforts, but in seconds she'd caught the rhythm he forced on Brad and there was a moment of absolute synchronicity, with all of them moving together, a wave of sensuality, a connection that went beyond the physical and took her outside of the acts themselves and into the very essence of the men.

She tasted Brad on her tongue and reached for Cain, lightly cupping his balls in her hand and following his thrusts even as he sped up, as he plunged harder and faster and Brad's mouth between her legs took on an edge that hovered between pleasure and pain. She felt his teeth and tongue and lips and increased her efforts, though there was no true effort involved.

Everything seemed to flow from one to the other, with Cain leading. He was the one who controlled this deeply erotic dance, his cadence, his need, his powerful love.

She felt it in his touch when he reached around Brad's waist and stroked her breasts, when he thrust hard and fast and Brad's cock swelled between her lips. Brad arched his back and cried out, but his fingers took the place of his mouth and he thrust deep inside her, once, twice, and on the third her body clenched in orgasm.

Cain's curse, Brad's shout, Cherry's muffled moan as she swallowed Brad's release and then swallowed his shrinking cock as well, taking him all the way until her lips touched the coarse hairs at his groin.

When she finally slipped him free of her mouth, Brad and Cain toppled to the side and all of them lay there, sucking air, bodies trembling, hearts thundering.

"Wow." Cain was the first to speak, the first to move. He leaned over Brad's thigh and kissed Cherry, sweeping into her mouth with his tongue, tasting his lover, tasting Cherry. "That was absolutely amazing." Then Cain got up and went into the bathroom to clean up. He was back a moment later and stretched out beside her.

Brad carefully turned around so that the two men bracketed her on either side. He propped himself up on his elbow, rested his cheek on his palm, and played with her nipple. "What Cain said. That was a first for us. You're doing amazing things for our sex life. For a woman who's only had sex once before this week, I've got to ask, where do you get your ideas?"

If she told him the truth, they'd laugh at her. All those sexy romances? She'd read scenes exactly like what they'd just done. She'd thought when she read them that they sounded sexy.

She'd had no idea. Not clue what it was really like with two men you truly cared about.

"I read," she said. "A lot."

"Cain, my friend. We need to borrow some of this lady's books."

Cain smiled. He lay close beside Cherry, one arm thrown over his eyes, the other holding her hand. "Nah. You were right. We just need to keep the lady."

CHAPTER 19

Friday

Thursday and most of Friday passed in a blur of hiking and fantastic meals, drinks and laughter in the dining room and on the big deck, and the most amazing sex any woman could ever imagine. During the days she'd had very little time with Brad and Cain, who were busy working, but they'd more than made up for their preoccupation with their jobs when they'd come to her last night.

She couldn't wait to see what they had planned for tonight, though she certainly hadn't been bored while they'd been busy. There'd been more beautiful wolves coming and going throughout the two days, almost as if they were checking out the women, and the Brad and Cain wolves had been her regular companions, which had Cherry wondering just how much actual work the human Brad and Cain had to do.

As far as the other wolves, many of them newcomers, Cherry wondered if any of them were the guys her sister and the others had met at Growl Wednesday night. Cherry had hardly had a chance to talk to them since they'd gone, at least not when there weren't men hanging around.

So far, she'd only gotten tidbits about the crazy fun they'd had at the bar.

She wasn't comfortable talking about anything personal in front of potentially eavesdropping wolves, but Cherry hadn't shared her suspicions about werewolves. She was having too good a time, and she hated the thought of starting rumors if her suspicions were untrue. She was actually enjoying the fantasy, if that's what it proved to be. A mystery she might never solve, once they all headed home.

Both Wednesday and Thursday nights with Brad and Cain had been amazing, so far beyond her expectations of what sex with two men could be she knew she'd never forget. She also accepted that what they'd had here would end when the three women left in the morning.

For all their insistence on calling what they did "making love," neither Cain nor Brad had vowed undying love to her. They talked of a nebulous future, but nothing she felt she could really count on.

That was okay. Today was her last day, and she planned to leave tomorrow with no regrets. There was no doubt in her mind that she'd miss them—both men were too good to be true and she knew she'd never find anyone to take their place. Which, of course, made it imperative that she not fall in love with them. They weren't hers to keep, and she really didn't want to spend her life yearning for two men she couldn't have.

Guarding her heart was still the only viable solution.

Cherry left out the loose yoga pants and T-shirt she planned to wear for the long drive home, along with the one clean dress she'd saved for tonight, but she carefully folded the rest of her clothes and packed them in her suitcase. She wished she didn't feel so much like crying. She'd known this night was coming, though at the beginning of the week she hadn't had a clue how she'd feel when it was time to leave this amazing place.

At least she'd gotten a lot of pictures of the people she'd met and Christa had taken a couple of great shots of her with Cain and Brad. One was good enough to enlarge—that one was going in her bedroom. Christa had caught both Cain and Brad wearing ragged cutoffs and work boots, their chests bare, strong bodies tanned, arms resting on each other's shoulders with Cherry in the middle. She'd been wearing her favorite dress, and she looked almost petite beside the two big men, her arms around their waists, all of them smiling, Cherry looking as if she didn't have a care in the world.

No one would ever know that, at the precise moment Christa snapped the picture, Cherry'd realized their vacation was coming to an end, and this picture might be all she had to remind her of her magical week at Feral Passions.

She turned on her phone and brought up the photo, just to stare at the image. She looked beautiful between her men. She looked like a woman in love.

Sighing, she flipped off the phone and took one last look around the room. She had everything packed except the few things she'd need for tomorrow. Dinner was in an hour. There'd be someone on the deck having a glass of wine or a drink. A last night with new friends.

Her last night with Brad and Cain.

She pasted a smile on her face, grabbed her sweater,

slipped on a pair of sandals, and headed down the trail to the lodge.

Steph, Christa, Suni, and Darnell had beaten her there. They were already drinking their margaritas on the deck when she arrived. She glanced around and realized one was missing. "Where's Fred?"

Suni rolled her eyes. "She's packing. She said she can't wait to get out of here, that she feels as if she lost a week of her life."

"Really?" Cherry caught Christa's disgusted look and noticed that the others seemed to share the feeling. "I've had the best time of my life this past week. I'm so glad Christa and Steph talked me into coming."

"We practically had to twist her arm off to get her here." Steph laughed and pointed at the door. "One of your men is inside making his magical margaritas. Go ye and get one."

"And see if he'll send out a pitcher for the rest of us," Darnell added. She held up an almost empty glass and pouted. "I'm exhausted from having fun all day."

"Yes, ma'am." Cherry saluted and went into the dining room. Brad was behind the bar, talking to Trak, Evan, and Cain, who'd taken three of the barstools.

"Hey, Cherry. I wondered when you were going to make it down here."

Brad leaned over the bar; she stretched up on her toes and kissed him. "I took a nap. Your relaxing activities have worn me out."

He laughed and held up a glass. "Margarita?"

"Yes, please, and Darnell wants a full pitcher. She said she's tired of having fun, but I think she's just trying to get back in shape for sitting on her butt at work."

Still smiling, Brad turned away to make the drinks. Cherry sat next to Trak. "I wanted to tell you what a terrific week this has been, Trak. You have a truly beautiful spot here, the meals have been amazing, and I've never had a better time in my life. I really hope Feral Passions is wildly successful for all of you."

Trak smiled, something the big man didn't appear to do all that often. "Thank you. I never did get a chance to ask you about your work. I'm wondering if your skills are something we could use here to boost our promotion, since we're looking for such a specific clientele."

Evan nodded. "What Trak is saying, I think, is how do we attract beautiful, young, single professional women like yourself, with a yearning for something different in their lives? Is there an algorithm for that?"

She laughed. She was really going to miss this, being treated like a beautiful professional woman. She didn't even get that at her job. "I'm sure there is, Evan. I'll work on it once I get back to the office Monday, but personally, all I think you guys need to do is post your pictures on the Web site and title the page 'The Men of Feral Passions.' The women will come in droves."

They were all laughing when Brad stepped out from behind the bar with a pitcher of margaritas and handed a filled glass to Cherry. "I'll carry this out," he said. "Trak, I'm taking a few minutes. Can you cover the bar?"

Trak merely smiled and waved as Cain got up and followed them outside. They moved the party to the big table and before long Lawz and Dr. Tuck had joined them, and then Ronan and Wils showed up. Trak and Evan eventually wandered outside, and a few new guys Cherry hadn't met arrived.

Christa and the others knew them from their night out at Growl, and it looked like they were all headed back there after dinner. Brad draped an arm around her shoulders and whispered in Cherry's ear. "Do you want to go to Growl? Cain and I can take you, if you'd like."

She turned and smiled. "What would you and Cain rather do? It's our last night and I know they're planning a party, but I've never been much for hanging around bars."

"Me, neither. Your place or ours after dinner?" He kissed her, right there in front of everyone. So she blushed, of course.

"Mine's okay." She glanced at Cain. "But I've never seen yours."

"Wherever you are, sweet Cheraza, that's where we'll be."

Dinner was a delightful celebration of good food and laughter. Again there was that amazing sense of belonging, of being part of something greater than herself, a part of the Feral Passions pack, as it were. She'd grown so comfortable with the wolves wandering in and out of the dining hall that she wondered if she should consider getting a dog when she got back to the city. She didn't live too far from a nice little park where she could walk one.

It might keep her from being so lonely.

She hated the thought of going home to her apartment, of walking in each night to an empty space. It had never bothered her before.

She'd never known what it was like to have a man in

her bed every night, either, much less two men. When they weren't there, the wolves somehow managed to find their way in. She'd awakened to wolves almost every morning since she'd been here.

No hint of their true identity, and for all she knew that's exactly what they were—wolves.

And she was exactly who she'd always been—Christa DuBois's chunky big sister, the math whiz more comfortable with numbers and her computer than real people in the real world.

At least that's what she'd be when she got home. Here she'd felt good about herself for the first time that she could remember. It truly had been a fantasy week. She glanced up as Cain and Brad walked across the dining room floor. They'd been in the kitchen serving dessert for some of the guests, but now they appeared to be headed straight for Cherry.

"We have something for you." Brad pulled out the chair next to her while Cain stood behind him with his hands on Brad's shoulders.

"For me? What for?"

"So you won't forget us. So you'll come back as soon as you can get away from work." Brad tipped his head back and looked at Cain, who sighed and then turned away.

Finally, he grabbed another chair and sat next to Brad. "We can't leave right now because of the work schedule, but we don't want you to think that this past week hasn't meant more to us than either of us can explain. You mean more to us, Cheraza. We don't want to lose you, but it's going to be at least a week before we can get away. We want to come and see you, spend some time with you in your world. If you'll let us."

It took her a moment to catch her voice. It seemed to have deserted her entirely. "I . . . I'd like that. A lot. You've got my phone number and my address. Let me know, okay?"

Brad handed her a small package wrapped in plain blue paper. She had no idea what it was, but she opened it carefully and pulled out an absolutely exquisite silk scarf. It was all shades of green and brown, and when she opened it out and laid it across the table the pattern became clear.

It was a beautiful hand-painted rendition of the Brad wolf and the Cain wolf racing along a woodland path. "It's amazing. I know these two! Who painted this?"

"Dr. Tuck. The big guy's quite an artist." Cain shrugged and glanced at Brad.

"We're glad you like it," was all he said.

"These are the two wolves that sleep with me when you're not there." Her eyes filled with tears and she brushed them away with the back of her hand. Maybe Brad and Cain really did mean what they said. Maybe they truly wanted forever. "I will treasure this. Thank you."

She wrapped the scarf back in the paper to protect it and set it by the door with her sweater. A few minutes later, Christa and Steph, Wils, and Ronan joined them at their table, but she didn't show them the scarf. It held too much meaning for her, and she wasn't ready to share it with anyone. Suni and Darnell came over with Evan and Dr. Tuck, but Cherry felt sort of detached from the last night of partying and the celebrating everyone was into.

She wasn't ready to celebrate anything.

She'd obviously done a pretty crappy job of protecting her heart. It would be so much easier if she could believe Cain and Brad when they told her she mattered, but she'd learned the hard way that words were easy, though when Brad suggested they go upstairs to his and Cain's suite, Cherry was surprised by the change in venue but more than ready. Cain had already gone on ahead and it was a simple thing to step into the kitchen and go up the stairs to their private rooms. She doubted anyone would even miss her.

"I had no idea that staircase was even there. I've never been up here before."

Brad walked her down the hallway with his arm around her waist. "I know. Cain and I just realized that this morning, that we've always gone to your cabin and you didn't even know how to find our rooms. He reminded me tonight, when you said you'd not seen our place."

"It's not a problem, but you're right. I guess I've had other things on my mind all week."

"You're not the only one." They paused in front of a door at the end of the hall, and he kissed her. "This is it. Cain told me you probably thought we were hiding something up here."

Brad opened the door and stepped aside so she could enter.

"You came." Cain stepped into the main room, grinned at Brad, and then hugged her close. He stepped back and shrugged. "I was afraid you wouldn't want to."

"Why?"

"We've thrown a lot at you the past couple of nights."

"And I've loved every minute. Have you heard any complaining?"

He took her hand, dragged her into the kitchen. "No. I think that's what makes me nervous."

Brad hung back a bit. She glanced over her shoulder and saw him standing there, watching her, smiling.

Turning, she put her hands on her hips and said, "What are laughing at, Bradley?"

"I was just seeing how you fit in here. I've imagined you in our home, but the visual is pretty amazing."

She sauntered across the floor and wrapped her arms around him, stood on her toes, and kissed him. In less than a heartbeat Cain was embracing her from behind and Brad was stripping out of his clothes. For a last night with these guys it was shaping up to be a pretty fantastic time.

CHAPTER 20

She lay awake long after both Brad and Cain had fallen asleep. Her body ached in the most delicious way. Tonight had been absolutely amazing, a truly bittersweet night knowing it was the end of this fairy-tale vacation. Both men had promised they would do their best to come and see her, that somehow they'd find a way not to lose what they'd been building.

She thought about staying the night, but she'd already talked it over with Steph and Christa and they wanted to get an early start. They all had to go back to work on Monday morning, and they'd need all day Sunday just to catch up on laundry and getting back to the grind.

Quietly Cherry gathered up her clothes and took them into the front room, where she dressed. She thought about leaving a note, but she'd see the guys in the morning. For now, she really had to get a good night's sleep before the long drive tomorrow.

Slipping out the door, she gently closed it behind her and went down the stairs. She started for the back door that would let her out through the kitchen when she stopped in her tracks.

"Damn." The beautiful scarf the guys had given her was somewhere out in the dining room with her sweater. A small light over the bar allowed her to see without turning on the bigger lights, but she heard voices on the front deck. It sounded like Fred and Suni.

It was easy to recognize Fred. She was always complaining about something.

With any luck, the women wouldn't see her and she could still leave by the back. She'd miss Suni, but not Fred. The woman had been downright rude to her on more than one occasion and seemed to excel at giving her dirty looks. Even Christa had noticed.

Walking quietly, Cherry found her sweater and the scarf right where she'd left them. Slipping the sweater on, she grabbed the scarf, but as she turned to leave she heard her name. She hated eavesdropping—no one ever heard anything good—but human nature won out over good sense.

Cherry stood in the shadows, listening.

"What a wasted week. Surrounded by good-looking men and I end up with Trak and his brother, and they're both sanctimonious jerks."

"No, they're not." Suni laughed, but Cherry thought she sounded uncomfortable. "They seem like really nice men. You took them back to your cabin often enough."

"Well, nothing happened, even when I let them know I was interested."

"You're kidding!" Suni laughed again, but Fred didn't sound all that pleased.

"Yeah, and like I said, the two best-looking guys here fawning all over Cherry. I don't get it. She's fat and she's ugly and she's got the men. What a waste—such beautiful guys with lousy taste in women."

"She's not ugly. She's a little large—"

"Suni, she's built like a fucking blimp."

"Anyone next to you is going to look like a blimp, Fred. You're skinny. Besides, I heard a couple of the guys talking about them. They said Brad and Cain are really nice guys who like to make even plain women feel special the week they're here. That's all it is—the guys are just giving Cherry good memories of her vacation. They probably figured, as pretty as you are, they didn't need to do anything to make you feel better about yourself, but why else would they spend all their time with her?"

Why else? Cherry clutched her scarf close to her chest—a scarf that was a gift from Brad and Cain—and thought about leaving it here. Except it was beautiful and, until this moment, her memories had been beautiful, too. Now she'd keep it as a reminder that she really had to be more discerning about men. She thought of confronting Suni and Fred, but what good would that do?

They were merely stating the truth.

Then Cherry thought of going back upstairs and telling Cain and Brad what she thought of them, but she honestly didn't have the energy, especially if they'd only been trying to make her feel good about herself. If not for Suni and Fred, they would have succeeded.

The women's conversation moved on to something else and Cherry crept silently out of the lodge, tears flowing as she took the beautiful path back to her cabin. The twinkling fairy lights swayed softly, only this time she felt as if they mocked her.

She called both Steph and Christa and left messages to let them know she wanted to leave really early, that if they wanted a ride home they needed to meet her at the car by five and she'd buy them breakfast in Weaverville.

Then she hung up and crawled between the sheets. If she was nothing but a job to Brad and Cain, then they probably deserved a raise, because they'd done a damned good job and she'd enjoyed every minute.

Until now. Now she just wanted to curl up and fade away.

Saturday

"Why do I feel as if we're sneaking out under cover of darkness?" Christa frowned at Cherry.

"Because we are," Steph grumbled from the backseat. "I was looking forward to a really nice breakfast and a last chance to see Ronan."

"I thought you were with Wils?" Cherry kept her eyes on the dark road, and wished she'd just kept her mouth shut. She really didn't want to talk to anyone. Not even Steph and Christa.

"She was," Christa said. "She still is. And she's with Wils, too. And so am I. With Wils and Ronan."

"She's with me, too."

Steph's soft voice from the backseat had Cherry doing something she'd thought she'd never do again—smiling.

"I know," she said. "I figured that out about midweek. In fact, I've wondered for years if the two of you were ever going to figure it out."

Christa turned in her seat and her focus on Cherry was laser sharp. "We might not have, if not for Wils and Ronan.

It took two men who were essentially strangers to pick up on something we still can't quite believe. How could you?"

"Observation, I guess. I've watched the way you two look at each other and wondered if maybe one of you was interested, but the other one wasn't. When I saw the four of you leave together the other night I wanted to cheer. It also probably explains why neither one of you has had a long-term boyfriend—you didn't really want one."

"See, that's where you're wrong." Steph was leaning forward now. "Christa and I've talked about it. We're both as attracted to men as we are to each other, but we have a lifetime of love to back up that attraction. Wils and Ronan are the first two we've met who feel the same way about their relationship. They love each other, but they love women, too."

"Except they were smart enough to figure it out." Christa sighed. "They said they want to see us again, but they can't get away for at least a week." She sounded hopeful. As hopeful as Cherry had been until last night.

Her sister turned around and faced forward, staring into the dusky dawn as their car reached the end of the gravel road. The sun was just peeking over the mountaintop when the automatic gate opened and Cherry drove out onto the two-lane highway. In the rearview mirror she watched Steph staring out the back window. Probably thinking about Ronan and Wils.

The same way Cherry was dreaming of Brad and Cain.

"She's gone." Cain raced into the bedroom and stared at Brad, who sat on the edge of the bed, trying to get his bearings. He'd been sound asleep until he heard Cain shouting at him. "Her sister and Steph are gone. Their car. I checked their cabins and they're entirely cleaned out. Hell, Cherry even stripped the bed. What the fuck happened?"

"I don't know. Last night was amazing. I was sure she finally understood how we feel, but obviously—"

"Obviously, we fucked up. I don't get it, Brad. What happened? Crap." Cain sat next to Brad with his head bowed. "I love her. I never thought I'd fall in love with anyone but you, but I love both of you."

"We have to get her back. That's all there is to it." Brad wrapped his arm around Cain and held him close.

"But how?"

"I don't know. We better find Wils and Ronan. I think they're in love with Christa and Steph."

"Shouldn't we follow them? We can be in San Francisco in less than five hours. We—"

"No, Cain. We added that one-week rule for a reason—to give women a chance to think about their feelings after they've left Feral Passions. Cherry must have really good reasons for sneaking away like she did. She has to—she's as honest and straightforward as they come, and she wouldn't have left for no reason at all."

"Fuck, Brad. I honestly thought Cherry was falling in love with us, but with her history with that jerk in high school, she's probably terrified of believing we mean what we say. Okay, we give her a week and then we go to her. But we need to find Wils and Ronan, too, and let them know."

"Wils and Ronan have just found you." Ronan shoved the door open with Wils right behind him. "You mean you're not the reason the girls left?"

"No," Brad said. "And obviously you two aren't, either."

"We're not." Wils stepped in ahead of Ronan. "But I bet I know who is."

Suni, Darnell, and Fred were already in the dining room, looking for coffee when Brad finally got dressed and made it downstairs. "Sorry, ladies. Had some problems this morning. I'll have coffee for you in a few minutes."

Brad went straight to the kitchen and filled the coffeemaker. Cain watched him for a moment and then went out into the main room with Wils and Ronan and sat at the table with the three women. "Something happened last night," he said, watching their faces. "Do any of you have any idea at all what could have upset Cherry badly enough that they'd leave in the middle of the night?"

"What? They're gone? I just thought they were sleeping late." Darnell's quick glance around the room made it clear that she was clueless, but the look of utter disgust that passed from Suni to Fred had Cain's senses on high alert.

"What happened, Suni? Tell me? This is important."

She lowered her chin and wouldn't look him in the eye. Not a good sign.

"Fred and I were out on the deck last night. The dining hall was shut down, but we were finishing off a bottle of wine, talking about the week."

"About the way you and Brad have been playing that hippo Cherry."

The breath left Cain's lungs in a long whoosh. Cain squeezed his hands into fists to keep from strangling the bitch. "You said that in front of Cherry?"

"Hell, no. She was upstairs, with you and Brad."

Suni shook her head. "No, Fred. I noticed her sweater by the door when we went out on the deck. I think she'd come downstairs to get it. I thought I saw a reflection in the glass, but now I think what I really saw was movement behind the window. I didn't think of Cherry until just now, but her sweater is gone this morning. She had to have heard us.

"Cain, I'm so sorry." She shot an angry look at the other woman. "Fred was talking trash about Cherry, getting herself all worked up, and I was trying to calm her down. I had no idea Cherry was listening, but I repeated something I'd overheard, that you and Brad were really nice guys who liked to give some of the plainer girls a memorable vacation."

"Fuck. She heard you and believed the worst." Cain flattened his palms on the table and stood, towering over Fred. "For what it's worth, Brad and I love Cherry and we want her here with us. Forever. We do not 'play' women. We enjoy women and we have tried to ensure that every woman here has a good time, but Cherry is different. She's beautiful, she's smart, and she's a good woman. She's certainly a lot more woman than you'll ever be."

He was so pissed he was shaking, and he knew he had to get out of there before he blew it. "Obviously, you don't know how to have a good time unless you're hurting someone else."

"Cain? What the hell's going on?" Trak stepped into the dining room and got right up in Cain's face. Cain had no intention of challenging his alpha, but the man needed to know.

"Talk to your girlfriend, Trak. She'll tell you what a

sweetheart she is." He spun away from Trak and headed
into the kitchen to tell Brad what he'd learned.

Cherry managed to drive and not cry almost all the way to
Redding, when Christa banished her to the backseat and took
over driving. By the time they got to Willows and pulled over
for Steph and Christa to trade places so Steph could drive,
Cherry was curled up in the backseat, beyond sobbing. She
hadn't said a word to her sister or Steph, and they'd left her
alone.

She was beyond talking about anything at that point.

She kept wondering if she should have gone straight to
Brad and Cain, if leaving without confronting them had
been the coward's way out. The women had almost reached
San Francisco before she finally admitted to herself that
yes, she'd been a coward.

She'd never wanted anything or anyone as much as she
wanted Brad and Cain. It had been easier to run than to find
out the truth, that they really didn't care for her the way they
said they did. That they'd just been doing their job and they'd
picked Cherry because she was fat and a loser and they were
truly nice guys.

But what if that wasn't it at all? What if they'd meant
everything they said? What if they really wanted her, but
they were as afraid to talk of love as she was?

And there was another option, one she hadn't even considered. What if that bitch Fred had lied? Except Suni had
been the one to bring up the guys just paying attention to
Cherry out of kindness and she wasn't a bitch.

But Suni was a peacemaker, always trying to make Fred

seem nicer than she was. Could she have made that up? What a stinking mess! Cherry curled into an even tighter ball of misery.

She didn't know. Damn it all . . . she just didn't know.

"Are you going to be okay here by yourself, hon? I'm worried about leaving you alone."

Christa had helped Cherry get her suitcases into her apartment and now her little sister sat on the side of her bed. Cherry had walked in and crawled into bed. She pulled the big comforter up over her and waited for Cissy to leave. Steph waited downstairs in Cherry's car.

"Just go." Cherry couldn't talk to anyone right now. "I'll be okay. I'm just really tired."

"Okay. I'll bring your car back in the morning. I checked your kitchen and you've got plenty in the freezer to eat until then. If you need me, if you want to talk, even if it's the middle of the night, you call me, okay?"

"Thank you, Cis. I really don't deserve you."

Cissy leaned over and kissed her cheek. "I know. I'm wonderful, and don't you forget it."

Cherry squeezed her sister's hand. "Never. Now go. I'll tell you all about it tomorrow." She sniffed. "I think that, right now, I need to wallow in my misery a bit and figure out what to do next."

Cissy and Steph left, and Cherry pulled the small package with that beautiful scarf out of her bag and laid it across the chair in her bedroom. Staring at the painted silk, at the picture of the two familiar, beloved wolves, she curled up on her bed and sobbed.

CHAPTER 21

Sunday

"Okay. We've got about four hours before the first of the new group show up. I want some answers. Cain? What the hell happened yesterday? You can't talk to one of our guests like that and think no one's going to notice."

Brad glared at Trak. While Cain had occasionally challenged their alpha, Brad had never before forced eye contact with the man, but he couldn't recall ever being so angry before, either. "You're right," he said. "But only because calling her what she is, a bitch, is an insult to every single female wolf here. Trak, you spent most of the week with Fred. You, of all people, should have figured her out."

"It wasn't by choice, believe me. I only stuck with her to keep her from leaving and taking her two friends with her. She's the one who arranged for the private plane. Look, I know she's petty, mean, and spiteful, but I have no idea what happened that put a bee up Cain's ass. Or why your woman and her sister and friend bailed out at the crack of dawn."

"Only because you didn't want to hear."

"Cain? Shut the fuck up." Trak glared at him and Cain

had no choice but to lower his eyes and bare his throat, but Trak wasn't through. "You've lost any right to this discussion, and you wouldn't even be here if not for your partner. Brad? I asked you. What happened?"

So Brad told him. About falling in love with a badly damaged young woman, feeling as if they'd finally gotten through to her when, inexplicably, she'd taken off without a word. Brad repeated what Fred had said about her, what Suni had admitted to saying.

Ronan and Wils were at the table, included because of their involvement with Steph and Christa, and both men listened closely.

"In Suni's defense," Ronan said, "and that's only because I really like Suni, she may have overheard me saying something to your brother, Trak. Lawz asked me what the attraction to Cherry was for Brad and Cain. At the time I didn't have any idea how you guys felt about her, and I said that you were both good guys and I'd watched you pick out the least attractive women in the past and show them a good time. It wasn't meant as an insult, and personally I think Cherry is a beautiful woman, but Lawz likes women who are a lot thinner, and my answer made sense to him."

Wils shrugged. "Face it, Lawz likes to see bones. We don't, but he can't see past a woman's figure to what's really important."

Trak nodded, and then he sighed. "Well, crap. You're right. He likes skinny women."

Trak turned to Cain, facing him head-on. "I apologize, Cain. I'm sorry. I had no idea what was going on, but it sounds as if Fred deserved your anger. Have you heard from Cherry since she left?"

Cain shook his head. "They wouldn't have gotten home until late yesterday afternoon at the earliest."

"Why don't you call her today? Let her know how you feel. That you'll be there next week. I still think a week's wait is a good thing, for both of you, human and wolf."

Sighing, Cain glanced at Brad. "We talked about it," Brad said. "We've never told Cherry we love her. We don't want the first time to be over the phone."

"Why didn't you say anything?"

Cain took Brad's hand and held on to it as if it were a lifeline. There were times like this when Brad thought he understood just how deeply Cain loved. The man had so many more levels to him than most people saw. Brad smiled at Cain and turned to Trak.

"Cherry had a horrible experience years ago with an absolute bastard, something that damaged her in ways we'll probably never truly understand. Neither of us felt she was ready to hear the words and accept them. The fact that she's as successful as she is shows us just how strong the woman can be, but I imagine Fred's hateful words have been harder for her to handle than something like this might be for another woman."

Cain sighed and glanced at Brad and then at their clasped hands. "My feeling is, we get through this week and then Brad and I want to take off at the end of the week. Plan on us being away for the weekend. Can you get someone to cover until at least the following Monday?"

"For us, too." Ronan looked at Wils and shrugged. "Hell, Trak . . . the entire point of Feral Passions is for us to find mates. I think we've found ours as well."

Trak leaned back in his chair and stared at the two men. "You, too? Cherry's sister and Steph?"

"Yep." Wils grinned at Ronan. "We're a team. Turns out Steph and Christa are, too, and they both like both of us. Face it, Trak. It just doesn't get any better."

Trak shoved his fingers through his hair and then pushed his chair back from the table and stood. "Okay. I'll make sure you're all covered. But that's one thing I guess we haven't thought through. Will you be leaving Feral Passions once you're mated, or do you think you can continue to work here, or maybe cover for some of the guys who haven't felt comfortable leaving their jobs to be here? At this rate, I'm going to end up shorthanded."

Brad glanced at Cain, who nodded. Then Brad grabbed Trak's hand and shook. "Cain and I are staying on. I think the women will be an asset, once they've gone through the change."

"I dunno," Ronan said. "Women? Change?" He shuddered. "Scary thought. Gentlemen, I think life as we know it is about to change."

They were all laughing by the time the meeting broke up.

Christa and Steph showed up just after nine with café mochas for the three of them. Cherry'd just gotten out of the shower and was trying to figure out where to go from there when the girls walked in without knocking.

There were times she was sorry she'd given Christa a key to her apartment.

This was not one of those times. She ducked her head

when they cornered her. "I'm sorry," she said. "I really am. Yesterday was so wrong on so many levels."

"Good. That means we might get some answers this morning." Christa handed her the mug topped with a layer of whipped cream and chocolate sprinkles. So what she didn't need, although she'd gotten on the scale last night and had actually lost a few pounds.

Good sex and hiking in the mountains must work for her.

"Cherry? What happened?"

Christa flopped down on one of the kitchen chairs and Steph took another. Cherry sat on a third and stared at the little chocolate sprinkles on the whipped cream. And then she told them. Everything—about the sex with both men and the things they'd said to her, that they wanted her forever. "And I believed them because they had no reason to lie to me. I was willing to be with them just for the week, because I knew it might be my only chance for such an experience, but then when I heard Suni and Fred talking—"

"Fred's an absolute bitch, and for what it's worth, Suni was always trying to make Fred look like she's nicer than she is." Christa grabbed Cherry's hand. "If the guys really love you, you'll hear from them, though I'd say to give it a week." She glanced at Steph. "Remember what Ronan and Wils were talking about, that day when they didn't know we were in the dining room?"

"I do." Steph grabbed Christa's hand and smiled at Cherry. "You know, I've wanted to hold your sister's hand in front of you for the past few years, but I wasn't sure how she felt about it, that I wanted to be her lover as well as her best friend. We learned a lot this last week that's changed our lives. I'm so glad you're okay with it."

Cherry gave her a wide-eyed, innocent look. "Think about it, Steph. Christa's my sister and I love her. You might as well be my sister, and I love you, too. This just means you're really going to be my sister, right? And now that we have that nonissue settled, what were Ronan and Wils talking about?"

"Sorry. Got off track. Something about there being a rule that they had to wait a week before contacting any women who'd been at Feral Passions because Trak didn't want anyone getting involved with a guest unless they were really sure of their feelings, although I don't know why that would matter."

Cherry's mind was spinning, and no matter how she tried to dissect the convoluted conclusion she was coming to, it always spun to exactly the same point. She'd suspected all along, but—

"I think I know why it matters, but you're going to think I'm nuts. First I want you to look at some pictures I took." She pulled out her cell phone and went to the photo album. "Just look through the first four pictures."

Steph and Christa scrolled through the first four shots Cherry had taken of wolves at the resort. "These are great shots." Steph raised her head and looked at Cherry. After a moment, she shrugged. "What am I looking at?"

"Their eyes. Specifically eye color."

Christa grabbed the phone. "Okay. Pretty brown eyes. This one has green eyes. This one's got grayish green eyes. And this one . . ." She raised her head and stared at Cherry.

"Bright blue eyes, right?"

"What are you saying?" Steph grabbed the phone and looked again.

"Brad has dark brown eyes. They're so pretty. They make me think of bittersweet chocolate. Cain's eyes are green. Dark green, like pine tree green. Ronan's are that really stormy grayish blue that reminds me of the ocean on a cloudy day. And Wils has—"

Looking at the picture, they all said, "Bright blue eyes," at the same time.

Steph swallowed. "Where are you going with this, Cherry?"

"Did you read that one paranormal romance that I recommended? *Alpha's Woman*? The one about the sexy werewolves?"

"Oh, Cherry. C'mon." Christa laughed. "You're not saying these guys are werewolves, are you? That's crazy! Werewolves don't exist."

"Did you ever see the blue-eyed wolf and Wils at the same time? Or the one with green eyes when Cain was around? Or the gray-eyed wolf with Ronan or the brown-eyed wolf with Brad? I'll bet you never did, because I'm convinced they're one and the same. I never saw man and wolf together, and believe me, I was watching for them. What else would explain wild wolves with manners? Wild wolves that cover their eyes when told not to look? Wild wolves that came to me when I was sad and stayed with me all night so I wouldn't be alone? I know you think I'm nuts, but if you can come up with another reason that these wolves are humanly intelligent and never appear at the same time as the people I believe they turn into, then I'm wide open. Except I don't think you can."

Steph had kept quiet, but she continued staring at the

picture. "It would explain that 'one week no contact' rule. I mean, I don't know if fictional werewolves have anything to do with real werewolves—assuming real ones exist, but in the fictional pack, and yes, Cherry, I read the book and I loved it. Anyway, in the fictional pack, when werewolves mate, it's for life, and generally includes biting the mate and turning them into a wolf, which sounds blatantly impossible."

"But if it is possible, imagine the life you could live. You and Christa would be mated through your mates, because Ronan and Wils are a pair, aren't they?"

Christa nodded. She didn't seem quite as disbelieving at this point. "They are. They're the ones who encouraged Steph and me to come out to you. I don't know why I worried about telling you the truth. It just felt like such a huge step. The parents aren't going to like it."

Cherry laughed. "Personally, I love it. You've always been the perfect daughter and I've been the huge disappointment. At least now we'll be on equal footing."

"Yeah," Christa said drily. "We'll both be pariahs!"

"Four-legged pariahs." Steph's droll comment had them all in hysterics.

They were all sort of mulling through the past week and trying to see things through the filter of werewolves. As much as she kept looking for proof she was wrong, Cherry couldn't find it. Her phone chimed, and she grabbed it out of her handbag. "Probably the office, checking to make sure I'm coming back to work tomorrow."

She stared at the text for so long that Christa reached across the table and took the phone out of her hands. "Wow! Steph, it's from Brad."

"What's it say?"

Cherry didn't wait for Christa to read the text. "'Don't give up on us. Cain and I love you. We'll see you at the end of the week."

"That is so cool." Steph smiled at Christa. "I wish Ronan and Wils would come, too."

"You never know." Cherry stared at her phone and sipped her café mocha, but when she raised her head she was smiling. "There never was a Gina, was there? You know, that mythical friend who dropped out of the three-person vacation package? The one whose spot I took?"

Christa and Steph looked at each other and then they both smiled at Cherry.

"I thought so. Thank you. Thank you both so much."

This was going to be a very long week.

CHAPTER 22

Friday

Cherry walked the last block to her apartment, convinced she might not make it. This had been the longest week at work she could remember, and the only thing that had kept her going was the hope that Cain and Brad might be here tomorrow.

She hadn't heard from them all week long, and she missed them with a fierce longing unlike anything she'd ever experienced in her life. Tonight she was going to take a long shower, have something easy for dinner, and then sleep. With luck she wouldn't look like death warmed over if—no, *when*—the guys showed up.

She had to believe. She couldn't *not* believe!

Normally she'd take the stairs—she was only on the fourth floor—but tonight she got into the elevator and made the quick trip to her level. She hung her tote bag over her shoulder and unlocked the door, closed and locked it behind her, and dropped the bag on the floor. Kicking off her shoes, she walked into her bedroom to get out of the long skirt and tank top she'd worn to the office.

Thank goodness the company wasn't too strong on dress codes. Days like today, the last thing she wanted to worry about was . . . *a wolf on her bed?*

Big and dark with soulful brown eyes, he stood alone in the middle of her bed with his head down, ears flattened to his skull, and his tail tucked between his legs, and all she could do was stand there with her hands over her mouth and cry. For about ten seconds. Then she flew to the bed, wrapped her arms around him, and sobbed.

"Brad! You came! Where's Cain? Is he here? I am so sorry I left without talking to you. I was wrong, but I was such a mess and Fred and Suni said a bunch of stuff and I should have gone to you first, but I was totally humiliated and I'm such a coward that I left. I was wrong and I'm so sorry."

"I'm here, Cheraza."

"Cain?" She whipped about and he was standing there beside the door, his hands at his sides, a half smile twisting his lips. "Oh, Cain." Trembling from head to toe, she stood there as if rooted to the floor. "This is Brad, isn't it? You can both turn into wolves, right?"

Cain reached her in two steps and she was in his arms, her mouth crushed beneath his kiss, her face wet with her tears and his. The wolf whimpered, and Cain ended the kiss, laughing.

"Yes, my darling Cheraza. I told Brad you had us figured out."

"I did, at least I was almost positive, but I wasn't sure until now. You're so beautiful when you're wolves. And I love you. I love you both so much. Will you forgive me? I never should have doubted you, but you just seemed too . . ." Shaking her head, she tugged Cain closer to the bed and buried her face in the thick ruff at the back of Brad's neck and sobbed.

He licked her face, washed away the tears, and she finally pulled it all together. She took a shaky breath and asked, "Is it hard to shift? I love you as wolves, but I want you, Brad. I've missed you both so much."

He stood and bowed his head and his body rippled and flowed, and with each ripple more skin appeared, and while it was soundless—thank goodness—his bone structure changed until it was complete. She'd thought the change would take a long time, but in less than a minute it was Brad on his hands and knees, gloriously naked on her bed.

He wrapped his arms around her and held her close, so close she felt his heart thundering in his chest, heard the break in his breathing as if his emotions threatened to overtake him. She couldn't let go of them—both men were even more wonderful than she remembered.

Cain pulled away far enough to look at her. His eyes were filled with tears and his voice broke when he said, "You need better locks on your door. Do you have any idea how easy it was to break in here?"

Laughing, crying, she kissed him. "What girl needs to worry about locks when she's got two fierce wolves to protect her?"

"Excellent point." He kissed her again and she tasted salt. Brad was right. Tough guy Cain really was a softy. They made love, the three of them as one, and Cherry realized there were no doubts in her mind or her heart. She loved both of them and they obviously loved her. They'd come after her, hadn't they? They all showered together. Brad got his clothes out of her closet where he'd hidden them earlier and dressed while Cherry ordered pizzas delivered. Cain opened a bottle of wine they'd brought, and finally the three of them settled in to talk.

"How did you know? Cain was convinced you'd figured us out from the beginning, but how?" Brad twirled her long, damp hair with his fingers. He'd not stopped touching her since his shift.

"Your eyes gave you away. Yours are dark chocolate brown and Cain's the color of pine trees. Two übersmart wolves hanging around with eyes that same color?" She laughed. "Impossible."

"As impossible as men changing into wolves?"

"No, Cain." She kissed him. "That's entirely possible. I'm a mathematician. All I need is proof. And you are absolute proof."

He laughed and then his expression went totally serious. "We're getting cable Internet installed in the lodge. Our quarters will be totally wired by the end of next week. There are rooms up there you can use as your office if you want to keep your job here and telecommute, and I know Trak wants to hire you for some contract work. Will you come back with us, Cheraza? Will you be our mate? Werewolf life isn't all that different from any other life. We do like to run under the full moon, but it's a choice, not a compulsion. Our children will all be boys, born to this life, though natural wolves like Brad and I don't make the shift until we're around thirty. Of course, we stop aging with the shift—you will forever be twenty-eight."

Cain kissed her. "Brad's got his architecture business, and I'm the pack enforcer, so that can take me away on occasion, but he and I also want to continue to work at Feral Passions. However, I promise no more naked massages with women."

Cherry sighed dramatically. "I wouldn't ask you to quit altogether. As long as I'm the one getting the naked massage, I'm okay with them. In fact, I really love them."

"Only for you." He kissed her again.

"You're the pack enforcer? What's that mean?"

He shrugged. "I'm the one Trak calls on when anyone gets out of line. They're all just a little afraid of me."

She laughed. "It's that tough-guy persona, but I can see right through you."

He kissed her. "Please, don't tell. You'll ruin my cover."

"Never," she said. "What's going to happen when you change me?" She wasn't afraid, but she definitely wanted to know what was coming.

"Brad and I will both bite you, which will make the three of us mates. All it takes is a small nip, just enough to break the skin. Usually, within twenty-four hours, you'll go through the change. It's not painful, though you might sleep a lot during that time. You'll awaken as a wolf with the knowledge of how to change back, but generally for the first change we'll take you for a run, introduce you to the wild wolves. That way they won't challenge you if they see you later."

"Can you communicate as wolves?"

Brad shook his head. "Not well. We're not really telepathic, though we do get better at understanding one another. Cain and I have been together for so long that we understand each other fairly well, but it'll take a while with you because we haven't known you all that long. Once you've changed, you'll live a long, long time."

She looked at them, both so young and healthy and way too sexy for their own good. "How long have you been together? How old are you guys?"

Cain smirked and glanced at Brad. "Rather rude questions, don't you think, Bradley?"

"Cherry, he's only saying that because he's sensitive about the fact that he's older than me. I was born in 1931. Cain and I have been together since I was about thirty, in 1961."

"And he doesn't look a day over eighty-five."

"Better than you, old man." Brad jabbed him in the ribs with an elbow.

"Personally, I think I look pretty good for my age. One hundred and six and I can still make Cherry scream my name."

"That you can." She gave him a sexy glance and slipped her fingers inside the collar of his shirt to tease. "But so can Brad. I think I need some more screaming demonstrations, if you're up to it."

They were both on their feet within seconds.

It wasn't all that many minutes later and Cherry was definitely screaming their names. Quite clearly.

EPILOGUE

Two nights before the summer solstice, at Feral Passions Resort

The summer solstice wasn't until Monday, but they held the mating ceremony on a Saturday night when there were no guests at the resort. Instead, the lush meadow was filled with strikingly handsome men, including a few older mated couples who'd made the trip back to the preserve just for this occasion.

Cherry wore a beautiful white gown and stood between Cain and Brad. Steph and Christa wore white as well, standing proudly between Ronan and Wils. The sisters and Steph had shared so much laughter all day while preparing for tonight, they'd decided ahead of time not to risk even a glance at one another until Trak completed the ceremony.

They'd all made their first shifts the weekend before, but tonight? Tonight was the real thing, more real even than growing fur and running on four legs. Tonight Cherry stood in front of the pack alpha, promising to love and cherish the two men who promised the same to her and to each other.

Brad and Cain had never had a ceremony of their own.

They told her they'd been waiting all these years to find her. Tonight was significant on every level possible.

As Christa and Steph repeated their vows beside Ronan and Wils, Cherry tightened her grasp on Cain's and Brad's hands. Then Trak stepped back to the middle once again and faced all of them. He'd worn a dark suit for the occasion, and he looked absolutely regal standing before them with silvery moonlight bathing a small meadow beside the lodge. Cherry thought of her dreams that first night, of running beneath a full moon with two wolves by her side, and she felt the power of Trak's words, as if by speaking them he created something magical out here. The moon, almost full this close to the solstice, was a silver beacon of light bathing the entire group of werewolves gathered for the ceremony.

Trak raised his hands, encompassing the newly turned wolves and their mates. "You have made your vows to the ones you love and to the pack you serve. Go forth secure in the strength of the pack and the love of your mates. My blessings and those of the pack on each of you for peace, good fortune, and love from this day forward. As Alpha of the Trinity Alps wolves, I pronounce each of you mated for life."

Brad and Cain kissed her and then kissed each other, and it was done. Cherry glanced toward her sister and caught Christa's eye. "Thank you," Cherry said.

Christa dragged her three mates with her. "What are you thanking me for?"

"For dragging me on a vacation I really didn't want to go on."

"You had a good time, right?" Steph slung an arm around

Cherry's shoulders. "I sure hope you did, sweetheart, because it's too late for a refund on the deposit."

The band started to play and drowned out the rest of Steph's teasing comment, but it was all okay, because Cherry learned something else she hadn't known about her two wolves.

They both really knew how to dance.

Two nights later, Cherry ran with her two wolven mates beneath the full moon. Pine needles crunched beneath their paws as they raced through the dark forest, winding their way along a narrow trail to the top of a rocky peak. There, surrounded by their wild brethren, they raised their muzzles to the silvery sky and howled.

Exactly as she'd dreamed.

THE
ALPHA'S
WOMAN

A. C. Arthur

PROLOGUE

The full moon

She had no choice but to run.

As a deafening howl ripped through her body, sounding throughout the small room she'd been allotted, Kira's long sharp black nails ripped through the curtains at the window until they fell to the floor in shreds. In an effort to release the pain burning deep inside she did the only thing she could, lashing out with wide swipes of her arms, deadly nails scraping along every surface they encountered.

Her lips peeled back from her lycan teeth, elongated and piercing as her mouth opened wide, another grisly growl breaking free. Around her she could hear furniture crashing to the floor, material and papers being torn, and the rapid thump-thumping of her heart. It was there that the pain had originated, beginning with the day her mother died three months ago.

Kira had believed she could go on even through the daily agony of not knowing for certain who had shot her mother down as she ran through the familiar forest. Kira's father had told her nothing, keeping his face stoic as he reported Tora's death to his pack as if it were just another announcement and he were some paid employee from CNN. But he had been Tora's mate, Kira's father. He should have felt something, yet he hadn't. Kira should have known then that something was wrong.

Instead, she'd tried to do everything her mother had taught her, tried desperately to be the alpha female she was born to be. She'd wanted to stand tall, proud of the extra-keen senses and strength she possessed over other lycan females. Coupled with the strategic planning and leader-ship skills she'd attained from watching her mother as she stood by Kira's father leading this pack, she'd had all the components to be a great alpha female. But Kira had failed. Pitifully. Irrevocably. Failed.

She'd been humiliated and disrespected, and when she'd finally spoken up she'd been betrayed by her own father.

Another guttural growl and she spun around, this time facing the mirror over her dresser, stopping cold. Staring back at her was the beast that was her counterpart, the ly-can with its feral snarl, protruding forehead and nose, eyes glowing light blue. Her hair was wild, sticking out around her face and falling in wild strands over her shoulders and down her back. She would have scared herself if that fear hadn't been replaced by the sting of lies and deceit. By the hatred she'd harbored for the members of her father's pack and for Penn himself. He wasn't a father to her, wasn't what he was when her mother had been alive. He'd changed in these months, so much so that allowing a member of his pack—his only daughter—to be assaulted the way she had been hadn't warranted so much as a double take.

"It's time you accept your fate, Kira. There will be no others, only them that are willing to take you and be what you need. Do not fight the inevitable," Penn had told her as she lay in the corner of their living room, her clothes ripped from her shivering body.

She'd kept her back turned to him, her head tucked low in disgrace as his words slammed into her skin like arrows. There would be no others because no lycan would want a female with her tall and curvy body. In Penn's eyes she'd appeared more dominant than she should have because she was almost as tall as the males with her five-foot-nine stature, and while she wasn't as muscular as they were, her body was built broadly. The fact that she was probably smarter than at least three out of the four betas in the pack meant nothing, nor did her abilities regarding the maintaining of the pack residence and the strategic planning skills her mother had taught her where their kind was concerned. She could be an excellent resource to the right alpha, a fact Tora cemented into her mind from the time she was a young girl.

But it wouldn't be any member of her father's pack. She'd realized that with startlingly clarity. They weren't who she was meant to be with, something Tora had also told her in the days just before her death.

"I've taught you everything I know," her mother had said, long lashes cloaking her soft brown eyes. "But there's more for you, Kira. More than I could ever teach you, more than you could have ever imagined. Beyond these walls and this pack, there is something for you. A destiny neither of us could ever have imagined."

"What?" Kira had asked, moving to sit next to her mother on the edge of the bed she shared with Penn. Fear and uncertainty had hung in the air like a dark cloud, just hours before they were set to attend Kira's college graduation. It should have been a time of joy, as she'd finished her courses early and would be receiving her BA in psychology. Tora had been so proud of Kira's goal to study the human psyche as well as the desire to probe deeper into the minds of the lycans. Yet today Tora looked so sad.

"Tell me what else there is?" Kira had insisted.

But Tora had only shaken her head and managed a shaky smile. "Not today, my child. Today is all for you. It is your beginning."

Three days later Tora had been killed and Kira had felt more like it was her end.

But it hadn't been. She'd survived in this house with this pack for three months since then. Every day knowing, sensing, that what had mother had said to her had been absolutely true. There was more for her than what was here. And after what had just happened to her, coupled with the fact that her father was condoning one of his beta's trying to forcibly claim her, Kira knew exactly what she had to do.

With a fist to the glass Kira broke the mirror, taking a step back from the shattering pieces. Her chest heaved as she struggled to rein in the beast, to yank it inside where it belonged. As an alpha female, she'd been trained and mastered controlling her shifts, so there was no doubt she could pull the beast back, but as the anger continued to rage, the beast was unrelenting in its claim over her. She lifted the mattress from her bed, digging her nails in deep and ripping it apart, tossing the remnants across the room. Next was the dresser that she turned completely over, standing atop it to howl into the night once more. Her pack mates would hear her, they would recognize her cry, but they would not come to her. Not to offer assistance or consolation, none of them, especially not her father.

That was just fine, because she didn't need them. Her mother had been the only one to ever give a damn about her. Tora had taught Kira everything she knew, just as she'd told her before her death. There was nothing here for Kira and she'd been a fool to let her father try to convince her otherwise. Her mother had been right, there was more for Kira out there, in the world, she supposed, and Kira was determined to find out what exactly that was. With that thought Kira backed up until she crashed into a wall, sliding down to sit on the floor. With arms propped on her knees, head hanging low, she breathed heavily, until her heart rate slackened, the sharp nails and teeth detracting slowly. She felt more like herself, like the self-assured and independent woman she planned to be.

Then she stood and she began to pack, because her choice had been made. She would leave this place and these people and she would find what her mother knew was out there for her. She would run toward freedom, toward the life meant for Kira Radney, not the one they'd tried to force on the alpha female.

And she wouldn't look back. Ever.

CHAPTER 1

Two weeks later

The more she squirmed the harder his dick became. His arms were wrapped around her tightly, the heavy weight of her breasts resting over them. His mouth watered, incisors biting into the skin of his lower lip, claws threatening to rip free.

"What the hell are you doing here?" Blaez growled into her ear, his mind warring with his body to keep his shift at bay.

"I was walking," came her clipped reply. "How about you? Is grabbing strange women a part of your regular routine?"

No, there was nothing routine about this. Blaez knew that for a fact. He'd been searching the woods, looking for something, following up on the feeling that had plagued him all afternoon. The one that had warned of danger.

And he'd found her.

Yet it was something else entirely clenching him at the throat just this second. Something so basic it might have been funny if he weren't who he was and she weren't where she should not have been.

He blinked once more trying to clear his mind of the

thick haze of lust that was now blanketed there. He took a breath and almost faltered. Her scent, so potent and intoxicatingly sweet, wafted straight up and into his nostrils, as if it were meant solely for him. Instinctively, his arms tightened around her, the soft globes of her ass like a cushion to his powerful erection.

If she was afraid she was doing a damned good job of hiding it. As for her arousal, that wasn't working too well for her. The scent of her dewy folds was what caused him to reach out and grab her close, to have the soft globes of her ass rubbing against his now-raging arousal.

Blaez held firm, grinding into her when she attempted to break away. The effort had him hissing through his teeth, and when she tilted her head to look back and up at him he almost moaned. Her eyes had glowed when she'd first turned to see him; hints of gold amidst the hazel color were bright and cunning in the seconds before he reached out and grabbed her. If her gaze had been meant to warn him of her anger and annoyance, he ignored it, opting to pull her back against him, enjoying the feel of her body against his for a second longer.

"You're not from around here!" he snapped. "It's dangerous to go traipsing around in someone else's territory. Didn't your alpha tell you that?"

She moved quickly, much faster than Blaez had expected, so that now she was facing him. But his reflexes were faster—much faster than even a lycan's should be—and he kept hold of her at the waist, her breasts flush against his chest. Her hair was disheveled, long dark strands framing her face to give her a distinctively wild and wicked look. At her sides now his fingers clenched and unclenched as the unfamiliar ache to run them over her scalp, tangling his hands in the dark mass and pulling her head back, threatened to take charge. Her mouth would open as she gasped from shock and he would take her then, his lips on hers, tongue stroking the moist recess of her mouth.

He shook his head quickly, as kissing was not something that Blaez did often. It wasn't something he'd ever wanted to do with any other woman, ever. Not in his dreams and certainly not in reality.

"No. I'm not from around here and I don't have an alpha. Are you going to report me?" she asked in a voice that was equally husky and sensual, snippy and cheeky.

"You're lucky I'm not the type to take and claim you for my own pack," he replied, the real reason for his anger toward her finally reaching the surface.

Lycans as a whole were not a domesticated bunch. There was no doctrine of rules or any thoughts of fair play when it came to building the most powerful and lethal pack. The same type of reckless abandon laid the groundwork for their insatiable desires. Next to hunting, their lust was a ruling factor in their lives, especially on the night of the full moon.

That, most likely, was not the intent of their kind. Then again, when a species was born of a god's selfish and arrogant rage it was no wonder said species didn't see life through rose-tinted glasses. Instead, the descendants of Nyktimos who had been lucky enough not to live in the deceptively utopic world of Arcadia now roamed the earth either struggling to find their place or threatening to kill anyone who crossed their paths—namely, their own.

This too was a result of their unnatural birth into a world that was neither ready nor equipped to deal with them. Had the battle between Zeus and Lykaon not gone to the extremes of the god using his power to turn Lykaon into a wolf and killing all but one of the king of Arcadia's sons, then maybe, just maybe, they would not be in the predicament they were in now. But Lykaon, angry and feeling hopeless in his new-found form, let jealousy overrule and bit his only remaining child, Nyktimos, turning him into a werewolf. In the vein of the apple not falling far from the tree, Nyktimos had taken his own anger and distress straight to the humans, settling in Seattle with the intent of wreaking havoc there, only to betray himself by falling in love with the most prohibited species—a human female—whom Nyktimos eventually turned into a lycan. From there the hybrid lycan was born and Blaez and his kind were doomed.

"I don't give a damn about you or your pack!" Kira snapped back at him, her stance and glare depicting nothing but distaste and disdain.

Her body, on the other hand, was sending off a totally con-tradictory vibe. She was aroused—there was no mistake—her body just about vibrated with the need. Her nipples had grown hard, brushing like tiny spikes over his chest, thighs trembling with the urge to be spread.

He wanted her.

And Blaez Trekas did not want anyone or anything.

"You will not be killed on my watch or my land. That's not the kind of attention I wish to draw. So you're coming with me," he said, easily stepping away from the tree she had him backed against. The temporary entrapment had only come at his allowance. The fact that her turn of defiance had only succeeded in bringing her body even closer to his had been his sole reason for allowing it at all. As he had no intention of dropping to the ground and riding her until she begged for his permission to come, Blaez knew it was time to get them out of the open, out of the scenting range of any other pack looking for a bitch.

"I am not coming with you," she said to his back, as he'd already begun to walk away. "I'm not a part of your pack, so I don't obey your commands. I don't obey anyone's commands!"

The last was said with every bit of defiance that lived within that soft, curvaceous body of hers, and it might have been commendable if it were directed at her enemy and she were the alpha bitch of her own pack. But she wasn't and Blaez was not a lycan to be toyed with or disobeyed.

Turning on her with the speed and agility only an alpha would possess, he lifted her clear from the ground, tossing her easily over his shoulder, and began his trek back through the woods to the lodge where he and his pack resided.

She squirmed, pounding her fists into his back, attempting to kick but for his arm wrapped tightly around the backs of her legs.

"Let me go, you idiot! You don't own me! I'm not one of yours!" she screamed as he walked, her perfectly rounded ass rubbing against the side of his face.

On instinct Blaez lifted his free hand to smack that delectable globe. The sound echoed throughout the woods, or was that only in his ears? His body certainly had its own reaction to the sting of his palm against the softest ass he'd ever imagined.

He did not stop walking, nor did he stop thinking of slapping her ass again and again, his dick growing harder against his thigh and his mouth watering at the thought.

———

"Sonofabitch!" Kira yelled and screamed and continued to fight back against what felt like a body of steel.

She knew the logic of what he'd said to her, had heard it just about every day of her life. So his saying it was not only tiresome and familiar, but it also really grated on that last shred of lycan patience she possessed. It had been one thing to hear this from her parents, another entirely to have him daring to speak to her that way when he didn't even know her, and now he was carrying her around like they belonged in some pre-historic time.

And he'd smacked her ass!

That had been the clincher. No, actually, that had been the moment Kira knew for certain she was in trouble. Because the action that should have enraged her to the point where she shifted and showed this alpha asshole just who she was and what she was about had instead aroused her to no end. Her vulva lips had pulsated, throbbing as the sting of his palm against her ass had sent spikes of pleasure throughout her body.

After he'd taken a few steps without even a hint of letting her go or another comment to keep their argument going, she figured she'd better rethink what she'd managed to get herself into this time.

She knew the rules; just like he'd said, he could "take and claim" her, and there would be no one to stop him and not much she could do about the situation. Except kill the sorry bastard!

Only something told her that wouldn't be as easy as she thought, not with this one. His physical strength was

obvious, the deep and commanding tone he spoke with another telltale sign that he was an alpha to his own pack.
What she was having a hard time pinpointing was this aura
that surrounded him. It had come quickly as she'd first
glimpsed him, seconds before he'd grabbed her, holding her
so tight against a very impressive arousal. In a flash it had
been gone, or rather her attention had been focused elsewhere, but Kira knew she'd seen it and now she wondered
at what it had actually meant.

"Look, why don't we try this," she said, hating this vulnerable position she found herself in and not too keen on
talking to his back either. "Put me down and we can talk
like mature adults. Instead of resorting to these basic primal instincts that are bound to get us all killed one day."

"I don't plan on getting killed, or letting you get yourself
killed. We can talk when we get to the house" was his clipped
response.

He had spoken to her like he was talking to a child or one
of the betas in his pack. No, she thought with a huff, even
they would receive more respect than he was currently showing her. That's simply how the packs worked and one of the
big reasons she'd decided as she'd been traveling that she
didn't want to belong to another one. She had never cared for
the hierarchy of the packs—the alpha male as the all-knowing
ruler; his alpha female just as strong and smart but relegated
to staying in the house and offering strategic hunting plans,
not going out to hunt or defend with her pack; and the betas,
male and female, who simply did what they were told, when
they were told, no questions asked. She was an alpha female,
which meant she was smart enough and strong enough to do

anything any alpha male could. Besides, her mother had told Kira there was more out there for her, more than simply being some alpha's mate. And she dreamed of more.

At least she'd thought it was a dream, because when it was over she'd been sitting on the wet ground, her back against a huge tree, head swimming in dizzying circles. She'd been standing on a deck or a porch of some kind, looking out into the night as the calls of an enemy pack had sounded their arrival. The battle plan was hers, spoken in her voice, a commandment to whoever was there with her. And then she'd run, wild and free, cool air ruffling over the thick layer of lycan skin that covered her face once she'd shifted. She was going into the battle, claws extended, teeth bared, the alpha female ready to strike.

That scene had made her believe all that her mother had said even more strongly. It had, in fact, inspired Kira to switch directions and to head to the Montana mountains instead of going farther south as she'd originally planned. Now she wondered if that had been a mistake after all.

"I didn't plan on getting dragged off into the night," she reluctantly admitted. "But we know what they say about the best-laid plans."

Her mouth was going to get her into trouble. Her mother used to tell her that and Kira had ignored her. It wasn't her mouth at all, but her too-round ass, too-big boobs, and the notion that she should be able to select whom she would give both to, that's what had gotten her into trouble. And now her mother was dead. Gone. Unable to help her only daughter in the time she'd needed her most.

Kira's fists balled once more, but she didn't slam them

into the alpha's back. She didn't open her mouth to curse at him or about what he was doing to her again. Instead, she clenched her teeth, fighting back the tears that threatened to fall, the self-pity that had begun to stalk her daily.

With one carefully aimed bullet Kira had become the most wanted piece of ass in Seattle, and Penn, her father, still wrapped in his grief and thirst for revenge against those he thought responsible for Tora's death, had done nothing to protect her. At least this alpha with his stony gaze, deep, authoritative voice, and the sexiest butt she'd ever seen had thought about her safety first.

Then he'd smacked her ass and the thought of her safety had slipped, no, dripped away as her vagina had immediately clenched at the contact, desire wetting her plump folds instantaneously. It shouldn't have aroused her and she used the fact that in two weeks there would be a full moon to explain the reaction.

"You shouldn't take me. Just leave me alone and I will be fine. I'll steer clear of the forest," she told him, knowing that was a lie. Even though she'd gone to human schools, done all the human teenager things—i.e., hanging out at the mall and going to boring as hell parties, then heading off to college, where she continued to do much of the same—the woods had always been home for Kira. They were her shelter, the only place where she'd ever felt any real connection.

"I'll do with you as I please," he replied quickly, his tone clearly intending to leave no room for argument.

Again Kira's fists were clenching, so tightly her nails almost broke the skin of her palm. She struggled for calm, knowing it was necessary, especially in this situation. Because this was no ordinary lycan. Of that Kira was certain. Any other alpha would have claimed her. It wouldn't have been about keeping her safe, but more so about keeping her, period.

"I don't belong to you," she told him finally. "As a species living in a human world we have to dislodge this notion of taking whatever we want, dominating whoever we can, just because we believe it's our right."

Kira half-expected him to drop her to the ground at that moment, looking at her with a mixture of bafflement and disgust just as Penn used to whenever she'd say these types of things to him. Her father was the alpha of a Hunter pack—which meant his sole purpose was to hunt those from the Devoted packs, the ones who were inclined to live in peace among the humans, while being certain not to cohabitate with them the way Nyktimos had. The Hunters believed in something totally different, they believed and craved total dominance, but to gain that they had to be rid of the Devoteds who would undoubtedly continue to preach their simplistic coexistence with the humans.

Penn hated not only that Kira had wanted to study the lycans' minds more deeply but also that she thought she could change his and the minds of the other Hunter packs with what he called "ridiculous words from human books."

"Our world lives by different rules," Penn had told her on one occasion.

"Rules of jealousy, vengeance, senseless killing and basic bullying," she'd replied. "Not so different from the human world at all."

"I'm not taking what I want; I'm protecting what I can," the deep rumble of his voice yanked Kira firmly from that memory.

"What if I don't need your protection? What if I'm as strong as you and can do just about all the things you can?" she countered.

As if saying in response that he didn't give a damn, his booted feet stomped upward. They were going up steps, although she could barely see them in the dark of night. She could scent, which worked better than vision for lycans anyway, to see if there were anything familiar about where he'd taken her. Instead, when she inhaled deeply her nipples tightened to painful peaks, her thighs clenching involuntarily, and confusion quickly set in.

"You are nothing like me. I can stake my life on that fact," he said only seconds before dropping her to her feet.

Kira struggled momentarily to land upright and not flat on her back. The book bag she'd hastily stuffed all her belongings in threatened to pull her down anyway. Righting herself, she took a precautionary step back. But in seconds realized that precaution meant absolutely nothing.

A light had come on, probably sensor motivated, and she could see that she was standing on a wooden porch. She could also see that the alpha standing in front of her—more like towering over her—was unlike any lycan she'd ever seen before. He was more than six feet tall, she knew because she was five feet nine inches tall herself and she still had to crane her neck upward to see into his eyes.

His skin was the tone of melted butter, smooth and taut over the bulging muscles of his biceps, his neck, his legs. He stood with his legs parted, his arms at his sides, fingers opened wide, ready to release his deadly claws if need be. He had a strong, clean-shaven jaw, a light mustache, and a bald head. He wore Lycra, shorts that fit his thighs and that toned ass and a shirt that melded over what she knew would be a perfectly sculpted upper body. He looked equally fierce and drop-dead gorgeous and she gulped in an attempt to keep her composure.

"I'm going to take you inside," he told her, taking another step toward her, closing the small space she'd managed to put between them.

"And you're going to sit down and tell me exactly why you were in my woods."

Her breathing came in quick pants now, desire pooling in the pit of her stomach like molten lava. She licked her lips, saw his gaze dip lower, then quickly pulled her tongue back inside. He appeared too good to be true, tall, strong, an alpha bent on protecting his alpha female . . . only she wasn't his and this was the last place she wanted to be.

"And what if I don't?" she taunted, refusing to give in to the arousal that had already taken over her body and was now ready for her brain to join the party.

He took another step, pressing his body flush against hers, reaching his hands around to grip the globes of her ass, pulling her so that she went up on tiptoe with a sharp intake of breath.

She couldn't help it; a little gasp sounded with his motion. Kira wasn't sure if it was those damned pleasure spikes shooting through her body from the point where his hands again made contact with her ass or the quick flash of bright blue in his eyes. At any rate, she couldn't speak, could barely do anything more than stare and wonder.

"Then I'll have no choice but to punish you for being disobedient. Is that what you want, *lýkaina?*"

Again words were just lost. Her mother would never believe it, but Kira's mouth remained closed. Until he moved in closer. When she didn't immediately respond he leaned in even farther. "Do you want me to spank you until you come?" he asked, his lips brushing the lobe of her ear, her mound rubbing flush against the thick length of his erection. "How quickly would you come if I did?"

CHAPTER 2

The door had opened behind her and Kira quickly backed away, going into the house instead of running when it was so obvious that she needed to get away from this male. Also quite apparent was the needle-point hardening of her nipples that she knew were visible through the thin material of her tank top, not to mention the thick cream now covering her plump folds that she knew the evil alpha could definitely smell.

In that moment she hated the lycan species. Hated how their scenting capabilities was one of their strongest attributes and that it was so blatantly connected to the insatiable sexual desires that coursed through their bloodstream like an incurable disease.

"Well hello," another male voice, this one measurably kinder than that of the alpha who was currently staring at her with a haze of simmering fury surrounding him.

She blinked at the sight as it reminded her of when they'd been in the woods and she'd thought there was some sort of light outlining his body. It hadn't been there just a few moments ago when they were on the porch, but she was just about certain she could see it now.

The alpha stepped inside as well, closing the double-wide door behind him with a quiet click. With every step she took back, he proceeded forward, taunting her with his dominating stature and steely glare, until finally she spun around. Kira's gaze immediately met the other male's in the room. He looked more relaxed, more approachable, than the alpha and she prayed he had more common sense.

"Hi," she said for lack of anything clever to add to his prior greeting. He was tall, with gorgeous blue eyes, light brown hair, and a terrific athletic build. His shirt was white and fit with the same alluring second-skin-like feature that the alpha's did. Only his was short sleeved and displayed two big and very detailed tattoos stretching the length of his toned biceps. There was markedly less dominance here, as there could only be one alpha male in any pack. Nevertheless, this beta was strong, he was perceptive, and he appeared to be nice.

Gulping quickly at the sheer masculinity of this guy while the corner of his mouth tilted in what she thought was going to be an excellent smile, Kira figured a coherent comment was the best she could do.

Next came an undeniable growl, low and threatening. "Who is she and why does she smell like that?"

Her neck almost cracked she'd turned so fast to see who had just criticized her. Not that she wasn't used to criticism; the betas in Penn's pack had dished out their fair share. This comment, however, Kira sensed was directly related to the alpha who was no doubt still glowering behind her. Had he not been so devilishly attractive, even while basically kidnapping her, she wouldn't be as aroused as she currently was and this second beta would not be commenting on that scent. Standing across the massive room, with its beamed ceilings, warm golden light, and heavy dark leather furniture, was another lycan. Another astoundingly good-looking—albeit pissed-off, as evidenced by the already-extended nails and the peak of sharp canines biting into his lower lip—male lycan. His eyes were green and piercing, his jaw covered in a neat low-cut beard, hair dark as night, and his scowl both menacing and sexy.

"She's a Hunter," the third beta said, coming from behind a wall, his sweatpants, tank top, and workout gloves giving away the fact that her arrival had interrupted his gym time.

Not that she thought any of the lycans in this particular pack needed to do any work on their bodies. They were all perfectly sculpted and beyond a pleasure to look at even though she knew one of the basic problems of her being here. It was the night of the full moon—which, as she'd recalled earlier, was coming in two short weeks—the one night when lycans were their most powerful and most aroused. It was also the only night a lycan mate could be claimed. Therefore, the days leading up to the full moon were tense, to say the least. It was akin to being addicted to some heavenly drug and having the next fix waved just inches from reach for days on end. That's what it was like waiting for the full moon, a slow and dangerous torture for unmated lycans and the blissful yet sometimes erratic prelude to mates reconnecting through the majestic power of the Luna goddess.

In essence, it sucked, and standing in the room with three unmated betas, as an alpha female up for grabs, was not the smartest situation for Kira to find herself in.

But that should have been the least of her worries, as

she just realized one of the differences that she should have known immediately when that cocky alpha had wrapped his arms around her—they were Devoteds.

This one, the third beta who seemed to know what he shouldn't, gave her an assessing gaze that raked over her body as if he were actually taking mental pictures. His skin was a golden tone, just a shade darker than the alpha's, his black hair cut close and precise, just like his goatee. He had thick eyebrows that were raised in question and a look that was a cross between pure hunger and unadulterated hatred etched across his face.

She didn't know what to do or say, how to feel or act. The only pack she'd ever been this up close and personal with had been Penn's. Hunters. And surely, Dallas, Cody, Kev, and Milo looked absolutely nothing like these hot-as-hell lycans. Perhaps if they had she might have considered having one of them claim her. But they weren't, and she'd left, and now . . . she was here. With four dangerous as hell lycans, all with their eyes set on her.

Kira swallowed, squaring her shoulders and refusing to back down. She was no longer a Hunter, no matter what they thought they could smell.

"My name is Kira," she told them. "And I'm no longer a part of a Hunter pack. I left them weeks ago and I have no intention of ever going back."

"Is that so?" the doubtful gym lycan asked. "You just left your pack and ended up here, of all places and with all lycans."

He was speaking of the alpha. Kira didn't know how she knew, but she did. She lifted a hand to brush back the wisps of hair that scraped along her face.

"I wasn't coming here specifically, if that's what you mean. In fact, *he*"—she said the word with every ounce of the disdain that she was feeling at the moment—"brought me here."

"Is she serious? They want to kill you . . . and us for that matter. And you brought her here?"

This was the angrier lycan, the one with the piercing green gaze who looked at her like he was ready to leap across the room and rip her throat out. His voice wasn't questioning, nor was it quizzical like that of the one with the pretty blue eyes. Instead, it was colder and more lethal, which meant he was the closest to the alpha. And thus more dangerous to anyone who threatened him.

For all intents and purposes, Kira knew she should be afraid. She was surrounded by four built-to-kill or built-to-fuck, whichever way the wind blew, lycans, which placed her in immediate danger. She should be calculating her odds on getting out of this situation alive, or at the very least thinking of what to say to get herself out of this predicament. Yet she was doing neither.

"He's Phelan," the alpha said from behind her, causing every muscle in her body to tense anew as he introduced the Green-Eyed Devil. "That one is Malec." The one fresh from the gym. "And this is Channing, who was just backing up."

Channing had still been standing directly in front of her with that boyishly cute smile that Kira figured was hella sexy when on full beam, and those insanely attractive blue eyes. He'd nodded and taken the advised steps away from her, while the alpha stood so close she could smell the soap he'd used to wash.

A lycan's sense of smell was everything. Their very lives

depended on how well they picked up scents, tracked, hunted. Kira felt like a colossal ass for not paying close enough attention to hers out in the woods. Since the moment he'd touched her she'd wondered how she hadn't picked up the alpha's potent and blatantly sexual aroma.

It had been the initial reason why she hadn't run, not the mere fact that he was an alpha. No, that wouldn't have been enough. She was already running from the leader of one pack; adding another wouldn't have made much difference, to her way of thinking. But the unfamiliar draw she felt toward him, as if he'd called to something specifically within her, had held her still for those precious moments when she could have gotten away. The moment he touched her, fleeing became a distant priority, a fact she figured she'd ultimately regret. It was confusing as hell, but it was also the honest truth.

"She was lost in the woods," the alpha stated.

"No, I wasn't," Kira replied quickly. "And while we're all making introductions, you are . . . ?"

The room was eerily silent as she'd turned to face him. He'd only craned his neck slightly so that he was now giving her a barely tolerant look. But there was so much more to that look, like another layer entirely to what he might have been seeing or thinking. It made her uncomfortable when his thick brows lifted as if he was intrigued, his lips fixed firmly like anger might have been his real reaction. Come to think of it, he'd seemed angry with her from the moment he grabbed her.

"He's Blaez and I'm not sure if it's a good or bad thing that you've been found by our pack when there's no other lycan around to protect you. There are no others, correct?" Channing asked, his tone still light compared to the intensely heated look she was still getting from . . . the alph—Blaez.

How fitting a name for this wickedly hot creature.

Those might have been the best words Kira had come up with yet to describe the simply seductive way he looked. The black clothes seemed to exemplify his power, while his body, every muscled inch of it, exuded every other cue that he was not to be fucked with.

And still, she'd continued to stare him down.

"As I just told you, I left my pack, so no, they are not with me. You needn't worry that they'll come here to hunt you down. They have no idea where I am and I'd like to keep it that way. Furthermore, I don't need protection," she stated evenly. "In fact, I don't need to be here. Nice meeting you all, but I'll be going now."

It was quiet again as if they were all waiting for something to happen. Kira wasn't; she'd just been blatantly reminded that she was once again surrounded by male lycans, the supposed top of their species. Wasn't this the exact situation she'd run from? No, these lycans were deliciously different from those in Penn's pack. They were also more lethal. She could tell just by the way they'd all seemed to surround her within moments of her arriving in the house—a pack descending on its prey. They were well trained—she'd give them that, because none of them had moved a muscle since Blaez had spoken. They all deferred to him unwaveringly as if he was not just their alpha but also someone infinitely more powerful. When she looked to the alpha once more, she realized with a heady start that he expected her to do the same.

Déjà vu immediately washed over her, to the point where she had begun to tremble, thinking instantly that deferring to another alpha was the absolute last thing she planned to do. She started moving to the door as quickly as she could without all-out running. None of them spoke for her to stay— even though she wouldn't have. None of them tried to stop her—even though it wouldn't have worked.

Penn had been cursing about her stubbornness for the better part of these last few months, in this instance his rangy pup pack following his lead with their own round of complaints. But she didn't give a damn; she didn't have to stay where she wasn't wanted, or *was* wanted, but for all the wrong reasons. And she damned sure didn't have to stay here, with these strangers who might just decide to kill her because of the pack she was unfortunately born into, just because Mr. Blaez, with his fine-ass self, proclaimed it.

She'd just reached forward, her fingers only inches away from wrapping around the doorknob, when she heard: "You're not leaving."

The words were barely out of his mouth when Kira felt herself being once again lifted and tossed over his shoulder like she was nothing more than a sack of old potatoes.

This time she did fight back, with every ounce of effort she possessed. Her heart beat wildly, fear slinking slowly along her infamous stubborn streak as she pounded her fists into his back. It was like hitting steel. His shoulders were broad, his stride even, as he carried her away. She'd looked up to see the other three watching them leave. Neither of them moving even when she called to them for help.

Blaez kept right on walking like he carried women away

without their consent on a daily basis. His running shoes were soundless on the wood-planked floors.

"You're an asshole, you know that!" she yelled at him. "This is kidnapping! It's illegal!"

His only response was to keep moving.

It was darker as he took the stairs, her head bobbing with each step, hair swaying all over until she felt like a wild woman. This time she kicked at him hoping she'd luckily land a groin shot, but that was unsuccessful.

"I'm not going to stay here," she told him with a huff. "The moment you put me down I'm leaving. I'm not a part of your goddamned pack!"

Her throat was beginning to hurt with all the futile yelling, but she could not give in. She could not go back to the same subservient position that she'd basically lived in all of her life. That's what her father wanted for her—to stay there in Seattle and to be claimed by one of his betas. That lucky beta would then become an alpha and Kira would become his mate. Her body actually shivered with that thought. It was wrong. It was not the way it was supposed to be. Not only did her mother's words confirm that, but something else, something deep inside of Kira, knew it to also be true. She'd been feeling it more and more in the weeks she'd been away from Penn and his pack. It was that confirming and guiding force that was getting her through each day.

It didn't take her degree in psychology to realize that yelling and screaming at this lycan wasn't going to work. No, she was going to have to deal with him on a much higher level than that. She would talk to him calmly, one alpha to another, regardless of the fact that she'd come from a Hunter pack, landing smack in the middle of a Devoted's territory.

"Why won't you listen to me? I cannot stay here," she said evenly. "It's just not where I should be right now."

She'd hoped her calm approach would work; still Kira was surprised when he abruptly stopped walking. He did not respond to her comment but opened a door and stepped into another room, closing it securely behind him. She'd just been frowning with disappointment when he unceremoniously dropped her on a bed. She fell back but then sat up immediately, swiping her hair from her face so she could keep eye contact with him. She probably should have been afraid of him, of the way he stood there towering over her, muscles bulging, eyes staring at her with a fierce glare. There was no mistaking this lycan's strength or his role in this pack, and if she was being absolutely honest with herself she'd readily admit that he was the most formidable and intimidating lycan she'd ever seen in her life. And yet she wasn't afraid.

"I am not a threat to you," he told her in that voice that was equal parts arrogant alpha and sex personified.

His brows had drawn close, his strong jaw stiff as he stood over her. That damned shirt molded over every muscle and curve like a glove, a well-fitted black glove that had her mouth watering. The shorts should have been a sin as well, hugging the tight roundness of his ass, denting in slightly on each side as if another muscle on his body needed pronunciation. And the bulge—the thick unmistakable proof of his arousal that had her creaming once more—pissed her off to another degree.

"I don't belong here," she said through clenched teeth, defensively pressing her thighs together tightly. It was no point, not enough friction as her body tingled with the slow burn of arousal.

"And you didn't belong there," he told her. "If you did you wouldn't have run."

"You don't know me," she said, flattening her palms on the bed before standing in front of him.

They were close. Too close. If she inhaled deeply the tips of her breasts would touch his chest. If she leaned in closer she would . . . what? What would she do with this alpha she didn't know and didn't want to be around but seemingly could not escape?

"I know that you cannot continue to roam around without a pack. It's too dangerous, especially now, with the way things are."

"I don't give a damn about pack law or what might happen if I'm found alone without a so-called alpha to protect me. I'm a goddamned alpha too; doesn't that count for anything?" she asked, totally fed up with the way things worked within this breed.

Humans chose whom to love, whom to marry, whom to spend the rest of their life with. In most marriages, they worked together as partners to raise a family and build a future. It boggled her mind as to why the lycans—the supposedly superior species—could not grasp that line of logic. At the same time, she warred with the facts of their heritage, the stories her mother had so proudly told her about their breed's fight to stay alive and to live in a world that they'd never asked to be brought into.

He grabbed her then, his strong palm bracing against the nape of her neck, pulling her flush against his body.

Kira shivered at the feel of his steely strength, the persistent throb of his cock pressing against her lower belly. His other arm remained at his side while he lowered his face so close to hers, Kira thought he might kiss her. She hoped he might . . .

She kept her eyes opened, refused to let them droop even slightly. Her heart was racing, her breasts so heavy with need they ached.

"Let . . . me . . . go," she whispered, hating the defeated sound of her voice.

If he ripped her clothes from her body and tossed her back on that bed, spread her thighs, and thrust deep inside her she would let him. Damn the logic, she would let him and she would enjoy it. She knew without one second's doubt that it would be good; he, Blaez the alpha, would be fucking fantastic! It was that simple for the lycan breed and that disastrous for the woman she wanted to become.

"Being an alpha means so much more than you know," he whispered hoarsely in her ear. "And because you're so naïve, I won't let you go to be hurt. And I won't . . . I . . ."

He faltered and she gasped. The sound of his voice had been rubbing against every sensitive, frayed, horny nerve of her lycan body. While she wasn't particularly keen on what he was saying, it was two weeks before the full moon and she was needing like she never had before.

"I won't stay," she said, because to remain silent and willing would be akin to admitting defeat.

"You won't run from me," he replied as if he'd regained something he'd momentarily lost. "And I won't hurt you."

He let her go then. As quickly as he'd taken her, he simply let go, turned, and walked out of the room. She fell back on the bed, taking a deep breath and still trying to get a grip on the desire burning deep down to her core, searing her from the inside. Her body trembled as with each inhalation she smelled him. Like earth and man and sex, a wicked combination that threatened to either strangle her or have her coming so hard and so fast she'd lose her breath.

She gasped with the potency of that thought, one hand going to her lower belly—she refused to let it go any lower, even though her wrist trembled with the notion. Another hand cupped her heaving breast. It overflowed her fingers; it always had. She was a full-grown female lycan and a full-figured twenty-one-year-old woman. And she was captured, once again.

CHAPTER 3

She was right next door.

A woman.

A lycan.

An alpha female.

Blaez had no idea where she'd come from or why she was on the run. All he knew for certain was that she carried the scent of the Hunters in the body of a goddess.

From the moment he'd seen her through the trees, watched her strong thighs and long legs carrying her briskly over the wooded terrain, he'd known he would approach. He would touch and goddammit he would taste. He'd known and he'd been pissed the hell off at the thought.

The women Blaez had sexual interactions with were studied and well versed in his preferences. They knew the rules, the limitations, the pleasure to expect, and the way out when he was finished. They came at his bidding, did what he required on command, and left without any complaints or further requests. It was the deal he'd worked out with them in the year since they'd moved to Blackfoot River. It was the way he preferred to handle his personal affairs because anything more, such as close emotional entanglements, was out of the question for him. His past had definitely dictated his future in that regard.

The decision to approach this female had come quickly, which in itself was unlike Blaez. He liked to consider all his options, then make the best plan of attack possible. Ten years of leading contracted covert ops with his specially selected team had honed his leadership skills to almost surpass the already-complex genetics of an alpha. He had been born to lead, or so his father had drilled into his head since Blaez was old enough to remember. It was in his blood and thus he couldn't escape it even if he wanted to, just as remaining a staunch member of the Devoteds was his destiny. It was the will of the Trekas pack before his and the one before that. Those were unchangeable facts.

But there were aspects of Blaez's life that he had been able to control, that he'd molded and designed to suit every one of his needs, even under these extenuating circumstances.

Grabbing the hem of his shirt, he pulled it roughly over his head; moving to the far end of his room where his dresser and wardrobe stood against the cedar-planked walls, he tossed it into the hamper and ran his hands down the back of his head. He breathed in slowly, out unhurriedly, trying to empty his mind. Only his body had another idea entirely. Gritting his teeth, he removed his shoes, then his shorts, until he stood in front of the window naked, exposed, every muscle in his body taut with a desire he'd never felt before.

Just on the other side of the window, forty feet to the west, about the same amount to the east, were the woods that surrounded and protected their lodge and property from the questioning eyes of the humans in town. He and his pack had moved into this building and had spent the last eleven months renovating and customizing it to suit their special needs. It had everything they required to survive and to not be found.

Blaez's space was on the upper level, a long hallway with three rooms and two bathrooms. His bedroom was the largest, with the king-sized platform bed he'd made himself from logs retrieved from the woods. There was a large flat-screened television mounted to the wall across from the bed with all news channels, local and international, programmed to its memory. Another room was private and remained locked at all times, the key kept on a silver link chain in a black velvet box on his nightstand. The other room, the one reserved for whom Blaez had never quite figured out, contained more custom-made furniture, including a queen-sized bed with rose-colored satin sheets and a black duvet, and now . . . her.

At his sides his fists clenched, his dick so painfully hard he had to gasp to catch his breath.

She'd been out there, he thought, in the dark of the woods, walking along as if she were on some nature hike. She'd been out in the open, her scent filling the air, traveling on the leaves. The night breeze was chilly, crisp, yet she wore no jacket, only the pants and top that both hugged her curves lovingly. Her hair lifted on the wind, the scent of the dewy dampness on her plump folds permeating and overruling his senses.

He licked his lips slowly, imagining his tongue moving over her labia instead. Another inhalation and his fingers flexed, his eyes growing heavy. He would spread her soft thighs, rubbing his cheeks along their smoothness. She'd opened before him like a newly bloomed flower, her arousal glistening on her folds, her pussy weeping with desire for him. He swallowed hard, his eyes going completely closed, his mind empty of everything except for her.

Moving in closer, he inhaled deeply of the heady scent that was all consuming and all hers. Or it had been hers; now, as it filtered through his flared nostrils, sifting through his body like fine mist settling along his raw nerves, twisting and twining into places inside him that had been long since dormant, Blaez declared that it belonged to him.

With his eyes still closed he began a slow descent, his head bowing farther, his tongue snaking out, moistened by the temptation, eager to taste, to fall, to enjoy. Oh, how he would enjoy exploring her with his mouth. His fingers clenched once more, his throbbing erection bobbing in anticipation, pre-cum dripping from its tip.

Blaez's chest heaved. Any attempt to slow his breathing, to recalibrate and get his mind right, was easily thwarted by her scent and how completely it had engulfed him. His body trembled, which was another first for the alpha, and he felt the prick of his extended incisors pressing against his skin.

"Dammit!" he cursed, shaking his head and opening his eyes. His breaths continued to come in heavy pants as he looked out the window once more, now fully aware of what he'd almost done.

One of an alpha's greatest powers was the ability to hold back its shift until the time was appropriate. She had shown that restraint in the woods. That and the way in which she'd confronted him toe-to-toe gave away her alpha status, without her ever needing to announce it. Alphas could be angered, injured, in danger, in captivity, on the night of a full moon, or not, and they would hold their shift perfectly until they were ready to strike. The training for this power had been ingrained and honed with each year the alpha grew into walking with its own pack. The betas who followed him did not have the same control, hence one of the reasons they needed to follow an alpha.

Only tonight Blaez hadn't exercised his total control, not the way he normally did. If he had, she would be dead in those woods or one of his betas would have been busily fucking her right this minute. He wouldn't have taken her himself because she didn't know the rules, didn't know his restrictive nature, and so could not have offered her consent. Blaez did nothing without consent.

Or at least he hadn't. Until now.

Kira.

He called to her and knew without any hesitation or doubt that she would answer.

"No," Kira whispered from the spot where she still lay on the bed.

She'd thought about getting up and using the shower in that bathroom she'd spied to the left when she'd sat up to face Blaez. There'd been a low light on beyond the partially opened door. That was the only reason she'd known it was there, because her rude host hadn't bothered to give her a proper tour of the facilities she'd be availing herself of to-night.

In fact, he hadn't done much but order her to stay here—against her will—and arouse the hell out of her.

And now this . . .

She shook her head from side to side as if he could see her. He could not, or at least she didn't think he could. This was what lycans called mindchatter—the ability of one to talk to the other without being in the same room. The range on this ability was pretty extensive too, somewhere around a ten-mile radius in the open and about six in a wooded area. This was the same for their scenting abilities. Only for alphas was the range farther, and the more powerful the alpha, the more intense its abilities.

She was rating Blaez as fairly fucking intense! Especially at this very moment.

Spread your legs and touch your pussy. That's what he'd just said to her.

She ignored him, yanking the hand that had been cupping her mound quickly away. He couldn't see in here unless he had cameras hidden somewhere, which she figured was a distinct possibility. Then again, maybe he did have the ability to see the lycan he was mindchatting with— some twisted lycan form of the humans' FaceTime abilities via cell phones. She'd already sensed something different about him; perhaps this was an alpha power she wasn't familiar with, as her mother had told her there was much more to learn about their kind.

Do it! he commanded.

No. She replied silently this time, clenching her teeth as if to show she meant business.

You're already wet for me, so you might as well do as I say. You need the release.

"I don't need a damned thing," Kira said out loud, because

406 A. C. Arthur

while they were mindchatting he could only hear what she said in her mind.

Open wide and let me see, Kira. Let me see just how hot for me you are.

"Oh hell no!" she yelled, then clapped her lips shut. He was taking arrogant to a totally new level. She'd just met him, if you called being carried over his shoulder and locked in a room in his house, as a proper meet and greet.

You wish I wanted you.

I don't do anything that's a waste of my time.

Then you probably should stop this conversation we're having, she quipped.

This isn't a waste of time. I can give you a moment or so to get acclimated. The fact that you want me and that I want to give you a little reprieve from the needing assures me that you'll do exactly what I say.

The needing had been upon her. It had come earlier this month, as the full moon was still a couple weeks away. Kira wondered if that had anything to do with what had happened on the last full moon or, rather, what had almost happened on the night of her twenty-first birthday. At any rate, the powerful urge to fuck or be fucked was there in full force. She'd known it the moment she'd awakened this morning to shaking thighs and heavy breasts. The full moon was hell on lycans who weren't claimed. Kira had decided she could handle it; after all, she'd been handling it for years now, on her own. Sure, the betas in her father's pack—one in particular—would love to end her self-imposed celibacy, but she'd been adamant about none of them being the one she would do it with. So pleasuring herself had become more than just a habit, almost like her only lifeline. And she was fine with that. Or at least she had been until him.

I don't want you. I don't even know you.

He was quiet for a time and she hoped he had found something more productive to do. But then—

You don't want to want me. I know how that feels. I also know that you're burning with your need. Your nipples are so tight right now they hurt. Your clit so hard and destitute you're having a hell of a time restraining yourself from giving it the release it craves.

Kira let out a slow breath, in an attempt to still the rapid beating of her heart. His words had been not only irritatingly accurate but also spoken through her mind in a deep, husky whisper—a private sound she had never experienced before—that was more enticing than her next breath.

The palm that she'd never moved from her breast squeezed and kneaded the plump mound. Her thighs had already been spread, only the barrier of her leggings and thong keeping her finger from her pussy.

Don't do this. It was a plea that she hoped he would acknowledge. This wasn't why she was here. It wasn't why she'd run from Penn's pack.

I have to.

She shook her head, her fingers pinching her hardened nipple, eyes closing. *No. You don't.*

Yes, he whispered. *I do. Just do it,* lýkaina. *Touch it for me, now.*

"No," she said aloud, but her traitorous hand was already moving, fingers slipping quickly past the band of her leggings.

Let your finger slide along your slickness. It's thick, like honey. Does it taste as sweet?

Kira lifted one leg, planting the sole of the flat boot she wore on the silk comforter without a second thought. She pushed at her leggings, lifting her hips and yanking them down with the one free hand, because it was going to be way too painful to remove the other hand from her breast. It was awkward and required a lot of moving to get it right, but she finally had the leggings down to the one ankle that was up on the bed.

It is sweet. He continued as if he knew she was now open and ready. *It's sweet and you want to be tasted, devoured. You want full consumption and a release that will leave you wilted and sated.*

"Yes," Kira whispered. "That's exactly what I want."

Her hand had already slid down her close-shaven mound, deftly slipping between the plump, wet folds, stirring the desire he'd described accurately as thick and plentiful.

Not yet, he all but yelled into her mind. *Don't go deep yet. Put your thumb on your clit, flatten the tip there, and rub.*

He sounded slightly out of breath as if he were enjoying this much more than she was. But that couldn't be true because the moment she pressed her thumb against the stiff hood and rubbed once, twice, her entire body began to tremble.

Her back arched as she continued to work the tightened bud, one hand moving so fast between her legs, while the other kneaded and squeezed her breast until she was gasping for air.

You're slick, dripping. He inhaled deeply, exhaled slowly. Every sound echoing through her mind as if there were some sort of microphone in there. *Ready for me?* he asked her. *You are so ready for me.*

The last was a statement, an arrogant and presumptive one that chafed against everything that Kira was, that she believed. And yet she hadn't stopped working her clit, hadn't even paused, but used her fingers to grasp her nipple, squeeze tightly, and shake. Her breasts were heaving now as she pumped against her own ministrations. Gasps that she'd been trying to keep silent sounding throughout the room.

"Dammit! I need this. I need . . ." The spoken words trailed off as she moved her thumb from her clit, letting her fingers slip through her slick folds, until one sank deep inside her pussy.

She lifted her other leg, so that now both feet were flat on the comforter, legs spread wide. She was just about to slip another finger inside, to really begin working so that the release she craved would finally be a reality, when he spoke again.

Your hand. My release. Remember that.

What?

Your pussy's drenched with desire for me. Your hands are now deep inside the pussy that craves my dick. It's my release you're about to have. Know that, lýkaina, *know that, and understand what it means.*

Kira wanted to yell back that he was an asshole. She wanted to scream it at the top of her lungs; then she wanted to find his room and slap that arrogant, all-knowing smirk she knew without a doubt he was wearing from his face. But she didn't.

No, there was only one thing for her at this moment, one

need that surpassed anything and everything else. She worked her fingers back and forth, switching sides to titillate her other nipple. So close, her vision clouded, her mind filling with nothing but the rush of pleasure, the burn of desire seeping through every pore of her body.

It took her breath away, giving her more than just the feeling of relief, but one of flying, soaring, in her lycan form, growling against the full bright moon in defiance of its power over her. She was free; finally and with a scream of elation Kira pumped her fingers deep inside her pussy once more, recognizing the second her muscles began to tighten, squeezing her as she came with an intensity that ripped through her entire body, holding her still as stone until it was complete.

Until she was complete.

Seconds later she was pissed the hell off by the mighty alpha and the declarations he'd proclaimed in the private recesses of her mind. With her chest still heaving she jerked up off the bed, heading to the bathroom without looking back. With shaky movements she switched on the shower and hurriedly stood beneath its spray, eager to get clean and to forget what was undoubtedly the best orgasm she'd ever experienced because of three simple words: *it's my release.*

She used the soap to scrape along her body, feeling the burn of anger that had her claws ripping free. She continued to scrub, hoping the sting of those sharpened tips raking over her still-sensitive skin would be enough penance. Because for all that Kira had thought she was on her way to total freedom, in the last ten minutes, with only her basic needs in mind, she feared she'd lost again. In fact, she'd lost more than she had before. She'd finally given an alpha what so many before him had wanted. Blaez's words had been right; her release—the best one she'd ever had—was because of him.

CHAPTER 4

The sun had yet to rise, but Kira was up, using the hairpin from her cosmetic case to pick the lock on the door. Her smile spread quickly at the click of its release. She had to tamp down on her triumph, focusing on moving quietly. Only when she was once again outside, in the deep covering of the woods, would she release the yelp of victory of escaping yet another overbearing brute of a leader.

She would find her own place in this world, her own destiny. Her journey would not end here; it could not. No matter the pull she felt toward Blaez and regardless of that low hum of arousal that had stayed with her throughout the night, even after that mind-numbing orgasm. He was everything she did not want in a mate—if she were even thinking along those lines, which she was not. Kira believed her mother's words that there was more for her and she hoped with everything she was that Tora hadn't simply been referring to her connecting with a male lycan. There had to be more to life for lycans than that simple link. Kira definitely wanted more and she was convinced that she wouldn't get it here.

The hallway was draped in darkness and the solemn

pre-dawn quiet. Kira tipped out of the room, her backpack over her left shoulder, a fresh pair of yoga pants and a hot pink T-shirt her runaway attire for the day. Two steps out into the hall, Kira stopped, looking behind her. She hadn't heard anything, hadn't picked up any scent—because today she was definitely going to keep her wits about her and pay attention to all her surroundings. But there had been something . . . there was only a door, about five feet away, dead center. It was closed, of course, and the fact that her heart rate had picked up just by staring at it was a sure sign she needed to stay the hell away from whatever was in there.

On the move again, she tiptoed over the wooden floors, noting the walls around her were also wood, pictures hanging at measured intervals, of what she could not readily make out. There were two more closed doors that she passed, one of which she was almost positive led to Blaez's bedroom. That thought only succeeded to hurry her along. If there'd been a tightening between her legs at the thought, she ignored it and kept on moving.

The staircase was grand for what she would definitely call a log cabin, only much bigger. About fifteen feet wide, it wound slightly to the right, ending in the living room area where she remembered coming in last night. For a moment she paused to look around. More wood, gleaming floors, high beamed ceilings, and a mixture of rustic and contemporary décor. Furniture pieces were either wood or leather, hard or soft, warm golden light pouring from antique wall sconces, plush rugs covering partial areas of the floor, a gorgeous wood-burning fireplace in the center of the living room, a mantel above holding metals of some sort.

This was their home, she thought fleetingly. She could

sense so much more here than just a structure where they lived. There was strength, loyalty, despair. The last sort of hung in the air, out of sight but still there making its presence known. Kira had no idea why that thought bothered her and so she took a deep breath and moved on to wonder something a little more mundane. There were too many lights on for everyone to still be asleep. The sound of his voice confirmed that assumption.

"Why are you running when you know the danger that awaits you out there?"

Kira turned slowly, an almost relaxed feeling coming over her as she knew to whom that voice belonged.

"Because I have no way of knowing what awaits me in here" was her calm response to Channing.

He looked great in the early morning, his dark denim jeans hanging low on his hips, white shirt baring muscled arms and suede moccasins. Yes, the shoes did strike her as a little strange as everything about him as he stood there, hands tucked in his front pant pockets, screamed male model or possibly movie star. Yet he looked totally comfortable in his morning attire, his neatly trimmed beard and piercing blue eyes giving him a youthful yet knowledgeable appearance.

"Well, I can tell you that breakfast is the most important meal of the day, so you shouldn't skip it. Especially if you're planning to be on the move for a while," he replied simply.

He'd moved his arm in a "come here" motion as he turned and walked away. He expected her to follow instead of heading out of that front door. She knew which one she should do and yet her feet were moving in the direction behind him instead. There was another room on this side of the stairway, a huge table, at least twelve feet long and probably six feet wide, with high-backed red-cushioned chairs all around. In the center of the table was a bowl full of fruit. To her left through a double-wide doorway was the kitchen.

After watching Channing go in this direction, immediately heading to a bank of white cabinets, she stepped inside.

"I'll be fine. I don't need to eat anything," she said at the exact moment her stomach made a very loud and extremely rude noise in contrast.

Channing chuckled, looking over his shoulder at her to say, "Come on; you know better than that. You're an alpha female, so you're too smart not to know that you'll be much more alert, more prepared to defend yourself should the need arise, if you're not also fighting low blood sugar."

Kira stared at him quizzically. "How do you know what I am?"

"It's fairly obvious to any lycan worthy of the breed," he told her with a nonchalant shrug. "There aren't many male lycans bold enough to stand up to Blaez the way you attempted to last night, let alone a female. We all knew you were an alpha the moment you stepped into this house."

"You knew I was a Hunter," she replied quickly.

Channing turned to look at her evenly. "Yes. We knew that too."

"And you wanted to kill me," she said with certainty.

"It's our job to protect the alpha. In that regard, we do whatever is necessary. Lucky for you, Blaez had other plans," he said before giving her that quick, infectious grin once more.

Kira didn't know what to say to his last remark. She didn't want to know what Blaez's other plans were. At least, she was trying valiantly to convince herself that she didn't.

Reminding herself that part of what Channing had said was true—she did need to remain alert—she looked around, making more mental notes of her surroundings. The kitchen was a bright space, filled at this moment with the lights Channing had already turned on. The moment the sun rose Kira suspected it would pour through the large window over the sparkling white farm sink, and the other window at the far end of the room, just above another table—significantly smaller than the one in the dining room—with bench seats. There were more exposed beams in here, jutting from the ceiling and even reaching down to serve as mounds for the eight-foot black granite-topped island. Again there was rustic and contemporary going on here. The cabinets were bright white with antique-looking handles, black and white subway tile backsplash, copper pots dangling from a wood pot rack above the island, and stainless-steel appliances, restaurant-style.

In addition to being well versed on the history of the lycans and on hand for whenever Penn and the pack needed tactical briefing, Tora had loved everything about decorating and designing. Their house had been an attestation to the sleek, clean lines she adored, each of the rooms decorated with her keen eye for colors that matched whichever person accepted its personality. Kira had paid close attention to everything her mother wanted to teach her, even the things—like decorating and most of the household duties an alpha female was expected to perform—that she could actually care less about.

Standing at the doorway of this kitchen, she knew her mother would like what had been done here, the warm welcome of the rustic theme that was carried throughout each room she'd seen so far blending seamlessly with the cool efficiency of the modern touches that promised whoever worked in this kitchen would provide nourishing meals for all who dared to enter.

Despite the title and all the enhanced power over their pack, the alpha female's main responsibility was to care for the pack by feeding them and taking care of their house. To some—namely, Kira—that might seem like an old-fashioned or maybe archaic mentality, but to the lycans it was the way of their world and it in no way demeaned the alpha females. Especially since another one of their duties was to direct the pack's strategic planning. If there was a confrontation ex-pected, the alpha female would give instructions on when and where it was best to attack. Of course, it was the alpha's choice whether or not to follow her directives, but since the alpha females had been trained their whole life for this job, their alpha usually respected that skill and did as they sug-gested.

It all seemed way too subservient for Kira, and as she had when her mother had explained these points to her time and time again, she shuddered, the beast in her already prepared to rebel. Shaking her head from those thoughts, Kira vowed once again that she would do more, be more, than what the lycan world mandated. She had to.

"You do the cooking here?" she asked after clearing her throat. There was no scent of another female here, and by the way they'd all circled around her last night she'd figured she was the closest in the vicinity. Of course, the way they'd all commenced upon her could have also been because they knew she'd come from a Hunter pack. Circling their prey was a definite possibility to which she supposed she might actually owe Blaez with his high-handedness last night an apology for sparing her life.

"I like to eat good food, so it made sense that I learn how to prepare it. The others, they aren't as interested in the taste of their cuisine as they are in simply getting the nourishment that they need," Channing continued talking in that light, casual manner she was beginning to associate with only him. As he still moved around as he spoke, Kira couldn't help but watch how familiar he was with this space and how completely comfortable he was with what he was doing.

He took down two frying pans, turned to the double-doored stainless-steel refrigerator to retrieve eggs and a carton of milk. After putting those on the counter he went back to the refrigerator, this time grabbing cheese and spinach. All the while his muscled biceps bulged and stretched with each movement. There was strength there, no doubt. Strength and complacency, two things Kira hadn't thought she believed a lycan could possess. How could one be content with living such a sheltered and solitary existence? But for their packs, especially for the Devoteds, lycans did not socialize with any other humans. If they held a job that required them to do so, then they did. If not, it was as if the two were living on separate planets. How was that considered a good thing? She wondered.

"It's still so early. Do you normally cook at this time?" Kira asked because it seemed the more she stood in this kitchen with Channing, the more she wanted to know about him, about this house and this pack.

"No," he told her. "You're in luck today because I'm preparing my famous cheddar and spinach quiche. Needs time to cook, so that's why I'm up early."

She nodded. "I don't like spinach."

He turned to face her, lifting a brow. "Sit down and tell me what else you don't like, Kira."

And he would listen, she thought as she stared at him contemplatively. This lycan who should have been her sworn enemy would let her sit in his kitchen and ask him question after question. He would answer her too, she realized. And it would be the truth, or the truth as to his way of thinking. Nobody in Penn's pack ever listened to Kira, unless she was telling them it was time for dinner. In the last few months they hadn't even spoken to her unless it was to put her down or come on to her. None of them had the common sense to know the two didn't go together and would most likely always end in her rejection of them. Then, it wasn't etched in stone that lycans were the smartest creatures on earth.

"No," she said, shaking her head. "I should go." Kira had to admit to herself that didn't sound very convincing; still a part of her had felt she'd at least had to say it.

Channing didn't immediately reply, but Kira still stood there. Why didn't she simply walk away? He wasn't doing a damned thing to stop her. She could go, walk out the door, and not look back. But her feet hadn't moved. She simply stood there as if rooted to this spot, watching this stranger prepare his morning meal.

"He's not going to let you," Channing finally said in a quiet, reserved tone.

"What? Are you talking about Blaez? I'm not a part of his pack, so why would he want to keep me here?"

My release. His words from last night echoed in her mind and Kira's entire body flushed as if he were once again directing her to a most delicious climax.

Thankfully oblivious to her discomfort, Channing had a glass bowl that he'd set on the island and he began cracking eggs and dropping them inside, as if she weren't here interrupting what was probably usually a solitary activity.

"He won't let you go back out there where you can be snatched by any other alpha, or beta for that matter, and either used or killed. That's not something he can allow," Channing continued.

"But he's a Devoted. Why should he give a damn what happens to me? I'm not his concern."

Channing looked up, tossing cracked shells back into the box. "You are now."

When she opened her mouth to speak again, Channing spoke up instead. "Listen, Blaez was born to be a protector. It's what he does, especially after what happened with his family."

"What happened to his family?" Kira asked immediately. She shouldn't care. Nothing about Blaez mattered to her. The only thing on her mind was getting out of here and getting on with her life.

"I'll just say that Blaez couldn't be there for them when they needed him most. He's never forgiven himself for that even though there was nothing he could have done differently to change the outcome."

"But I'm not his family. I'm nothing to him," she said, the words ringing oddly in her ears. "And I can't stay here, regardless of whatever guilt complex he may be nursing." With those words Kira turned and walked out of the kitchen. She didn't wait for Channing to respond or even look back to see if his response was a questioning look. No, she had to leave at this instant. She'd stood in that kitchen too long, looking at all the dishes, the notes on the refrigerator, the cups in the cabinet, all remnants of a home. One in which she was the outsider, a feeling that was all too familiar to her.

She came to the front door and pulled on the handle.

Nothing happened, so she pulled again. She pressed the latch and pulled once more. The door would not open and she cursed.

Kira kicked the door once, then again, screaming in frustration. She'd just lifted a fist to pound on it—ignoring her mother's training to keep a calm head in all circumstances— when Channing grabbed her wrist.

He held it gently, speaking in his quiet tone. "It's an electronic lock. You need the code to get in or out. It's specially designed for our safety," he told her. "Whatever his reasons are, you can trust that Blaez will not let anyone hurt you, Kira. You'll be safe here until he can figure out what to do with you."

She whirled around then, yanking her arm from Channing's grip. "I don't want him to figure anything out for me. I don't want anyone to make decisions for me. Why can't anyone understand that?"

"I do," Channing told her. "Believe me, I know all about wanting to make your own way in this world and to your own destiny. Been there, done that, and from the looks of things should have written a book about it." He chuckled at himself as if it didn't matter at all that she was smiling in response. "Now, come on, put this heavy bag down, and let me fix you a cup of my delicious homemade hot cocoa. Then you can sit with your feet up and listen to some of my infamous celebrity stories."

Kira looked up into his smiling face. Her head throbbed

with the stress of the situation, yet her heart warmed toward him and his totally confident yet blissful attitude. He seemed genuine, his tone and actions toward her nothing but respectful. She wasn't used to that from betas, or at least not the ones in Penn's pack. Each of them had wanted to get her into bed so that he could claim her and lead the pack. When she repeatedly thwarted their advances they showed their truest colors, criticizing her weight, degrading her for not being as svelte and sexy as Tora had been, swearing Kira should believe she was being granted a privilege if any of them would even consider sleeping with her. She hated each of them and she hated her father for allowing the treatment in his house and among his pack and, worse, for commanding that she allow one of them to claim her for the sake of them all.

"Come on," Channing said again, reaching for her hand. "You have nothing to fear here. I promise."

Kira had never been made a promise before but was leery of them just the same. But as it stood she could not get out of this fortress, not at the moment anyway. She'd have to figure out the electronic lock system, and that might take some time. On a huff, she readjusted her bag on her arm and reluctantly took Channing's hand. Couldn't hurt to play at being cooperative. Besides, his hand was warm and strong as it clasped around hers and he smiled even more warmly at her.

"You are not going to believe the dirt I know about them, and it's all true," he was saying, about the celebrities, she supposed, as he headed for the kitchen once again. She followed him, reluctant and interested but determined to not let down her guard and to keep true to her purpose. To keep moving toward finding her own freedom, from men and from lycans.

"Why did you bring her here?" Phelan asked Blaez the moment he stepped out of his bedroom. "You know she's trouble."

His longtime friend and right-hand pack mate had absolutely no idea how true his words really were. The trouble had begun the moment Blaez had touched her, and this morning Blaez was just as angry about that as he had been when he'd finally fallen into a fitful sleep last night.

He hadn't meant to reach out to her as he stood at that window staring out. His original thoughts had been on the danger she'd been in out in the forest alone. Any lycan could have happened upon her; he could have forced her into a claiming, taken her as his alpha female, and nobody would have ever known. Blaez had no idea why she'd been out there alone, but he damned sure planned to find out. In addition to that knowledge, Blaez also wanted to know what pack she'd come from. He knew exactly what Phelan was thinking right now because he'd thought it himself.

What if she was a decoy amidst a bigger plan to attack his pack? Blaez was a wanted man. There were some who if they knew who and where he was would kill him on the spot. Or they would try. He also knew that he'd kill every last being that came at him trying to take him down. Blaez's father, Alec, had been a Devoted, committed to upholding everything his father, Lyktimos, had originally wanted for the lycans. By birthright Blaez was obligated to do the same—even though on some levels he hadn't agreed with Lyktimos's actions—but he had no plan to lose his life in the name of an old feud that had absolutely nothing to do with him personally.

How Kira fit into his life's plan Blaez had no idea. The only thing he knew for certain where she was concerned was that she needed protection and it appeared that he would be the one to provide it for her.

"Would you prefer I'd left her out there alone?" he asked Phelan in a clipped tone as he closed his door behind him and stepped out into the hallway.

Kira's scent was here already, lingering on the air until his entire body vibrated once again with need. He had intended to hit the gym for an hour or so in an attempt to work off some of this residual tension, but since Phelan was here, demanding answers, that probably wasn't going to happen.

"I would prefer if we didn't have a Hunter sleeping under our roof!" was his heated retort. "This might be exactly what her pack wants. Hell, she probably positioned herself out there in the woods knowing you liked to do a nightly perimeter check, and used the damsel in distress bit to get you to bring her inside."

Blaez frowned at Phelan's words. "Don't insult me," he said with the baseline simmer his tone often took when he was becoming irritated. "Or her for that matter. Does she look like any part of her is a 'damsel in distress'?"

"No. What she looks like is an alpha female traipsing along in our woods by herself. Oh, did I forget to add an alpha female from a freakin' Hunter pack? Hell, man, you know they want you dead. You're watching them walk right up on you and not doing a damned thing about it."

They were still standing in front of his room, Blaez hearing his close friend's words while battling with his body's need to be close to Kira once more. Reaching into her mind last night had pushed Blaez into a very unfamiliar place. That's precisely why he'd made it a point to never mindchat with the women he was with. Blaez had only ever had sex with lycans; it was part of the Devoteds' credo, to stay true to their lycan nature at all times. Nyktimos had declared that after he watched his mate suffering through her life as a lycan before finally hanging herself. The guilt over having changed her without her permission had continued to plague him even after she was long gone.

Still, Blaez had started that conversation with Kira knowing how it would end, but not knowing the ultimate effect it would have on him. His body had reacted to her every response and not just her words. He could hear her breathing and smell her arousal, and when he closed his eyes he could see her lying on that bed playing with herself. The more she'd fingered herself, the harder he'd stroked his cock. When she came, her heart pounding, chest heaving, fingers drowning in her pussy, Blaez had come too, arcs of his thick white semen splashing against the windows in front of him.

Even now the thought had his body hardening, so he started walking, knowing Phelan would follow.

"If she's a decoy we'll know soon enough. And we'll have leverage when they attack," he told his second in command.

Phelan grabbed his shoulder then, but when Blaez turned, looking at him with narrowed eyes, the beta let his hand fall slowly down to his side.

"We don't negotiate with them. We kill the sonsofbitches!" Phelan exclaimed.

"No. We try to live peacefully until there is no other choice but to defend ourselves. And rest assured, if this is a plan to attack us by the Hunters, we will do just that," he said in a tone that should have ended this conversation.

But Phelan continued, "What if it's more than that?" he asked him. "I saw how you looked at her."

Blaez moved immediately, stepping closer so that the few inches he was taller than Phelan were noticeable. They stared eye to eye. "You. Saw. Nothing."

Phelan's reply was a muscle twitching in his jaw, the scar beneath his left eye that had been left by a very angry fury years ago pulsating. He was angry, which wasn't new for Phelan. The lycan had joined the Marines to quench the rage that simmered inside him. Twelve years later, Blaez was sad to report it hadn't worked. Phelan was just as pissed off as ever, and considering he'd joined a pack of Devoteds, there weren't too many outlets he could find in the mountains of Montana to assuage that particular ailment. But Blaez didn't give a damn; his goals where Kira was concerned were going to be made clear, here and now.

"I will handle this," he continued. "I will handle her. Do you understand?"

Phelan nodded just as there was a loud screech coming from downstairs.

Blaez moved with lightning-fast speed, descending the steps with his feet barely touching them, stopping in the kitchen his gaze already intent on her, as she'd been the focus of his chase. He'd known Kira had left the room he'd locked her in last night, had known the second she'd popped that lock and attempted to sneak away. Of course, he'd also known that she would never make the escape she planned, since she had no idea how to disengage the locks on the doors and windows of the house.

Nobody could get in or out of the fortress he and his pack mates had renovated without them knowing, as was their plan. A year ago, when the existence of the Shadow Shifters— half-human, half-feline shapeshifters—had been unveiled to the human world on national television, all otherworldly beings that walked this earth alongside humans had been put on notice. Their time was coming soon. And just like what had happened since the Shadow Shifters were discovered, the human's mass panic, combined with the interspecies fighting, had created a world in a constant state of war, a place of mass hysteria, confusion, death, just as Lykaon had tried to tell the people of Arcadia before Zeus had arrived to permanently shut him up.

If the human world thought living among big, deadly cats that looked like humans most of the time was scary as hell then they could never be prepared for all the wickedness that came with Blaez's world. The one where lycans were the norm along with furies, demigods, age-old rivalries, and gods that did not take kindly to being ticked off.

The idea to cease the contracted covert operative work they'd been doing for the U.S. government had been Blaez's, moving far away and steering clear of the chaos that was brewing in the human world his main goal. He would not be a part of the fighting, would not be forced to kill more lycans because half of them wanted revenge for what started from a god's wrath.

Blaez's fellow soldiers, the ones who had been a part of him since day one in the Marine Corps, had decided to come with him. They were committed to his cause. Together, the four of them had transformed the old run-down log cabin into a sprawling estate that could easily rival any lodge or resort situated in the picturesque mountain range. Only they did not take visitors; with all the money they'd earned over the years for the private contracting work, added to Blaez's inheritance, the pack members rarely needed to leave their oasis. Some would call it hiding, running away from the problem, quite possibly cowardice. Blaez and his pack called it self-preservation, because otherwise the training of the human killers combined with the hybrid wolf genetics would most assuredly make them public enemy number one.

The moment Blaez saw Channing's arms around Kira's waist, his face nuzzling way too damned close to her cheek, a grin on his pretty-boy face, all of Blaez's genetics and military training came bubbling to the surface. His claws broke free, teeth elongating, sideburns and hair sprouting instantly until he looked every bit the alpha male he was. Right there in the middle of the country-style kitchen.

"Release her!" he stated, his voice deeper, raspier, when he was in this form.

Channing had looked up instantly the moment Blaez's telltale pissed-the-hell-off growl echoed throughout the room. However, Channing hadn't immediately dropped his hands from her waist. No quick movements that could be construed as defensive. That was a rule when dealing with a lycan, as such movements would most assuredly get the person killed. Even if it was a beta in that alpha's pack. Instead, Channing had kept eye contact with Blaez, moving slowly away from her.

Kira had been the one to step forward instantly, getting

in Blaez's face as if his teeth, claws, and growling didn't scare her one bit.

"Good morning to you too," she quipped, seemingly not impressed at all at his appearance.

Blaez's head tilted, the unfamiliar feeling that had coursed through him at the sight of Channing's hands on her ebbing only slightly, being replaced with something else Blaez wasn't used to and therefore could not pinpoint. As he pulled the beast within back as quickly as it had appeared, his claws retracted, hair along his face and head vanishing, teeth drawing back inside his mouth. His nostrils still flared, her scent powerful as she stood this close, even over the aroma of whatever Channing was preparing for breakfast.

"Leave us," Blaez directed both Channing and Phelan, who he'd known stood a few feet behind him, most likely ready to pull Blaez off of Channing had it come to that. Blaez would thank the one beta later and apologize to the other. Only after he made it perfectly clear to each of them that there was a hands-off rule where Kira was concerned.

Channing nodded his acknowledgment while casting a quick glance at Kira. He moved past Blaez on his way out and Blaez remained silent until Channing and Phelan were both gone.

"Wow, somebody sure did wake up on the wrong side of the bed this morning," Kira said before turning to walk away from Blaez.

She moved with what felt to Blaez, and his growing arousal, like blatant sexuality. The pants she wore today as tight over her plump ass as the ones from yesterday. Only

430 A. C. Arthur

these were longer, flaring at her ankles and draping over her tennis shoes. Her shirt was just as tight as the tank from yesterday as well, its bright and perky color only highlighting breasts that his mouth watered to suckle. Clenching and releasing his fingers at his sides, he thought of palming the delectable globes, watching as they overflowed from his large hands, dark nipples peeking up at him teasingly.

The sound of her knocking a spoon off the island as she moved her arms—to probably fold over her chest, since he'd been staring at her tits like a horny teenager—broke through his lust-filled haze. Only to replace that intense feeling of need with one of shock and then . . . Blaez wasn't quite sure what.

As Kira had bent down to retrieve the spoon her shirt rode up her back, her pants dipping lower on her hips. That's how he was able to see it. The crescent-moon shape centered at the small of her back. Blaez sucked in a breath as realization hit him. She was not only an alpha female; she was also a *Selected* alpha female.

Damn.

"I asked you not to run," he said through clenched teeth, now more annoyed than ever that she'd been in the woods alone. "And yet you tried."

There was a quick jolt, one Blaez knew he hadn't shown but he'd felt ricochet throughout his body. All of his feelings, his thoughts, his actions, could usually be held in check. He was the alpha after all, he reminded himself once more. It was his birthright and this was what he was meant to do. If he said that to himself more than a dozen times a day not only would he believe it, but so would others.

Except her.

"I wasn't running; I was leaving; there's a difference. I don't belong here, and if you can't see that your pack sure can. I know they've warned you about keeping a Hunter here. If you won't listen to me, I'm curious as to why you won't listen to them either," she said, long lashes brushing over her high cheekbones as she watched him.

"Because I'm the alpha," he told her, inwardly berating himself because he still sounded like he wasn't totally convinced by that fact. This had never happened to him before and he didn't like that it was happening now. "I know what I'm doing, Kira. And I know that you being here is safer than you being out there."

"Are you positive?" she asked, lifting one elegantly arched brow. "Because Phelan looks like he's ready to claw my heart out at the first opportunity. And Channing, well, he's very nice, but he's also suspicious. And the other one, Malec, he acts like he's pissed at me for being a Hunter. Or he's pissed at me because he's in his needing. Either/or wouldn't exactly lead to this being such a safe haven."

She was right. Every word she'd spoken was absolutely correct. Blaez had seen it all for himself, so there was no sense denying it.

"And yet I can assure you that none of them will put a hand on you. And if, or should I say when, your pack comes for you, those three guys will actually protect you as they do me," he told her seriously. They would do just as he said because he would order them to do so, regardless of what they might truly think of her on the inside. And to be perfectly honest, Blaez had no idea why he planned to ask them to protect her that way, as if she were *his* alpha female.

"They won't come for me," she said, momentarily looking away from him.

"Why?" he implored. "Tell me what happened to make you run."

Her gaze was back on him, that stubborn chin of hers jutting up as she did. "They didn't make me run. I decided it was time to go."

"Because you thought that was the only choice you had." He moved closer, finding himself just as entranced by the smooth buttertone of her skin and almond-shaped brown eyes as he was with her seductive and curvaceous body.

She stayed on the other side of the island, her hands flattened on the wood top. On the surface she looked calm, but Blaez could hear the quickened beat of her heart; he could smell the almost instantaneous drip of her arousal.

"You're trying to find something," he told her. "Something you want more than your own life."

"You don't know me," she replied, her voice a breathy whisper.

"But I do," he told her, realizing now why he'd been so drawn to her from the start. It wasn't simply the burning desire that he'd first thought. It was so much more, so much deeper, and that much more annoying to him. "You're running from who and what you are."

"No."

"Yes," he continued. He recognized the look in her eyes, the persistence in her words, the bravado barely masking the fear. Blaez recognized all of these signs because once upon a time he'd felt them himself.

"Look," she said, balling her fists, then releasing her

fingers flat on the island top. "I don't have to stand here and bare my soul to you. You think you know so much. Fine." She shrugged. "You're right; I am running. I'm running to the life I want to lead. The life I'm entitled to. Is there something wrong with that, Blaez? Aren't you allowed to live the life you want to lead?"

"That, right there," he told her with a nod of his head, "is why you fail."

"What? You're why I failed. If you hadn't been creeping around in the woods like you were searching for something or someone, I would have been halfway to my destination by now."

"Or you would have been dead, or taken" was his simple reply.

She folded her arms over her chest, the action pushing her breasts up even higher, the mouthwatering rise of cleavage a momentary distraction.

"I'm so sick of hearing about this. Sick of the way all lycan males think." She'd dropped her arms then, letting them slap against her sides, then raising both hands and running her fingers through her long tresses.

She was sick of the lycan males she'd known because they weren't the ones she had been Selected for. The thought had Blaez cursing inwardly. He did not want to think about this. Did not want to be faced with an ancient legend on top of everything else. And yet he couldn't walk away.

"Come with me," he said, turning immediately away from her.

"What? No, I'm not coming with you, Blaez. You're not my alpha," she insisted.

Her words raked over something inside of him, adding to the unfamiliarity, doubling his intentions, cementing in his mind a plan he never thought he'd make.

"If you want to live on your own terms and be success-ful, I will show you how," he told her slowly, matter-of-factly. "I will show you what you need."

CHAPTER 5

"I don't need a teacher," she called after him, following him through the dining and living rooms and into an extended hallway.

He took long, deliberate strides with his shoulders squared, authority oozing from his every pore. As agitated as that made her, she had to admit he looked damned good doing it.

As the lycan had roared behind her in the kitchen she'd known it was him and had not been afraid but intrigued. Alphas possessed practiced control over their shifts, so why, when she turned around, had she looked right into the bright blue eyes of his wolf? Even with his teeth fully bared, hair where there normally was none, and his muscled legs spread wide in the prepared-to-fight stance, he'd awakened something inside her. Something that had immediately sat up and taken notice. It was arousal and a little bit more, which again irritated the hell out of her.

Now he had the audacity to be ignoring her, which only pushed more of her buttons. What was it about this guy that had her so ready to yell with consternation one minute and more than eager to pant with desire the next? She'd asked herself that question too many times throughout the night. And now here she was following him to who-knew-where, to do only he knew what. She hated the act of following altogether, hated the implications, and yet she couldn't turn away.

Besides, if she did turn away, where was she going to go? Channing had told her that not only were all the doors in the lodge on that electronic lock system, but so were the windows. In addition, there was a perimeter monitor that would also alert them to strangers approaching their property. There were cameras outside the house, heat sensors along the floorboards of the front porch and upper and lower back decks. The trees were another source of security, lodgepole and ponderosa pine so tall and thick the only way to see the lodge was if someone knew it was there from overhead. In essence, it was a well-guarded fortress, one she found herself trapped in.

Temporarily.

She would figure a way out; she had to. But first, she had to put this guy in his place once and for all. Sure, he was right in that he was the alpha of this pack; she couldn't deny that and generally wanted to respect it. He just kept pushing her, kept saying things and looking at her like she was . . . like he wanted to— She huffed and stopped right there, trying to get herself together.

Stop thinking. You're wasting your energy on things you cannot change.

"Stay the hell out of my head" was her quick retort just as he stopped in front of two double doors.

He turned to her partially, his silhouette just as breathtakingly perfect as the rest of him. He wore jeans today, dark denim that looked as if it had been cut and sewn perfectly over his sculpted physique. His shirt was royal blue, fitted to his skin just like the one he'd worn yesterday. At his wrist was a watch, silver, on his right ring finger a ring. The alpha insignia ring that Kira knew from tradition was passed down to the eldest alpha son of each family.

"Stop stalling. If there's something you want bad enough, figure out how to make it happen. Lesson one, learn how to keep me and any other lycan out of your thoughts," he said in a crisp, stern tone before pushing through the swinging doors knowing she would continue to follow him. Gritting her teeth, she did so, determined to not back down from him and his high-handed demeanor. And not to let those smoldering dark as night eyes excite her each time he looked her way. One of those tasks was going to be a lot harder than the other to achieve, she thought as she walked through the doors.

"Sit down over there," he told her as he moved around the room.

"I know how to block mindchatter," she told him. "My mother taught me."

He turned to glance at her, a marginal look of shock on his face. "Your mother taught you how to hone your alpha skills?"

"Yes, she did," Kira told him. That had been a mother's job; Kira was certain that was a lycan tradition. Why that caused him pause she had no idea.

"What else did she teach you?"

"Everything I needed to know," Kira replied.

He raised a brow. "You sure about that?" Blaez asked before continuing his trek across the room.

The room looked like one of the state-of-the-art gyms that cost a small fortune in membership fees every month. She remembered a place like this back in Seattle. Its industrial-carpeted floors and intimidating-looking equipment pulling her into the most competitive environment she'd ever been forced into. It had been two months after her mother's death when Penn had unceremoniously snapped, "You need to get in shape if you hope to get claimed!"

Kira had immediately bristled at his words because being claimed wasn't something she had been looking for, especially if he was talking about her being claimed by one of the members of his pack. There was nothing attractive to her about Dallas, Cody, Milo, or Kev. Each of them was just as ignorant as the other. But one was clearly meaner and more determined than the others to rule. Kira had found that out the hard way.

"Look, my mother was great. She did everything she was supposed to do." And yet she'd been gunned down like a rabid animal, Kira thought with a pang to the center of her chest that almost took her breath away. "Besides, I'm almost positive that a workout is not going to keep you out of my head," she said, still looking around, searching for a possible exit.

There was none, she realized after a full survey. There were four of everything in here, treadmills, ellipticals, weight benches. Mirrors lined one full wall, while tinted windows filled the other right across. The two smaller walls housed shelves with towels and hand weights, tension bands, and more gym paraphernalia; two rows of drawers were at the bottom of each set of shelves.

That's where Blaez was standing. All the way toward the

back of the gym, staring down at one of the drawers he'd opened. Kira walked that way, passing several pieces of equipment, her feet silent on the carpeted floor.

"You're right; a simple workout is not what you need. This is a more serious lesson, one of many that you'll need to enter this next phase of your life. Take a seat," he told her, still in that restrained and authoritative tone. Only this time it was tinged with what she thought might be a touch of agitation.

He acted as if she'd done something to him, not the other way around, which was simply ridiculous. After all, he'd gotten her to stay the night here and if she was being totally realistic it looked as if this was where she would be for the foreseeable future. In addition, he'd had the pleasure of knowing all he had to do was say some dirty words and she'd masturbate for him on command. Remembering that moment caused her cheeks to warm, humiliation bubbling inside of her. And he hadn't mentioned last night at all, making her even more embarrassed by the arousal she still felt when he was around. All of which, combined with her obstinate nature, had her remaining perfectly still where she stood.

When Blaez turned to her, his eyes flashed the mystical blue glare of the lycan and she took a quick, defensive step back. It was only a flash of light, perhaps meant to do exactly what it had done, put a bolt of fear inside of her. Now she was pissed. "I'm not afraid of you," she told him.

"Good!" he snapped. "Now, I want you right there, on that bench. Sit."

His muscles looked even more pronounced, the dark slashes of his eyebrows above his now-normal eyes giving him a wicked aura. Suddenly his words didn't just seem like words anymore; they raked over her body like the softest of fingers even though they were spoken in the harshest of tones. She should just leave. Kira knew when to cut her losses; she wasn't a total idiot. And yet again she did not move.

"How does taking orders from you help me gain control?" she asked.

This time, he came to her. His arms down by his sides, his gaze locked on hers as he approached.

"An alpha, whether male or female, needs to have complete control over their own mind, their thoughts, and their needs." He spoke slowly, as if he were reading from a manual but believing wholeheartedly every word that he said. "Emotion drives you, Kira. Every thought you have, every step you take, is guided by your emotions. I've been told by some that's not a bad thing. As long as you have control. Not having that is going to slow you down. It's going to prevent you from becoming what and who you really are."

He continued moving toward her, with every step Kira moved back, until the weight bench bumped the backs of her legs.

"If you want to learn, you will take a seat," he said to her, his warm breath fanning over her forehead as she looked up at him.

She felt flush all over, just as she did each time he came close to her, each time he looked at her. Dammit, she wanted to wrap her arms around his neck and pull him down for a kiss. A greedy, hot kiss, the kind she'd dreamed about but never really experienced. Then she'd wrap her legs around his waist and sighed heavily as he thrust deep into her waiting pussy.

"Why do you care if I learn this control or not? And why should you be the one to teach me?" she asked, her chin tilted in defiance.

He looked as if he could not believe she was, one, still standing and, two, questioning him as if she had some authority.

"You will never be safe from what or who you are running from without the ability to control the situation. I have that control. It's what I do and who I am. Which makes me the best teacher you could ever find."

"Confident, are we?" she quipped.

"Most definitely" was his immediate reply. "And soon you will be too."

He'd been standing so close, smelling so delicious, that Kira had forgotten what the hell they were discussing. Her gaze had fallen to his lips, watching as he spoke how they moved, the quick peak of his tongue, and her breathing increased, her nipples tightened, breasts growing fuller with need.

What she really wanted right now was for him to fuck her. It was that simple and at the same time that strange. Sex with a partner had never been high on her list of priorities. She'd learned how to bring her own pleasure a long time ago. But that pleasure had paled in comparison to what she'd felt last night with Blaez's voice in her head, her fingers firmly ensconced in her pussy. That was a dangerous realization she knew but could not deny. He said she needed to learn control, and since her thighs were now quaking, her pussy throbbing with need, she agreed that he might be right. Blinking slowly, feeling as if she'd been drugged, Kira felt her legs bending, her body lowering to the bench until she was sitting.

"Lie back," Blaez continued.

Kira hesitated only a second before doing as he said, lying back on the bench so that her upper body was reclined, her feet still flat on the floor, legs bent at the knees as the bench ended there.

He moved quickly then, taking one of her wrists and lifting it upward. She turned, only to frown as she saw him using a stress band to bind her wrist to the weight holder beside the bench.

"Wait? What are you doing?" This wasn't what she'd thought would happen next. How would she have control if she was tied down?

"Trust me," he said as if that task were as simple as night and day.

"Are you kidding me?" she snapped back, yanking at her arm.

Blaez was fast; he had that band secured in seconds. It was tight but not painful.

"That's not how I work," he replied firmly.

"Well, I'm not your job," she continued her protest as he reached for the other arm.

Kira moved futilely, yanking so hard this time her shoulder screamed in pain.

He'd already tied her by then, so he rested a hand over her shoulder, heat pooling in that spot immediately.

"Relax," he said, staring down at her.

He was so close and yet, she sensed, so damned far away. His eyes were growing dark again, his jaw firm, his lips barely parted. He smelled like man and beast and everything in between. His power surrounding him like a cloak and thus pulling at her, wrapping around her body and her mind as well. Her legs shook the second she thought about kicking at him as if in warning for her not to even try it.

"If I tell you to do something you do not want to do, you tell me to stop. But do not deny what you know deep down that you want simply out of fear of the unknown. Embrace the courageousness of your alpha spirit. It's the most powerful part of you."

And most likely the craziest thing Kira had ever heard, but her body was already making its own decisions, leaving the questions whirling around in her mind in the dark. She didn't give any sign of acquiescence, but she did not resist again. Not when that hand slid from her shoulder, down to cup her breast. His hand remained still, not groping or grabbing, simply holding as if it might have been a prized possession.

Up and down her chest moved, her other breast aching to be touched like its partner. He wasn't in her mind, she knew, because she felt totally alone there but for her own thoughts. But his other hand moved to the twin orb as if he'd heard her speaking of its need. He held both her breasts, squeezing lightly this time. When she looked down it was to see his light-complexioned hands in stark contrast to the hot pink of her shirt, overflowing with the weight of her breasts.

For one instant, a quick pang in her senses, she felt like it was too much, like she was too much, physically, that is.

Old doubts breaking through the dark like beacons. What if he didn't like what he was feeling? What if her size disgusted him?

No, she thought as he grunted, his face twisting as if he was confused. He wasn't disgusted. What if he was aroused?

Blaez pulled his hands slowly away from her, not as if he'd been burned and hated the sensation, but slowly, almost reluctantly. He moved quickly again, this time tying her ankles to the legs of the bench. Kira was shaking now, wondering what would happen next, wondering if she'd actually be able to find part of what she'd been looking for all her life.

When she felt his hands at her waist, pulling down her pants and panties, she stiffened. He did not stop, simply kept pulling the garments down her legs until they were at her ankles, similar to the way she was last night. Only then she'd been in the privacy of that room, alone, but for Blaez's words in her mind.

"How is this . . . what are you going to do . . . I mean, I don't understand," she spoke quickly, the words tripping and tumbling from her lips.

"Trust me," he told her once more.

Kira didn't know trust. She thought she had, when her mother had been alive, but Penn and his pack had taken all that away from her. She trembled with that memory, with the darkest one of all, biting on her bottom lip to keep from screaming that she wanted Blaez to stop whatever he was doing, to get the hell off of her and let her go. That was the fear clawing at her, that dark ban of betrayal that had so recently ascended over her life. She didn't want to feel that again. Didn't want to put herself in the position to be so egregiously let down. But, she realized, she needed to see where this lesson would lead so much more than she wanted to protect herself. She wanted to know if there truly was a power inside of her that would keep her safe.

Blaez's hands were warm as he slowly pushed them up her legs, over her calves, cupping her knees, along her thighs. Kira shivered, her body tingling with heat that traveled like sparks throughout her entire body.

"The moment I do something that you do not want or that hurts you, all you have to do is say 'Please.' That's your safe word, Kira. Just say it and I will stop," he told her. "You can control every bit of this moment."

She wasn't so sure about that.

Kira couldn't control the excited thumping of her heart or the involuntary quivering of her thighs as his hands had moved upward, his thumbs just whispering along the crease of her legs. When he applied the barest but most titillating pressure she opened her legs wider, as if knowing that's exactly what he wanted her to do.

"That's a good little *lýkaina*," he whispered.

She clenched and unclenched her fingers, taking a deeper breath, closing and reopening her eyes. When she looked at him this time and saw the hungry way in which he was looking down at her, Kira wanted to come right then and there.

"So pretty," he was saying as he continued to stare at her pussy. "So pretty and so wet because you want to fuck."

It was an unpretentious statement, a candid and lurid one that had her pussy pulsating, dripping with even more desire, embarrassing her just a smidgen more. She felt her cheeks warming and shifted slightly, not used to being so totally open to anyone's perusal—and ultimate scrutiny—before.

"Ah, that's not nice. Don't try to hide from me. This is exactly what I want to see," Blaez continued, this time using his thumbs to separate the plump lips of her vagina until she could hear the slickness of her own desire.

"Just relax and let me see. Let me see how good you're going to be."

He stroked his fingers up and down her slit and she trembled, gasping at how hot the fact that he was touching and watching her so intently made her feel. It was all about sensation at that moment. The tendrils of heat spreading throughout her body with the gentle touch of his fingers. He said he wanted to explore and yet she was the one feeling as if she was on some type of journey. As he circled around her clit, not touching the tight nub, but spreading her slickness all around it, she'd hissed in a breath, her eyes closing momentarily with how good that very simple motion felt. Around and around his fingers went, as if he was not only stirring her rapidly producing juices but also churning something else deep inside her. She felt it approaching like a door had just been opened, the first tentative rays of light just able to seep through. When he slipped a finger deep inside her pussy, Kira bucked up off the table, the sensations having quickly grown intense. Used to only having her smaller fingers there, she was tight, and she gasped when another of Blaez's fingers slid alongside the first.

"That's right, open for me, my *lýkaina*. Stretch around my fingers, so hot and so tight," he whispered. "All that sweet nectar," he continued. "All that loveliness you have to give."

Kira's head moved frantically from side to side. On instinct her arms yanked at the restraints as she desperately wanted to grab the back of Blaez's head and push his mouth down over her waiting mound. She'd seen the act done and had often wondered how it felt, but she'd never had a man eat her pussy before. Never thought she would crave it like air, until this very moment.

So when Blaez abruptly pulled his fingers from her she wanted to cry, which made the sob that escaped her only natural and mortifying at the same time.

Shhhh. I won't leave you like this, sweetheart. I won't let you go.

His words were spoken so softy, just along the edges of her mind where the intense desire had already begun to take over. It was like last night, but stronger. He hadn't commanded this reaction as he seemed so eager to direct everything else, but his words, his voice alone, had changed something in this moment, something Kira couldn't quite explain.

Take me slowly, he continued. *So slowly.*

He was inserting two fingers inside her now, two thick and powerful fingers that filled her so completely she wanted to melt right there in his hands. In response her muscles clenched tighter, gripping his fingers as if trying to lock him inside. To hold on to this full and completely delectable feeling for as long as she possibly could.

Do you feel me inside you, Kira? Do you feel me filling you?

Yes! she replied immediately. *Yes!*

With the pad of his thumb he touched her ultrasensitive clit and immediately jerked upward against him. Her body hummed with sensation now, her arms and legs shaking as quick breaths slipped through her lips. Tension spread quickly, the need to find her release of upmost importance.

Do you want me to stop? he asked abruptly, his fingers still strumming her like a master guitarist.

No! she yelled. *Hell no!*

You want me to keep on until you come, don't you? Yes! Please! He stopped then, pulling his hand out of her immediately, and Kira's eyes flew open, waves of panic surfacing the second that connection was broken. "What . . . what are you doing?"

"I told you that 'please' was your safe word. You said it, so I stopped," he stated as plainly as if he were giving her the time of day.

She gulped, letting his words register. "No. That's not what I meant."

"Say what you mean, *lýkaina.* Mean it with everything in your heart and soul. If you want me or anyone else out of your head, you shut us out. You give the command and it will be so. Take the control of all aspects of your life in the same manner," he instructed her.

Do you understand? he asked after endless seconds of her breathing heavily, trying desperately to figure out what the hell was going on.

Answer me, lýkaina. *Tell me—*

His words were cut off, just as quickly and succinctly as the pleasure he'd taken from her when he removed his masterful fingers from her pussy.

Kira held his gaze then, feeling triumphant at the immediate silence in her head.

"Good girl," Blaez said. "Good job, my hot little lycan. Now tell me what you want. Tell me what I can give to you."

"I want to come," she immediately admitted in a breathy whisper. Then with more strength and clarity she added, "Can you make me come, Blaez?"

He shook his head and Kira sucked in a breath.

"Ask me can you come," he told her. "Ask me and wait for my permission to do so."

Kira immediately chafed at his words. She was an adult, one who was capable of bringing herself to climax—when she wasn't tied down and thus rendered virtually helpless.

"Ask me?" he prompted.

"How am I learning control, if that control only comes at your command?"

He didn't immediately reply but brought his fingers to his lips, licking each one from the base to its tip.

"Sweet and satisfying," he said, and she realized with a rush of moisture between her legs that he was tasting her.

Her thighs trembled and she licked her lips.

"I know that it's burning inside you. The need so strong and potent sometimes you can barely think straight. You will not be able to deny it much longer, nor will you be able to slake it on your own as you tried to last night. It is in your control to quench your tremendous thirst, Kira. All you have to do is ask."

Kira didn't know what to say or how to say it. How did she ask a man she'd just met for permission to do something with her own body? Was this who she really was in the end? And if so, why hadn't she been able to submit to the will of what Penn and his beta had planned for her?

Blaez remained silent, his gaze going back to her pussy causing more ripples of desire to fill her body until she thought she might actually combust from this need.

The words sounded foreign, but before she could give that any more thought his fingers were on her clit, pinching the tightened bud until she yelled his name. He held right there, the sting of pain radiating throughout her pussy, up her body, to settle in heated spirals in her breasts.

"Damn you, Blaez! I asked the question!" she yelled at him.

He released his hold on her leaning so close she almost climaxed at the very sight of his face so near the clit that begged for his attention.

"Only when I say so," he told her. "Only then."

Before Kira could reply this time Blaez blew a whisper-soft breath over her. Kira tensed all over, shivering like putty in this man's hands.

Those devilish fingers snaked inside her once more, this time working with fierce intensity in and out of her opening, coaxing and guiding her to release. Kira felt like she was flying. High above the mountains she'd loved so much, she soared, her body busting with the tingling sensations of pleasure. She licked and bit her bottom lip in equal intervals, her fingers clenched so tight she was sure to have broken her own skin. Her mind was void of any reasoning, logic, or planned reactions. All she could see, hear, and breathe was him and the moment he would allow . . . the second he would finally say:

"Come, *lýkaina*. Clutch me deeper inside you and give me all your sweet nectar. Come for me, now!"

Kira thought she felt his hand trembling inside of her. She might have even imagined a bead or two of sweat on Blaez's brow. Those thoughts melted away as the tidal wave of release hit her full force. Her body shook and trembled, her essence gushing out of her so that she could hear his fingers drowning in the outpouring as she continued to work them deep inside her.

It seemed like an eternity that she lay bucking and moaning on that table, her body still shaking in the aftermath of that powerful release. She was afraid to open her eyes at first, afraid this might have been one tortuously delicious dream.

Only she knew that it wasn't. This was real; every one of her heightened senses could attest to that. And so she did open her eyes and with a start saw that Blaez was staring at her. His human eyes boring into hers as if he was searching for something that only she possessed.

She wondered what she should say. Not only was this the morning after for them; it was also the after of the most soul-shattering release she had ever experienced. Somehow, "thank you" or "this was nice; maybe we should try it again" didn't quite seem appropriate.

"You should get cleaned up. Breakfast should be ready soon," he said as he backed away.

He removed the bands as quickly as he'd attached them, going over to the shelf to put them back where they'd come from.

Kira had been just sitting up when he paused in front of her.

"Do you need help?" he asked, his words cool and aloof.

"No!" she snapped quickly, the humiliation from earlier returning full force. "I'll be fine."

He'd nodded curtly, then muttering an, "I'll see you at breakfast," before walking toward the door.

Kira pulled up her underwear and pants quickly, standing so that she faced his back before he could leave.

"Now that I've had my lesson," she said, anger bubbling inside of her, "can you let me go now?"

Blaez stopped but still faced the door.

"Did I ask correctly?" she continued. "Or is there a special word I need to say for this request to be granted also?"

She was beyond pissed. She felt used and discarded, in spite of the wonderfully sated buzz that hummed just beneath her skin.

"I can't." was his solemn reply.

"Oh really?" she said, moving closer to him. "I thought you were the alpha. I thought you could do whatever you damn well pleased."

"It's about your protection."

"Or is it about your dick?" she continued, spurred on by the mixture of embarrassment and bafflement. "With less than two weeks until the full moon your need is just as strong as you claim mine is. How lucky of you to happen upon an alpha female traipsing along in the forest at just this time. Were you tracking me, Blaez? Were you planning to complete your pack with the naïve little bitch?"

Her mouth snapped shut when he spun around, grabbing her by the shoulders. "I'm protecting you, dammit! It's not my job and I don't know why you showed up when you did, but I'm trying to keep you safe."

"Protecting me from what? I'm not in danger of anyone at this moment but you. Carrying me in here like I'm some sort of stray, locking me inside this wooden fortress you've built, and giving me all this bullshit about teaching me, helping me! You're using me, Blaez, just like the rest of them planned to do. You're no better than them," she said finally, her heart pounding in her chest.

If what she'd just said were true, she was in more trouble now than she had been before. Because Kira was certain there had been nothing between her and the betas of her father's pack but disgust, a feeling that had made packing up and leaving all the more easier. Yet here, now, with this lycan whose actions were contradicting what he should be and do, she was afraid of the fact that she didn't feel that way. Blaez didn't disgust her; he intrigued her. Even now, at this very moment, as much as her mind screamed she must be insane, Kira didn't want to break this heady connection that had so quickly formed between them. In fact, there was a part of her, a deep down in the recesses of her soul part, that wanted to reach out to him. To grab hold and take what she wasn't even certain he knew he was offering.

His lips had grown thin, brows furrowing as he glared down at her. "Don't," he said in a warning tone. "Don't ever compare me to anyone else you've known. I'm better and stronger than they are." He leaned even closer to her, so close she thought he might kiss her. "And when they come for you, which we both know they will, they'll catch my scent all over you. That, Miss I-can-do-whatever-I-want, will keep your fine ass alive! And then, when it's over, you can thank me."

He released her so abruptly then that Kira almost fell back on her ass. Instead, she managed to right herself just in time to see Blaez walking away, saying, "Get cleaned up and be down for breakfast. Smells like it should be just about ready," without ever turning back to her.

Kira frowned at his retreat. She cursed his arrogance and the strength he'd bragged about and she'd sensed. She closed her eyes to the memory of how good his ass looked in those jeans, how intoxicating his fingers had felt inside her, and how totally awakened her body had felt when she came. And then she dragged her hands through her hair, knowing he'd been absolutely right.

Penn and his pack would come for her, and when they did she would be here, like bait in a trap, because Blaez and his pack would kill them. There was no doubt in her mind that Blaez and his pack's strength clearly outweighed that of Penn's pack. With a rush of breath she wondered how she felt about that fact, about knowing that the man she feared she was now irrevocably connected to would kill her father and his pack, the very men whom she'd come to hate.

CHAPTER 6

Blaez ran until his lungs screamed for mercy, and even then he pushed on. Uphill, around sharp bends, down lethally high inclines, through chilly creek water, circling back to where he'd started at the base of the mountain. He relished the burn and tightness in his thighs, his buttocks and calves, felt the sting of air escaping his lungs through his partially opened mouth, and blinked away the sweat that dripped down from his forehead.

She was a Selected.

That had been a surprise. And it was a problem.

The gods and goddesses thrived on their control over all in their domain, the battle for more domains an ongoing quest for them all. But for some the battle wasn't how many they could control, but how best they could try to prevent the constant uprising in the meantime. Selene, the Luna goddess from which the lycans' very strength had thrived, had not been strong enough to stop Zeus's wrath against the king of Arcadia, but she had done something that she'd thought would counteract the new battle the mighty god of thunder had unwittingly begun. She'd Selected specific alpha females to be paired with certain alpha males. The Selected female could never be claimed by any other alpha but the one she was Selected for. These were matches that would enhance them both, creating a mighty force that could hopefully keep the peace among the warring breed. It was said that each one Selene had Selected was marked.

Kira's crescent-moon marking came instantly to his mind.

If she was Selected bringing her into his house was an even bigger mistake than he or the pack could ever have imagined. Kira could not have been Selected for him. That was the last thing Blaez wanted. He'd decided long ago that intimate or emotional connections were not for him. He'd failed the people he'd loved most in this world once; no way was he going to put himself in the position to endure that type of pain and heartache again. Besides that, things were different now—this situation dictated that it be so—and not even a Selected was going to change that for him.

"Let's stop here," he heard Malec say from just a few steps behind.

With a frown Blaez turned, still running in place to see two of his closest friends, chests heaving in a similar fashion to his, bodies built for this type of brutal exercise, eyes trained on him, etched only slightly with worry.

After breakfast Blaez had gone into his office, locking himself there while he did some research. He'd needed to know where she'd come from, which Hunter packs were closest to their region. Phelan would have already begun similar research, without Blaez having to instruct him to do so, because that was his job within the pack—to know whom and what they were dealing with at all times. That's why Blaez hadn't been at all surprised when e-mails from his second in command appeared while he'd worked on his laptop. Malec, on the other hand, only knew that there was a guest in the lodge. An overnight guest who was most likely going to be there in the long term. True to his nature, as the contemplative one, he'd simply sat at the breakfast table, watching Kira interact with Channing.

The two of them had acted as if they'd known each other for ages, like today was their reunion and Blaez and the others were somehow intruding. Blaez treated the heated ball at the pit of his stomach as hunger, instead of acknowledging what it really was. She'd changed after their tryst in the gym to pants that hugged her ass and a button-down shirt, one that, this time, barely held her voluptuous breasts in place. His mouth had watered the moment she walked into the kitchen, just as it did each time he laid eyes on her. A more alluring female, lycan or human, Blaez had never seen.

There was a grace to her that was unlike that of the slim and sexy vixens he'd usually entertained himself with. A naïveté that both shocked and enticed him. She hadn't been vetted; no agreement had been discussed and sealed before their first meeting. It had all simply happened, so fast and so intensely that Blaez was still wondering what the hell he was doing. She'd obeyed his commands and masturbated, then she'd tried to run away, and then she was lying there, tied down, spread wide for him. Only him. Asking his permission to come. There was fear—he'd sensed it marginally at first—but then there was intrigue and pleasure, the likes of which had almost taken Blaez's breath away. She'd been so beautiful when she'd come, so hot and tight, that it had taken all of his training and living experience to keep from tearing off his pants and fucking her right there in front of those open windows.

458 A. C. Arthur

It had taken even more control for him to walk away from her moments later. The uncomfortable half hour he'd sat at the breakfast table while she and Channing chatted and laughed, Phelan eyeing him knowingly, and Malec questioningly, had been enough for Blaez. He'd had to be alone. And once he'd found out about her past, he'd had to run.

"There are five of them," Phelan immediately began when Blaez had stopped running.

A couple feet away from him Malec had already begun his stretching, one leg extended in front of him as he lunged. In addition to being contemplative, Malec was the fitness guru of the pack, constantly getting on Channing about the unhealthy dishes he prepared for them, while also consuming those meals with unabashed fervor. To the rest of them it was humorous, but to Malec eating those meals just meant more hours in the gym for him. More often than not, Blaez figured that was just Malec's way of escaping the group setting, heading off to be alone to work off a debt he believed he owed, to someone who didn't matter worth squat.

"Penn Radney, the alpha. Cody, Dallas, Kev, and Milo. They run an auto mechanic shop in Seattle and live on one of those historic houseboats. Penn's mate was Tora Hepprin from another Hunter pack in the region. She was shot and killed three months ago in the forest near the Olympic Mountains. Penn suspected Devoteds, but the authorities ruled it a possible hunting accident. Kira is Penn and Tora's only child," Phelan stated as if he'd memorized the recap version of the reports he and Blaez had compiled before coming out here.

"Wait," Malec said, standing straight and gazing from Phelan to Blaez. "I knew she was from a Hunter pack. But you're saying she's their alpha female now?"

"No," Blaez replied instantly, his tone clipped, agitated. "She's not their alpha female. She's simply the alpha female in that pack, or at least she was. There are no claimed connections."

"You sure about that?" Malec asked. "What if getting into our pack is their plan? We're only twelve days out from the full moon; every lycan that's breathing is in need right now. It would be simple to flaunt a female in front of us to get her inside. And then what?"

"Ambush? Maybe?" Phelan asked. "If they knew you were here all along, she could be just what they needed to get close to you. To kill you."

Blaez shook his head, already having considered this very scenario. In fact, he and Phelan had been discussing it on and off all day. What Blaez hadn't shared was that if Penn knew his daughter was a Selected, if the alpha subscribed to that theory and he was a Hunter, the very last lycan he would want her around would be Blaez, with his pure-blood status. Sure, the Hunters would still want Blaez dead based solely on his bloodline, but Penn certainly would not want to risk his only child being claimed by Blaez first. Connecting a Hunter and a Devoted would be as big a catastrophe as connecting a lycan with a human—at least in their minds.

No, Penn and his pack would come first and foremost because they'd want Kira back. Once they followed Kira's scent to Blaez they would undoubtedly realize who he was, or at least part of who he was. Killing a Trekas, to hit the Devoteds in the very heart of their breed, would be a coup worth bragging about. And then they would celebrate in whoever claimed Kira. Blaez only frowned, because he had no intention of letting any of that happen.

460 A. C. Arthur

"It's not an ambush if we're ready," Blaez told them.

"Why don't we just let her go?" Malec asked. "Send her back to them with a message to keep away before the demise of their pack becomes imminent."

"I can— I'm not letting her go," Blaez said, clenching his teeth at the thought of what he'd almost said. "She ran for a reason. Letting her go puts her in danger from not only unknown lycans but also most probably the ones she's known all her life."

"So she's having some sort of temper tantrum and we're going to ultimately pay the price for it? Since when do we settle domestic disputes?" Phelan asked, with a shake of his head. "I don't know if this is such a good plan."

"It's *the* plan," Blaez said adamantly. "I will deal directly with her; you make sure all of our security measures are in place. It'll be the night of the full moon, when we're strongest."

"When we're rabid and horny, you mean?" came Malec's curt reply.

"I mean when Selene's power for once shines brighter than Zeus's and we are the dominating species," Blaez said, feeling like he had to give them both lessons on their true origin.

Phelan nodded. "Right, the Luna goddess will prevail. She always does."

Blaze ignored the flippant comment as it was the norm for Phelan, who for so long had held a grudge against the women of their world. As if he had learned nothing from dealing with one of the goddesses of revenge, who had left him permanently scared. While their kind usually healed almost instantaneously, Phelan's scars, both inside and out, were permanent because of the powerful being who had inflicted them.

"And in the meantime, she gets to play house with us and Channing. How do you think she's going to like that, if she didn't like living with her own father's pack?" Malec interjected.

Blaez didn't know the answer to that question. What he knew, and what he wasn't about to relay to his pack, was that there was no way he could let Kira leave, especially not after what had transpired between them earlier today. He wanted her. And for Blaez that was all that mattered at this moment.

"I'm heading back," he told them without further discussion, taking off at a run, pushing his body further beyond its limits because something about the burn and the strain was keeping him from totally losing control. He had no idea if the others followed and didn't really care. Running was a release; the air upon his face, the wind in his ears, was freeing and almost relaxing. It was another way that he coped.

Still, heat burned inside of him, need pressing against his bones until he felt them threatening to break. Kira's scent was leading him like a besotted puppy back to the lodge, back to her.

Tonight, instead of masturbating and then falling asleep in the wonderfully comfortable queen-sized bed, Kira had showered and slipped beneath the fresh, new sheets. She figured Channing had been responsible for changing them while she'd been enjoying the extensive library located at the far end of the lodge, near Channing's and Malec's rooms.

Channing had clearly taken over the alpha female's role in the pack. This was only slightly surprising to Kira, because in any pack where there was no female one of the betas had to take on that supervisory role, it was just their way. More shocking had been the hard-on he'd unabashedly been sporting when she turned around after leaning over the counter in the kitchen earlier this morning. For a moment she'd thought it would be kind of nice to have a lycan like Channing with his honest good looks and perfectly sculpted body want her.

He'd smiled at her as if it was only natural, which she figured it kind of was for him, and he'd be attentive to her every need both in and out of the bedroom. The lycans were a very sexual bunch, some more promiscuous than others, since they weren't bound by human social protocols. It was nothing to have pack members sharing a female, or a male for that matter. The anything-goes mentality was like their mantra. While Kira had never experienced anything on that level personally, or seen it done for that matter, she'd heard Dallas and the other betas in her father's pack talking about it often enough. In fact, she suspected they'd done quite a bit of sharing themselves.

In the end, she'd simply smiled at Channing and the oddly familial bond she'd felt with him instead of the intensely sexual one she'd felt with Blaez. That's when she'd asked about books or anything she could do to pass the time here. What she really wanted was to see other parts of the lodge to confirm for herself that there was no way out of this fortress.

"If you like to read we have quite a library," Channing had told her. "I love books. Blaez has a thirst for knowledge too, but other than his personal collection of books, he prefers his computers for research purposes. Malec, of course, favors the gym and Phelan, well, he doesn't like much at all." Channing had followed that up with a chuckle, but Kira suspected that fact was a little more troubling to him than he let on.

"I love to read. My mother always read poetry to me. I prefer mysteries myself," she admitted, then clapped her lips shut, hating that she'd said those words to anyone. It was odd talking to Channing as if they were actually friends, as the members of her father's pack only saw her as an object to be claimed, especially in the last few months.

Channing had shown her to the library and left her alone there, trusting her, she thought initially. A few seconds later she realized the trust wasn't necessary, since she'd likely set off a million alarms if she so much as cracked a window in this place. Not that she was even paying attention to the large windows with the same tinted glass that she'd seen in the gym. No, Kira was much more fascinated by the gleaming wood floors and bookcases that matched, reaching up to the ceiling. There were aisles just like in the university library she remembered studying in for the past couple of years. Yet this place had a more elegant touch, curving corners that led to even more books in a room that she'd had no idea was as large as it turned out to be.

By the time she'd made it to the other end, she'd passed through the room's center where four leather couches sat facing one another, a huge area rug covering the floor beneath them. There was also a fireplace nestled deep into the back wall surrounded by an intricate rock design. As gorgeous as it all was, Kira found herself going farther, to the end of the room, to a section of books that looked terribly old and for some odd reason appeared the most interesting.

There were leather chairs in this part of the room as well, single high-backed ones the color of rich caramel. Reaching out, she let her fingers brush lightly over the tattered spines of a couple books, stopping as if by no control of her own on one. The name TREKAS was printed in letters so worn she could barely see them all. Kira pulled that one from the shelf without a moment's hesitation. Before opening it, as if knowing already that this was going to take some time, she'd backed up until she sank into one of those high-backed chairs.

The book was clearly old, so she'd had to turn the pages slowly to keep from ripping them. A couple of those pages were written completely in Greek, which she found only a bit odd, and she wondered what else could surprise her in this place. Her mother had tried to teach her to read in Greek. But Penn hadn't thought it was necessary, so the lessons hadn't gotten very far. Names that appeared early on in the book were familiar as she remembered her mother telling her the story of the lycan origination when she was just a little girl. But as she continued to read the story changed, switching, she thought, to Nyktimos's point of view as he explained why he'd come to the states and fallen in love with a human. A woman whom he'd been unexplainably drawn to; one who made everything he'd thought he believed in "fall to ashes on the ground" was what he'd said.

Kira's heart beat faster as she watched the love story unfold, saw Nyktimos's ultimate mistake, and felt his broken heart as if it were her own. She read about the sons who had been born to him through his wife before she'd taken her own life and how those sons had sons, continuing the pure bloodline until it came to Alec Trekas and his three sons: Cabe, Blaez, and Ryer.

"Hey there, bookworm, you've been in here all day. I left you some dinner in the microwave, since I'm sure you're beyond starved right now."

Kira looked up, her neck aching from having been in the position of staring down into that book for so long. It was darker in the library then it had been when she'd come in, and as Channing's words had registered in her mind she'd looked to the windows to see that night had already fallen.

"He's a Trekas, isn't he? My father's pack are trained to hunt anyone from the Trekas family. You don't just think I'm here to kill your pack; you think I'm hunting him," she said slowly, the realization of where she was and whom she was with finally hitting her full force.

Channing stared at her a moment before speaking, leaning against one of the bookshelves. "Are you saying you didn't know who he was? Is that what you want us to believe?"

If that was the case Channing certainly wasn't buying it. "It's the truth," she replied vehemently. "I left my pack and was headed to the Midwest. My mother had some family there, but I got sidetracked," she said, not wanting to admit the still-unnamable force that had changed her route so that she'd ended up in those woods where Blaez had found her— similar to the way Nyktimos had described feeling about the human he'd fallen in love with. "I wasn't looking for him," she said, a shiver snaking down her spine.

Channing shrugged. "The Hunters want him dead. That's not something Blaez takes lightly."

"He doesn't take anything lightly," she whispered, thinking of Blaez's intensity, of the serious and almost dour personality he possessed. She'd originally seen that as just another trait to dislike about him; now she realized by his birthright that it might be warranted.

"He's in a precarious position," Channing told her.

Closing the book and letting it sit in her lap, Kira shook her head. "I know how that feels."

"Maybe the two of you have more in common then you thought," he said.

"I doubt that Blaez's family chased him away," she said, then went silent, looking away from Channing's inquisitive gaze. "Anyway, what does he plan to do with me? Am I now going to be part of some revenge plot?" Kira just couldn't believe it. What were the odds that of all the lycans in all this world, she would walk right into the path of this one, landing in his arms . . . and liking it way more than she was ready to admit?

Pushing himself away from the shelf, Channing leaned forward, slipping the book from her lap before saying, "You should have dinner and get some rest. I hear there's more training for you tomorrow."

For the billionth time today Kira had felt embarrassed, now wondering if Channing had any idea what type of training Blaez had taken her through this morning before breakfast. It was a good thing Channing had walked out— carrying that book with him—that at least had saved her a little bit of pride. But now she couldn't ask the questions flitting around in her mind.

On Channing's instructions, she'd stopped in the kitchen on her way back to her bedroom, and had been pleased to find a meatball sub drenched in provolone cheese, baby carrots and celery sticks on the side of the plate that had been covered with a plastic lid and sitting in the microwave. The bright green sticky note that read "For Kira. Eat Me." was what caught her attention, and she'd smiled at Channing's thoughtfulness.

She'd eaten the carrots, which she suspected were actually Malec's idea after she'd heard him talk relentlessly about physical fitness and healthy eating during breakfast. Celery was just not tasty to her and so she'd left that alone and enjoyed the sub after she'd reheated it. The hot shower that followed her meal felt heavenly in the bathroom that looked as if it were meant to be in a five-star hotel, instead of this rustic lodge. She was beginning to think "rustic chic" was a better description of this place.

Now she was in bed, but she'd feared sleep would not come. Greek words replayed in her mind, the story of Nyktimos and the love of his life, the mate he felt he'd been bound to find but too cursed to keep. But sleep did come and with it a dream that felt so real, so deliciously tangible, Kira had wanted to scream.

The wolf had pushed open the door to her bedroom, its large head, the first she saw of it, held high. With a majestic gait, it entered just as if she'd invited it or, no, rather as if it belonged.

On the bed she sat up, noting how thin the nightshirt she wore was when a breeze coming in from the hallway chilled her until she shivered. She felt her nipples growing hard and crossed her arms to cover them. The wolf, with its piercing sapphire blue eyes, zoomed directly in on her, turned then, using its muzzle in a sideways motion to push the door closed.

It walked around to the side of the bed, its very movement speaking of power and dominance. With every quiet step of its paws over the carpeted floor Kira's gaze remained transfixed. She'd never seen a wolf this close up before. A lycan—a human who through a bite or scratch from another lycan possessed the ability to take on wolf-like characteristics and powers—yes, but not a full-grown wolf, such as this. She thought about this fact and vaguely remembered something she'd seen in one of those Greek books in the library. Among its differences and perhaps the most intriguing point of all was the immediate connection she felt to this wolf. As if she'd seen or communicated with it before.

Pausing only momentarily to look at her from a closer range, the wolf turned, going to the other side of the bed, repeating the same action. Kira inhaled deeply, the wolf's very primal and earthy scent permeating her senses, inciting every sexual spark in her body until she felt like a firecracker, fizzing and sparking, waiting until the final pop. She jerked with that thought, her thighs shaking, pussy throbbing. Grabbing the sheets, she made sure they covered her legs, tucking them between her thighs and squeezing tightly to assuage the need growing there.

The wolf moved again to the end of the bed, its cheeks lifting slightly as it bared its teeth. Kira sucked in a breath, still staring because it was next to impossible to tear her gaze away. When the wolf lunged forward grabbing the sheets and ripping them from the bed she let out a yelp and scooted back on the bed, grabbing a pillow—as if that were actually going to provide protection—and placing it in front of her.

In the next moment the beautiful gray and white wolf had shed its glorious pelt, the four legs shifting in a blur to form arms and legs, all muscles rippling as they stood and stretched. The body of the wolf had also changed to that of a man . . . one hell of a fine-ass specimen of a man. Every part of him looked chiseled as if some deity had taken not just a day or two but possibly months to design every inch of its perfection. From his narrow waist to the wide splayed shoulders, back down again to the contoured thighs and very pleasantly endowed—possibly too much—cock that jutted forward with full-on arousal.

Kira swallowed, her gaze fixated there, mind soaring with the possibilities. It wasn't until the man knelt on the bed, crawling across the mattress toward her, did she venture to look at his face, the carefully sculpted jaw, thin nose, medium-thickness lips, and those eyes. They remained the piercing blue searing through her as if they possessed X-ray vision, making her shake with vulnerability. All lycans had blue eyes in their shifted form, but none like this. Kira was certain she'd never seen eyes this brilliant and alluring before.

"Blaez." His name came on a whisper, her fingers shaking as she grasped the pillow tighter.

"Don't hide from me," he said, his voice deep, clear, dominant.

He pulled the pillow away and still on his hands and knees lowered his head to nuzzle between her breasts. The thin material of her nightshirt stuck to her body as she arched upward, loving the feel of his warm breath against her skin. Falling back, Kira braced herself on her elbows, her mouth opening with a gasp, eyes still fixated on the top of Blaez's bald head. He moved lower, rubbing his cheeks, one and then the other, his lips, his forehead, over her torso, her abdomen, and farther down until she was panting with anticipation.

His hands abruptly grabbed her thighs, spreading her legs wide, lifting her until her ass was up off the mattress, her weight supported partially by his strong hands. She was completely available to him, her pussy open, wet, and waiting and him staring down hungrily as if he'd known he would end up here all along.

Those eyes, piercing and hypnotic, as blue as a jewel, found hers again as he looked up and whispered, "Mine."

Kira didn't know what to say or do. Her fingers were clenching the sheets as if they were her new lifeline, her thighs quivering in his hands, breasts tingling with the rush of arousal. When his tongue extended, long and thick, curving slightly at the tip like a ladle, Kira shivered. He licked her then, from her dripping wet center up excruciatingly slowly to the hood of her clit where the tip of his tongue made a swirling motion that drove her wild. He repeated that action again and again, taking turns looking up at her, then down at her pussy. He could see the throbbing of her vulva lips, lapped up each drop of her essence that dripped incessantly. She gasped each time the pad of his soft tongue touched her awaiting heat. Her breasts jiggled with each tremor coursing up and down her spine. She wanted more, so much more, and she wanted it right now!

"Once I claim you there's no turning back," Blaez said seconds before thrusting his tongue deep inside her, lapping up every drop of her release as it racked through her body like a violent storm.

She'd barely caught her breath, teeth were still biting into her lower lip, hands pulling the sheets completely from the mattress, when he pulled back, moving closer so that the bulbous tip of his dick, dripping with a thick white drop of his arousal, was now aimed at the entrance his tongue had just left weeping. Her eyes fluttered open, once again finding his magnetic gaze.

"No turning back," he repeated. "Ever."

Kira blinked, her chest still heaving, heart thumping wildly. His eyes had changed. They weren't that brilliant sapphire she'd been drawn to, but a lighter, duller shade. His body was the finely sculpted bronze tone she'd first glimpsed, but darker, less contoured. She closed her eyes once more, opening them slowly. He was closer, his breathing coming faster, more erratic. His jaw was covered with a light layer of hair, dark hair, that also covered the top of his head. His forehead wrinkled, swelling into its lycan form, his teeth elongating, eyes burning with a mixture of lust and disgust that had her stomach churning.

"You're gonna be my alpha bitch!"

The voice was different, not as deep, not dominant, but angry and creepy as hell. She squirmed, trying to get away because this wasn't the same . . . this wasn't Blaez. Oh no, no, no! It was him . . . it was . . . he wanted to claim her and become alpha of his own pack. He wanted to use her because she was there, not because he loved her . . . in fact, he'd told her time and time again how much her body disgusted him, how she was too much woman and lycan.

Kira shook her head and felt herself scooting back on the bed. He followed, laughing, taunting. "I'm gonna get you. I'm . . . gonna . . . get . . . you!"

She opened her mouth then and screamed so loud and so long her throat burned, her neck cracking as her head arched back.

CHAPTER 7

"Kira! Kira!" Blaze yelled into her face. "Wake up, dammit!"

He was shouting, anger at the fear that he'd not only smelled as he'd slept in his own bed but that had also assailed him like a plague when he'd stepped through the adjoining door into her room. The sight of her flailing wildly into the air, pillows flipping off the bed, sheets tangled in her legs as she continued to scream had incited something deep and intense inside him until his muscles had actually vibrated as he moved quickly to get to her.

Now his arms were holding her tightly, her back against his front, her head thrashing over his shoulders. The screams had subsided, but her fear was still live, still potent enough to have her eyes closed tight, tears trickling rapidly down her cheeks.

"I'm right here," he told her. "Right here. Nobody will hurt you as long as I'm with you. I promise you."

Her heart was still hammering against her chest. He could hear it and feel it as his hand stroked along her arms. He had no idea when he'd begun rocking her back and forth or why, but the movement seemed to calm her, so he continued. Her hair tickled his cheek and Blaez leaned into it, until his cheek rested against the top of her head.

"They'll never hurt you again," he said when her sobbing had ceased, her body jerking slightly with her heavy breathing.

He moved so that he was now sitting on the bed, his back against the headboard, her body still cradled against him.

"Tell me what they did to you, *lýkaina*?" he asked after a few more moments. "Tell me so I can make them pay."

She didn't speak at first, the silence slicing through Blaez like a painfully familiar knife. He gritted his teeth against his own personal memory and vowed to focus only on her, on what she'd been through and what had ultimately brought her here to him.

"It's all so stupid" was her response. One Blaez had not expected. He'd half-expected an argument before the admission because since they'd met that seemed to be the formula that worked for them.

"What's so stupid?" he asked.

She shook her head, attempting to turn away from him and to move out of his grasp, but he held her firmly. Not to cause her further harm, but to keep her close because every instinct he possessed said he needed her to be near him.

"A beta can become an alpha and form his own pack if he claims an alpha female. He can claim her without her permission, without her love! It's stupid!" she yelled.

Blaez clenched his teeth, temples throbbing at her words. She sounded just like his mother as she'd made that declaration, but he didn't want to think of that. "Someone wanted to claim you, and you disagreed."

"Yes," she sighed. "That's why I left, because he wanted

to claim me. He waited until the night of the full moon, my birthday." The last came out quietly and she closed her eyes momentarily as if wishing whatever emotion she was feeling would go away. "The others had already been sent away. He'd made some plans for them at some bar where they could have sex with whomever they wanted as much as they wanted until dawn. They knew about those kinds of places. I didn't."

"And the bastard tried to force you." Those words stuck in Blaez's throat in a wad of disgust, threatening to actually choke him as the visions of someone attempting to forcefully claim her surfaced in his mind.

"He was going to take what he wanted regardless of how I felt, or what he truly thought of me. He didn't like me. Never had. Called me names to my face and behind my back. Told me that I would change the moment I was his bitch. I would lose weight and I would wear the clothes he wanted me to wear, cook the food he wanted me to cook. I would be his and there would be nothing I could do about it."

Blaez felt the rage boiling inside him as he listened to her words, heard both the anger and fear in her voice as she remembered that night.

"He was wrong," she said, taking a shaky breath. "I stabbed him in the shoulder and would have killed him if Penn hadn't shown up and stopped me. He said that I was a disgrace, that my mother hadn't done her job training me, and that I should accept whoever wanted me despite whatever my mother told me, because that's the best I was ever going to get. I told Penn and the rest of the pack to go to hell."

"Bravo!" Blaze almost cheered. "Fucking bravo!"

Her father sounded like an ass, a clueless alpha whose

pack was probably itching to turn on him. Blaez remained quiet, letting her words sink in, as he cursed inwardly when her body had gone tense in his arms.

"Which one was it?" he asked, trying like hell to sound as calm as he possibly could. The last thing she needed right now was to see how pissed he really was about what she was telling him.

She took in a deep breath and said, "It was Dallas. He's closest to Penn and probably had Penn's blessing over the others."

"You ran away because a beta in your pack tried to force himself on you and your alpha, the sorry bastard, did nothing to stop it! Even when he knew—" Blaez didn't finish the sentence. What if Penn didn't know his daughter was a Selected? After all, it didn't seem as if Kira knew herself what she really was.

"Yes, he knew that I didn't want Dallas. I didn't want any of them and I'd made a point of telling them on more than one occasion. They'd backed up for a while, but then after my mother's death . . . I don't know, it just seemed like they became more determined after she was gone. At least Dallas had. I hated how he looked at me," she said, pressing the heels of her hands into her eyes.

"Dammit. I didn't mean to tell you all that. I'm fine now," she said, clearing her throat. "Sorry I woke you with my nightmare. You can go now, I'll be all right."

"I won't leave you," he told her adamantly. "I will protect you."

"From the boogeyman?" she asked with a light chuckle. "Seriously, I'm good now."

She'd turned a little, so that she was now looking right

up at him. He glanced down, saw her hazel eyes, still red from her crying. Honey-toned cheeks streaked from tears, hair a wild mass that for all that it was worth, aroused him just as much as the feel of her soft body pressed against his. No, Blaez did not believe in the selection process because if it were true she wouldn't be here with him; of all the lycans in the world it would not be him.

"I'm not leaving," he replied adamantly, ignoring his thoughts. "Turn around and go back to sleep."

She huffed and acted as if she were about to say something else. Blaez only stared at her with every bit of intent that he possessed. He meant it. Alpha female, Selected, homeless woman on the streets, who- or whatever Kira was, Blaez had no intention of leaving her or letting her go. It was that simple. And that damned complicated.

He'd never slept with a woman before. Never held one in his arms in this way before either. Had never wanted to.

"You cannot sleep if you keep staring at me," he said, this time not looking down at her.

Something happened when he looked deep into her eyes, something stranger than what was happening now, and Blaez figured he could only deal with so many anomalies at one time.

"Are you really planning to stay with me every second of every day from now on?" came her tired inquiry.

"I already told you I don't plan on letting anything happen to you."

"That's not an answer to my question, Blaez. Why would you want to keep me here knowing that my family is intent on hunting and killing yours?"

The question had caught Blaez off guard, but he didn't

show it. He should have known she knew who he was. She was a Hunter after all. Gritting his teeth, he said, "This is not the time for a question-and-answer session. It's the middle of the night. You need to get some sleep." And he needed to think. He needed to figure out what the hell was going on here and how he actually planned to deal with it.

"And what do you need, Blaez?" she pressed.

He was the one to stiffen this time.

"Why are you doing this when there's a very real possibility that I could be setting you up to be killed?"

Blaez looked down at her this time, ignored the urge to push a few thick strands of hair from her forehead. "Are you setting me up?" he asked her simply, seriously.

She shook her head. "No. I'm not."

He believed her. That was simple and also very serious.

"Then go to sleep. Tomorrow you're going to tell me all about your pack and why one of them was stupid enough to try and claim you against your will."

"Why do you care?"

Blaez had no answer to that question. None that he was ready to admit anyway. "We'll talk more later. Go to sleep now, *lýkaina*."

She blinked up at him. "Why do you call me that?"

Another question. Blaez should have been amazed, but nothing about her was as it should have been. Nothing was normal or self-explanatory. That was a big part of the problem.

"Because you're one spitfire of a lycan."

"It's the Greek translation of the word," she continued. "There are books in the library written in Greek. They're yours, aren't they?"

"Yes."

"I could tell some things from the pictures and a few words looked familiar. I think I'd like to know what they say." She paused momentarily. "I read the book about your family."

And that's how she knew who he was. Or had she always known? Blaez couldn't think straight, not with her lying so calmly in his arms, her body soft and warm against his. He knew who she was and who he was. For all intents and purposes that alone caused a problem. If that sign on her back had any real significance, the issue was magnified. When all of this came to a head the damage could be irreversible. His head pounded, even while his body hardened reacting to her proximity, the innocent whisper of her voice in the still of the night. It had been a very long time since Blaez had been this conflicted, since the decisions that he needed to make weighed so heavily on his mind.

"I can teach you the Greek words," he said finally. "After you get some sleep."

She actually looked as if she was contemplating his response, her brow furrowing slightly. Blaez slid down so that he was now lying on the bed, pulling her to him, and settling them both against the two pillows that still remained on the bed.

"Good night, lýkaina," he said, this time praying to every god he did believe in for her questions to cease. At least for tonight.

She moved then, an action that pressed her flush against his hard cock, her back to his chest. The fear was gone now and she smelled like rain. Her hair brushing against his chin smelled like coconut, which matched the shampoo that he knew was in her bathroom.

"Good night," she replied finally, the sound of her voice like a fresh breeze on a summer's day.

Minutes ticked by, then hours, Blaez was sure. He did not sleep, did not close his eyes or even relax. Instead, he remembered.

His mother had been born in Greece, in a small town at the base of Mount Olympus. His father had moved there after years of traveling, attempting to find solitude from the role he'd been cursed to play. Alec Trekas had no idea that he'd been going to the very place he needed to be to continue his part in this war that Zeus had begun. Kharis was a believer in the Moirai, or the Fates. She knew that meeting Alec on that summer's day was a thread in the life she was meant to lead. Ten years later Kharis and Alec had moved to the United States to raise their three sons and daughter. And Kharis had begun to tell her middle son, Blaez, the stories of the Fates, explaining that his life had a purpose and that he would one day find that purpose and act accordingly. He would live up to the power of his bloodline.

And on that fateful day while Blaez was in basic training at the Marine Corps, his family had been killed by a group of Hunters. In the blink of an eye his fate had been sealed. He'd tried to run from it, joining the human military and getting as far away from his family and their beliefs as he possibly could. Yet he had been unable to run from the threads of fate that were steadily twining together to form his life.

Kira was a thread.

The thought had hit him some time just before dawn. The Moirai had brought her here and that knowledge was the intrinsic reason why he could not let her go. He'd held back a curse as once again what he wanted no longer mattered. His destiny had been pre-ordained by powers beyond what even he and his many books on their history could comprehend.

So, yes, he would keep her close and he would protect her and he would face the pack of Hunters that he knew were coming for her. He would face them, all the while praying that they had no idea who and what he really was, because that would be a game changer.

That would be the beginning of the end.

Kira awoke with a whoosh of breath escaping her lungs, her eyes cracking open to see a great ass . . . naked, flexing much closer to her face than she thought was good for her sanity. Or anyone else's sanity for that matter. Her palms itched to touch each tight globe, to run her fingers along the deep dent on each side. She'd just been moving her arms closer, her fingers wiggling with anticipation, when it dawned on her what was going on.

A door slammed and she jolted upward, or at least she tried. A strong arm across the back of her legs and the fact that she seemed to be moving despite that had her about to scream. Only something told her that she wasn't in danger, at least not in the traditional sense. No, this was different; this was the type of trouble that started with a capital *B* and seemed to be right up her alley as of late.

"What the hell are you doing? Put me down!" she yelled at his back . . . the exceptionally great-looking backside of this man she couldn't seem to keep out of her mind or her personal space.

482 A. C. Arthur

"I need a shower," he said while he continued walking.

"You've got to be kidding me," she said just after her feet
hit the cool ceramic tiles. She looked down at her feet, light
against the dark gray of the floor, then up to see that mouthwatering ass again as Blaez leaned over into a shower stall
that looked the size of half the room she was staying in. He
turned the silver handle and looked up as water instantly
began to fall . . . from the ceiling.

Kira looked up then to see one of two sleek silver shower-
heads that blended seamlessly with the stark white ceiling.
The walls surrounding the shower were gray tiles that
matched the floor, clear glass doors encasing the entire structure. A bench lined the entire wall, with three inlays that
housed bottles of body wash and shampoos, she presumed.

"You can't take a shower from over there," he said, and
Kira looked up at him.

He was naked. Totally. Deliciously.

Had he been naked last night when he'd come into her
room? More important, had he been naked the entire time
he'd lain in that bed next to her? Oh yes, she recalled immediately, he definitely had. The inside of her thighs were
still wet from that knowledge, as she'd continuously pressed
her ass back to rub along the mouthwatering length of his
arousal. He'd been hard and hot all night long and she'd
wondered how she'd managed to fall asleep at all. Easy,
when she slept she dreamed of him slipping every inch of
his thick cock deep inside of her, sort of like that wolf in her
nightmare had done with its tongue.

"You can stare at me from inside the shower as well" was
Blaez's final irritatingly cocky statement before he stepped
through the glass door, to stand beneath the spray of water.

His words bothered and aroused her, and before she could analyze them any further Kira found herself doing exactly as he'd said, again. She stood there staring at him as water sluiced over his ripped abs, down his toned thighs. When he turned she sucked in a breath to see a line trickling down the crease of that perfect ass of his. Hell, she wanted to scream that he shouldn't look so damned good and be so freakin' irritating all at the same time. No, what she really wanted to do was fuck him.

It was a startling truth, and since she'd decided long ago that she wasn't in the business of lying or betraying or any of that other stuff her father and his pack seemed to thrive on, she had to start by at least being honest with herself. No matter how she'd come to be here or how much she thought leaving was the only answer, she wanted to be beneath Blaez with her legs spread wide, willing and waiting for him even more.

With that thought and the realization that it was morning so she would need a shower anyway, she pulled the nightshirt up and over her head, moving slowly until she was opening the shower door and stepping inside, with him.

He'd already grabbed the soap and stood just a couple inches away from the water rubbing it all over his body. There was nothing seductive about his movements, they were purely functional, and yet she could not stop watching every swipe of his hand over taut muscles, sculpted peaks, and that rigid gloriousness of his shaft. Her mouth watered at the sight.

Kira had never gone down on a guy before. She'd seen it of course, as her father's pack were absolutely shameless in their sexual exploits. There'd been more than one occasion when it had been late and she'd gotten up for a snack—or because she'd known what she'd see—and she'd found them in the living room. All of them. Together. Of course she'd seen more than she'd ever personally experienced. Dallas sitting on the couch, his head tilted back, mouth open as he groaned, some unknown female between his legs sucking his hard cock until he was coming into her mouth. Cody would be behind the same female, spreading her ass cheeks as he thrust his length into her from behind. While across the room Kev and Milo would touch and suck each other, until finally they were both howling with release.

She'd been both aroused and alarmed by the sights at first but over time had grown more accustomed to seeing how lycans were together, how her father said they were meant to be. But when Dallas had come for her that night she'd wanted him off of her. She'd screamed and fought back and done everything in her power to resist becoming a part of the circle these men had formed, no matter how normal it was said to be for their kind.

"You like what you see?" Blaez's deep voice pulled her from her reverie and her gaze snapped up to his face to find him staring intently at her.

His eyes were usually brown—she'd noted that during yesterday's breakfast—but in the gym and again last night when she'd looked up at him they'd been almost black and clouded with what . . . she thought might be desire. Was Blaez as attracted to her as she was to him? How could that be possible? He was an alpha of his own pack and she was just— On second thought, yeah, he could want her. He could want to claim her just like the others. If nothing else, she was an opportunity to any pack, a rise in their power and a key part to whichever side that pack was on. How was that for knowing her worth? However, Kira sensed something different here, something more intriguing than anything she'd ever seen the members of her father's pack doing before.

"What are we doing?" she asked in response because she simply wasn't sure. Her plan had to be to find her mother's family, to possibly stay with them while she figured out what else was out there for her, what her mother had said was her true destiny.

"You're just about salivating while staring at me," came Blaez's reply.

"Even in the shower you're an arrogant ass," she quipped, turning away from him and reaching for one of the bottles of body wash. She was just reading to see what scent it held when he reached an arm around her, taking it from her hand.

"But I wasn't lying," he said. "You were staring at me like you wanted this dick for yourself."

She opened her mouth to say something, but he touched two fingers to her lips after replacing the body wash. "Shh, just listen before you argue."

Kira did not want to listen to him, not again, and certainly not now when he was so close to her and the thoughts of him pounding hard and fast into her pussy were still running rampant through her mind.

"Like I told you yesterday, part of taking full control of your life is knowing what you want and taking it," he said, water trickling at his back.

They were both wet and standing only inches from each other. The water was hot and steam had begun to fill the stall, so that she could no longer see anything outside the space they now occupied.

"I do know what I want," she told him defiantly. "I know that I do not want to be here. I never planned to be here . . . with you."

"And yet, you want to touch me," he told her, his gaze going dark as he stared down at her. "You want to wrap your little hands around my hard cock and stroke until I come. Or do you want to suck it? You do, don't you? You want to suck me dry, *lýkaina*."

His voice had deepened as he'd continued, his gaze falling to her lips that as if on command had opened, not wide enough for him to slip his length inside the way he'd suggested, but enough so that even if she denied his words he would know she was lying.

"I don't understand," she replied with every ounce of honesty she possessed. "Why me?"

His gaze came back up to meet hers, his lips pressing tightly together before his next words seemed to be ground out, "Why not you?

"I'll bet that smart mouth of yours is hot as hell. And wet, just like your pussy. Ever since that night in the woods I've been unable to get the scent of your arousal out of my head. It's driving me insane!" He had raised his voice and Kira took a precautionary step back.

"I don't belong here."

"You do," he replied.

She was shaking her head, refusing to hear his words, wanting desperately to focus on the sound of the water hitting the tiled floor.

"I don't belong with you."

"That's what I originally thought," he said, reaching out to grab her wrist in his hand. He held it firmly while their gazes remained locked. When she could feel him pulling her hand closer Kira swallowed.

"I vowed to never let anyone in. I had no choice." His voice sounded strained, almost tortured, and Kira's heart beat wildly as she stared at him, seeing that strange glow outlining his body once more.

"But then you showed up," he continued, and Kira blinked. She tried to focus to hear his words, to understand what they meant, what this aura surrounding him was supposed to mean to her.

"I didn't expect you," he said, his voice growing deeper as he placed her hand at the base of his dick. "You," he repeated, clamping his lips tightly once more.

Kira gasped when her fingers scraped along the turgid length of his arousal. Her body trembled, her mind warring with what she should do next. Part of her thinking she should pull away, kick through the shower door, and run like hell, doing whatever she could to get out of this house and away from this man. Another part demanding she stay right there, that she touch him, be with him, accept him. It was weird in a long line of unexplainable things that had been happening to her—Tora's death, Penn's betrayal, her running away and ending up in the midst of a Devoted pack, the dreams that seemed so real, and him, this lycan who should have been so wrong for her but felt so damned right.

Her fingers extended, wrapping around the base, loving the warmth that immediately spread from him to her palm, up her arm, and throughout her body. She held him tightly, her lips trembling, eyes trained on his face.

"Take it, *lýkaina*. Take what you want," he said through gritted teeth.

Kira stared at him, amazed at what she thought she saw. His face was contorted, in pleasure, she thought, as his breaths were coming faster, a muscle in his jaw twitching as she tightened her grip on him. When she pulled her hand back, stroking her palm along the veined length of his cock, stopping to rub her thumb over the bulbous head, he closed his eyes, shaking his head slightly from side to side.

She repeated the motion again and again, moving faster, watching his shoulders bunch, his Adam's apple shift up and then down each time that he swallowed.

"I want your mouth. Now," he told her. "Right, fucking now!"

His words had been spoken in a guttural tone, raw with something she wasn't totally familiar with. When his eyes opened and he caught her staring at him, he licked his lips slowly. Kira thought she remembered that tongue and felt her pussy clench in response.

"Put your mouth on me, *lýkaina*."

Kira wondered if he meant on his lips, which he'd just licked again, or on his cock, which she was thoroughly enjoying stroking.

"Where?" she whispered, her throat going dry with the simple word.

"There," he said the moment her thumb rubbed over his tip again. "Right. There."

Never in a million years would Kira have thought she would be here, doing this, with an alpha like Blaez. She'd been told she would never get anyone better than a beta and that even then he wouldn't really want her for anything other than the status her birthright could provide.

There were so many questions, so many obstacles that should stand between her and Blaez. She didn't know the answers to any of those questions, and right at this very moment Kira didn't care. Her body had already begun to lower, her knees planting firmly against the wet tile, her hand still tightly gripping his dick. His gorgeous long and heavy cock with the thick veins stretching like rope along the sides and the tip that at this very moment wept a drop of white cum that she couldn't wait to taste.

So dipping her head lower without another word, Kira extended her tongue, licking the tip of Blaez's cock and taking that drop as if it were there especially for her. His hands were immediately in her hair, tangling and wrapping the strands around his fist until his blunt nails scraped along her scalp and he began to slowly push her down farther over his dick.

Having never done this before, Kira simply went on instinct, opening her mouth, letting her tongue slide along the underside of his length, the head reaching the back of her throat where it seemed to tap and ask for entrance. Blaez helped her this time, by tipping her head back slightly, pressing forward as he did. She looked up at him, shivering at how hot and hungry his intense gaze on her made her feel. His teeth were bared, the sharp tips of his incisors clearly visible through the steam rising around them.

He worked her head slowly, easing himself in and out of her, like he was spoon-feeding her. She could tell he was holding back, that maybe he wanted to pump more deeply into her mouth. That thought had her thighs shaking, her pussy dripping. Her nipples scraped against his legs, sending tendrils of pleasure flitting throughout her body.

With a start she realized she wanted more, needed more. She sucked him in deeper, loving the feel of his turgid skin sliding sinuously against her tongue, pressing back along her throat. Her hand worked up and down his shaft in conjunction with her mouth, until her lips were as wet as his length, the suckling sound echoing in the stall.

When his dick began to pulsate in her mouth, his hands gripping her head more firmly, holding her in place, Kira shivered all over. She wanted desperately to reach between her legs and thrust her fingers deep inside. She would come instantly, she knew; her arousal was so keen she was ready to explode.

"I don't . . . do . . . this," he said, his voice strained as his hips jutted forward, his balls slapping against her chin as she took him completely inside her mouth.

Kira had no idea what he didn't do. All she knew for certain was what he was doing to her at this very moment. Every nerve in her body was on alert, her breasts so full they ached and her pussy creaming so heavily she was certain the moisture on her thighs was not water from the shower.

"Never before," he continued, this time pulling her head back again.

She could see him looking down at her, saw the twist of his lips, the muscles bulging in his neck as he looked to be fighting something. Whatever it was he was working against must have been strong; the struggle looked so intense that Kira almost let him slip from her lips.

"No, *lýkaina,* you cannot stop. It's too late for that," he told her, thrusting forward one more time so that he was once again filling her mouth.

Kira sucked hard and deep, her cheeks hollowing as she held him still right there.

"That's right; you're gonna suck it right out of me," he said, his teeth gritting between his words. "Whether I want you to or not!"

And she did, without even knowing what to expect or how to complete this task. Blaez stiffened over her, his hands firm on the back of her head, a growl reverberating throughout his chest as the heated jets of his release shot straight to the back of her throat. When she swallowed once, then twice, it was with a spike of something new coursing through her body, something more powerful than she'd ever imagined.

She held him in her mouth until his fingers loosened in her hair. Then with a few last licks along his still-stiff cock, she pulled back slowly, only to gasp when he lifted her up quickly from the floor. He was staring at her intently as he locked her ankles around his back and moved them until they stood just beneath the spray of hot water.

"I'm going to fuck you now," he said with a growl quickly following his words.

A sound that sent heat spikes straight down to her pussy, stalling any reply she hoped to make.

CHAPTER 8

Blaez had no idea what he was doing.

That was wrong, he thought as he sat back on the bench, his hands firmly planted on Kira's pliant ass as he positioned her over his throbbing length. He'd carried her across the shower stall only seconds after watching her take every spurt of his cum into her mouth without blinking an eye. With each swallow something had shifted inside him, something more than the beast that resided within. He'd decided in that moment he would have her, here and now, regardless of the restrictions he'd put on himself or the consequences that might come from this act.

"Dammit, so fucking tight!" he gritted through clenched teeth. "So good and so tight!"

Her nails dug into his shoulders and he pushed her down slowly over his length, sucking in a breath each time another inch of his cock was buried deeper in the warmth of her. His arms threatened to tremble, his eyes closing. Blaez willed it all to stop, forcing the thoughts of why this was wrong and possibly dangerous out of his mind.

None of it mattered at this moment. He was doing it. He was steadily sinking inside of her, loving the tight grip her

heated walls had on his cock, the sting of her nails breaking his skin, and the look she was currently giving him. Her
eyes were wide open, bright with arousal and anticipation.
Her body was willing and pliant and she scooted even closer
to him, his dick buried to the hilt inside of her. Her thighs
were so soft around his waist, her breasts high and heavy,
jiggling each time she moved, holding his gaze like a dog to
a bone.

"It's perfect," he heard the words, knew they were spoken from him, and yet still couldn't believe it.

He kneaded her ass, loving the feel of the globes in his
palm, remembering with startlingly clarity how it felt the
first time he'd touched it.

He'd slapped her ass. The thought hit him mid-thrust
and Blaez growled, wanting to do so again. Yet she hadn't
disobeyed him in any way this time. In fact, she'd been giving him everything he wanted, from the moment she stepped
into this stall. It wasn't right, he thought, trying desperately
to concentrate on her hips gyrating above him, his deep
thrusts in and out of her. He considered pulling his hands
away to remove the temptation, but they wouldn't move, as
if it were their turn to be defiant.

He pumped harder, going deeper, as she gasped, biting
her bottom lip to keep from screaming out loud. Blaez didn't
like screaming or moaning or any other faked response
from females. He tended to go only for the true evidence of
their pleasure—their puckered nipples, wet pussy, and release that vibrated through their body. Anything else was
not tolerated.

"Let it out!" he told Kira. "Let me know how good I feel
inside of you!"

She continued to grip his shoulders, her teeth still biting into her lower lip, her eyes halfway closed as she bounced on top of him, taking every inch of his dick as if it were something she did every day, like this was somehow owed to her. She did not scream or yell.

Blaez raged on the inside, grasping her at the hips and pushing her up off his dick. His body reacted and he growled, his release not at all happy that he'd put a pause to its second act. Oh, how he wanted to come while buried deep inside her. While her mouth had been warm and wet it was nothing compared to how juicy her pussy felt, how tightly it gripped him, threatening to milk the remaining cum from his body.

He stood, still holding her by the waist, and she looked at him in surprise.

"Turn around," he told her once he'd stood up.

For a second she looked as if she might argue, but then she turned away from him. He pressed at the base of her back, the point where her hips splayed outward, the most enticing of her curves beginning—his palm covering that crescent-moon mark. She gasped, most likely because he hadn't been gentle when he'd pushed her forward. Her hands flattened on the bench, her ass jutting up and out, ready for him to sink between its creases to find her waiting pussy once more.

Instead, Blaez smacked her right cheek and almost groaned as he watched it jiggle in response.

"Blaez!" she yelled his name, looking back over her shoulder.

"I told you to let go," he said, lifting his hand, flexing his fingers at the heat burning in the pit of his palm. "And you disobeyed me."

The cracking sound of his hand on her other cheek came and his dick jutted forward with excitement. Kira turned then, twisting her body so that she was almost facing him.

"Don't," she said through clenched teeth. "Don't do that again."

"Why?" he asked, his heart beating wildly, the combination of her scent and the sight of her rounded ass turning red bringing him even closer to release. "Because you like it, don't you? You've never been spanked before and you like it."

She shook her head, but she was no longer yelling at him. Blaez placed a palm flat on her ass and kept his gaze trained on her. "Tell me you like it, *lýkaina*. It's okay to like what I do to you."

"No," she whispered. "It's not . . . I don't . . ."

He began rubbing his palm over the reddened spot on her buttock, then leaned forward, moving his hand so that he could kiss that spot, tracing his tongue along the heated flesh.

"I won't hurt you, Kira. I would never hurt you," he told her. "Trust me."

She'd sucked in a breath when his mouth touched her flesh; now she trembled as he continued to lick and kiss her intermittently, his other palm planted firmly on her other cheek.

"I don't know how to do this," she said on another hiss of breath. "Or how to be this person."

"Just let go," he told her. "You're safe with me. Just let go and let me give you everything you've ever desired."

Blaez had no idea what that really was. For the first time in his life he wasn't totally certain of what he could or should

496 A. C. Arthur

do for a female . . . for *this* female. Because he suspected what she really needed was far beyond the physical.

"Let me give you pleasure," he whispered, not willing to question himself any further.

He continued to rub her bottom, using long, slow, gentle strokes. The waning steam still misting around them. "Just relax and let me give you more."

She looked as if she wasn't certain, her lips partially parted and wet. He wanted to kiss her, the realization slapping against him with surprising clarity. But he didn't do it; he couldn't. Instead, he rubbed a hand up her back and over her shoulders to continue to calm her, all the while positioning himself behind her, spreading her bottom so that his dick could slip through the warm crease, down, down until being sucked into her waiting pussy.

Blaez grabbed her hips then, thrusting deep and fast inside of her until his teeth cut through his bottom lip, her moans growing louder and louder.

"Come for me, *lýkaina*. Come for your—" His words cut off abruptly. He was not her alpha. Did not want to be. Could never be.

"Come for me!" he yelled, his hips slapping wildly against her ass, "Come for me now!"

"Bla-a-ez!" His name was a long, loud wail as she stiffened beneath him, her lycan nails scraping along the tiled bench with a high-pitched sound.

He loved that sound, coupled with her voice screaming his name again and again. Blaez moved faster, his dick pistoning in and out of her slickness with a smacking sound that only added to his arousal. His entire body vibrated while his nostrils flared, filling him with her scent. He would never forget this, never forget her. Ever.

Dammit!

"I'm going down to the library," Blaez said twenty minutes after he'd left her standing in the shower.

Kira was now in her room and, thankfully, completely dressed, while he stood in the doorway, blocking any entrance or exit.

Replacing the embarrassment she'd felt yesterday after their training session when he'd walked away from her was a heated ball of agitation from the way he'd simply fucked her and left this morning. The pattern with him was more than disconcerting. At the same time, Kira couldn't help but wonder what it was she actually expected from him. Was it candlelight and romance, a prelude to a claiming? No. That's not what she'd been looking for; she'd been adamant about that fact from the beginning. But now—

"You need to join me," he continued, sounding exasperated.

He thought she would get up and follow without comment. Just as there'd been no doubt in his mind that she would melt in his hands as he'd smacked her ass in the shower. Well, okay, the spike of pain had seared straight through to her clit, causing her to shiver and almost come as if on command. But that didn't mean she had to follow him blindly all the time.

"No. I'm not simply going to follow you down to the library, Blaez. I didn't come looking for another lycan to dictate what

I do and how I do it. I didn't ask you to keep me locked in this house whether for protection or whatever other reasons. None of this was a part of my plan." She took a deep breath and then released it. "But I'm not so rigid or blind, for that matter, as to not see that there's something else at play here. Something that I don't think either of us planned. Wouldn't it make more sense if we talked about that instead of operating on this hot and cold system that's been going on between us?" Kira wanted answers and she wasn't going to follow any more of Blaez's commands—even the ones that aroused her tremendously—until she received them.

He looked so damned good standing there, so powerful and authoritative, legs spread slightly, muscles bulging and flexing she suspected without any direction from him. Her father had not exuded this authority or strength, for that matter; neither had any of the other alphas she'd ever met. And while it wasn't there at this very moment, there was that glow that she saw every now and then when she looked at Blaez, that not so subtle reminder that he was a force to be reckoned with. Well, it looked as if she'd be going up against him now whether she planned to heed that warning or not.

"You were the one who said you wanted to know what the books written in Greek said," he told her calmly, without addressing her current questions at all.

But he was agreeing to another one of her requests. She wondered if this would be the only way to deal with him, on his terms and in his time. If it was, she wasn't sure how she would deal with that, but for now she asked for clarification, "You're going to teach me how to read Greek?"

"You said you wanted to learn so that you would be able

to read all the books in the library. Come down to the library with me and I'll teach you."

Of course he left her standing there to contemplate a reply that he wouldn't hear either way. A part of her, a distant part that she was feeling less and less connected to the longer she remained in this house, wanted her to stay in this room, to continue to search for a way out. But another part, the stronger part, she admitted, pressed her to go forward. It actually felt more like a push against all that she'd thought she was and believed to go with him, to possibly learn more.

Minutes later, Kira was in the library.

"Whose idea was it to make this a library?" she asked him.

Yesterday she'd wondered this same thing as she'd walked into this space with its darker, heavier-looking wood shelves. Today she stood in the center of the room, the plush Oriental rug cushioning her feet; the two love seats positioned in the middle of the floor directly across from each other were dark brown leather. There was a large round coffee table between the love seats and on the opposite sides two sets of the same high-backed leather chairs that matched the one she'd sat in yesterday.

"Did you hire a decorator?" was her next question, and she turned around to see where Blaez was and why he hadn't answered the first one.

When he turned to face her he was already holding a book, the one on the Trekas family she'd been reading yesterday. "Channing's mother is into designing. His father's a contractor, so they helped with the remodel. Each of us agreed on the library."

"What do you all do for a living?" she asked, since he'd

opened the door with mention of Channing's parents. "Are you all sickeningly wealthy?"

"Not all of us" was Blaez's calm response. He sat on the couch, opening the book, and began flipping slowly through its pages. "You said you read this book last night," he said without looking up at her. "I know that parts of it are written in Greek. My family loved the language and made sure that each of us knew how to read and speak it. So I'll have to teach you the Greek alphabet before you can read. For now, I want to tell you the story of how the lycans came to be in existence."

Kira sat beside him, moving closer to look down at the page. "We all know the story, Blaez," she started to say even though she distinctly remembered reading things she hadn't known before in that book last night.

He nodded then, sitting back on the couch. "Tell me what the Hunters taught you to believe."

The Hunters—her parents and their pack had been Hunters. She had been a Hunter. Ignoring that fact, she began,

"Lykaon pissed Zeus off. Zeus sought revenge in his usual brute way by killing all of Lykaon's sons but one, and turning Lykaon into a wolf. Nyktimos was Lykaon's youngest son and had been saved from Zeus's wrath by Gaia, who hid him in the river. She should have been smart enough to hide him from Lykaon, who was now bitter and still irritated at having lost his reign as king of Arcadia and was now relegated to walking around on all fours howling at the moon." Kira paused when she noticed how intently he was staring at her and noticed the quick warmth spreading throughout her body as a result.

Clearing her throat, she continued, "Lykaon eventually found Nyktimos and out of anger and jealousy bit his only living son, thus changing him into a werewolf. Nyktimos, now angry at his father in turn for the fact that now on the night of the full moon he would shift into a hideous beast, left Arcadia and Olympus and all its battling gods and demigods and helpless mortals. He ended up in Washington State, where he met and fell in love with the human Aleya, whom he eventually bit. Thus began our hybrid breed of part wolf, part man, otherwise known as the lycan."

She left out the part where Nyktimos had felt an instant connection to Aleya and only bit her because his love had grown so quickly and so deeply for her that he never wanted to lose her. When Kira looked at Blaez this time there was a brief change. His eyes were blue again, his face contorted until he looked more like a wolf than a lycan, and he lay on the ground, not moving, dead. A quick and potent wave of grief washed over her and she bit down on her lip to keep from gasping.

"The lycan breed then began to grow throughout the world, continuing the ridiculous feud between Zeus and Lykaon in their own self-destructive way," he said, slamming the book closed on his lap and not noticing the few strange moments she'd just experienced.

Kira chanced another look at him, just to make sure what she'd seen wasn't true. Blaez wasn't dead. He couldn't be, because he was sitting here talking to her. His shirt today was light gray, a color that made his dark eyes brighten only slightly, even though his brow was still furrowed, his jaw stoically drawn.

Maybe she was hallucinating since they'd skipped

breakfast. Yes, that was it. Her blood sugar was low and so now she was seeing things.

With a shake of her head Kira replied, "Mortals that were forced into being animals coming to an even bigger population of mortals, thus cursing some of them to the same dastardly fate, were supposed to do what else exactly?" She asked because she hated this story.

"Your pack, the Hunter packs, are attempting to kill off the Devoted lycans. Are you trying to say that's because they have nothing better to do and that we should all simply blame Zeus and let the killing ensue?"

"No." Kira shook her head, turning in the seat so she could face him. "That's not what I'm saying."

"Then tell me, Kira. What are your thoughts on the Hunters and the Devoteds? Where exactly do you stand in this little war?"

He was speaking as if he already knew the answer, watching her closely like he had a plan for the moment she responded. It was like he had this all sorted out in his mind and was just waiting for her to walk to his beat. Just like Penn had.

"I don't give a damn which one of you kills who," she shot back quickly, loving the slight widening of Blaez's eyes, which said she'd managed to shock him. "It's not my fight, hence the reason I could so easily walk away."

"Was it easy?" he asked, tilting his head slightly as he continued to stare at her. "Walking away from your pack?"

Talk about being caught off guard. His voice had changed with the blink of his eyes, from the cool, aloof interrogation to what she thought might be genuine concern. Kira fidgeted. Well, she clasped her fingers, then unclasped them.

And when she caught herself doing that she pulled her hands apart, tucking each one beneath a thigh as she looked back at him.

"Nothing in this life is easy, Blaez. I'm sure you know that considering you're a leader of your own pack. You know better than I how all the decisions rest on your shoulders, how you are responsible for the lives of those who follow you."

"Why would you feel responsible for your father or his pack? After what they did to you."

She was already shaking her head, regretting the moment he'd come to her last night in the midst of her nightmare. She'd said things to him then that she shouldn't have. Blaez was not her friend. Sure, she'd had sex with him, so maybe that kind of made him her lover, at least temporarily. But a friend was different. It was intimate and personal and there was nothing like that between them. Was there?

"Look, my situation is different from yours and probably from anyone else's. I wasn't what my father wanted or needed in his pack, I guess. And the others, well, they were down for making the best of the situation."

"But you're not a situation," he said vehemently. "You were their alpha female. They should have cherished and protected you."

His words, because they were so true and so exactly like the way her mother had been treated, hurt as if he were cutting directly into Kira's chest with a heated blade.

"Yeah, I know," she said with a wavering smile and a chuckle that didn't spark any humor inside. "They shouldn't have felt like it was a chore to decide which one of them would claim the big girl. Alpha female or not, a man knows what he likes."

"And an idiot will soon see what he lost" came Blaez's automatic reply.

Kira grew quiet, looking down at her thick thighs and shaking her head. She'd never been thin and hadn't convinced herself that she was beautiful. Cute, yes, especially in the right outfit; pinks and vibrant blues were really her colors. So she didn't have self-esteem or body image issues, but that didn't mean she was stupid to the way of the world or the way most men thought when they looked at her. Hell, her father had even suggested diets and gyms to her on more than one occasion. Kira had declined both. She ran on a daily basis, sometimes in the forest—where her mother had been killed—and Kira loved to cook, which gave her ample excuse for also loving to eat. She was healthy according to her latest physical with the human doctor, a healthy size 16, with a mind much sharper than all the lycans in her father's pack and a sweet spot for love songs.

"They were all idiots," she replied finally. "Even my father. And so I left. Case closed." She shrugged when Blaez didn't immediately say anything and looked across the room.

"They'll come for you," he said.

She nodded. "I know. That's why you should let me go. I can move surprisingly fast, thanks to my daily runs in the forest, which I'm missing out on being stuck in this lovely but locked-tight log fortress of yours. If I leave now I'll be gone before the full moon."

"Because there's no way they'll come before then," he said.

Coming from anyone else, it would have been a question, but since Blaez seemed to know everything about everything, it was a statement.

"They're not as strong as you and your pack," she told him.

"How do you know how strong we are?"

She did chuckle then, honestly. "I can see, Blaez. Each of you is built like you stepped right off the pages of a workout magazine. And you carried me at least two miles back from the woods to this place and then again up the stairs, where you so eloquently showed me my sleeping quarters. Believe me when I say you're much stronger than any of my father's pack."

"You're not proud of your father at all. You speak almost as if you have no feelings for him. Why is that?" Blaez asked her.

"Because I don't," Kira immediately replied. "I loved my mother and she was killed. I believe my father knows what really happened, but he refuses to tell me. For that, and for—" Kira stopped. She took a deep breath and continued, "I'll never forgive him for that."

She was looking across the room again, trying to tell herself that this feeling like Blaez might actually be a nice guy, a guy she could on some level really like, was most likely way off base, when he surprised her yet again. His fingers slipped along her shoulder, moving until he was rubbing the nape of her neck. As she'd pulled her hair high into a ponytail today, each brush of his skin against hers sent a shiver of excitement straight down her spine.

"Sometimes people do what they think is best to protect others," he told her.

When she looked to him again she was shocked to see that he'd moved even closer, without making a sound. His face was only inches from hers and she blinked away her astonishment.

"I don't need protection," she told him adamantly. "I needed the truth."

Blaez stood then and said, "The truth is overrated and is rarely what one expects." He walked away at that point, going to put the book back on its shelf, she presumed.

Kira also figured that Blaez thought this conversation was over. He probably assumed she would leave since he'd walked away from her yet again. But no, that was not happening, not today. And especially not after she'd just about emptied her soul to him about what had gone on in her life. No, she was going to get answers from Blaez Trekas right here and right now, if it was the last thing she did.

CHAPTER 9

"Tell me why you're doing this," Kira said coming up behind Blaez, cornering him at the far end of the library.

He'd been thinking about her as he'd slipped the book into the empty space on the shelf where it had been. He'd known she'd read it even before she told him because Channing had come to Blaez's room, tossing it onto his desk before saying, "You should tell her why you're being such a dick. She's a lot stronger than you think and she deserves better from you."

Blaez had looked at the man he'd known for years, the lycan who had been raised by humans and had no clue of what he was until his fifteenth birthday, when his first shift had almost inadvertently exposed their breed to the human world. Blaez had found him when he'd shown up at Channing's high school recruiting for the Marines. From that moment on they'd been together, like brothers, which was why Blaez hadn't broken Channing's nose for speaking to him that way.

"It's none of her business," he'd told Channing. "It's none of anyone's business."

Channing was already at the door when he turned back

to Blaez. "So you've always said. But she's different, Blaez. All of us sensed that the moment you brought her in here. And it seems to me that whichever greater entity selected to send the two of you into the woods at the same time may have done so for a good reason."

Blaez had frowned at the door long after Channing had closed it, rubbing his hands over the book and contemplating the beta's words. Kira was different, but in ways that nobody besides him really knew. He'd already been pissed off about seeing that mark on her, about wondering each day if she had been Selected for him or someone else. Because Blaez had wanted her. He'd wanted more than just touching and tasting her, oh, so much more. But if that mark meant what he knew it did, she wasn't his for the taking.

He'd returned the book to the library, dropping it onto the table instead of returning it to the shelf because he'd wanted to return to his room, to stay locked behind that door in the hopes of keeping his hands and mind off her again. But then she'd screamed and he'd gone to her and he'd stayed. He'd held her, watched her sleep, felt everything from the curve of her chin to the bright pink polished toenails creep inside of him, winding herself so securely around his heart he'd thought he would never take another breath again. But he did breathe; he'd watched her enter that shower, seen her in all her naked glory, touched her, felt her touching him, until none of that was enough any longer.

"I'm not leaving just because you're choosing to be quiet. I'm going to stand right here until you tell me the real reason why you're keeping me here. Why you want me desperately one moment and then do everything in your power to pull away from me in the next. Dammit, Blaez, I want to know why when I should be breaking these windows in an attempt to get the hell out of here, I'm not, because the thought of walking away from you, what I see when I think—" She sighed, but she didn't back down.

She was right up in his face, her body pressing against his, not sexually—although his dick was getting hard because, like she'd sort of just said, there was something strong between them—but close enough to act as a barrier if he should try to move past her.

"There's nothing—" he tried to say, but decided to start over. "I told you it was about protection."

"But that's not all, is it?" She pressed. "I can see it in your eyes when you look at me. I can feel it each time you walk into a room I'm in. I'll admit that right about now I don't like it any more than you do, but at least I'm not trying to deny it."

"The only reason you aren't trying to break out of here anymore is because you know it's impossible," he said, hating that on top of her confronting him, he could still hear Channing's warnings last night, as if the two were somehow working in tandem.

"That's not the only reason," she said, this time pressing against Blaez in a *very* sexual way.

Blaez cupped her ass in his palms. "This," he said, leaning so close he could lick her lips if he wanted to, "is the needing."

She surprised him by being the one to go for it, moving in to tug on his bottom lip with her teeth. It was as close to a kiss as Blaez had been in for he didn't remember how long. He couldn't understand why she'd done it or why he'd just been thinking about doing it a few seconds ago.

"It's not simply the needing and you know it," she whispered.

It was like a taunt, a dare for him to tell her what this really was between them. For Blaez, however, actions had always spoken louder than words.

He moved quickly, lifting her into his arms, until she'd wrapped her legs around his waist. Turning, he pressed her back against the bookshelf, grounding the thick bulge of his erection into her. She was wearing jeans today, the denim giving to every curve of her ass and thighs. Thrusting a hand between them, Blaez had the jeans unbuttoned and unzipped before she could whisper his name.

"This is what you wanted, right?" he asked, pressing his hand down between her legs. She sighed the second he touched her mound, moving farther to separate her plump folds. Wet and hot and waiting for him. Blaez almost shivered with that knowledge.

"You want me to fuck you right here in this library; amidst all this history and knowledge you want to scream my name," he told her.

She shook her head, surprising him yet again today. "That's not what I want," she told him.

He clenched his teeth. "Then say the word. Say what's necessary to make me stop."

Until that moment he would continue to stroke her, loving the feel of her thick juices dripping onto his fingers, the quick suction when those fingers moved farther back to her core, sinking deep inside of her. She swallowed, lacing her arms around his neck, her eyes wide open and tinged with desire.

"Is this all you plan to give?" she asked him. "You want

to make me come. You want to come. And then you walk away. Is that all you have, Blaez?"

He growled.

Couldn't help it. Her words pissed him off. Her pussy felt too good.

He pulled his hand out of her immediately, letting her stand on her own feet once more, and turned to walk away. He wanted to give her more. Blaez could close his eyes and think of laying her on this floor, licking her pussy until she was sated with pleasure, until he was crazy with needing to be inside of her. Only then would he get what he wanted, sinking his length as deep inside of her as he could go, to the point where he felt like they were one.

He gritted his teeth again and went totally still when her hand touched his back.

"Don't do that," she said quietly. "Don't walk away from me again, Blaez. You're a better person than that, a better alpha."

She said the words and, like what Channing had said and the simple fact that she was here, now, Blaez wanted to believe them. He wanted to accept that she was here for him, that maybe, just maybe, this was his destiny. But that was a dangerous thought, one that he wasn't certain he was ready to have.

"My mother's name was Kharis. My father was Alec, Nyktimos's grandson; first-generation blood runs deep and fresh in my veins. The more descendants that spun from him, the more diluted their blood became, the less power they possessed." Blaez began talking slowly, his eyes closing as he refused to turn around and look at her.

She kept that hand on his back but did not say a word.

She would listen intently to what he had to say, but would she understand?

Blaez took a long, deep breath, letting it out slowly before continuing, "Zeus wanted to rule Arcadia. To do so he needed Lykaon and all of his descendants out of the way. The egotistical god thought he'd done that, but Gaia saved Nyktimos. It was not until Nyktimos claimed that mortal and they began to procreate did Zeus realize his misstep. He began his search for Nyktimos and all of his offspring, but as the bloodline became diluted it was harder for Zeus to find them all. So he focused on the pure bloodline, the same way the Hunter packs began doing. When Zeus learned that my father had not only claimed someone but had produced children, he was angered once more. He sought them out and had them killed. My parents, my brothers, and my sister."

Kira gasped. "Oh, Blaez, I'm so sorry."

He shook his head, not really knowing what to do with her sympathy.

"When I came back," he continued, now since he'd started down this path, the words coming out softly, "I came home from the service and they were gone. All I had were my memories. My brothers' playful tendencies. My dad's quick wit. My sister's smile and rich laughter. My mother's words of wisdom."

"Blaez," she whispered again, both her hands moving along his back now.

"I didn't want this. I wanted my family to live and to be there the way they'd always been. I would have done anything, everything, to protect them from him, to save them. But I didn't know. I didn't realize that he would come for them. So I wasn't there to save them. By the time I arrived there was nothing I could do," he said, finally turning to face her.

"Nothing but continue on. My mother was a believer in destiny and for a while I'd believed in it too, but how could my destiny include so much pain and grief?" He gritted his teeth. "There are threads to our lives, you know. The Moirai made it so. They piece those threads together and so our destiny is already planned. That's what my mother taught me. So my destiny was to form a pack. I came here and I decided to do my part, to live the way they wanted me to. But that was as far as I planned to take that destiny trail. I decided that if I was going to give up everything I'd wanted to live the way my parents and the Fates so deemed, I at least deserved one thing for myself. I deserved not to endure that type of pain or loss ever again. No emotional or intimate attachments, ever. Unlike my father and Nyktimos before me, I would never claim anyone, never bring another life into this dismal world that we've been forced to live in. Not ever."

For a brief moment Kira looked as if his words had caused her great pain; then her facial features had relaxed, her gaze softening as she said, "So instead of running like me, you'll just hide. Here in this beautiful mountain region, you'll stay with the pack that can fight almost as well as you; each of you will stay here with the vow to protect each other. But nothing more." She lifted a hand to touch his cheek as she finished.

Blaez almost pulled away, but the warmth of her palm felt too good. It felt too right.

"I'll do whatever I have to do to keep them, and now you,

safe," he vowed. "That's what I was meant to do. I know that without a doubt now it's my purpose. To protect. But I don't have to subject myself to anything more. I won't."

She gave a slight nod. "And what's my purpose, Blaez? Am I a part of your destiny? Maybe I'm another part that you refuse to accept."

If he believed in praying to the gods he would have, right at this very moment. He would have prayed that his answer to her could be yes. But there was so much more she didn't know and could not possibly understand.

"Kira," he began, searching for the words to end this conversation, her questions, everything, in the hopes of getting back to what he'd decided was his normal life.

When she came closer, cupping his face in her hands, and tilted her head up to touch her lips to his, Blaez didn't know what to do. For the first time in he didn't know how long, he didn't know how to react, how to proceed, what to say or feel. She kissed him again, her lips soft against his, her tongue just barely brushing across the seam.

"Ki—" He'd been about to say her name, to tell her this was a colossal mistake, when he heard another voice.

"Blaez," Phelan said from somewhere pretty close to them. "We have a problem."

Kira jumped as if she, or rather they, had been doing something wrong. And Blaez cursed.

He turned to face Phelan, giving Kira a moment to refasten her jeans.

"I'll be there in a moment," Blaez said, glad that Phelan had turned his back to them.

"I'll wait up front," the beta said.

"No need," Kira told them, coming from behind Blaez. "I

was just leaving," she said, moving hurriedly toward the front of the library.

Phelan had turned around at her words, staring at Blaez when she left them alone with a knowing and disapproving look.

"I should change that to say we've got *another* problem," he said, and only frowned when Blaez growled his response.

"Headache?" Malec asked, his voice just shy of being raspy, and all the way sexy.

Kira stopped massaging her temples, letting her fingers run through her hair instead as she sat back on one of the sofas in the living room. She had no idea how long she'd been sitting there after leaving Phelan and Blaez in the library. But as she'd walked down the hallway it had happened again and this time what she saw had taken her breath away. She'd had to sit immediately to get herself together. Only now, however long afterward, she still felt edgy, like there was something about to happen, something big that would change everything. And she had no idea what it was.

"No. Just thinking," Kira replied.

She looked up slowly to see the lycan with the great washboard abs leaning with his arms crossed over his bare chest against one of the wooden beams in the living room. She flattened her palms against her thighs, keeping perfectly still as they stared at each other. Malec looked good— that was obvious—and he was powerful; his muscled legs and arms and his overall demeanor told her that. He would be one hell of an opponent to another lycan. But he was sad. That she could also see by the look in his eyes and the blurry yellow haze outlining his form. That was what had her holding his gaze so intently.

"Are you thinking about how to tell your Hunter pack to attack us? Maybe you're reconfiguring your original plan now that you've been on the inside for a while," he said.

She relaxed as the haze that had been surrounding him ebbed, slowly disappearing. "Is that really why you keep this place secured like Fort Knox, because you're afraid of the packs coming to attack you?"

"We're not afraid of Hunters. So if you have any contact with your pack, let them know that the moment they step onto this property their asses are mine!"

His lips had peeled back with that statement, his sharp teeth baring. For anyone other than a lycan, and perhaps other than a stubborn and tenacious alpha female, such as herself, that little display would have been frightening. But Kira stood up, taking a few steps closer to where Malec stood.

"You don't trust me," she said when she was standing only a few feet away from him. "You think I'm here to set you up."

"Your pack is no match for us," he told her. "So whatever your reason for being here, it won't end the way you think."

"You know it was not my choice to stay here and yet you still think my intentions are corrupt. That tells me either you have trust issues with everyone or your senses aren't worth a damn. Either way, Blaez should watch you closely, because in this state you may be more of a danger to him than I could ever be," she told him.

"Blaez wants you here, so you stay," he told her. "But you're right; I don't trust you."

"Fine," Kira replied. "I don't trust you either." Which wasn't exactly a lie. It wasn't him she didn't trust per se, but more like what she could see was really bothering him instead.

"Fine!" he snapped in return, pushing past her.

She stumbled back because she'd been so busy trying to decipher that rapid glimpse of Malec standing at a window watching Channing with an unknown female that she hadn't really been paying attention to the Malec that was directly in front of her.

When she thought he had left her there alone, his voice had her turning to see that he'd stopped, looking over his shoulder.

"You need to strengthen your inner body. One of the reasons he caught you, outside of the fact that he's an alpha, is because you weren't prepared. You're not strong enough to fight on your own, without a pack. I can teach you how to fix that in the gym."

Each of his words was clipped, like he was being forced to say them, his body being held in that spot against his will. Yet what he was saying was an offer, one that he shouldn't have been offering if he really thought she was here to set them up.

"Are you saying I need to lose weight?" Kira asked, her hackles immediately rising as his words caused unwanted feelings to surface. She'd endured Dallas and the other betas of Penn's pack insulting and berating her because Penn had never did anything to stop them. As the alpha he should have demanded respect for his daughter. Since he didn't, she hadn't. Not until she'd had enough and left. This time around, with this pack that wasn't hers, in this place where she hadn't asked to be, there was no way in hell she was letting anybody get away with disrespecting her.

He smirked. "That would be predictable, wouldn't it? You expect everyone who looks at you to say that first. Not that you really care about what they think, but you expect it."

Again she realized that this one saw too much, at all times. It was her turn to frown.

"Just meet me in the gym at noon. Every day. I'll show you how to be stronger, not skinnier," he said tightly.

"And now that we have that settled, you wanna come into the kitchen and talk about what we can have for dinner tonight, Kira?"

Of course that was Channing interrupting, with his sexy-ass grin and baby blue eyes. He wore jeans and a T-shirt, which seemed to be the general attire of this pack, and he'd come to stand so close to Malec that Kira had raised a brow at both of them. The vision she'd had just moments ago of Malec watching Channing had been startling as well. As for Malec, he'd continued to frown, until he figured it made more sense to walk away.

"He likes you," Channing told her. "So he'll get used to having you here."

Kira didn't believe the first part of Channing's comment for one minute. If Malec liked her he sure had a funny way of showing it. "He doesn't have to like me. I'm used to that," she told Channing.

"Some people are specially selected to be picked on," Channing said, draping an arm around her shoulders. "My mother used to say, 'You were picked out to be picked on.' I didn't know it then, but now I believe that meant I was special. Very special."

Kira couldn't help but smile as she looked up at him. "You're special all right," she said, pleased that she was able to joke when it seemed like everything around her was spiraling out of control.

"And so are you. Don't argue with me," he warned before she could open her mouth to reply. "Us special people are able to recognize each other. Now, like I was saying before, I think you and I should put our heads together and come up with something fabulous for dinner!"

Kira walked with him, but before they made it to the kitchen she stopped, placing a hand on his arm, and said, "I didn't come here to be your alpha female. That's not what I want to be."

His smiling eyes sobered a bit as Channing stared at her. "What if you were selected to be something more than you ever dreamed of, something beyond what your mother or any other lycan could explain?" he asked. "Would you want to run from that too?"

Three nights later Blaez had been staring at his laptop for hours as he searched for the proverbial needle in the haystack. Phelan's announcement of a problem when he'd interrupted Blaez and Kira in the library had been an understatement.

In the days since she'd been here Blaez had searched her name not only on the Internet but also using the CIA classified networks that he, as a contract operative, still had access to. He knew everything about her—everything that appeared in the human world, that is. That's how he'd found out about her pack. Penn Radney had been listed as her next of kin. Tora Radney, her mother, was deceased. Because that death had been so recent and Kira's admission to him last night about her past had made it seem like most of her trouble with the pack had started after Tora's death, Blaez had sent a message to Phelan this morning to look into the lycan's death.

What Phelan had found out—through his own research and from another Devoted pack that lived in the Seattle area—was that Tora Radney's death had been ruled accidental, although no autopsy had been completed. That was no surprise to Blaez, since the alpha of the pack would have been certain to ensure that there was no chance of the humans finding out about their kind. Penn Radney would have declined any investigation and he immediately buried his mate nine feet beneath the earth's surface, three feet deeper than a human body in the hopes of avoiding anyone mistakenly stumbling across the body.

So Tora Radney had been shot dead in the forest, her body found by Dallas Muldron, one of Penn's pack mates. Dallas, the beta who had attacked Kira. Blaez had immediately stiffened, rage brewing just beneath the surface.

Phelan had not noticed the flaring of Blaez's nostrils and clenching of his fingers as he'd continued to talk once Kira had left the library. "When Penn Radney reported this incident to the authorities he said his wife had been accidentally shot and blamed it on possible illegal hunting in the area. You know about the conservation and management of the gray wolf species in the northern Cascades and Eastern Washington regions."

"The Radneys lived on a houseboat in Seattle. What was she doing all the way out there running?" Blaez asked, trying desperately to keep his voice steady, his mind focused on receiving all the information before reacting.

Only minutes ago, Kira had sat right beside him telling him how she believed that her father had lied to her about her mother's death and that she could never forgive him for that. And now Phelan was confirming that the documented circumstances surrounding Tora Radney's death might well have been a lie.

"Penn claimed she loved it in the mountain region and would often take weekend trips there, alone. He called it her 'me time' in the report written by the forest rangers."

"How did you get a copy of that report?" Blaez asked Phelan.

"That Devoted lycan I mentioned before, he works in the ranger's office as a janitor and was able to scan and send me a copy this morning."

Blaez nodded. "I presume that Penn would have sent one of his betas to watch over Tora on this trip. Since Dallas was the one to find her and brought her back to Penn, I'm assuming that was him. So how did the rangers know about the shooting at all? And why would they travel all the way to Seattle to question Penn?"

"This is how," Phelan said, pulling a folded sheet of paper from his back pocket and handing it to Blaez.

Blaez accepted the paper as Phelan slipped his hands into his front pockets.

"What the hell is this?" Blaez asked after reading the words of what looked to be a photocopied letter.

"It's an anonymous tip that the ranger department received about the murder," Phelan informed him. "The same Devoted lycan that's been helping me actually witnessed the murder, and even though they were Hunters, or maybe because they were, I'm not sure, he wanted the rangers to know the truth."

"So he sends a tip to the human rangers that Penn Radney killed his wife? But Radney wasn't even there." As Blaez spoke, more facts began to click into place. "Dallas was with her. Dallas is Penn's second in command. So did Penn tell Dallas to kill his wife? Why would he do that?" Blaez wondered.

"That's a good question," Phelan had said. "Another question I had for the lycan was why he wanted Penn Radney picked up by the human police. Didn't he know that a Hunter in captivity—for whatever reason—wasn't going to turn out well for the lycan breed? He said it was one less Hunter for them to be on the lookout for. No regrets there and not a lot of common sense when it comes to how lycans react to things like bars, handcuffs, and restrictions."

Blaez had agreed, but as he'd told Phelan before leaving the library, their priority was to figure out why Penn would have wanted Tora dead. An alpha could no more kill his mate than he could kill the members of his pack. It just wasn't what they did. They were leaders through thick and thin and killers only when they needed to be. Had Penn found a reason to kill his mate? And if so, how would all of this affect Kira when she found out?

For the next few days Blaez had thought a lot about alphas and their mates. About the selection process and the probability of whether it was true or not. And even though he'd told Kira about what had happened to his family in the hopes that she would understand why he'd made the decisions he had to live the way he does, he still couldn't stop thinking about being with her. About how soft her lips had been on his and how tempted he'd been to fold her in his arms and take that kiss deeper, to take whatever was happening between the two of them further.

Keeping his distance from her for the past days had been one of the hardest things Blaez had ever had to do, but he felt like he owed her that much. After all her father and his pack had put her through, Blaez had no business messing her life up even more with his desire for her, the desire that he could never act on. That distance had come to an end earlier tonight as they shared a meal alone because the others had gone into town for the evening.

Do you like it?" she'd asked as she was taking her seat at the large table in the dining room.

It was made to seat up to ten people, with Blaez always sitting at the head with his back facing the steps. The guys usually sat on both sides when they shared meals. Since Kira's arrival, Channing and Malec had each moved down a seat, allowing her to sit on Blaez's right side. Tonight, however, she'd set her place at the opposite head of the table, where the alpha female would sit, but Blaez suspected that was because of the distance he'd been putting between them.

For endless seconds he'd watched her there, picking up her napkin and placing it in her lap. Moving her glass just a little farther away from her plate. Then picking up her knife and fork, holding them in hand as she waited for his response.

"Well?" she prompted him. "The food, Blaez. Do you like it?"

With a frown he snapped his own napkin in the air before letting it fall to his lap. He picked up his knife and fork and cut through the meat and noodles, putting a bite into his mouth and chewing.

"Channing said you favored Italian, so I took a chance when I decided to make this. He also said you guys weren't big food fanatics like he was, so even if I wasn't a great cook you'd probably scarf it down without any complaint. But I'm hoping you actually taste it and that maybe you might really like it."

He'd heard her talking and seen her mouth moving as he chewed, but his mind had been elsewhere and so when he spoke he feared he might have confused her. "That's a lovely color on you," he'd said. "I like you in dresses."

She'd blinked. Confused, just as he'd thought. Then looked down at her clothes and back up at him again.

"Channing again," she said with a shrug. "I only packed three outfits, figuring I'd buy more things when I got settled with my mother's family. He said that was ridiculous and we shopped online. I have credit accounts, but he suggested I not use them. A good idea, I guess."

"So he paid for your new clothes?" Blaez asked, already not liking how much interaction she'd been having with Channing.

"Oh no," she told Blaez, shaking her head as she cut into her own pasta. "He used your credit card, since I'm your guest and all that."

When she looked up at him again, food in her mouth as she chewed, eyes alight with humor, Blaez felt something deep inside. It was peculiar and yet a part of him felt like it should have been expected. The Moirai, he thought with a slight start. If Kira was a thread in his life's fate, each time they created another stitch together he would know. Until eventually there would be absolutely no doubt.

"That's fine. You can buy whatever you need," he told her.

"Really? So if I need a car to get me across the country instead of moving about on foot, would you buy me that?"

"I had wondered why you were running on foot instead of taking a flight or a bus to your destination," he said.

She shrugged. "I've always loved to run and after my mother's death I felt even closer to her when I did. So I figured I'd do a combo of running through the mountain areas, then find a bus or train to take me the longer stretches."

He nodded, admiring the way she thought. "To answer your question, if you needed a car to take you back and forth into town I would make sure you had one." He took another bite of his food, sitting back in the chair and watching her as he chewed. He preferred her to be closer, he thought with a start.

Her shoulders were bare but for the thin straps of the dress she wore. It was a beautiful blue color that stretched tight across her heavy breasts, clasping her waist even tighter before falling straight to her ankles with slits up both sides. He'd seen naked women and women posed in lingerie and thousand-dollar dresses. None of them had come even close to how sexy Kira looked tonight in a simple dress with her hair piled high atop her head.

"So you really plan to keep me here," she said quietly. "How long?"

"Excuse me?"

She gave him a direct look. "How long do you want me to stay here?"

Blaez lifted his glass of wine, sipping it slowly, enjoying the warm bitter taste as it slipped down his throat. "Until it's safe for you."

Blaez took another bite of his food, chewing as he contemplated all that he'd just found out about the pack she'd left. Penn Radney had ordered his wife killed and then attempted to give his daughter to the lycan who had murdered for him. But Kira had run. She had no idea how much danger she had put herself in by doing that and no idea the lengths Blaez would go to keep her safe. He hadn't been able to save his family, but he'd be damned if he lost her too.

"This is really good. Did you know that I love Italian food?" he asked, pushing the darker thoughts from his mind.

She blinked. Then she smiled and the room grew warm and much lighter.

"Uh-huh, I knew. I make a scrumptious lasagna too. I'll have to write down the ingredients so Channing can get them for me. Tell me what else you like, Blaez?"

He could tell her so many things. Most of them would probably frighten her, like the fact that he wanted to tie her up again. He wanted to watch her spread wide open for him and then take her to the brink of ecstasy, listen to her beg him for release, before he would finally let her come all over. No, not all over, into his mouth, he thought while taking the final gulp of his wine. He wanted every drop of her release in his mouth, slipping down his throat like the thickest, sweetest honey.

His dick was painfully hard with that thought, his body strung tight with tension at having gone so long without slaking his basic needs. Sure, he'd fucked her in that shower, had felt her tight pussy strangling his cock until he had come harder than ever before. But it had not been enough. He'd known that it would never be enough and yet he'd done it and then attempted to forget.

That was a futile attempt.

Blaez had managed to regain his composure. He'd continued to have banal conversation about food, drink, and more food, listening as she talked about preparing more things for him. About what Channing liked and what Channing said the others enjoyed. He was sure she didn't know it, but she sounded like she was the alpha female of this pack. *His* alpha female.

Only they both knew that would never happen.

Ever.

He'd frowned now, remembering the time spent with her and still looking for a reason why her father had done what he did. The sound of a door opening jolted Blaez from his thoughts and he remained still, listening as her feet moved softly over the wood-planked floors. She couldn't get out, he knew; he'd checked the alarm system himself before coming upstairs. Malec, Channing, and Phelan all had the codes to get in and reengage the system. If Kira tried, none of the doors or windows would open. But she already knew that. So what was she doing up and why was she going down the steps?

Closing his laptop, Blaez stood, heading for the door before he could convince himself it wasn't necessary. She couldn't run away from him the way she had from her family. It didn't matter that he couldn't keep her because he just wasn't the keeping type. No, that didn't matter at all.

He was at the top of the stairs when he heard it.

Moaning, heavy breathing . . . *dammit.*

He took the steps two at a time, coming to a complete stop just two more from the bottom because that's where Kira was standing. She had on one of those short nightshirts she liked to sleep in and fuzzy slippers he figured were a part of her new wardrobe courtesy of Channing's generosity with Blaez's credit card. After his parents' deaths he'd inherited a great deal of money, property, and jewels. He'd banked it all under a corporate name and used one of those credit accounts for the household items. That's why Channing had access and the good sense to do what Blaez should have done to ensure she had everything she needed.

Her back was to him, one hand on the banister, her gaze trained on the living room where a low light burned.

Malec and Channing were home.

And they'd brought company.

Malec had leaned against the back of the sofa, holding the female lycan, as evidenced by her extended claws running through Channing's hair, on his lap. Malec's hands were at her hips, pressing her center into what was most likely his erection. While Channing stood behind her, his fingers grasping her chin as he tilted her head back, kissing her hungrily. Malec had just dipped his head to lick the bared skin between her breasts when she let out a low growl that Blaez knew would only egg the two betas on.

He took the last two steps, reaching out to touch Kira's arm lightly.

"Come with me," he told her.

When she turned it was with a look of such lust and hunger Blaez wanted to growl himself. Her eyes were wide and glazed, her mouth partially open so that her breath could come in quick pants. Through her shirt her nipples were clearly puckered, her legs shaking slightly.

"Blaez," she whimpered.

"I know, *lýkaina*. Just come with me," he said, taking her hand.

He led her up the steps and down the hallway to his bedroom. Her arousal was obvious; even if he hadn't picked up the scent the moment he'd heard her footsteps, it was apparent in the way her body trembled, the glazed look in her eyes when she'd turned to him. From the looks of Malec and Channing the needing was taking its usual hold on the pack, and regardless of Blaez's reservations or Kira's past, this distance he'd tried to put between them simply wasn't going to work.

CHAPTER 10

Kira blinked once and then again.

She sucked in a breath, letting it out in shaky little spurts that hissed through her teeth. Blaez still held her hand, his palm warm against hers after he'd closed the door behind them. They walked past his desk area straight to his bed. With a rush she turned immediately, pressing her body against his.

"I know that you don't want any connections," she whispered, her heart pounding in her chest as she spoke. "I heard everything you said and didn't say in the library that day. Because you couldn't save your family you don't want to get your feelings involved with anyone else. You don't want to risk the pain of not being able to save someone else you love."

She inhaled deeply, picked up the scent that seemed to filtrate through her every second of every day. Her body trembled; she couldn't stop it. She felt as if every nerve ending was exposed, every sense she possessed heightened. Her nipples were hard and ached through the material of her nightshirt and the T-shirt Blaez wore, her thighs quaked, pussy pulsated, and she swallowed deeply to keep from ripping his clothes off in the next seconds.

"I know where you stand and that I don't belong here. What I can't figure out is why, with all of that between us, do I still want you?" She sighed with the weight those words had produced along her shoulders, resting there for the past few days even though she tried valiantly to ignore them.

She hadn't been looking at him while she talked; her gaze was more focused on the rise and fall of his broad chest. Now she'd tilted her head slightly, her gaze reaching for his. He had turned away, standing there in front of her rigidly but not looking at her. Lifting a hand, Kira touched his chin, turning him until he did look at her.

"I still . . . need you," she said her voice surprisingly steadier than she imagined it would be in this moment.

Kira could see the muscle twitching in his jaw, felt the tension rolling from him in waves, and she wanted to scream. Was he really going to deny this, deny her, again?

"You don't understand," he told her, his face tight with something that appeared like torture to her.

Desperately she cupped his face in her hands. "If you don't want me, just say it. If you would rather not throw me down on this bed and sink deep inside of me, just say it!"

He moved then, his strong hands clasping her arms as he lifted her clear off the floor, tossing her back onto the bed she'd just spoken of. He was over her in seconds ripping her nightshirt completely off. The coolness of the room touched the heated pores of her skin and she shivered.

"You want to know if I want you," he said through clenched teeth, his chest now heaving with the same quickening of breath as hers. "You want to know if I can think of anything other than my dick pounding inside of your wet, hot pussy."

He was touching her now, his palms grabbing her breasts,

532 A. C. Arthur

squeezing to a point that was almost painful. "The answer is no!" he roared, and Kira half-expected his teeth to elongate, his eyes to change to that brilliant blue she saw each night before she fell asleep.

His hands moved from her breasts, tracing a heated path down her torso until he cupped her juncture, heat pooling instantly at the contact.

"No, dammit," he continued, dropping his head. "I've tried everything. Denial. Recrimination. Grief. Anger. None of it stops this; none of it makes this go away."

It was a struggle, Kira thought, to hear his words and most likely for him to say them. Blaez was a very powerful lycan. She'd seen it the moment she arrived in this house, from the way he'd dealt with his pack to the restraint she'd watched him wield each time he touched her. Even though that day in the shower she'd thought they were both giving in, Blaez had still held back. No other lycan could have mastered that.

"None of that matters now," she told him, lifting her legs until her feet were flat on the bed.

She touched a hand to his wrist, holding him still the second he'd attempted to remove his hand from cupping her. "There's a reason," she told him. "A reason I'm here with you at this moment. I didn't want to see it at first, didn't want to accept that something could be happening without my permission once again, but it just is, Blaez. We—this thing between us—just are."

His head shot up then, his gaze dark and aroused. "Tell that to the goddess," he said, pulling his hand away from her.

"What?" she asked quizzically.

He moved away from the bed then, going to his dresser and grabbing something out of it before returning to her. "Stand up," he told her.

Kira didn't know what the hell was going on now, but she did as he said, standing and going with him a few feet away to a door that he opened. There was a body-length mirror there and Blaez grabbed her shoulder, turning her back toward it.

"Look," he said, holding the smaller mirror he'd retrieved from his dresser in front of her. "You see that?"

She did look and she did see it, but she was still confused. "It's a birthmark, Blaez. I've seen it before."

"Is that what your parents told you it was? A birthmark?" he asked, staring at her with furrowed brows and clenched teeth.

"That's what it is," Kira said, stepping away from him and going back to the bed. Suddenly she felt extremely exposed.

"It's the mark of the Selected, Kira. When you were born—"

Her temples throbbed and she wrapped her arms around her body, now chilly as she climbed back onto his bed. "I was born on the night of the full moon. My mother said that meant I'd be blessed with great luck." She gave a nervous chuckle. "She'd be pretty pissed to see how things were working out for me now."

"Selene, the Luna goddess, Selected you on that night," he said, coming to stand at the foot of the bed.

Then he turned his back to her, sitting on the edge of the

bed, leaning forward, his elbows on his knees. "My parents talked about Selene and her powers, the powers of the moon that feed the lycans each month. It is because of her that we are rejuvenated and strengthened through her phases."

Kira pulled the sheet up and around her, not sure where this was going but knowing she wasn't going to like it. Not one bit.

"I don't understand what you're saying," she admitted.

Blaez took a deep breath, expelling it slowly, his broad shoulders rising and falling as he did.

"You were specially Selected to be with someone, a lycan. Selene made this choice and branded you so that all would know."

"Only my mother," she said quickly. "Only my mother and I know about the mark. My . . . Penn . . . he never cared about me either way. I was a girl, not a son to carry on his bloodline, to take over his pack. He despised me for having to one day give up his pack because I was born of the wrong sex."

Blaez looked over his shoulder at her. "He may have despised you for much more than that. You and your mother."

Kira shook her head, not wanting to hear any more. "Stop," she said softly, closing her eyes.

"You have to understand," he continued. "You may be meant for someone else. No matter how much I may want you, how much . . ." His words drifted off and she could hear movement although she refused to open her eyes.

"I don't think of anything but you," he continued, his hands clutching her shoulders, shaking her until she looked up at him. "That night in the woods I felt you before I saw you. I should have turned away, but I couldn't. You were right,

I shouldn't have brought you here, because you were meant for someone else."

There was no more air.

Kira's chest heaved, but it was a reflex, nothing more. She felt no incoming or outgoing, just the suspension of their locked gazes, her mind whirling around all he'd just said. He was wrong; that crescent shape on her back was a birthmark. It had to be, or her mother would have told her differently. She would have let her know if she was meant for . . . wait a minute.

There's more for you, Kira. More than I could ever teach you, more than you could have ever imagined. Beyond these walls and this pack, there is something for you. A destiny neither of us could ever have imagined.

No, her mother would have told her. She would have explained all of this to her. This would not be the first time she was ever hearing about this.

"I don't understand, Blaez. I don't understand what you're telling me," she said, even though Kira was deathly afraid she was starting to understand. "You're wrong," she said, leaning into him. "This isn't a true story. It's just something that maybe your parents heard in passing. Maybe someone made it up. It wouldn't be the first time myths have been faked. If I were meant especially for someone I would know. Wouldn't I?"

"Or you would know who that someone was not," he told her.

She gasped and he dropped his forehead until it rested on hers.

"I want you," she whispered, because with every fiber of her being that's what she wanted. She knew that now without a doubt. It didn't matter what was on her back or what some goddess who had never even met her might or might not have pre-ordained. She wanted Blaez.

Lifting her hands, she cupped his face again, tilted him up, and went in for a kiss. Her lips touched his and he didn't respond. Her heart pounded once again, her entire body shaking. "I want you, Blaez," she whispered. "I. Want. You."

He opened his mouth to speak and Kira took the plunge, her tongue dipping inside to tangle immediately with his. He grabbed her then, wrapping his arms tightly around her and pulling her onto his lap. Kira gasped and fell deeper into the kiss, deeper in love with this lycan whom she'd sworn she would hate for holding her captive.

This was her first kiss. The first real, live soul-searing kiss of her life. Blaez held her tightly, like maybe he was as afraid to let her go as she was. He licked her mouth, every crevice and every core, stroking the heat that had been steadily brewing there. She wrapped her legs around him, loving the feel of his strong arms wrapped tightly around her. He pulled her closer, took the kiss even deeper as she gasped for air.

"Blaez," she managed to whisper when he finally tore his mouth from hers, kissing along the line of her jaw and down her neck when she arched in his arms.

"I'm going to have you," he whispered over her bare skin, his tongue snaking out to touch her nipple. "I'm going to suck your plump tits, and lick your wet, juicy pussy."

Kira was on fire. Every inch of her body quaked at the sound of his voice.

"I'm going to be so deep inside of you, there will never be another you want fucking you besides me."

"Yes," she whimpered. "Yes. You. Just you."

Blaez didn't give a damn about the moon, the sun, the stars, or anything in between.

He had to touch her, to feel the tight walls of her pussy clenching him. He needed to taste her, to lick the sweet, thick honey from her plump folds, drowning in the pure bliss that only she could offer. This was why he was here, why he had not been killed with his family. For this moment, to lay her back on the bed, strip his clothes off, and return to her again. In this second, this infinite time in space that they would never get again, this was his sole purpose in life.

"Open wide for me, *lýkaina*. Show me that beautiful pussy," he told her, a growl rumbling loudly in his chest.

When she spread her thick thighs apart it was like heaven on earth. Her vulva lips opening like the most delectable flower, glistening with her arousal. He lifted her by the backs of her knees, dropping her legs onto his shoulders as he went in, inhaling deeply of her intoxicating scent before licking the sweet nectar from her skin. She bucked beneath him, lifting her hips to feed him properly, and Blaez was grateful.

He licked her long and slow, loving the feel of her smooth, soft skin along the contours of his tongue. His lips were wet with her juices, his chin, cheeks. She was all over him, just where he'd wanted her to be.

Kira arched up off the bed, his name falling from her lips in a guttural moan that echoed throughout the room.

Blaez held her close, drinking her release like it was the sweetest wine, knowing he would never taste anything as wonderful again. The softness of her inner thighs cushioned his face as her climax continued to wrack through her body, his lips gently kissing her now, praising everything that was her.

When she'd gone still, her hips moving only slightly against him, Blaez pulled back, looking down to her once more. Her breasts were large; her dark, pert nipples staring back at him. He moved between her legs, letting his dick tap lightly against her clit. Her eyes opened wide, her tongue stroking along her bottom lip.

"I want you to watch as I sink inside you," he told her, and she came up on her elbows, her gaze fixed between her legs. "That's good, *lýkaina*. Look how hard you've made me. How crazy I am with need for you."

She gasped. "This is not just the needing, Blaez. It's so much more," she told him.

He heard her words, heard the truth laced in them. "Right now I need to be inside of you. Watch me slip inside of you."

They both watched as the bulbous head of his cock pressed between the saturated folds of her pussy. He moved slowly, loving the sting of the torture it was to wake against the promise of the pleasure once he was tucked securely inside. She lifted her hips ready to take him in. He pressed farther, his dick sinking into her; the sound of her sucking him deep joined their gasps for air.

Her hands grabbed the sheets, her legs shaking beneath his arms. And Blaez went deeper, dipping into the heat, feeling her cream coating every inch of his dick.

This was where he was supposed to be, where he desperately needed to be. The wolf inside threatening to howl its ultimate pleasure, dangerously close to wanting to claim her completely.

With that thought Blaez began to move, thrusting in and out of her, circling his hips, pulling almost completely out before sinking back in once more. He lifted her legs high, spreading them into a V shape so that he could have more freedom to move inside her at his will. A glimpse at her and he saw that she stared up at him, her eyes glassy with desire, her lips parted slightly, breasts jiggling with their motion.

His mind was flooded with Kira, her smile, her laughter, the way she chewed, the way she smiled. If he closed his eyes she was there, lying against the soft pillows of her bed sleeping soundlessly. When he opened them again she was coming from the gym where she'd been working out with Malec, her body slick with sweat, those damned pants she liked to wear molded to her body. He saw her cooking in his kitchen, laughing with his pack, smiling up at him when she thought it was okay. His arms trembled first, then his legs, and Blaez knew he was about to come.

He pulled out of her quickly, moving them so that she was now standing, bending forward onto the bed. He gripped her ass, loving the feel of her plump cheeks in his hands, spreading them wide apart. Leaning down, he licked her crease, down past the rim of her anus, wet from her cream that had coated her completely. He suckled her there, at her entrance, his tongue dipping deep before coming out to lap quickly over her clit. She shivered, her ass cheeks bouncing against his face. Blaez groaned, pulling back and sinking his rigid cock inside her again. Holding her ass tightly, Blaez pumped deep inside of her. His hips rocked against hers and he fucked her with every ounce of desire he possessed, every thought of intimacy, every inkling of emotion that dared seep inside his soul.

And when he came he emptied everything he had inside of her, giving her the man and the wolf that he was. Giving her his all, knowing damned well they would both eventually pay the ultimate price.

CHAPTER 11

"Where's Channing?" Kira asked as soon as she entered the kitchen the next morning after she'd showered and dressed.

Blaez had already left by the time she'd awakened, which hadn't surprised her. What had been different this time was that he had left her a note telling her that her clothes and personal belongings had been moved into his room. She'd read the note a couple of times before finally getting out of bed and going to see if what he'd said was true.

She dropped the sheet and padded to the now-familiar bathroom. There were fluffy towels and more body washes in the stall, she noted as she leaned inside to turn the water on. Coconut-scented shampoo, cocoa and shea-butter body washes, the ones she'd selected from that online store when she was shopping with Channing, all lined up neatly in Blaez's bathroom as well as the private one she had in the room where she'd been staying. She'd smiled at the sight, ignoring the sense of dread that was clinging to the back of her mind.

After the long steamy shower she'd found more of her things in one of Blaez's bureaus. All of the items that she and Channing had ordered, blouses and slacks, jeans and dresses, were hanging neatly inside. There had been a flurry of questions crowding her mind by that time. About her future with Blaez—if there was one—and about what he'd told her last night. Some pieces to the puzzle of her life had appeared and she was anxious to try them out, to see what fit.

First up, she had some questions and she knew Channing would know the answers; after all, he'd been the one to mention something about "being Selected" the other night. She hadn't caught the meaning then, not until Blaez's announcement last night.

"It appears he's not here," Phelan told her.

Kira had then moved to the coffeepot, remembering where the filters were kept and putting on a pot of dark roast as she knew was both Blaez's and Phelan's preference. For herself, she liked a glass of orange juice first thing in the morning, so she went to the refrigerator remembering that Malec and Channing had been busy last night, which was most likely why Channing wasn't already in here preparing breakfast himself. The meals that she'd prepared in the last couple of days they'd talked about first because Kira hadn't wanted to intrude. Actually, she'd denied wanting to cook at all, but Channing—in his kind and almost unassuming way—had been steadily pushing her to do more around the house, to take more responsibilities . . . the alpha female responsibilities.

"What's on the menu this morning?" Phelan asked from the doorway.

"I'm not sure, since I wasn't made aware that I would be preparing it," she replied as she poured herself a glass of juice.

"Something's bothering you," he said, surprising her even more than the fact that Channing wasn't already down here cooking. "Thinking about how close it's getting to the full moon and your pack eventually coming to make their move against us?"

Phelan was wearing all black today, jeans and a long-sleeved shirt. The dark clothes added to the short black hair on his head and the expertly groomed low-cut beard gave him a very ominous look, a dangerous persona that reached to the crisp green of his eyes and the grim turn of his lips. The scar just beneath his left eye that looked like three jagged claw marks was prominent and scary, and yet Kira felt like that made him the most vulnerable of each of them.

"No, actually, I'm thinking about Blaez," she said in an attempt to take that smug look off Phelan's face.

It worked. At least momentarily, as Phelan blinked once, then leaned forward to rest his elbows on the table.

Five days ago Kira would have felt defensive; she would have stood her stance prepared to do and say whatever she needed to prove her point or to make it known that she wasn't afraid. This morning, she simply took a sip of her juice and continued to watch him.

"Do you know what it means to be Selected, Phelan? Have you ever heard of the process?"

His silence, coupled with the twitching of that rugged scar on his face, said he did, so before he could deny it or say something else designed to piss her off instead of answer her question, Kira continued.

"Blaez thinks I've been Selected."

"For him?" Phelan asked, raising his brow.

"No," she replied quietly, even though there was a part of her that wished like hell that was true.

"I know that you're doing something to him," Phelan countered. "He's not the same since you've been here."

That had her moving slowly, setting the glass down on the counter. "I'm not the same as when I first came here," she said, because it was true. In the days that she'd been here, reading those books in the library about the lycan history and Blaez's family, cooking and talking to Channing, training in the gym with Malec, Kira had begun to feel very differently about herself.

"What do you think is going to happen now? Are you planning to become the alpha female of this pack?"

Kira immediately shook her head. "I'm not sure that's what he wants."

"Is it what you want? Are you going to stand there and tell me that you're in love with him, that you want the same things he does, that this is where you think you belong? Because just a few days ago you were going around here checking every window and door, searching for a way out."

"A captured wolf will try to escape," she quipped.

He raised a brow. "Or it will kill everyone in its way to get what it wants."

"I'm not a killer."

"No," he replied tightly. "But you are a Hunter."

"You're wrong. My father's pack were Hunters. I am me, a female born into a society of which I did not create the rules, nor can I change them. I didn't choose which pack to be born into," she told him, anger slowly building.

"But you remained loyal to them. It was a choice."

"Just as me leaving was a choice. Does it matter when we decide to make the right one?"

He paused then and Kira wondered if they'd made some sort of progress, crossed an invisible bridge of some sort, because the corner of his mouth lifted and she thought for one moment that maybe Phelan might just give her a smile.

"She asked you about being Selected, Phelan, not to badger her about the pack to which she was born," Channing said, finally making his appearance in the kitchen, Malec not far behind him.

"You knew, didn't you?" she said immediately. "That's why you said what you did the other day. What I don't understand is how? There's no way you could have seen my mark."

"That's where you're wrong," Malec said, heading straight to the refrigerator to grab a bottled water. "We both saw your mark. Those yoga pants you wear don't exactly keep you covered when you're working out."

"Or bending and reaching for things in the kitchen," Channing added.

"So everybody knew but me?" she asked, looking from one lycan to another. They were certainly a hot bunch, but right now she wasn't very impressed with them.

"It's not for us to get involved in," Phelan told them, looking pointedly at Channing and Malec and then finally to her. "Your status is your business. Just like Blaez's is his."

"But you're his family," she said.

"We're his pack. We protect him and fight beside him; we do not interfere in what has been put on his shoulders to handle," Phelan continued.

Channing set the cup of coffee he'd just fixed down so that it clinked against the marble countertop. "She asked a general question about the selection process. I can answer that."

Kira sighed. "Then would you, please? I'm sick of being the only one not knowing what's going on."

"The Luna goddess Selects a mate for a lycan. It's a match she believes will be powerful and will somehow aid the breed in their struggle. It is her way of arming us against Zeus and his unstable attitude. Selecteds are also given extra abilities, ones not found in the other lycans; this is what sets them apart from the rest. It's what makes them so valuable to the mate they are promised to."

When he was finished Kira was shaking her head. "I don't have any special power."

Malec looked at her then. "The Selected comes into their power the first full moon after their twenty-first birthday."

"How old are you?" Channing asked.

Kira swallowed. She licked her lips and tried like hell not to twist her trembling fingers together, a sure sign of her nervousness.

"I turned twenty-one three months ago," she replied softly.

Everyone in the room went quiet. Kira thought about what Blaez had said last night, what her mother had said before she died and what she'd just learned. She also thought about the things she'd been seeing, the weird feelings and—

"What matters right now is what's for breakfast," Phelan said loudly, as if he knew he was interrupting her whirling thoughts.

"That's exactly what I was going to say," Channing added, his voice suddenly even more cheerful than usual.

Malec chimed in, joining the let's-talk-about-something-else bandwagon. "I could make smoothies for everyone. Fresh kale, flaxseed, mango, blueberries. It'll be great to get the metabolism going."

"And great to send me straight to the bathroom," Phelan quipped. "No, thank you. I'm sure Kira can come up with something better."

What she did was look at Phelan with surprise, then to Channing, who was smiling knowingly. She still had questions, but she respected the pack for pulling back after they figured they'd told her as much as they could. This was her journey, her destiny, as her mother had said. If this was where she was supposed to end up all along and if Blaez Trekas, with his painful past and bounty on his head, was the alpha she was meant to be with, she sure as hell wanted to know for sure. But not now, she decided after taking a deep breath and releasing it slowly. Now she had three hungry lycans looking to her for breakfast, or was it something more?

"How about pancakes?" she asked, letting her lips spread into a smile and for the moment pushing all her questions and concerns to the side.

The entire Selected legend and the fact that she was probably involved in it had come as a surprise to her, just as the fact that everyone in this house had known about it but her, and just when she thought she could not be shocked again so soon he caught her off guard one more time.

"Pancakes definitely sounds like a plan," Blaez said,

coming inside, moving past everyone until he was near the cabinet where the mugs were stored, taking down the taller, black one he always used.

He'd thought about skipping breakfast. As he'd worked out, bench-pressing just over two hundred pounds for the thirty-second time, he wondered if he could continue with this charade. This wasn't who he was, it wasn't what he'd wanted from his life, and here he was, sleeping with a woman in his bed and looking forward to eating the food she prepared for not only him but also his pack.

This was the life his parents had wanted for him, his mother especially. It was the one she'd talked about all the time.

"Supreme power deserves a partner, Blaez," she'd told him when he was sixteen. "Someday you will find the one that matches every part of you. It won't be because she agrees with all that you say or do, or that she even likes everything you say and do, but because she will understand you. She will know your heart and your destiny and she will agree to walk beside you, to combine the threads of her life with yours."

He'd closed his eyes, gritting his teeth as the bar and weights slammed onto the stand once more. His biceps screamed with the stress of his hour-long workout and all that he'd put his body through in those sixty minutes. But Blaez did not get up; he'd lie there for endless moments still thinking, wondering, hating himself for the duplicity and blaming himself for having put these things in motion in the first place.

He should have left her in that forest.

But he'd known he couldn't. Neither his body nor his mind was going to agree on that action. The connection between him and Kira had been too strong for him to ignore.

Now she was here, in his house, in his bed, in his soul. That was the clincher, Blaez thought. For all that he'd sworn against any intimate or emotional connections, Kira Radney had shown up and slipped seamlessly inside, threatening to undo that shield he'd worked so hard to erect. So what the hell was he supposed to do now?

Wiping sweat from his face, he'd decided to do what he always did, persevere. He'd gone to the shower, seen that she'd already been in and out. He touched the bottle of body spray, the one called Amber Romance, and replaced the top that had been sitting right beside it. Inhaling slowly, he let the warm scent permeate his senses, knowing that as soon as he was near her he would recall this very moment. When he was in the shower, beneath the hot spray of water, he'd reached for his soap, only to bump the bottle of coconut shampoo. He'd washed and stepped out, going to the bureau to retrieve his clothes for the day. Out of habit he reached for the door, pulling it open expecting to see the neat rows of jeans, shirts, suits, and ties. What he found were dresses and colorful blouses. What he scented was Kira.

He remembered waking in the middle of the night and moving everything from the room next door to his while she'd slept. It had been an impromptu action, one in the light of day he still could not explain. Closing that door quickly, he'd gone to the next bureau, found his clothes, and hastily chosen an outfit. Next, he was on his way down the steps when he heard the murmur of voices, the female one included. Then he'd heard something that he hadn't had the pleasure of hearing before, her laughter. He had no idea who had said what; all he knew was that he loved the sound. It was genuine and full of life and flanked him like the warmth of the sun. He'd immediately headed for the kitchen, needing desperately to see her, to see that smile and how it might possibly light her hazel eyes. To see what she'd selected to wear from that bureau, how her curves looked in the clothes, how she moved, and to wonder again, Why now? Why her?

The sight of her amidst his pack was another sucker punch to his gut. He liked it, way too damned much. Malec had been closest to her, just lifting his cup to his lips, his stance casual. Channing was at the island, leaning over it, flipping through one of his many cookbooks. And Phelan, he was sitting at the table looking over at Kira with a smile. Phelan never smiled.

Blaez had tried to play it cool, to enter as if this were the easiest thing he'd ever done. Like this scene wasn't some sort of déjà vu. Now, as they all sat at the table eating, talking about things like hiking up the mountain and possibly camping out for a couple of days, Kira eagerly agreeing with the excursion, he was back to contemplating again. No, it was more like fighting with what he knew he was capable of and what his mother, and now quite possibly the Luna goddess, believed to be true.

"What do you say, Blaez? Right after the full moon we pack up and head out?" Channing asked while at breakfast. "I'd have to do some massive shopping to stock up to be sure we have everything. What are we talking, a week maybe?"

"A week away sounds good," Malec replied, finishing the last of his pancakes and turkey sausage.

"It depends" had been Blaez's reply. "We will wait and see how things play out."

"You mean you'll wait to see if my father's pack makes an appearance on the full moon," Kira said quietly.

Blaez wanted to kick himself as the light he'd been so enjoying seeing in her eyes this morning had quickly faded.

Phelan cleared his throat. "He's right. We need to get that out of the way first. Things may change and they may not. We should be prepared either way."

Malec nodded and Channing frowned, placing a hand over Kira's. She pulled hers away slowly, standing to take her plate and glass to the sink.

"I'm gonna go for a run," Malec said then. "Come with?"

Blaez knew what would happen next, even without him telling them to do so. Channing nodded, him and Malec taking their plates and putting them in the dishwasher. Phelan gave Blaez a look that said he wasn't happy, which wasn't really new. Blaez gave him the "who's the alpha?" look and Phelan stood. He was just about to follow in the others' footsteps and take his dishes over, but Kira was there, removing them from the table for him. He gave her another damned smile and Blaez felt his fists clenching. Phelan only frowned at him as he walked out of the kitchen, Channing and Malec following behind him.

Kira had crossed the room again, closing the dishwasher and grabbing the towel to wipe off the counter, when she said in a level tone, "Did my father not try to stop Dallas from trying to claim me because he knew I was Selected?"

Blaez rubbed a finger over his chin before letting his hands fall to his lap. "It's possible."

"Channing said that Selected females come into some type of special power on their twenty-first birthday." She talked while continuing to drag that towel over the counter, even though it was already clean.

"That's what the legend says. The Selected's power combines with the alpha she is matched with to make them some sort of supercouple. It's the gods interfering once again," he said with more distaste then he'd meant to.

"Our lives are possible because of the gods," she replied neutrally. "I used to think that was all unbelievable. How could we, our species, be here amidst this unknowing human one? Why weren't we trapped in Arcadia? Why were we allowed to come here?"

When Blaez didn't answer right away she continued, turning around to lean against the counter, hands grasping the sides of the marble slab.

"Humans keep dangerous animals locked in cages at the zoo. They go out and kill the others under the premise of keeping the population down. That's how they rule," she told him.

And because Blaez knew exactly where she was going with this analysis, he added, "Zeus and the gods kill the ones they want out of their way and rule the others with ancient legends and powers instead. We're not that different from them."

She shook her head. "But we're not the same either."

"No. We're not the same."

"I want to know what happened to my mother and why. And if Penn is responsible I want him to pay," she told Blaez.

"Because you've always thought he knew more than he told you," Blaez said. The last thing he wanted to do was tell her that he believed Penn had Tora killed as well. Only in the early-morning hours had he thought he figured out why. Now he wondered if he should tell Kira without having any real proof, or wait until he had the truth, then present it to her. Either way she was going to be hurt and would possibly grieve her mother's death again. Just as Blaez had done all those years ago. He wished he wouldn't have to watch her go through that but didn't know that there was a way to avoid it.

"Why don't we go out for a run, clear our heads, and stop thinking about this for a while?" he offered, standing from his seat and walking over to her.

"Is this a test?" she asked, looking up at him skeptically.

"I don't understand what you mean."

"Are you asking me if I want to go outside with you to see if I'll try to run away?"

Blaez was quiet for a moment, taking the last step that closed the space between them. He reached up, touching a soft curl of hair that fell over her shoulder. "Channing took you virtual shopping, Malec's been helping you work out, and Phelan, well, he's not talking about you betraying us every five minutes anymore, so that's his contribution. I haven't given you anything."

She looked absolutely flabbergasted at his words, which made two of them, because Blaez had no idea why he'd admitted that.

"I . . . I didn't ask you for anything," she replied.

How could he tell her that he felt guilty for everything he'd done to her since that very first moment? That if he

554 A. C. Arthur

could he'd give her the world to make it up to her, for giving her what he knew was false hope, he would.

"I know," he said instead.

"I can't do this hot and cold act anymore, Blaez. I don't know for sure if I was Selected to be here or not. Or how I would know if I were. When I left Seattle a week ago I had no idea what I'd find or if I'd ever end up where I was supposed to be, and I certainly never imagined someone like you." She took in a deep breath, her eyes closing momentarily before she sighed.

"I don't know what you want me to say" was the only reply he could come up with.

"Then I guess you shouldn't say anything."

She turned away from him then and Blaez felt like a colossal ass. He was always in control; he knew what to say and what to do at any given moment. He was the fucking alpha! So why was he standing here so helplessly, trying to figure out how to tell this female that he'd messed up, not only for himself but for both of them? There were too many things at play here, too many situations that were bigger than both of them and that prevented the fate of falling in love that his mother had predicted—and quite possibly the selection the Luna goddess had ordained—from coming true.

He didn't know how to say it. How to tell Kira something he didn't completely understand himself. So instead he touched her shoulders.

"Please do not give me another command," she whispered. "Don't make me do something else that will push us further in a direction you obviously do not want to go. Just don't," she said, a slight hitch in her voice. "Please."

It was her safe word. He knew it and so did she. And she'd said it twice. Blaez inhaled deeply, let that breath out as slowly and as calmly as he could, before deciding to hell with it.

One arm snaked around her waist, turning her quickly to face him, while the other instantly went to the nape of her neck, tilting her head upward as he pulled her closer. She gasped, her lips parting, eyes staring up at him in question. Blaez didn't have answers. He didn't have a sustainable plan. And he didn't give a damn. His lips crashed down on hers, his tongue plunging deep into her mouth without malice or afterthought, without anything but the pleasure and some other powerful emotion that had been rippling like a steady stream throughout his body. He kissed her with a fervor he'd never experienced, his eyes closing, mind wrapping around a scene he'd only ever dreamed of once before.

The dream where he was happy. Finally.

CHAPTER 12

The full moon

She was killing him.

Slowly, but surely, Blaez thought as he lay on his back in the center of his bed, Kira and all that had happened between them in the two weeks since he'd met her were going to be the death of him.

Of course, said death had come with him walking slowly but assuredly directly along the path set for him. It had led him to her and he'd been led by her ever since. The past five nights, since that heated kiss they'd shared in the kitchen after breakfast, had all ended the same, with moans of ecstasy, each of them being pushed to the brink of their control before diving off the cliff together into memorable climaxes, and then the emotions began. Like a bottomless pool Blaez felt like with each passing night he was swimming, no, treading water, toward an ultimate destination that he was previously convinced he did not want to visit.

"I want you to ask my permission to come this time," Kira's voice sounded through the muddled thoughts of his mind.

A few moments ago he'd assumed she was asleep, half

THE ALPHA'S WOMAN 557

her naked body draped over half of his, her breathing even against his bare chest. Now, however, she was climbing on top of him, spreading her legs so that she straddled him, looking down at him with heavy-lidded eyes, flecks of gold— he'd only recently learned were there—sparkling in the dark room. Her hair was a wild mass around her face, just the way he'd come to like it. There were so many moments throughout the day, especially yesterday morning when they'd all gone out for a run, when he'd wanted to see her hair this way. Malec, who wanted to test the hour-long workouts he'd been having with Kira each day, had challenged her to a race. Blaez had followed along because he hadn't wanted to let her out of his sight. He watched her break out in a gust of speed, her long legs eating up the ground as if she weren't really touching it at all. Every part of her body had stretched and flexed and he'd had to slow down his own speed be- cause the instant punch of arousal had taken his breath away. When she'd stopped, Malec beating her by a millisec- ond, if that much, she'd leaned over, hands on her knees, taking in air, before standing straight. Her signature pony- tail had swung back and forth and Blaez's fingers had itched to rip the band that held it together free, to ruffle his hands through her hair before tossing her to the ground and fucking her right there where she stood.

It was like that more often than not as they'd slipped into a sort of routine, culminating tonight—the evening of the full moon—when they'd had an early dinner and all re- tired to their rooms without too much to say. Blaez had thought of going over a strategy but figured he and his pack had been together so long, they'd planned this place specifi- cally for the day it was attacked, so they knew what to do and when to do it. More important, he was the one who needed to adjust his thoughts, because now he had someone else to protect, someone who meant more to him than Blaez ever thought anything or anyone ever would.

"Oh really," he finally replied to her statement, his hands going instantly to her hips, where his fingers dug into the soft skin there.

"Yes, really," she told him, reaching between them to grasp his hard cock, aiming at her pussy.

She would already be wet; she always was, a fact he also loved about her. No matter when or where he'd taken her, in the kitchen that day after her pancake breakfast or in the shower once more after yesterday's run.

"You know that's not how it's done," he told her, his teeth clenching at the pleasure of feeling the tight, hot walls of her pussy sucking the head of his cock in slowly but surely.

"Someone once told me that I should take control of my life. I should figure out what I wanted and go after it," she said, lowering herself down over the last inches of his dick.

She was settled in so tightly the plump lips of her pussy rubbed along his groin, his balls tapping against the curve of her ass. He wanted to sigh with that pleasure alone. Instead, he moved with quickness, holding her close and flipping her over so that her back fell to the mattress. She frowned up at him as he clasped her legs behind his back.

"Not fair," she told him.

"No," Blaez said, pulling out of her, then sinking back in slowly, tortuously to them both, he suspected. "Not fair. But good. Pleasure is good." He was moving in and out of her, taking his time, savoring every single moment.

The sun had not completely set, but the sky had already

begun its transition of colors, the dark orange melding into a purple-like explosion across the horizon over the mountaintops. In just a little while the sky would be full-on dark, alight only by the full moon. And then . . . Blaez didn't even want to think about what might happen.

So for now he was where he wanted to be, doing exactly what he wanted to do. When he leaned back, resting on his knees, his hands going to her thighs, lifting them so her ankles would disengage from behind him, and pushing them back so that her ass was off the bed, her pussy tilted, offering him an even deeper range inside, he growled. The animal within feeling every bit of its power and energy from the upcoming night.

"I'll always give you pleasure," he told her. "Always."

She'd been cupping her breasts, squeezing them in her hands so that her nipple was visible through her fingers, the dark circle of her areola a sharp contrast against the much lighter tone of her skin. He loved how she looked touching herself, but he felt jealous at the same time.

"Feed me, *lýkaina*," he told her, leaning forward between her legs, his dick still pumping in and out of her.

She immediately followed his directive, which made Blaez even hotter for her. As his dick slid in and out, her arousal providing more than enough lubrication for the smooth entrance and descent, he opened his mouth, taking the nipple of the breast she'd groped once more, arching in offering to him. His tongue slid along the tightened nub seconds before his teeth latched on and he bit down. Just enough to hear her gasp; then quickly his tongue licked over the pebbled tip, his mouth opening wider to suck her deep inside. His thrusts continued inside her pussy, her walls hugging his dick so tight at some points he almost felt like he couldn't breathe. He definitely could not see anything other than her, the sultry tilt of her almond-shaped eyes, the slight parting of her pert lips. That was permanently emblazoned in his mind. As for when he opened his eyes, it was the heavy mounds of her breasts, moving with each thrust inside of her. Leaving one breast for the other, he continued to watch as he quickened his pumps, her breasts moving faster, the growl circling in the center of his chest coming louder. When he was finally able to pull his mouth from hers there was only one word he could say, and he meant it with every fiber of his being. "Mine."

Settling her legs on his shoulders, Blaez continued to move inside of her, with quick, deep strokes that had every part of him, from his ankles to his spine, tightening in anticipation of his release.

"You. Every part of you. Everything you are. It's all mine. Just mine," he continued, watching her through half-closed eyes as her head thrashed against the pillows.

"Blaez," his name came as she panted, her fingers squeezing her nipples, probably as tight as he'd been biting them in the hopes of re-creating that sensation.

Kira loved the pleasure/pain stimulus. She loved being pushed to the point of almost no control, before he replaced it with a desire so phenomenal she'd had no choice but to submit. That thought aroused Blaez more than anything. How this feisty, headstrong, and independent lycan—who might be promised to someone else—had completely submitted to him and all the pleasure that he offered her.

"Say it!" he told her. "Say it or you don't get to come."

She opened her mouth; only sound came out. A low howl

that he'd never heard before. She snapped her lips shut, cutting it off, and Blaez wanted it back. He wanted that call that he sensed was going to be specific to him, to this moment of pleasure she was about to experience. He wanted it all.

"Again!" he yelled to her. "Again, dammit!"

He was holding her ankles now, working in and out of her so fast the slick sound of his skin slapping against hers echoed throughout the room.

"I . . . ," she whimpered. "I . . . can't."

"Say it or it stops. The pleasure, the need, everything. Say it!"

"Yes!" she yelled as he'd begun to pull his dick from her sweet embrace. "Yes! I'm yours!"

"I want the sound, *lýkaina*. I want everything. Now!" he told her, feeling his own body tense knowing that he wasn't going to hold on much longer. She had that control over him whether she knew it or not. He'd always prized himself on being able to hold out until he was absolutely ready to offer his release. With Kira there had never been that sense. From the moment he'd jerked off in the open window to right now when the base of his spine was tingling, his balls drawing so tight he could barely speak, he realized she had something over him. Something pretty damned powerful that he'd never given anyone else.

She made the sound. A low and long howl that ran along his spine like a bow to a violin, creating a perfect melody and a perfect moment.

"Yes," he sighed. "Yes, *lýkaina*. Come for me now. Come all over me."

Her legs began to shake, her walls tightening around his

cock with such fierceness Blaez could only throw his head back and growl with the extreme pleasure. In seconds he was following her lead, his own cum shooting in thick spurts deep into her pussy, his body jerking with the intensity of his release.

"You didn't claim me," she said in the silence of the room minutes later, when Blaez had pulled out of her and rolled onto his back.

He didn't speak.

"I thought with everything in me that I was Selected for you," she continued. "I spent hours in that library reading everything I could find on the selection process. That really old one that's written mostly in Greek—I used the site you bookmarked on the iPad to help me with the letters and I read most of it. It said that the alpha female would know. She would feel it all over the second her Selected alpha claimed her."

Blaez tensed all over.

"But you didn't," she said, her voice so quiet he almost hadn't heard her. "It was time; the full moon is up now. It was time," she finished, and he knew she was looking toward the window.

Blaez didn't need to look; he could feel it. Like water filling an empty fountain, pouring in until he was full, his body and his mind in tune to the transition, to the night and all that would come of it.

"You will remain here," he told her. "I want you safe."

"I'm not claimed," she said again, her voice a little more shaky this time. "I'm not part of your pack."

He moved quickly again, rolling over until his face was

hovering just inches from hers. "You are a part of me," he stated vehemently. "Don't you understand that?"

She opened her mouth then, about to answer him, when her entire body stilled, her nostrils flaring. Blaez did the exact same thing, every part of him on instant alert.

"They're here," he whispered.

Channing spread a map over the kitchen table, his long arms stretching as he used the salt and pepper shakers to hold the rolling edges of the paper flat. The bottom half he secured with the silver holder that Malec kept his sugar substitutes in and a bottled water. When Channing stood back, he looked directly at Kira.

She was at the head of the table, her arms folded over her chest. Fifteen minutes ago she'd been lying in the bed, Blaez over her, inside her, and everything had been . . . Now she was here looking down at the layout of this property. She'd been calling it a fortress, but really, she had no idea. This house was not only huge; what looked like simple log walls were reinforced by six-inch steel slabs, the windows— that film over them that prevented anyone from seeing inside—covered in the thinnest bulletproof shielding there was. In fact, Kira doubted this particular product was even on the open market in the United States. Twenty feet out in all directions were motion and heat sensors. On their boat in Seattle they'd had cameras. Out here in the wilderness that wouldn't have been enough.

She felt him the moment he stepped into the room, coming to a stop just beside her. Out of the corner of her eye she

564 A. C. Arthur

saw Phelan continue past them, going to the side of the table. He, Malec, and Channing now all looked at her. Kira knew what to do. She'd watched her mother do this so many times before. Closing her eyes slowly and taking a deep breath, she felt her mother's presence with her as surely as the other lycans standing in this room. She could almost hear her voice, strong, clear, concise, giving the pack instructions, fully confident that she was guiding them in the most effective way possible.

It's your turn now.

It sounded as if Tora were mindchatting with her, but Kira knew it went much deeper than that. Since the day her mother had died she hadn't heard her voice, could only hold on to those things she had said to her the day she graduated, three days before her mother's death. That she was doing so now meant something, and Kira completely grasped that meaning.

With a slow exhalation she rolled her head on her neck, lifting her shoulders slightly, hearing the crack of her bones, clearing her mind.

"They'll spread out. A simple circle formation is their favorite. Stalk, surround, attack," she told them.

When she leaned over the table similar to the way Channing had, her hip brushed against Blaez's leg, the warmth from his body immediately transferring to hers, adrenaline sizzling through her like she'd received some sort of transfusion.

"Dallas is his second," she said, looking up to Phelan. "He'll come in here." Her finger pointed to a spot near the front door. "Penn will stay close to him. He's been—" She stopped, sighed heavily.

"Dallas will be his shield," Blaez added.

Kira nodded, taking another deep breath. When she closed her eyes this time she saw her mother, standing with her shoulders squared, her mind focused on the matter at hand. Kira did the same. "The others, Cody, Milo, and Kev, they'll come around back. Of the three Cody is the fastest. He sneaks up and he attacks. Kev and Milo usually attack in twos, so watch for both of them. Dallas has something in his nails. It's a poison. He was born with it. Nobody knows where it came from because he was orphaned at three years old, so they don't know anything about his lineage. If he scratches a human, they're not likely to transition into a lycan on the next full moon; they die." It was a solemn announcement, one she delivered while looking at each one of the betas standing around the table . . . each one in her new pack.

Thinning her lips and inwardly slapping down on that thought, Kira continued. "On us, it'll paralyze you for about thirty to forty minutes, depending on your inner strength." This she directed at Malec, a silent thank-you for all the days he'd had her in that gym, working on strengthening exercises.

"You and Channing take Milo and Kev," she continued. "Phelan, you need to be on Cody. Remember what I said; he's the fastest. Blaez and I should go out the front door."

Up until this moment she'd been the only one speaking while the others stood around watching her intently. Blaez behind her, his presence felt in every inch of her body. It was as if he were a part of her, his mind with her mind, her breath matching his, even though he hadn't claimed her. It was a strange feeling, one Kira was determined to work around.

His hand touched her shoulder. A light but oh, so authoritative touch and instantly she knew what was coming next.

Don't you say it, Blaez, she warned him through mind-chatter, not wanting to have this argument in front of the pack.

You know what you're doing. You know where your place is was his quick response.

"Go!" Blaez yelled to the others, who immediately filed out of the kitchen.

The alpha stood as the alpha female did the debriefing. She offered the strategy, and if the alpha accepted it he was the one to send the betas out. It had been the lycan way for hundreds of years. That part of the job had been done seamlessly, as if she and Blaez had been together for years on end. The other part, where the alpha female sat and waited for the pack to return from the fight, well, that was proving a little harder for Kira to carry out.

"This is my fight," she told him when they were alone. "The only reason they're coming here is because of me."

He looked like he was about to say something, then clamped his lips closed. Lips she'd just kissed not too long ago, which had whispered that she was his.

"You are the one I swore to protect," he replied.

A part of her wanted to tell him she didn't need protection, but she knew that's what he did. That's what he needed desperately to do. Blaez took his position seriously. He was their leader and he would act out every part of that title, no matter what. And he hadn't been there to protect his family. Kira knew Blaez carried that guilt like weights permanently implanted onto his shoulders. It was that guilt that kept him from giving himself totally to her, from claiming her. She respected Blaez and his sense of loyalty and dedication; that's why she said in as level a tone as she could muster, "We can protect each other."

He nodded. "You from here and me from out there."

She shook her head. "If someone's coming for me, I'm not going to run. Not anymore. I won't sit down, Blaez. My mother did it and look where that got her."

His hand had slid from her shoulder to the nape of her neck, where he held tighter, pulling her up close against him. "If anything happens to you . . ." he ground out through clenched teeth.

"It won't because you'll be right there to protect me, remember?" She'd given a light chuckle even though she knew that laughing was the last thing Blaez wanted to do right now. And that made two of them.

CHAPTER 13

Kira watched as a section of the wood-planked wall right beside the front door pulled away with a clicking sound, then slid slowly aside to reveal a control pad with lights and long numbered buttons that she knew would disengage the alarms throughout the house. It was the first time she'd seen this, and standing right beside Blaez as he punched in the code she wondered if maybe she should have looked away. She didn't and Blaez made no effort to hide the combination he was putting in from her view. Another button was pushed and the wall went back to normal, not so much as a seam showing to give away the panel access.

The breeze was cool as Blaez opened the door, lifting the hair off her neck and sending a chill down her spine. It had grown dark quickly, the trees out ahead looming like taller, stronger entities, the grass like an ominous field that would soon see blood. For right now it was quiet as she stepped out onto the porch behind Blaez, the moon shimmering in the sky, a giant orb of power and energy. She inhaled deeply, remembering now more of what her mother had taught her.

"She will be with us tonight," Blaez said as if he were reading her mind.

"Who?" she asked abruptly.

"Selene. The Luna goddess. It is her power that keeps watch over us on these dangerous nights. Zeus doesn't know, just as he has no idea that . . ." Blaez trailed off, staring out toward the line of trees.

"What else?" Kira asked. "What else doesn't Zeus know, Blaez? And how could that affect us tonight?" She'd always thought that Blaez had more thoughts in his head than he'd ever expressed to her before. He always seemed to be holding something in, and as she stood by him, ready to fight or to do whatever was necessary for their continued existence, she wondered what that was.

The first lycan, teeth bared, face affixed in what to any human would be considered a scary-as-hell scowl, stepped through the trees, throwing his head back and howling long and loud.

Blaez had gone completely still while Kira took in a deep breath, her fingers wiggling at her sides. "He's telling the others that it's time."

In the seconds that followed, there was another, deeper howl that rang shorter than the first and closer to her because it was louder. Phelan, she thought. Blaez must have used mindchatter instead of his own howl to communicate with his second.

"And so it is," Blaez said, stepping down the steps slowly, intently.

He hadn't shifted. It was odd that she noticed that even as the other lycans from Penn's pack had also materialized from the dark veil of the trees. As the threesome approached, Dallas, Penn, and Cody, the skin at her fingers itched, her claws struggling to remain inside. She rolled her head again, feeling the burn of her shift pressing hard against her human frame.

Keep your mind clear. Focus on something you love with all your heart. Focus on your mother.

Blaez's voice was in her head again. Her heart skipped a beat at the realization that just like in the kitchen, it was because she'd allowed him there. She'd opened herself for him to communicate to her this way. There was a slight thumping in her temples and she faltered slightly.

He stopped, turning to her immediately.

He's trying to talk to you. Your alpha.

She shook her head immediately at those two words.

He's no longer my alpha. That was over the day my mother was killed.

Blaez only nodded, touching his fingers to her temples, then letting them slide down to her cheek.

"You can do this," he told her. "Find your control."

Kira let out a breath and nodded to him. "I got it."

And it was a good thing too, because in the next second, like flashes of light through the darkness, Penn and the others had closed the space between them, racing across the field to come to a quick stop. Dallas stood directly behind Blaez while Penn had materialized behind her. Without even blinking at her, Blaez bent forward, wrapping his arms around to grab Dallas behind the knees, then flipping the lycan over so that he landed flat on his back on the ground between them.

Penn wrapped his arm around Kira's neck, pulling back hard so that she had to gasp for breath.

"This is mine," he said over her shoulder to Blaez, and her body screamed with rage.

Her claws instantly extended and she raked them across the arm that was clutching her neck until he yelled, letting her go abruptly. She turned out of his arms, looking back at him with all the pent-up anger she'd held for the past year. "That's a lie!" she shouted back at him, then staggered slightly when something flashed before her eyes.

It was her parents' bedroom back in Seattle. Tora, tall, slim, beautiful with her straight auburn hair reaching down to touch the small of her back.

"You're a liar!" Penn had come through the bedroom door yelling at her. "All these years you've been lying to me about my own child."

Tora had stood straight, shoulders squared as she stared at her alpha. "I don't know what you're talking about."

"The hell you don't!" he roared, storming across the room to get right in Tora's face. "She's marked and you knew! You knew she bore the mark of the goddess and what that means."

"No," Tora had whispered, her eyes blinking furiously, hands fisting at her sides. "How did you find out?"

"It doesn't matter how I found out!" Penn continued to bellow. "I know now and I know exactly what it means."

"Penn, you have no idea what it means for her, for the future of the lycans," Tora tried to tell him.

"It means that she's going to be powerful. In a few months when she turns twenty-one she's going to be a powerful bitch that was made to rule. That's what I know! And I'll be damned if I let her go and rule some other pack."

Tora shook her head. "It's not up to you," she said quietly, and moved around the alpha to head out of the room. "Her fate has been sealed by the goddess. She will come into

572 A. C. Arthur

her power and she will seek her alpha, the one that has been Selected for her. And there's nothing you can do to stop that, Penn. Absolutely nothing."

Kira gasped. Her father had known she was Selected.

"You're a liar," she whispered before her temples throbbed once more and another scene flashed in front of her.

"She's going to tell her and then she'll leave. You promised her to me, Penn. You owe me." Dallas had frowned, his wide nose flaring with his words. "Tora has to be eliminated."

"I don't know how this selection process works," Penn had told him. "My family wasn't big on passing down any of the stories of the gods, since all of them are controlling bastards that we'd kill if we could."

Dallas had stared at him for a couple seconds, his dark eyes assessing, calculating. "I have to claim her. On her twenty-first birthday I can claim her. Then I will rule the pack; the power stays right here with you and me."

"Are you certain?" Penn had asked, looking as if he hadn't actually believed what the beta had said.

"I can claim her," Dallas had said, lifting his hands so that his deadly nails detracted with a clicking sound.

Penn seemed to contemplate, only for a minute, because then Dallas with those nails had stepped closer to him, aiming the nails at his neck. Penn had immediately shifted, growling at the beta, but Dallas had only laughed. "I could have killed you at any time, you old fool. But I kept you alive. Last night when I snuck into Kira's bathroom, about to make her see which beta she should be with once and for all, I saw the reason why I hadn't killed you. That little moon hovering right over her fat ass was all I needed to know. The time has come for me to take my rightful place in this pack, and claiming your thick-assed daughter is going to be the one that puts me there."

"You bastard!" Kira yelled the second the vision faded, her eyes trained on Penn. "You killed my mother! You killed her so that you could give me to this beast!" She swung an arm catching him off guard, her lycan nails scratching his face the same way she'd done his arm.

The "beast" being Dallas, who was just about to mimic her scratching motion with his claws aimed at Blaez as he leapt up off the ground. Of course Blaez was faster, reaching out and grabbing both of Dallas's wrists, lifting him up off the ground, then tossing him even farther away.

Blaez grabbed Kira then, pulling her close to his side. "You don't want to do this," he told Penn.

For the first time in she couldn't remember how long she saw what might be true emotion in her father or, rather, the alpha lycan who stood across from her. His mane of wild black hair stood up wildly, his fangs long and sharp as he opened his mouth to howl his response back to Blaez. His body surrounded in a gruesome dark haze depicting that of the evil and demented, sparks of red representing his deep anger adding to the mixture. She knew what it was she saw now, knew what she'd been seeing for the past couple of weeks. It was the lycan's true form, his most inner emotions displayed on the outside for only her to see.

With her heart pounding at what Kira realized must be the power she was promised as one of the Selected, she spotted Cody in her peripheral, charging forward. He too had looked red in the night, his quickness met by Phelan's mighty growl as he crashed into the younger lycan's chest full on, knocking him off his feet. As for the others, Kira heard growling and thumping in the distance and knew that they were fighting.

Channing and Malec were battling to save her. Phelan had just taken a blow from Cody but was retaliating with double blows of his own, jumping on Cody as he fell on his back this time, growling with the full force of his beast in Cody's face. That's when Kira felt it, the pull and tug against her own skin, the ripping of her claws as they extended even longer. Unlike Dallas's, hers weren't poisonous, but they were still deadly and inches longer than the other lycans'. Her claws were like knives attached to her fingertips, and as her own fangs elongated she opened her mouth to match the growls sounding around her, rolling her head once more, this time feeling the immediate growth of her hair, the drooping of her forehead, and the bunching of her muscles.

"Mine!" Penn said again with more persistence before reaching out to grab her arm.

Dallas surprised them all by moving from his place near Blaez to stand in front of Penn. "No, old man. This is my bitch!"

The air around her sizzled, like there was a lightning bolt or some strange sort of energy emanating in the area. The cool breeze that she'd felt the moment Blaez had opened the door picked up until even the trees rocked back and forth, the ground beneath her shaking so hard she stumbled forward, landing on her hands and knees.

Cool grass ruffled beneath her fingers, the surface still vibrating as a familiar scent permeated her senses. That feeling of togetherness, of being two connected instead of one, washing over her immediately. It was strange and then again it wasn't. A part of her knew exactly what was happening, exactly what needed to happen.

And that's when she saw it. Standing right next to her, with a body as tall and broad as hers, its fur a glistening white and gray, eyes sparkling sapphire blue. It was a wolf, the same one from her dreams. Its flanks moved in and out, in conjunction with her own breaths, its fur blowing in the breeze. There was a great power in this wolf; Kira felt it in the air around them and going deep down to the ground beneath. This was definitely the wolf she'd dreamed about. The one that now bared its teeth, leaning toward Dallas in a definitely predatory way, its power rippling straight through the earth, surfacing where she stood, and wrapping its protective aura around . . . her.

CHAPTER 14

The first bite was to his leg, knocking Dallas onto his ass, in a more permanent nature this time. The lycan fell back, howling in pain as Blaez, in his wolf form, climbed atop him, growling down into his face.

"No!" Penn yelled. "Don't!"

"He tried to rape me and you still protect him!" Blaez heard Kira yell. He knew she was talking about Dallas and that's why he'd bitten the lycan the first time. Now Blaez continued to growl, thoroughly enjoying how afraid and confused Dallas was looking up at him, just before he took a bite out of his other leg.

There was no other lycan walking the earth who could turn into a full-fledged wolf. None who had the strength, the cunning and intuition that he had. They didn't have the power of a god because the only blood that ran through their veins was that of Nyktimos with the wolf traits he'd inherited from Lykaon.

Blaez had so much more.

"You lied to me about my mother's death and now you're protecting him. You don't give a damn about me!" Kira yelled.

"You belong to our pack; there's nothing you can do about that," Penn responded.

"Not anymore. Not without my mother," she countered.

"She's dead because she betrayed me and the pack. She should have told me what you were and she should have let me decide how to deal with you. Instead I let Dallas deal with her," Penn continued. "I'm not going to let you destroy what I've worked so long and so hard to build. And I'm certainly not going to watch you join forces with this disgusting spawn of Nyktimos! I'll kill you myself first!"

Before Penn could do anything Blaez was on the move. In the back of his mind he'd heard her scream, even though her father had yet to strike. Blaez had felt her pain like shards of glass pelting his own skin. He growled loudly before leaping away from Dallas, to land on Penn, Blaez's teeth sinking into the alpha's neck with deadly accuracy to its jugular vein. And as Blaez knew Penn's life was draining out of him he heard Kira's growl.

"You bastard!" she yelled. "You killed my mother, didn't you? Didn't you?"

"She was as hardheaded and uncontrollable as you are. But I will control you, Kira. I will claim you and bend you to my will. With you I will leave the world of a lowly beta to transition to the most powerful alpha this world has ever seen," Dallas informed her.

The lycan must have begun healing from Blaez's bites, enough so that he could get up off the ground.

"Never!" she yelled, and when the wolf turned this time it was to see Kira, mouth wide, fangs sharp and glowing in the moon's gaze, jumping on Dallas.

578 A. C. Arthur

This time the lycan did not fall but swatted his beefy arm just in time to knock Kira onto the ground. He jumped on top of her then, ripping at her chest with his deadly claws. The wolf saw the moment Kira's body went still and growled before jumping on Dallas's back and sinking its teeth into his neck, then quickly administering another bite to the back of his skull. The lycan growled loudly, lifting up off of Kira, arching his back with the wolf still attached biting into each of his shoulders and when he finally fell to the ground once more the wolf tore off his hands, rendering the poisonous claws defenseless and their owner dead.

"We'll get her inside!" Phelan yelled. "And we'll take care of the others. You go. Go!"

The wolf looked at Kira as Phelan lifted her still-paralyzed body from the ground.

"Go! Before they see you too!" Phelan yelled at it once more.

Blaez growled again, before taking off at a run into the forest, away from the house where the betas from Penn's pack were obviously still alive. They couldn't see him like this. If they did they would have to die. Nobody could know who and what he really was. That wouldn't be safe for anyone.

"What time is it?" Kira asked, her throat and lips dry as she tried to sit up.

Channing was sitting beside her, pressing hot, wet towels to her chest, which felt like somebody had taken a good punch at her.

"Whoa there," Channing said. "Let's take this slowly. I

don't know what aftereffects those poison claws usually have."

"Dammit!" she cursed, lying back on the pillows with a thump and closing her eyes. Dallas had scratched her. In those moments she remembered the razor-sharp tips of his claws sinking into her skin, felt the heat of the poison seeping into her bloodstream only seconds later.

He'd been on top of her, glaring down at her the same way he had the night of the last full moon when he'd tried to claim her. Tonight, even in lycan form, his dick had been hard, his heart beating wildly to match the look in his eyes. He was going to do it, right there in the open. He was going to attempt to claim her.

But he would have failed. He was not whom she was Selected for. Kira knew that as certainly as she knew her own name.

He'd bared his teeth to her the second he decided to cut into her with his claws. She'd lifted her arms, wanting to catch him in the face or somewhere else with her own claws first, anything to give her a few seconds to roll out of his reach, but that hadn't happened. She'd been too slow and he'd paralyzed her. In that moment he'd thought he'd won.

Except the wolf had been there. It had come soaring through the dark sky, its bright eyes and coat of fur like some type of god coming down from the heavens. It had killed Dallas, but Kira had not been able to get up and go to it or to even turn her head and see it before it ran off. She hadn't been able to thank it . . . him . . . Blaez.

"Where's Blaez?" she asked quietly, her eyes still closed. She knew they were all there, could feel their steady gazes on her. But none of them spoke.

She opened her eyes then, looking around to see that she was lying on the big sofa in the living room, the one she'd seen Channing, Malec, and that female leaning against a week ago. Channing was still sitting beside Kira, his hands seemingly frozen over the towel on her chest. Malec stood behind him, his face fixed in a grim frown. Phelan she had to turn her head slightly to see standing closer to the door. He was waiting for Blaez.

"Will he come back on his own?" she asked Phelan specifically. He'd turned to her; his scar looked puffier, redder, than she recalled ever seeing it, his arms folded over his chest.

"He always does" was Phelan's clipped reply.

She blinked, took a deep inhalation, and was glad when she didn't feel that deep pang of pain again, which meant she was already beginning to heal. "When?" was her next question.

"When it's time" was Phelan's reply.

"Just relax," Channing told her. "We're here and we'll take care of you."

"Penn," she said in an almost whisper. "Where is he?"

"Dead!" Malec snapped. "Him and that bastard that tried to take you!"

There was definitely malice in Malec's voice, laced with the anger that was still simmering around this room. So it was over, she thought with another slow blink of her eyes. Then why were they all standing watch over her like they expected something else to happen?

"Cody and the others? Where are they?" she asked, but was met with total silence.

She moved again, this time slowly, lifting up the upper

half of her body, giving Channing a gaze that dared him to try to stop her. "I want to know what happened and I need one of you to tell me." She put her hand on top of Channing's, moving the towel from her chest so she could look down at it.

Four jagged scratches showed, ripped flesh still raw and puffy but no longer bleeding on the tattered pieces of her shirt. She grabbed the pillow from behind her head, quickly putting it in front of her chest as she looked at them again. They looked tired but still lethal as hell, with muscles protruding and glares so angry and tight the tension just about radiated from their skin.

"We had to kill them," Malec told her. "There was no other choice."

"I don't think the two we had saw anything," Channing added, his lips drawing in a thin line after he finished.

"They would have figured it out!" Phelan snapped. "We all know what that means. So they had to die."

She'd been looking from one to the other even as Channing took her hand in his. "They can't know who or what he is, Kira. There's too much at stake if anyone ever finds out."

Her heart was slamming against her chest at this point, her mind whirling with the things that they'd been saying. "What . . . what is he? Why can't anyone know? Tell me, Channing!"

"It's his story to tell," Phelan said dryly. "When he wants and to who he wants."

"But I'm . . ." she started. "I'm his—" she attempted to say, then stopped. She knew, without any doubt; at this very moment Kira knew.

It was like a light, that bright light that she'd seen radiating around him that very first night in the woods, filling her completely on the inside. That light brought knowledge, a warmth settling over her as everything became clearer. Her. Blaez. The day she'd envisioned seeing him hurt. The dream of his wolf. It was all very clear and very meaningful.

She had been Selected for Blaez. And whatever he really was, however dangerous he perceived that to be was why he continued to deny it, to deny her and their destiny. It wasn't only what had happened to his family; it was his wolf that now stood between them.

They all looked at her expectantly, like there was so much hanging on her next words. And there was, she thought clearly. Her next words, her actions, all of their lives—this pack that she was so ready to call her own and Blaez's included—depended on what happened next.

"I'm going to get him," she said.

She tossed the pillow down and was trying to move her legs to get off the couch, but Channing was still sitting there, blocking the way.

"Where . . . you don't know where he is. None of us do. We just wait. He always comes back; as soon as the moon is gone once more, he always comes back," Channing told her.

"This is the first time he's killed like that," Malec added as if that made a difference.

"Like a wolf," she said. "Blaez is a wolf."

The realization hit her just like that cool breeze of air had earlier this evening. She wasn't shocked, but she knew she should be. "Why is he a wolf? None of us have a complete shift like that. Why does he?"

"It's his story!" Phelan yelled as if he was exasperated with her in particular.

Kira didn't care; she pushed Channing to the side and

stood from the sofa, stalking over to where Phelan was standing to get in his face. "Let's be clear here, Phelan. I'm in love with him, whatever or whyever he is. I was Selected for him," she said, feeling the truth of those words trickling into every pore of her body.

None of them spoke for what seemed like endless moments.

It had taken her a little longer than it should have for her to get up the steps, change her shirt, and come back down. She was still a little light-headed from the poison, but the scratches were continuing to heal and would most likely be gone within the hour. While she was in Blaez's bedroom—the one she'd been sharing with him—Kira glanced at the clock to see that hours had passed since they'd first gone out to greet Penn's pack. The sun would be rising soon. And Blaez would come back. That's what Channing said.

But the full moon would be over.

Kira wasn't going to wait. She knew where Blaez was. That same light that had filled her and told her that she'd been Selected for him gave her knowledge of where she could find her mate. He would be there; she only had to go to him.

"He wouldn't want me to let you go out there alone," Phelan said, still standing watch by the front door like that was his designated spot for the night.

Kira nodded, respecting the second in command of Blaez's pack in a way she never had before. "Then let's go," she said. "You'll have to keep up."

Kira broke into a run the moment she'd cleared the door, calming her mind as Blaez had taught her and focusing on that light still blossoming inside her. It seemed as if the moon shone its brightest here in the thicket of trees, as she was able to see perfectly while moving along an untraveled path. His scent was different now, yet she'd still held it, from the moment that wolf had stood beside her. She continued to run wondering how she'd missed what was so clear to her now. How had she not realized? Her mother had told her there was something more out there for her and then he'd appeared as if, at the same time, that she'd been searching, he'd been looking too. Blaez would probably never admit to that, but Kira knew it to be true. In her heart and soul she knew that she and Blaze were meant to run into each other that night in the woods; they were meant to spend these weeks locked in that lodge together. That time was preparing them for this moment, for this slice of time that the goddess had carved out for them. The moment they would become one.

That realization still hummed along her conscience, pushing her to go even faster, to find him before it was too late.

Kira moved faster until her arms and legs burned with the exertion, her chest beginning a dull ache. Then, as suddenly as she began, her feet were skidding to a halt, dirt and rocks being kicked up as she came to a stop, only inches before going over a cliff with a steep drop down. Phelan was right there, grabbing her arm to keep her from toppling over.

She looked up at him in thanks and he nodded as if neither of them needed to actually speak a word. He thrust a backpack toward her and for a second she looked at it and wondered if he was sending her on her way. But the backpack wasn't hers; it was black instead of blue like the one she'd carried here.

"He's going to need these," Phelan told her.

She nodded, realizing the backpack must contain Blaez's clothes, and the memory of that beautiful wolf that had saved her life appeared in her mind.

"Thanks. I'll be all right now," she told Phelan, looking back down to the lake and knowing now why she'd really stopped. Blaez was down there somewhere; his scent was stronger here. And when she'd looked down into the dark ravine again, she would swear she'd seen the quick flash of his blue eyes.

"Be careful," Phelan told her as if he too knew that Blaez was down there, which would be the only reason he would leave her alone.

"I will," she told him as she turned and headed down.

It was steep and rocks crumbled rolling downward as she moved. With each step her heart beat just a little faster, Blaez's scent grew stronger, and that full moon above shone brighter. When Kira made it to level ground she walked in the direction where she'd seen the flash of blue. She hadn't glimpsed it again, but it didn't matter. There was a copse of trees just ahead, beside what looked like a cave driving into the side of the mountain. That's where she was headed.

Her thighs burned as she continued, wisps of hair plastered to the back of her neck while the length of it swished behind her. Kira had no idea what to expect. Would it be Blaez the man? Or the wolf? What would she do in either instance? What would she say? How would she react? There were so many questions and so many feelings going through her at the moment. Her father was dead. Dallas had killed her mother on her father's orders. Why? Because she was a Selected, a powerful lycan ordained to join with another powerful being.

Blaez.

She continued to move, stepping over two rocks being smacked by the quick-moving water that sluiced its way through this passage. She'd just jumped in the hopes of landing on steady rocky ground on the other side of the water when she felt herself being lifted into the air.

In the next instant she was staring down at the ground she'd just been traipsing along, being carried deep into the cave that had looked so gloomy just a few moments ago. Unlike the last time she was in this position, when her heart had beat wildly as she wondered what was going to happen next, this time her heart beat wildly because she knew who it was that carried her. She recognized him with every fiber of her being and wanted to scream with joy that he was all right. Instead, she bit her lip against the swell of desire building in the pit of her stomach and when he set her down slowly in what she figured, when she looked around, was the end of this cave she let out a breath and stared up at him.

He was gloriously naked, his body streaked with what looked like mud but might have also been blood. His chest heaved, pectorals rising and falling in a heavenly display of manhood as he breathed in and out. Every inch of him was beautiful, sculpted, alluring, just point-blank sexy as hell, and she had to take another gulp of air to settle herself.

When he took a step toward her, Kira moved in, adrenaline coursing through her veins right alongside the light that had led her here. Sure, she was certainly happy to see him alive and standing and she was elated to finally know that he was the reason she was here, that they—as the Selected couple—were going to be the reason that things changed for the lycans in the future. But she was still pissed with him.

"You liar!" she yelled. "How dare you hold me captive all this time, telling me to trust you, to find my control, to do this and do that, when all the while you were lying to me about everything you were! Everything you are!"

He caught her wrist the second she finished, holding it tightly in his hand. She tried to yank it away, but he held tighter. She swung her other fist, almost catching him in the jaw before he grabbed that wrist, holding it just as tightly as the first.

"You done?" he asked, looking down at her.

"No, I'm not done," she continued, unable to yell or to quiet the fear that had bubbled deep inside her when the pack refused to tell her what he was.

"I should hate you," she admitted, the anger that had appeared so quickly, dissipating just as fast.

"But you don't" was his quick reply.

"No," Kira sighed. "I don't. And see, that's the thing, Blaez. I never hated you. I wanted to leave that lodge because you told me I had to stay there and I thought there was something somewhere else I should be looking for. But I wanted you. Every step of the way and as much as it irritated the hell out of me, I wanted you. Always."

"You shouldn't have," he said, zeroing in on her, his eyes now brown with swirls of something in the center. It looked like an orb or kind of like the moon. She gasped once more and this time he let her pull away from him.

"I know I should have told you the truth, all of it, that day in the library. But I didn't want to see . . . I knew I wouldn't be able to stand you looking at me like I was an abomination. I'm an alpha and I can do just about anything, but that, Kira, that I wasn't going to take well," he told her.

"Tell me now," she replied. "Just tell me everything right now."

There was silence in the cave, the remnant echo of her last words having dissipated into the air. In the distance she could still hear the rustle of water, but there was nothing else. No words.

"You already know that my mother was Kharis. I didn't tell you that she was the daughter of Artemis and a farmer she met in Arcadia, when Zeus had gone there to seek out Lykaon."

He spoke quietly, his tone resigned as he eventually looked to Kira again.

"My father was a pure-blood descendent of Nyktimos and my mother was a demigod. The blood that runs through my veins is more than that of the wolf, it is mingled with the gods, so I'm not just a lycan."

"No." Kira shook her head. "You're not."

"I'm part lycan and part demigod. The only one left of my kind," he replied grimly. There was that look that she'd seen him get often. It usually went as quickly as it had come. But not this time. His thick brows furrowed, his lips set in a thin line.

"Zeus knew who my parents were and that they'd produced more like me. He knew and that's why he really wanted them dead. He can never risk anyone being as powerful as him, or that could somehow be a threat to him. The children of a lycan and a demigod would be powerfully different from anything he or the mortal world had ever seen. So he killed them, and just like with Lykaon and Nyktimos, he forgot about me."

Kira shook her head. "But Selene did not forget about you," she told him. "On the night I was born she Selected me for you. She sent me to help you go against Zeus whenever he comes for you."

"I told you before that I didn't want this. I didn't want to be an alpha of a pack, didn't want to have to fight anyone, to defend anything. I just wanted to be . . . whatever," he said, finally turning away from her.

"But that wasn't your destiny," Kira told him. "It wasn't yours and it wasn't mine. Here, right now, this is what is meant to be, Blaez. *We* are meant to be."

He shook his head. "We can't. And not for the reasons you think. It's not that I'm afraid of Zeus finding me or of what he will try to do to me when he does. I'm much too powerful for that to happen with just a blink of his eye and he knows that, which is why he had to use trickery to get to my family. No, when he comes for me I'll have no choice but to fight back and that fight will involve the world I've chosen to live in. People will die. Mortals will suffer. Lycans will falter. And anyone I'm close to, connected to, might be—"

Kira moved forward, touching a hand lightly to the back of his shoulder. "All this time I've been thinking that you were just being an arrogant ass. I thought this thing I felt inside whenever you were near and even when you weren't was just nothing. A result of the needing that would be slaked the moment we finally had sex. But it didn't," she said, circling her finger on his skin, loving the tautness and the warmth she felt there.

"Then you told me about what happened to your family and I thought I could relate to you not wanting an intimate or emotional connection after that. Who would willingly put themselves in a position to be hurt that way all over again? But you know what, Blaez? You have put yourself in a close relationship with others. You care very much about your pack, just as you had about your family. And then I came along," she told him.

"And you shouldn't have. She has no right dictating who and what should be. None of them have any right. They don't rule; the gods only know how to control," he told her, his body bunching with the intensity of his words.

"But don't you see, Blaez. They won't control us. We were Selected to be together, but nobody could predict what bringing two powerful lycans together would do, let alone a lycan and a demigod. It's never been done before, so there's no way they can know what to expect. We can fight Zeus together. I've seen it, Blaez; we can be good together," she said softly, a smile ghosting his lips. "My selected power is of vision, so that I can see clearly who we are dealing with at all times and pieces of what was and what might be. With that, together with your wolf and godlike instincts we will change the course of the lycans' lives. And when the time comes, we will combat Zeus. Together."

He turned at her words then, staring at her quizzically. "I can't be that, Kira. I can't be the alpha that has an alpha female, another vulnerability. The pack, the betas, they stand their own ground, choosing the ground beside me. I cannot build a family like the one my parents had only to have it snatched away from me again. I could not survive it another time."

She cupped his face just as he had begun shaking his head, his eyes blinking between the brown and blue as the beast within him grew desperate to shift and possibly run.

"You once told me to find my control. That when I found it I could have whatever I wanted." When he stopped shaking his head she continued, "Tell me what you want, Blaez."

He was quiet, but she felt his body reacting, felt the thickness of his growing arousal pressing against her lower belly, saw the complete shift in his eyes to that ominous black that she'd become used to. Stepping even closer, she pressed her breasts against him, lowering her head to kiss his bared chest. "Tell me, what the alpha demigod wants," she whispered.

"Kira," he warned through gritted teeth.

"No," she said with a shake of her head. "*Lýkaina.* Call me *lýkaina,* like you always do. Say it and tell me what you want, Blaez."

That muscle twitched in his jaw once more and this time when he spoke it was with that gruffness she recognized, that authority that never failed to send sparks of desire shooting straight to her pussy.

"I want you, *lýkaina.* I want to be so deep inside of you I can't think of anything or anyone else. I want your pussy holding my dick so tight neither of us can breathe."

"Yes," she whispered, tilting her head and leaning in to take his lips. "Take control, baby. Take control of what you want. What I need. Take it, now."

CHAPTER 15

She was giving him everything, arching in his arms as he licked along the line of her throat. Her words had said it all, and later he'd replay them in his mind. As for now, Blaez could only do one thing. It would be the first time, but he didn't give a damn; he would take her command and give her what she needed, what he had so desperately wanted all this time.

His kisses continued along her collarbone, down farther to the soft skin between her breasts. Inhaling deeply, he let every nuance of her scent be permanently embedded in his mind, his body, and his soul. She was everything, even when he'd tried to convince himself that she was nothing.

One arm held her in place, gripping her around the base of her back, while he reached the other one up to rip the front of her shirt completely. He pushed it off one arm, grabbing her bra and giving it the same treatment, his mouth already open and ready to gorge on the dark-tipped nipple, already puckered and ready for his assault. She locked a hand behind his head, pushing him closer, feeding him like she'd become accustomed to doing. He wondered if she knew just how much she'd done for him in the short time they'd been together.

Two weeks ago he was determined to live his solitary life, to lead his pack, and to keep his promise to his parents and his birthright. That had been enough. Until the moment he'd seen her, scented her. His cheeks hollowed as he sucked her breast as hard and as deep as he possibly could, loving the feel of her in his mouth.

When she lifted a leg, wrapping it around him, he growled low and deep inside. Then he finally managed to tear his mouth away from hers, grabbing her by that lifted leg and thrusting his thick length against the pants she'd worn. He kissed her mouth then, hungrily, possessively, placing nipping bites along her bottom lip before sucking that into his mouth similar to the way he had her breast. She was gasping and whispering his name and his mind was caught in a frenzy of desire and want and destiny.

"I knew it," he rasped, his tongue tracing a heated path along her jawline, down to her neck once again. "The moment I felt your presence in the woods and then when I saw that mark. I knew and I should have just let it be."

"It is now," she replied. "We are right now."

They were and yet they weren't and Blaez opened his eyes with a start. The cave was still alight with moonlight even though it should have been dark. It had been rumored that Artemis and Selene were great cohorts, the moon often being mentioned when speaking of Artemis and her great hunting triumphs. While Kira had received her powerful gift solely from Selene, Blaez's came from both, his grandmother Artemis making him a powerful hunter and leader while a significant source of his strength came from the moon. So the inside of the cave would stay alight, until the very last second that the full moon hung in the sky. After that it would be too late, until next time.

Blaez was not going to let that happen.

He tore his mouth away from Kira once more, his hands moving in frantic motions to get her naked as fast as he could.

"I won't do this," he said abruptly, cupping her face in his. "Not without your permission."

She licked her lips, blinking those beautiful eyes as she stared up at him. "We have been Selected," she told him. "But even if we hadn't, I want this, Blaez. I want you and all that you are."

If he were inclined to such things it would have been like music to his ears; as it stood, his body tightened with more than just arousal this time. He felt that sensation again, as if he were being filled, not just completely this time, until overfilling. The threads had weaved together, the bond was born, and all he needed was that last connection, that one last act that would seal their fate forevermore.

He lowered his forehead to hers at that moment. "I didn't think I could," he whispered. "Didn't think there was anyone that I could love, or someone who could love me. Someone that I would be willing to risk it all for."

"But I do, Blaez," she said immediately. "I do love you. As much as I wanted to fight it, to run and keep going forever and ever. It's here, right here is where I belong, standing beside you ready for whatever comes. I know that now. I know that this is our destiny."

He let his hands slide down, brushing past her breasts,

spanning her torso, her waist, the curve of her hips, then between her legs. He kept one at the base of her back, letting his fingers slip through the folds of her vagina, each of them moaning as his fingers touched her warmth, the wetness. He loved how she felt in his hands, his mouth watering at the knowledge of what she would taste like. The flat of his palm rubbed along her clit, while two of his fingers delved deep inside of her.

She grabbed his shoulders, her nails sinking into his skin. He pressed deeper, deeper, his fingers splaying, stretching her. His teeth ground together, his eyes closing, emotion so thick and so hot rushing over him Blaez actually shivered. He pumped into her fiercely then, his fingers slipping in and out of her wetness as she leaned her head forward to fall on his shoulder, her tongue tracing over the spot where she'd just scratched. If she'd drawn blood, the claiming would begin. Her saliva, mixing with his blood, the connection. But it would not be complete without him.

His dick was hard, dripping pre-cum as he continued to work inside her, loving the sound, the scent, every damned thing about her. When she was so wet it was hard for his fingers to stay inside, Blaez pushed farther back, his wet fingers pressing against the tight bud of her anus. She hissed in a breath, arching her back in his grasp.

"Relax and open for me, *lýkaina*. Open for me," he said, his voice tight with emotion, his muscles tense with anticipation. "Open for your alpha."

It took a moment, but Kira's body went almost slack against him, her breaths still coming fast, her kisses against him like swipes of a feather. Blaez applied more pressure, felt the tightness giving way to his pursuit. He held her close, enjoying the feeling of her breasts pressed against his chest. "Breathe for me; breathe in deep."

She did and at the same time he pressed his fingers all the way inside of her. She stilled momentarily. Then she relaxed again and he knew it was all right to insert another finger. He stretched her when she'd calmed again signaling she was ready to take him.

"I won't hurt you," he told her, wishing like hell they'd been back in his room where he could use more lubricant, prepare her more for this moment. The thought of causing her any more pain than she'd already endured was threatening to tear him apart.

"I know you won't," she told him. "Just do it. I want to be claimed by you, by my alpha."

Her words had his balls drawing tighter, his spine tingling with lust and anticipation. He pulled his fingers out of her then, tilted her chin so she could receive his kiss. The soft one, the one that said everything he felt for her in this moment with such sincerity and gentleness that it almost broke his heart.

"Do it," she whispered against his mouth when he'd pulled slowly away.

She began kneeling down, pausing the second his dick bumped against her cheek. Turning, she kissed along its length. Licking the drops of pre-cum from his tip. "Now, Blaez, just do it now!"

Deep, hot, wet, that's what Blaez thought the second she closed her mouth over his cock, pressing farther, taking him all the way down. Then she pulled back, his cock slipping from her lips with a distinctive pop, before she went all the way down on her hands and knees, her ass up and waiting, just the position he loved seeing it in.

Blaez knelt down quickly, grabbing the rounded cheeks of her buttocks, squeezing, inhaling, loving the feel of their wealth in his palms. Spreading her wide, he looked down, saw the glistening path of her arousal he'd made with his fingers, and clenched his teeth.

"I love you, *lýkaina*," he said, pulling one hand back to position his length, still glossy from her heated kiss at her back entrance, Blaez pressed gently at first. "I love you."

Pressed a little harder.

"I love you."

Then another push, until the crown of his cock was fully ensconced. She hissed, arched her back, and sighed, "I love you."

He moved slowly then, thrusting inside her slowly until she'd taken him completely. It was then, with the glow of the moon shining on them both, that Blaez lifted a hand. Staring down at his fingers, he watched as his claws descended and without another thought scratched Kira down the center of her back. At the same time he'd pulled slightly out of her, thrusting back in at the exact moment she howled in pain and in pleasure.

Leaning forward, he licked the scratches, while pumping in and out of her, loving the tightness that gripped him and the way she pumped back against his movements. He licked and pumped and licked and pumped until her back was void of any blood, her ass jiggling back against his motions.

"Blaez," she moaned. "Can I?"

Normally he would wait; he would push her further, bring out every second of the pleasure between them. Not tonight.

"Come, *lýkaina*. Come for your alpha."

Then he pumped wildly into her because they weren't only words this time. Kira was officially his *sheyla*—his claimed alpha female. He'd claimed her, or rather, she'd claimed him first. It didn't matter; they were together, locked tightly at the moment. His dick was so full when it exploded, his cum shooting in thick, hot spurts, he'd arched his back too, howling long and loud.

"You are my destiny. My mate. My life," he whispered seconds later, when he'd pulled out of her, sitting on the floor of the cave, and cradled her in his lap. He kissed her forehead, her cheek, and finally her lips when she'd turned to him.

"You are my alpha" was Kira's whispered response as she leaned in for another kiss, wrapping her arms tightly around his neck. "My alpha forever."

ABOUT THE AUTHORS

Eve Langlais is a *New York Times* bestselling Canadian author who loves to write hot romance. She enjoys strong alpha male heroes, shifters, and a happily ever after.

Kate Douglas lives in California and loves "happily ever after" endings.

A. C. Arthur was born and raised in Baltimore, Maryland, where she currently lives with her husband and three children. Determined to bring a new edge to romance, she continues to develop intriguing plots, sensual love scenes, racy characters, and fresh dialogue.

Made in the USA
Monee, IL
07 October 2023

44120231R00353